PROBABILITY
MOON

By Nancy Kress

NOVELS

Prince of Morning Bells
The White Pipes
The Golden Grove
An Alien Light
Brainrose
Beggars in Spain
Beggars and Choosers
Oaths and Miracles
Beggars Ride
Maximum Light
Stinger
Probability Moon
Probability Sun
Probability Space
Crossfire*

STORY COLLECTIONS

Trinity and Other Stories
The Aliens of Earth
Beaker's Dozen

*forthcoming

PROBABILITY
MOON

NANCY KRESS

A TOM DOHERTY ASSOCIATES BOOK
NEW YORK

PROBABILITY MOON

Edited by David G. Hartwell

A Tor Book
Published by Tom Doherty Associates, LLC
175 Fifth Avenue
New York, NY 10010

www.tor.com

Tor® is a registered trademark of Tom Doherty Associates, LLC.

ISBN: 0-765-34341-X

First edition: July 2000
First mass market edition: September 2002

Printed in the United States of America

0   9   8   7   6   5   4   3   2

For Charles, who certainly earned it

Men love liberty because it protects them from control and humiliation from others, and thus affords them the possibility of dignity. They loathe liberty because it throws them back on their own abilities and resources, and thus confronts them with the possibility of insignificance.

—THOMAS SZASZ

PROLOGUE

LOWELL CITY, MARS

The aide materialized beside General Stefanak at a most inconvenient moment. The girl with him was too schooled to react; she'd been with her company for two years now, and it was the most popular and discreet first-class company on Titan. The girl took no notice of the intrusion, but the general lost his erection.

"I'm so sorry, sir," the holo said, averting Malone's eyes, "but there is a level-one message."

"You are not to blame," the general said ritualistically. "One moment."

The girl was already pulling on her dress, eyes properly downcast. She would, of course, be paid anyway. Stefanak put on a robe and bowed to her; she returned the gesture and left through the side door. Her long black hair flowed down her back, the ends glowing with tiny holographic beads. There had been nothing holographic about the rest of her. This level-one had better be important.

He walked into his outer office and waited for Malone, who probably had to travel across the base from Communications. Level-one messages were physically encoded and hand carried. This one must have just come through a few moments ago. While he waited, Stefanak poured himself a drink, thinking about the girl.

Maybe he needed his hormone levels adjusted again. He wasn't eighty anymore.

Malone appeared with the communication cube, bowed, and left. Stefanak activated the security shield. While it was on, nothing could enter or leave his quarters. No electromagnetic radiation, no compression waves, no air, not even neutrinos. Then he switched on the cube, using level-one protocols.

It was from a recon team to a remote and unimportant planet, funded and mounted by soft-science professors at Princeton University, for the usual squishy "research." But every recon team had a line-rank military representative on it. Usually junior officers fought not to go on recon. Usually it was an E-year of irrelevant boredom on primitive planets, most of them uninhabited.

Not this time.

Stefanak viewed the cube once, and then again. He sat thinking for a full five minutes, very carefully. The *Zeus* was available, or could be made available, without attracting significant attention. A command-level line officer could not be made available, but there were ways around that. Physicists . . . leave that to Malone. But maybe the whole mission could be made to look like just another low-priority scholarly expedition. Yes. Salernos would be the one to arrange that, she had plausible contacts . . .

When Stefanak finished his planning, he released the security shield. Malone waited outside. The general told him to put together an immediate meeting with the Solar Alliance Defense Council, highest-ranking officers only, all participating governments urged most strongly to attend.

This might change everything.

ONE

RAFKIT SELOE

When Enli came outside at sunrise, her flower beds had been destroyed. The curving line of border stones had been pointedly straightened. The jelit bushes, not yet in flower, sat broken into pathetic piles of twigs. No one, of course, would harm the ollinib or pajalib, now in full glorious bloom; they must have been transplanted to some neighbor's garden, Enli studied the holes where the broken jelitib had been. At the bottom of one hole was something dark and matted, vaguely damp-looking. She fished it out with a stick. A dead freb. Enli poked the little mammal carefully, to see how it had died, and eventually she saw the place in the flopping neck where the knife had gone in.

So her neighbors even knew about Tabor.

Enli's neckfur prickled. She glanced around. No one in sight, even though the sun was above the horizon and the weather clear and warm. There should have been people riding to the fields, to the soap manufactury by the river, to Rafkit Seloe. Children should be playing in the village square, eating their cold breakfasts together, grudgingly minding smaller brothers and sisters. Instead, there was only silence and emptiness, as pointed a message as the straightened stone border and missing plants. Her neighbors were waiting for Enli Pek Brimmidin to leave.

She walked around the flower bed again, pretending to study it, working to calm her breathing. It was always a shock. Not an unexpected shock—this was, after all, the fifth time that a village had discovered who she was and forced her to move on. Sometimes they did it this way, stopping all real activities in her presence. Other times they just looked straight through her, pretending not to see her, carrying on the life of the village as if an unreal person were not among them, as if Enli were a ghost. Which, of course, she was. She was unreal.

Well, she couldn't stay here any longer. Her neighbors had the right of it, after all. How much did they know? That she was unreal, yes. That she stood convicted of killing her brother. That Reality and Atonement had, for reasons of their own, not put her in Aulit Prison for the crime. Did the neighbors know that she was working to earn back her reality? Probably not. Although the brighter ones might guess. Old Frablit, for instance. Not much got past that one's grizzled neckfur. Maybe Inno. Maybe Glamit.

Enli sat down on the bench outside her hut to consider where she should go. Farther north, maybe. Word about her might not travel north as easily; most people in this village seemed to have family toward the south. She looked again at the straight line of border stones, where last night there had been a long, graceful curve. Ugly, ugly. She should leave soon, this morning, now.

Already her headpain had burst past what the government pills could control. Maybe she should raise the dosage. Reality and Atonement had said she could do that, if the unreality hurt too bad . . . So far, Enli had made do with the lower dosage. You had to be tough to stay unreal and not go mad. Well, Enli was tough. You had to be tough to kill your beloved brother, too.

No, don't think about that.

Enli jumped to her feet. She would go now, this minute. Pack her few belongings—the hut and furniture were leased, of course—get her bicycle from the shed, and go. Before her neighbors started getting headpain, too. She owed them that much.

Someone was bicycling toward Enli's hut.

She shaded her eyes from the sun's low, red rising and squinted along the road. As she did so, she caught again that gleam in the sky, a flash of sudden light . . . what *was* that? She'd seen it before, always at sunrise or sunset, like something shiny high in the sky. Not one of World's seven moons, not a bird . . . There was nothing else it could be. *I don't see it,* old Frablit had said to her, and Inno, and even the children. But Enli had better eyes than even the children. Strong, ugly, sharp-eyed, that was she. Oh, and, of course, unreal.

The approaching traveler was identifiable now. A young man on a government bicycle, his neckfur barely out of child-brown. If he was from Reality and Atonement—and of course he was, no other government section would write to Enli while she was unreal—then he knew she was unreal. If he took notice of Enli, even to deliver a government message, he would be tacitly admitting that the illusionary woman sitting on a bench existed, which of course he couldn't do. It was a nice point.

The messenger did the right thing. Ignoring her, he tossed a letter, neatly addressed to Enli Pek Brimmidin, down by the dusty road. Then he pedaled back toward the city.

The letter was shaped into a utilitarian circle, very businesslike, with a generic government seal. Enli opened it. A summons: They had a job for her.

She let out a long thankful breath. Sometimes the flowers of the soul bloomed just when you most needed them. A job would take her away from here. A job would give her something to do. Most important, a job would earn more atonement toward completing her sentence. If it was a big enough job, it might even finish her punishment, setting her free to become real again. And, of course, setting Tabor free as well.

Enli packed her shoulder sack, wheeled her bicycle out of its shed, and started for the city. Probably she would never see this place again. There was still no one around. Well, let them hide. She didn't care.

But she had to stop her bicycle to take another pill. Damn the headpain! Boring right between her eyes, it was almost bad enough for tears. So much unreality, so much isolation . . . No. She wouldn't think about it. She would think instead about the job ahead, about the beauty of the wildflowers along the road to the city, about anything at all except that she was unreal, and alone, and had murdered her brother.

All morning Enli rode steadily. It was Am, that luscious season, and the larfruit was ready to harvest. Villagers swarmed over the orchards, singing and picking. Between the villages and orchards lay long lush stretches of uninhabited road, glorious with wildflowers. Shade-blooming vekifirib, yellow mittib, the flaming red bells of adkinib. The warm air smelled sweet as shared reality, and in the sky the sun burned clear orange. Enli passed few bicycles or handcarts, and made good time toward Rafkit Seloe. She could be there by noon.

But then, just a few miles shy of Rafkit Seloe, she turned her bicycle off the main road, toward the village of Gofkit Shamloe. Suddenly, desperately, Enli wanted one more look at Tabor.

The house of Enli's sister, Ano Pek Brimmidin, stood in the very heart of Gofkit Shamloe, off the central square. At this time of day, the square frothed with harvesters back for dinner. Old men cooked and women weaved and children made nuisances of themselves by chasing each other between the solid brick hearths. Delicious dinner smells floated on the warm air. A group of young people danced, giggling, to the rather inept piping of old Solor Pek Raumul. In Gofkit Shamloe, meals were always the best time, for as long back as Enli could remember. The time of life and warmth, the time when shared reality filled the air as strongly as the scent of roasting meat.

She rode through the villagers as if she were invisible. No one stopped her, spoke to her, glanced at her. No one barred her from slipping through the open door of Ano's house.

Tabor lay on his bed in the back room. He rested on his

back, his strong young legs straight as trees, his fingers lightly curled. His neckfur, more golden than either Ano's or Enli's (unfair—why had the boy gotten all the beauty?), floated in the bondage chemicals of his clear coffin. He looked no older than when the servants of the First Flower had imprisoned him, making him as unreal as Enli, for their mutual crime. When Enli leaned over the coffin, Tabor's unseeing dark eyes stared back at her.

"One more year's atonement, Tabor. Less thirty-six days. Then you will be free. And so will I."

Tabor said nothing. But, of course, there was no need. He knew as well as Enli did the time until his burial, when he would be released from the chemicals and glass that bound his dead body and so could rejoin their ancestors. Enli had heard that some of the unreal dead complained and recriminated, especially in dreams, making the houses in which they lay a misery. Not Tabor, Enli thought. Tabor had always been a well-mannered person, and he wouldn't trouble Ano's house. Nor would he trouble Ano's sleep with fear and dreams. Only Enli's sleep.

The door to the bedroom creaked. Enli's nephew, small Fentil, came into the room, took something out of a wooden chest, and left again, carefully not seeing her. His mother had taught him well. But above his soft childish neckfur his little head must hurt, and his real presence made Enli's headpain even worse. Clearly, it was time to go.

She walked back through Ano's house, not looking at its flower altar—she owed Ano at least that, to not pollute her flowers with unreal gazes—and rode her bicycle down the road toward the capital.

To Enli's surprise, the clerk at Reality and Atonement addressed her by name. "Pek Brimmidin, you may go in now."

Usually the man, very old and very sour, with neckfur gone beyond yellow or even gray right up to a sparse sickly no-color dun, never spoke. He looked at the unreal who came to petition or object or report in; he must look at them in order to enter their comings and goings in the records, just as he must know Enli's name. But never before had he addressed her by it.

"Thank you," Enli said, to see if he would say more. But his eyes went unfocused again, the brief period of shared reality over.

Why had it happened in the first place? What did the sour old man know about Enli's upcoming job? Possibly quite a bit. Long-retained clerks always did.

Cartot Pek Nagredil's office was empty when she entered, which gave her time to examine the extraordinarily ugly sculptures on his table. Curves too exaggerated, colors too harsh. Enli felt a sudden, delayed pang for her vanished pajalib, with their exquisite curving petals. There were not, of course, any flowers in Pek Nagredil's office, where they would be exposed to the gaze of the unreal. Nor would anyone offer her a hospitality flower. Not her.

"Pek Brimmidin. I have an informant job for you." Pek Nagredil never wasted words. He was only middle-aged but so solid, so immovable, that Enli wondered if he even needed pills to talk with her. Was that possible? Could Pek Nagredil be so coarse that he didn't feel the large, dull pain in the soul, like gravel grinding inside the skull, or even that sharp hard shock between the eyes, when it became evident that two people did not see World the same way? No. Not possible. To be a Worlder was to share reality with other Worlders, or to suffer the physical pain of not doing so. Pek Nagredil was a man; he could be no different from anyone else. He had a soul. He must use the pills.

Enli asked, "What is the job, Pek Nagredil?"

"To inform on the Terrans that are coming to live in the household of Hadjil Pek Voratur."

Enli felt her mouth fall open. She tried to speak, but no words came out.

"You may have heard that the Terrans have returned," Pek Nagredil said, imperturbable. He moved a sculpture a tiny bit to the right, stepped back to observe the effect, and moved it back to the left.

"No," Enli finally managed. "I had not heard that." She had never seen a Terran. Hardly anybody had seen a Terran. They had come a half year ago, to a village on the other side of Rafkit Seloe, in a metal boat that flew down from the sky. They were amazingly ugly, ran the reports, and amazingly ignorant, but apparently not dangerous. They asked a lot of rude questions but also gave some very nice presents, which induced some people to answer the questions. After a few tendays, they had abruptly packed up and left in their flying boat. The most important questions, of course, were not theirs but Worlders': Were these Terrans real? Did they have souls? The priests of Reality and Atonement had only just begun their inquiry into this when the Terrans, without so much as a farewell flower, had left World.

Now apparently they were back.

"We knew the Terrans would return," Pek Nagredil said. "They were overheard to say, 'We will come back for the manufactured item.' They're great traders, you see. Now, Pek Brimmidin, you can see that this is a sensitive job. That's why we asked you, Pek Brimmidin. You have done good informant work. And Reality and Atonement allows me to say this: If you also complete this job well, then your debt to shared reality will be washed away. You will again be real, and so will Tabor your brother."

Again be real. Enli lowered her head. She didn't want Pek Nagredil to see her face. To be real again . . . and Tabor, too. Tabor, who lay in his coffin preserved in the bondage chemicals that kept his body from decaying and so releasing his soul. Tabor would be broken from his coffin, washed clean, buried under a mound of flowers. His soul would be released to join their ancestors. And Enli would live again in Gofkit Shamloe with Ano, cooking at midday on the communal fires and dancing on the green and growing flowers openly, without guilt, without shame . . .

A hunger so fierce swept over her that, had she not known better, she would have said she still had her soul.

"I accept the job, Pek Nagredil."

"Good. This is what has happened. A Terran who visited

World before, one Ahmed Pek Bazargan, came yesterday in his metal flying boat to a village south of here, Gofkit Jemloe. He asked to live in the great household there, the Voratur, in return for any rent they chose to ask. Household Oversight approved the request, and naturally Hadjil Pek Voratur accepted."

"Naturally," Enli said. Even in Gofkit Shamloe she had heard of the Voratur. They were a great trading family, rich and respected, and the Terrans had already demonstrated their willingness to share marvelous trade goods. Enli heard her own voice, and was glad it again sounded normal.

"Six Terrans will live with the Voratur. Many sections of the government besides Household Oversight are interested in the Terran visit, as you can perhaps imagine."

Enli certainly could. So the question would bloom all over again, like the First Flower: Were the Terrans real?

"You will live in the Voratur household, Pek Brimmidin," Pek Nagredil said, "and you will inform on everything the Terrans do and say. Your position in the household will be cleaning servant, with special attention to the crelm house where the Voratur and Terran children will live."

"The . . . children? *Terran* children?"

"Yes. You will—"

"There are Terran children? What Terran children? Why would the Terrans bring children?"

For the first time, Pek Nagredil looked slightly discomfited. "They say to raise them as Worlders. Along with the Voratur children."

Enli and Pek Nagredil stared at each other, the air heavy with what neither said. Children were not born real; they must grow to participate in shared reality. A few tragic empty ones never did so and must, of course, be destroyed. If the Terrans wanted their children "raised as Worlders," did that mean they wanted them to become real? And did that in turn mean that the adult Terrans *weren't* already real? That they had no souls?

"You will report here every tenday," Pek Nagredil said, taking visible refuge in normal routine, "and report everything you have learned about the Terrans. Every detail, no matter how small."

"Pek Nagredil," Enli blurted, "am I going to be supplying information that actually determines whether or not Terrans are real?"

"That's not for you to know," Pek Nagredil said severely, and Enli saw his skull ridges throb slightly. She knew he was right. She had no right to expect to know why she was informing, or what the information would be used for. To tell her those things would be to make her a sharer in reality, and she had excluded herself from that by her own crime.

"Yes, Pek Nagredil," Enli said. "I will report to the Voratur household tomorrow morning."

"You may go, Pek Brimmidin." No farewell flower.

Enli bicycled thoughtfully away from Rafkit Seloe, toward Gofkit Jemloe. The Voratur household did not expect her until tomorrow, but no one had said how early tomorrow. She would present herself at sunrise.

By the time she reached the edge of Gofkit Jemloe, it was sunset. Enli found a quiet field, unrolled her bedsack, and cooked dinner on a small fire. As she worked, she kept glancing at the sky. Another clear night. Four moons were up: Ap, one of the two fast-blooming moons that raced across the sky more than once in a night; Lil; Cut; and luminous Obri, Home of the First Flower. Enli lay on her back in the bedsack, watching Obri. The sun sank below the horizon. Enli watched carefully, but no matter how hard she searched overhead with her splendid eyesight, the mysterious sunrise-and-sunset gleam in the sky wasn't there.

TWO

ABOARD THE *ZEUS*

Forty-five thousand kilometers above Rafkit Seloe, David Campbell Allen III stood in a bathroom aboard the Solar Alliance Defense Council ship *Zeus* and breathed deeply to calm his panic.

Damn it, he shouldn't be feeling any panic! He had given a lot of thought to this morning's Discipline, carefully designing the neuropharm mix for a dynamic balance between stability and hyperalertness. He took his neurological responsibility toward himself very seriously. (*The boy's a prig, Diana,* he'd once overheard his father say. But then, his father would.) So why wasn't the mixture right?

Stepping to the wall, David stuck his finger in his biomonitor for another check. All readings looked fine: glutamate, serotonin, dopamine, cortical suppressant, amygdala regulator, P15, BDNF to strengthen the synaptic connections for learning in the hippocampus. All the rest. Maybe a touch too much noraldin, but within range for the state of mind he wanted. All right, then, the panic must be normal, too. He would handle it. He breathed deeply, bending his head toward the floor. Today, of all days, he wanted to be at his best, do his best.

(*The boy's too earnest. Too rigid.*)

Why was he thinking so much about his father?

All at once David realized the answer. It was the *bathroom*. It had been in a bathroom that he'd first told his father, the revered Barlin Prize winner in astrophysics four separate times, that his son was entering Princeton to study the squishy-soft field of alien anthropology. They'd been in the men's room at Selfridge's Restaurant, in Lowell City on Mars. David had picked a public bathroom for his announcement for a very good reason. It was the only place he could be sure his father would take a few more moments before turning around to face him.

"Mr. Allen," the system said melodiously, "message."

"On."

"The shuttle will be delayed five minutes."

"Thank you. Off."

David knotted his hair on top of his head and pulled on the Solar Alliance Defense Council civilian dress uniform, an ox-ymoron if he ever heard one. The official rationale was that a scientific expedition was always a representative of the home solar system, whether it was military, political, or Trans-Planetary University Foundation. They all received tax dollars from somebody's government. The unofficial reason, David knew, was that uniforms reminded the expedition of what they were representing: the solar system in toto, not Mars or Luna or the Belt or the Confucian Hegemony or the United Atlantic Federation or any of the other possibilities. United in science. Officially, anyway

The problem was that the equivalent of an officer's uniform was completely unsuited to fieldwork in anthropology. Stiff, intimidating, and equipped—God help us!—with a small ceremonial sword. Well, he wasn't wearing *that* down to World. Obviously nobody had consulted a xenoscientist about designing the uniform. A *sword*. Might as well show up in a native village shooting a lasercannon. Anyway, after today the team would wear native dress.

Time to go. His first trip as a xenologist, not counting university fieldwork. By any standards, a coup for his first time out; most graduate students had to be content with doing their practicum with well-worked-over aliens like the Tel or the

Sien-Tu. Tame stuff. But here was David Allen on World, practically virgin territory. And he had gotten it on his own, without once asking his father to intercede. In fact, his father hadn't even known he'd applied for the post. Didn't know now, either, although that part of the expedition was a little vague to David. It had to do, Dr. Bazargan had explained, with the military presence aboard ship, and the war. Sensitive data. Secrecy was essential.

David had nodded, but the truth was, he didn't really care. As long as they didn't encounter the Fallers on World—and he'd been assured they wouldn't—the war was as remote to David as to most people in the solar system. It meant skirmishes fought only rarely, and elsewhere. He'd been too busy with his coursework to follow it closely. Anyway, science was concerned with knowledge for the ages, not with temporary political situations. Science was above all that.

(*The boy's a prig, Diana.*)

He was ready to show them all.

Dr. Ahmed Bazargan greeted his team as they assembled in the shuttle bay. Around them, the hydroponics workers loaded masses of cut flowers into the shuttle. "Good morning, Ann. Ready to begin?"

"Completely," Mellianni Sikorski said, smiling. She was the team's xenobiologist, an American, competent and experienced despite her youth; she was only thirty-seven. Bazargan had campaigned to get her. He'd worked with her once before, and she was invariably a calm and amiable presence. Perhaps she was simply unusually good at the Discipline, but Bazargan didn't think it was that. Her stable sweetness seemed to go deeper, down to the bedrock of character. He had a nose for these things.

Ann Sikorski specialized in the xenobiology of neurosystems. So far, it had been a disappointing field. Through the space tunnels, humans had discovered thirty-six other sentient species, and thirty-five of them had been, in essence, human. They possessed only minor variations in skeletal structure, biochemistry, genome, and neurology. The prevailing theory was that something—or some race—had seeded the galaxy with a common pseudo-human ancestor, and subsequent evolution had diverged only as various planetary conditions favored. The thirty-five sentient species ranged from stone-age cultures to middle industrial.

That made sense. The mathematics of probability was not Bazargan's field, but he did understand the inspection paradox: In any statistical distribution, entities that have already begun their lifetimes will have longer-than-average lifetimes. It applied to middle-aged people, and to middle-aged species. The probability had always been that Sol was thus one of the more advanced galactic civilizations.

Except, of course, for whatever vanished race had done the initial seeding. And for the Fallers.

Bazargan watched Ann smile at the approaching geologist for the team, Dieter Gruber. Unlike Ann, who had a long, plain, washed-out face (no genemod enhancements for beauty in her family, obviously), Gruber was an impressive physical specimen. Enhanced? Probably, although that very personal information was not in the team files. Gruber, a German, looked like somebody's idea of a Teutonic prince: big, blond, blue-eyed, with an irreverent grin. His scientific record was good, even brilliant. Capable and agreeable, he nonetheless showed flashes of stubborn independence. Still, Bazargan anticipated no difficulties in working with the geologist, who in any case would spend much of his time off alone at promising sites.

Bazargan wasn't quite so sure about David Allen.

The young intern walked too quickly toward them. Allen, who had grown up so internationally that it hardly mattered what country or planet he'd been born on, had showed competence in his student fieldwork. He also had an unusual flair for languages, better than Bazargan himself. In the team's preparatory language immersion on Earth, judiciously aided by chemical and digital boosters, Allen had mastered World astonishingly fast. He'd also done exceptionally well at reading World facial-and-skull-ridge expressions on the recordings made by the first team.

But against all that, Allen was mostly untried, and there was a quality about him that made Bazargan uneasy: an intensity, a fervid idealism that Bazargan suspected was capable of reaching hysteria. It was a quality familiar to Bazargan; in his native Iran it was possessed by politicians and ayatollahs, revolutionaries and generals. It had caused Iran centuries of bloody unrest, and Bazargan, himself a careful and methodical realist, distrusted David Allen's capacity for idealism. Look at the way the boy obsessively practiced the Discipline, monitoring his neuropharm mixture several times a day, turning a tool for mental acuity into a religion. If Bazargan had had a choice, Allen would not be filling the obligatory graduate-student position on this scientific expedition, which already had too many anomalies surrounding it.

But Bazargan had not had a choice. Science, no less than Solar Alliance Defense, had its politics. Anthropology was perpetually underfunded. There was a war on (there was always a war on). The word came down from the Trans-Planetary University Foundation: *David Campbell Allen's father wishes his son to be a member of this expedition. Funding may depend on this.* Bazargan had made the best of it. David Allen would be the backup anthropologist for the nursery study.

Of course, Bazargan had expected that the babies' mother would be alive, running the study. But anthropologist Dr. Hannah Mason had died in a freak electrical accident aboard the *Zeus*, and Bazargan, stuck with deploying his small team as efficiently as possible, must needs make do with David Allen because the senior Allen wanted it so.

And Bazargan understood. That was how it still worked in Iran: family first. But he wondered if the boy knew. Probably not. Allen struck Bazargan as capable of an enormous amount of self-delusion.

"Sorry I'm late," David said.

"You're not," Bazargan said pleasantly. "Leila hasn't come down yet with the twins."

"David," Ann said, smiling at him. "Ready to go down?"

"More than ready. You aren't wearing your sword, either, I see."

"A sword," Dieter Gruber said, grinning. "Well, at least we don't need to be armed against tanglefoam or proton beams."

Ann said, "What *were* the uniform designers thinking of?"

"The Solar Alliance," Allen said. "Or rather, solar reliance—relying on a uniform to remind us that our separate governments are supposed to be anything but."

"Which is only one reason you should be wearing the sword," said another voice behind Bazargan. "A uniform is not an à la carte menu, mister."

Bazargan turned, although of course he already knew who the speaker was; there was no mistaking that note of authority. Colonel Dr. Syree Johnson, military physicist, headed this scientific expedition, although she would not be descending to the planet. Why not? *Space physics,* Bazargan had been told, vaguely and unconvincingly. One of the expedition anomalies.

David Allen flushed. "A sword is inappropriate to fieldwork, Colonel. It sends the natives the message that we are unfriendly."

"It is part of the uniform for dress occasions," Colonel Johnson said. "The first meeting of your scientific team with the natives is a dress occasion. You need not wear the uniform for your fieldwork."

Allen began, with too much heat, "It's more important to—"

"Put on your sword," Bazargan said clearly. "You, too, Ann and Dieter. And I will get mine."

Ann and Gruber both nodded and started toward their quarters. David, still flushed, set his lips together and also obeyed. Bazargan had been curious to see if he would.

When the three returned, swords at their sides, Colonel Johnson was in conference with Commander Rafael Peres, captain of the *Zeus,* and Chief Engineer Major Canton Lee. David Allen said, sulkily but low, "There. I'm adequately armed, just to please the colonel. Why does she limp, anyway?"

"I don't know," Bazargan said, although he did.

"Easy enough to grow a replacement leg, and the Alliance would pay for it. Looks pretentious not to fix that limp."

"Here comes Leila," Bazargan said pointedly.

Corporal Leila DiSilvo entered the flight bay, pushing the twins. Ben and Bonnie Mason lay in a double flight seat, both asleep. Ann looked down at the sleeping babies, fourteen months old, strapped in for the flight down. "Poor pumpkins."

"What's a 'pumpkin'?" Allen said, with a shade of defiance left over from Colonel Johnson. "And why 'poor'?"

"A pumpkin's a Terran vegetable, not grown much anymore. And 'poor' because any child who loses its mother and never knew its father is poor."

"You wouldn't say that if you'd had my mother and father," Allen said, and Bazargan saw that the boy instantly regretted saying it. He didn't want Ann Sikorski, ten years older and female, to pity him. Ann, always tactful, merely said lightly, "Ben and Bonnie will have you, and the World children as well. They'll be fine."

Bazargan smiled. Americans dismissed family so lightly. He was used to it, but he still didn't understand it.

Colonel Johnson finished her conversation with the ship's officers and turned again to Bazargan. "Good luck, Doctor."

"Thank you, Colonel."

"Do you wish to go over the emergency recall signals again?"

"No. We are fully prepared."

"Then Allah be with you."

Bazargan was surprised. There was more to Colonel Johnson, that military martinet, than he had supposed.

"Thank you. Ann, David, Dieter . . . we go."

As the shuttle, piloted by the popular and easygoing Captain Daniel Austen, pulled away from the *Zeus*, everyone looked down at the planet below. A scrap of Persian poetry came to Bazargan, as it so often did when he reflected on anything at all: *Be fearful of trouble when all seems fair and clear, / For the easy is soon made grievous by the swift transforming fear.* Khusrau, eleventh century.

Although there was no reason to expect either fear or grief on World, the most idyllic civilization scientists had ever discovered. The planet was lush and fertile, the monolithic (why?) civilization peaceful and comfortable. No, this would be just another routine field trip. Gather data, go home, analyze, publish.

And yet . . . there were those anomalies. Why had the recon team been ordered back to Earth after only two months? The scientists had assumed some dire development in the war, and had undoubtedly fretted during the entire eight E-day travel time from World to Space Tunnel #438. But there had been no dire developments in the war. Nor had there been any explanation of the hasty departure from World, although the scientists aboard had fumed and petitioned and filed official protests. The team had never published: "insufficient data."

The scientists hadn't even been able to agree among themselves on the central issue of World culture: Why was it so uniform? Was the "shared reality" that dominated Worlders a political control mechanism, a religious belief, or—Ann's hope—an actual unique biological development in the aliens' evolution?

Insufficient data.

Why was this replacement team so small, and so hastily assembled, and so covert?

Insufficient data.

Why did military physicists outnumber anthropologists on what was supposed to be an anthropological expedition—moreover, military physicists listed on the ship's roster merely as "chief engineer," "third officer," and "shuttle pilot"? Bazargan had his own sources of information; in Iran you did not survive without them. But why was the secrecy deemed necessary?

Insufficient data.

Bazargan turned to Gruber, Allen, and Ann, strapped in beside him in the shuttle, crowded by masses of genetically engineered red roses, yellow dahlias, and orange snowballs. "When we make planetfall," he said quietly, "you can leave your swords in the shuttle."

* * *

Syree Johnson followed the shuttle trajectory on the bridge displays. Automatically her mind reviewed the planetary data. Point six nine AUs from its primary, a G8 emitting .48 of Sol's energy per unit area. Maximum energy reaching the planet at intensity .66 micrometers, roughly the same as Earth. Point seven three Terran mass, 5,740 clicks in radius .9 Terran gravity on the planetary surface. Rotation of 26.2 Terran hours, period of 213 rotations, inclination to the ecliptic of 3.2 degrees. One major almost-circumequatorial landmass plus coastal islands, some of them large. Unremarkable composition, except for some strong radioactivity in the second-highest mountain range, identified by the flow of neutrinos registering on the *Zeus*'s detectors.

None of it mattered.

Despite what the anthropologists thought, the only thing that mattered about "World" was something currently known only to Syree, her military physics team, and Commander Peres. Something so potentially momentous that it had equipped and funded this expedition to a backward planet in a remote section of space served by a little-traveled space tunnel. Something that could tip the balance in the far-off war with the Fallers, those peculiar and aggressive and dangerous aliens.

The planet that its natives ethnocentrically called "World" had seven moons. Only one of them wasn't.

And now that the anthropologists had left the *Zeus,* Syree Johnson and her team could get to work finding out what the seventh moon actually was. They had a hypothesis. Her job was to prove it right.

THREE

GOFKIT JEMLOE

All of Gofkit Jemloe turned out to welcome the Terrans. Hadjil Pek Voratur, Enli realized, was a very important man. He walked toward the Terrans a few steps ahead of the village priest, a short man with unfortunate ears, whose name Enli had forgotten.

Pek Voratur was portly and tall, with well-fed skin that looked oiled and neckfur that undoubtedly was. With his handsome tunic he wore a magnificent woven vest that must have been imported from Seuril Island, a belt studded with gold, and a flat wide hat decked with perfect saji blossoms. Beside him walked his wife, Alu Pek Voratur, dressed with similar richness. Both carried armfuls of perfect flowers in the hospitality colors, yellow and orange, plus a nosegay of sacred blue frimpil flowers to bless the visitors. The priest should have been carrying those. That Pek Voratur did, instead, told Enli quite a lot about the man.

But it wasn't Pek Voratur she was interested in. These were the first aliens she'd ever seen.

At first sight, they were disappointing. Too much like real people (or, rather, like people already proven to be real, Enli reminded herself; the distinction was why she was here). Big, but not as monstrously huge as rumor said. Two arms, two legs, torso, head, two eyes, one mouth . . . Enil had secretly been hoping for monsters. Or at least something exotic.

Pek Bazargan has told the servants of the First Flower that Worlders and Terrans grew from the same seeds, long ago, Pek Voratur had said to his assembled household, but it had been clear to Enil that he didn't believe it. How could he? What an idea! If that was the kind of things these Terrans believed, the priests of Reality and Atonement would most certainly decide they were unreal. Still, Pek Voratur might have misquoted. The Terrans deserved a chance. Souls were at stake.

Enli craned her neck over the crowd; as a lowly cleaner, she stood near the back. But she was tall.

When they approached closer, walking from their flying boat toward Gofkit Jemloe, the Terrans appeared more satisfyingly alien. Their skins were various shades of brown, from dun to dirt, rather than the normal pale yellow. Their foreheads were strangely flat. Most shocking, they had no neckfur, but did have fur on top of their heads, covering their skull ridges. The headfur was evidently long enough to pull into curving bundles. Rather pretty, if you didn't mind not seeing people's expressions.

The Terrans knew enough to bring yellow and orange flowers with them, masses of blooms of types Enli had never seen before. Why, if they gave Pek Voratur seeds for those plants, that alone could make him the richest man on World!

One of the Terrans pushed a cart, an ugly vehicle of straight, utilitarian lines. The cart was covered with a blanket and more flowers. Enli couldn't see what was inside. The Terrans and Worlders met, and Enli strained to hear.

"I honor your flowers," Pek Voratur said. Speaking before the mayor or the priest did! But neither winced with the sharp onset of headpain that Enli knew so well; shared reality had not been violated. All must have been agreed on and rehearsed.

The oldest Terran, probably male, replied correctly: "I rejoice in your blossoms." His accent was strange, but no stranger than Coe Lijil islanders.

"You are welcome to the flowers of our household," said Alu Pek Voratur.

"Your beautiful blossoms rejoice my spirit," another Terran said. Female, Enli decided.

"May your garden bloom always," the mayor said.

"The petals of your flowers are beautiful," said a third Terran, amazingly huge, in a terrible accent. Didn't they know any other flower words beside "beautiful"? Were they then stupid?

"Your flowers transport my heart," the priest said.

"May your blossoms always please the souls of your ancestors," said the last Terran, who was pushing the cart. His accent was quite good.

"I am Hadjil Pek Voratur. You are welcome to the flowers of my household."

"I am Ahmed Pek Bazargan. You are welcome to the flowers of my heart."

The ceremony went on, followed by the ritual exchanges of flowers. Enli noted everything, for her report. The Terrans certainly *acted* real.

Finally Pek Voratur removed a blanket from a World cart—much more attractively curved than the Terran cart—and said formally, "Here are the children of my household."

He meant, of course, the ones too small to be pronounced real, all those still isolated in the crelm house. There were seven: four walking and three still in infancy. They peered shyly from their seats in the cart. One little girl looked frightened and puckered her face to cry; the older children were not used to being away from their crelm house. Only the babies looked unaffected, two staring with wide dark eyes and one asleep, scrunched in its basket.

Pek Bazargan said, "Here are the children of my household," and the Terran pushing the cart pulled back its blanket.

Two babies, much plumper and bigger than the World babies. They lacked neckfur, but because they also lacked very much fur on their heads, they looked to Enli far more normal than the Terran adults. Their eyes were pale but filled with shining light, like reflections on clear water. Each stared

around with exactly the same round-eyed, unblinking stare as
World babies, and this further endeared them. People in the
crowd hummed softly, *"hhhhhmmmmmmmmmmmmm,"* smiling despite themselves at the pretty infants.

If Enli had been making bets in a pel house, at that moment
she would have bet on the Terrans' being declared real.

"Let us go home," Pek Voratur said, and everyone shifted
positions by rank to follow the aliens to the Voratur household. Enli took her place farthest from the dignitaries, at the
far right end of the fan-shaped crowd escorting the Terrans.
As it happened, she was well placed to see everything that
happened next.

"Look! See! See!" the child cried, running toward them.

She was easily over eight years old, and big for her age,
her shift torn. Dirt smeared her clothing and face; blood clotted
on one bare arm. She drooled constantly. Enli looked away.
The child's eyes were both wild and empty, without a soul.
She was clearly unreal, and her family had not yet held the
necessary ceremony. How could they have waited? It was
cruel, it should not be allowed.

No one looked at the girl. The crowd continued as before,
walking slowly toward the household of Hadjil Pek Voratur,
chatting or humming. But a sorrow rippled over them, like
wind in grass. Enli could feel it in her every pore. The dark
eyes around her deepened and mourned, together, in shared
reality.

The girl stopped, saw the Terran babies, and made a small
gargled, "Oooooo." She had no more language than that, evidently. She moved toward the Terran visitors.

Silently, never breaking stride, never looking at her unreal
and empty husk, Worlders prevented her. The crowd of them
shifted and flowed, so there were always one or two adults
between the girl and the cart with the Terran infants. The girl
pushed and butted with her head, but she could not break
through. Finally she stood still and broke into loud wailing.
Worlders did not hear her. The crowd moved on.

And then it happened. The Terran pushing the infant cart,
David Pek Allen, stopped and *smiled at the unreal husk.*

"Let her see the children," he said. "I'll hold her so she doesn't hurt them."

Everyone froze.

Pek Allen reached between two men and took the unreal child by the arm, drawing her firmly forward but restraining her from coming too close. "See, little girl? These are Terran children."

Enli could feel her head begin to pain, even through the government pills. What then of the others without pills? Faces began to pucker. An old woman closed her eyes and pressed her withered hands between her eyes. Couldn't Pek Allen *feel* how he was violating shared reality? Couldn't he feel it inside his own head, the discomfort between the eyes that quickly became pain at being out of belief with the village, with reality?

Pek Allen went on smiling, talking to the unreal thing beside him.

That could mean only one thing: Pek Allen did not share reality. He himself was unreal.

Enli's mind whirled. Was this the answer, then—so *quickly*? No, no . . . The other Terrans hadn't addressed the unreal child. In fact, Pek Bazargan now moved toward Pek Allen, putting a hand on his arm. He said something, too low for the crowd to hear. Pek Allen's face below the absurd headfur turned red, and he dropped the girl's arm.

Someone shifted between the girl and the Terrans. Then someone else. A man came forward, shoulders bent in the attitude of extreme atonement. Somehow the unreal girl disappeared.

Again the crowd moved forward, shared reality restored. Once more everyone acted from inside of belief. On the faces of those nearest her, Enli saw the headpain ease. Skull ridges smoothed, smiles tremulously returned. A man clutching his stomach—it took some people that way, in the gut—eased his arms away from his body. Still, the crowd was not the same as before. Enli could feel it, the uncertainty, the strain. No one walked quite as close to the Terrans as they had before.

And so the hospitality procession came to the gates of the Voratur household, and the aliens went inside.

It was surprisingly difficult being an informer in this place.

On her other jobs, Enli had informed on only one person. Here there were four Terrans, not counting the babies, and they were not often together. How could she be in four places at once? It was impossible. Reality and Atonement asked too much. Plus, the Terrans themselves made informing harder.

The huge Terran, Dieter Pek Gruber, wasn't even in the household at all. He had been given a room, in which he placed many objects of obscure purposes. Then he rode off on the most beautiful bicycle Enli had ever seen, to travel to the Neury Mountains to "look for rocks." What sense did that make? There were plenty of rocks right here in Gofkit Jemloe; the farmers picked them out of the fields and piled them into crude walls. Rocks choked the river, tripped the bicycler, dotted the marshes. Why did the Terran need to travel all the way to the Neury Mountains to gather rocks? The sacred Neury Mountains, the place the First Flower inhabited since coming down from Obri, were also unhealthy, as everyone knew. People who went into them usually sickened and died. Their neck-fur fell out, their bodies burned with sores, their throats thickened and tongues blackened. Thus did the First Flower guard her sacred beds. Pek Gruber had been told all this. Yet he went into the mountains anyway. For *rocks*.

Then there was the youngest Terran, David Pek Allen, who had raised such grave doubts at the hospitality procession. He worked and ate and slept in the crelm house, with the two Terran infants and the seven Voratur children who had not yet been declared real. In the villages, infants were treated with a casual lovingness, cared for while the adults worked and played, but it was different in rich households. The crelm house was separated from the big house, with its own gardens and courtyards. Until a servant of the First Flower certified that the Voratur children did indeed become discomfited and upset when they were out of belief, the children were isolated from shared reality. Their parents visited them most days. Otherwise, the crelm house had its own staff of nursemaids, cook, and cleaners. Enli was not among the cleaners assigned to the crelm house. She had not so much as glimpsed Pek Allen during the last tenday.

That left Ahmed Pek Bazargan and Ann Pek Sikowski. They at least lived in the sprawling big house, as honored guests. But Pek Bazargan accompanied either Pek Voratur or his wife nearly everywhere: to the docks when the Voratur trading fleet set out, to the market, to the gardens, to Rafkit Seloe, to visit friends. Pek Bazargan, in fact, was rarely home. And even when he was, she couldn't learn very much. Cleaners, she discovered, did not clean rooms at the same time the household family occupied them.

Pek Sikorski's rooms she didn't clean at all. The Terran female had been given apartments on an outer courtyard, close to the outer wall that circled the vast household. One chamber was Pek Sikorski's personal room. The other two she filled with strange objects, plus plants and animals that she killed and dissected. Well, Pek Sikorski was a healer; that was how healers made their pills and potions. But the Terran healer requested of Pek Voratur that no one else enter her workrooms, not even to clean. Probably she didn't want her healer's potions stolen before she was ready to sell them to Worlders herself. No one could blame her for that. However, it meant that by the end of her first tenday, when Enli was supposed to report in to Pek Nagredil, she had nothing to report. At best she had only glimpsed the Terrans in passing through corridors and courtyards.

Gloomily Enli rode her bicycle toward Rafkit Seloe. The trip seemed to take a long weary time. As she had expected, Pek Nagredil was not pleased.

"You observed nothing of the Terrans? Nothing at all?"

"I told you about the hospitality procession," Enli said.

"The sunflashers told us about the hospitality procession," which of course they had. Enli had seen the woman in the tunic of Annals and Sunflashers, racing on her bicycle toward Rafkit Seloe. From there news of the Terrans had flashed by mirror glass from hill tower to hill tower around all of World. Before nightfall, the Voratur hospitality procession had been shared reality.

Enli said feebly, "I told you about the personal rooms each Terran received in the Voratur household."

"But nothing beyond that? Not even that Pek Sikorski hired the kitchen boy to catch frebs and bring them to her to kill?"

"How do you know that?"

"Pek Brimmidin," Pek Nagredil said severely, "you are not the only informant we have in the Voratur household."

Enli felt stupid. Of course she was not the only informant; for a job of this importance, Reality and Atonement would use others as well. Who were they? She knew there was no point in asking.

Pek Nagredil walked across his small office, absently touched a statue, squinted at a wall hanging. He had not combed his neckfur very well. His skull ridges wrinkled. Enli waited.

Finally he said, "We will have to try something different. Here is what I want you to do, Pek Brimmidin."

He unlocked a heavy wooden chest in a corner of the room.

Enli waited until midafternoon, when there was a lull in the cleaning routines and the family was often out of the house. Quietly she slipped through the maze of interconnecting courtyards and treed parks to Pek Sikorski's apartments near the east wall. The Terran worked at her bench. Enli looked, then looked away. A dead freb lay pinned to a board, its belly slit to show the insides, from which pieces had already been removed. Alien objects littered the room. Enli stamped her foot to make her presence known.

"Oh!" Pek Sikorski said, turning swiftly. "Who are you?"

"Enli Pek Brimmidin, household cleaner," Enli said humbly. "Forgive me for startling you."

"Come in," Pek Sikorski said. Her manners were good; she plucked a yellow pajal blossom from the hospitality bush by the door and offered it to Enli. "You are welcome to the flowers of my rooms."

"Your blossoms rejoice my soul," Enli said, taking the flower, and felt a sharp stab of pain between her eyes, even through the pills. Her words violated shared reality. She had no soul, not while she was unreal.

Pek Sikorski waited. Clearly she expected Enli to also produce a flower. Well, that was why Enli was here. But for a moment she hesitated, struck by the weird strangeness of a Terran seen close up.

Pek Sikorski had light-colored fur above her eyes, as well as on her head. And how much of the headfur there was! Instead of being tied on top of her head, as during the welcome procession, the long pale headfur streamed down her back. But most peculiar of all was Pek Sikorski's naked neck. Didn't it get cold? And didn't it feel immodest, exposed like that? Usually only intimates saw a person's neck: mothers nuzzling infants, lovers exploring each other's bodies.

Also, the Terran smelled odd. Not unpleasant, just odd, in a way Enli couldn't describe.

Also, there was a small, empty hole on the soft ugly extensions of her ears. What were the holes for? What were the extensions for? A deformity?

"Pek Brimmidin?" the Terran said gently.

"Forgive me, my foolish brain blinks," Enli said, embarrassed. "Accept the flower of a visitor, Pek Sikorski." She held out the palm of her hand, on which sat a white cloth. Carefully she unwrapped the blossom that Pek Nagredil had taken from his locked chest.

The flower was dried, not fresh, such as were used only in the most sacred of ceremonies by the most holy of priests. The drying had preserved the bloom perfectly: its tiny crimson petals and long, curving tongue. Casually Pek Sikorski reached for it. "The color is beau—"

Clearly she did not know what it was.

"Don't touch it, please!" Enli commanded. Astonished, the Terran pulled her hand away. "The petals are poison."

Pek Sikorski's pale eyes sharpened.

"This is a camorif flower," Enli explained. "It only grows on Kikily Island, far to the south. The servants of the First Flower make a powder of the tongue, unmixed with even a tiny taste of petal, and it takes them deeper into shared reality, so they may return and share their knowledge with the people. Camorifib are only used on holy feast days. This flower has belonged to my family for two generations. My grandfather was a priest." Her headpain was sharp now, boring more deeply with each unreal sentence. But she must finish. "No one ever talks about giving camorif flowers, of course. It is not a hospitality flower, and no one talks about owning one. Never. I give this camorif flower to you, Pek Sikorski."

This time the Terran took the bloom carefully, transferring it and its white cloth covering from Enli's hand to hers. Then she looked levelly at Enli.

"Why do you give me this, Pek Brimmidin? It is a valuable gift."

"I would ask something in return, Pek Sikorski. A piece of information. But if you do not wish to answer, the gift is still yours."

Pek Sikorski nodded, apparently accepting the ritual formula. Perhaps she'd been told it by the other Terrans, the ones who came a halfyear ago. Or perhaps she'd already heard it herself in the Voratur household. Pek Voratur, after all, was a trader.

"I may ask my question?"

"You may ask your question."

Enli said, "Are you Terrans here to learn about the headpain that comes when reality is unshared?"

For a long moment Pek Sikorski did not answer. So Pek Nagredil had been right. He had told Enli exactly what to say, the question put together from whatever information Reality and Atonement already had about the Terrans' behavior. Finally the Terran said, "May I ask, Pek Brimmidin, why you think that?"

"I don't know," Enli said, and felt for a moment the blessed cool sweetness of shared reality. It was the truth. She did not know.

Pek Sikorski said, smiling now, "You are a sharp observer. We Terrans are very interested in shared reality. Tell me about the headpain, if you will."

"I cannot. I must go back to clean now."

Pek Sikorski nodded. She must know that the bargain was fulfilled: the camorif flower for an answered question. More information really could not be expected. But there was more, to Enli at least, in the quick way that Pek Sikorski said, "Of course, we are not interested *only* in shared reality. As we have said to everyone on World, all of World interests us."

"Yes," Enli said, smiling back. "Of course. May your flowers bloom in glorious profusion."

"May your garden please your ancestors."

Enli left. Yes. The first part of Pek Nagredil's plan was accomplished.

She approached Pek Voratur after dark, after Pek Bazargan had strolled through the courtyards to the crelm house. The portly trader sat in his wonderful personal garden with his oldest son, Soshaf, talking business. Around them burned lamps of vegetable oil in beautifully curved iron holders. The perfumes of skillfully chosen night flowers blended on the air with the quiet hum of lifegivers' wings. As Enli walked toward them, both men looked up, astonished to be approached by a servant in the tunic of a cleaner, although not as astonished as the servant Enli had passed leaving the garden with empty pel glasses.

"Pek Voratur," Enli said, "I would share reality with you."

"We share reality," Pek Voratur said ritually. "Who are you?"

"Enli Pek Brimmidin, household cleaner. I wish to tell you something about our Terran guests, that reality may be fully shared." Enli had taken a double dose of the government pills for this interview. She was violating reality more than at any time since she and Tabor . . .

She would not think of that now.

"What have you to tell of the Terrans?" Soshaf Pek Voratur demanded.

Enli made herself look troubled. "I heard Pek Bazargan in

talk with Pek Sikorski. He said, 'If we can only learn about the shared-reality headpain, this voyage will have been worthwhile.' "

"The shared-reality headpain?" the older Pek Voratur said. "What is there to learn? Headpain just is." But then his eyes narrowed, and Enli saw the successful trader gleam in his lamplit eyes.

"Pek Brimmidin," he said to me, "where did you hear Pek Bazargan say this?"

"In the garden by Pek Sikorski's apartments."

"And why were you there?"

Enli lowered her eyes. "I was there to look at the flowers, Pek Voratur. I used to have a noted garden."

Pek Voratur hummed softly, thinking. Enli saw him exchange glances with his son. She said, eyes still lowered, "I am good with plants."

"Yes. Pek Brimmidin, the Terran healer uses many plants in preparing her potions. Although not, of course, flowers."

"Yes," Enli said, as if she already knew this well. Which, of course, she did.

"It may be she could use someone who is good with plants to help her. Would you prefer that job to cleaner?"

"Oh, yes, Pek Voratur!"

"And it may further be," the trader continued, "that Pek Sikorski will talk again, another time, about things she is interested in, or needs, or would like to have. It may happen you will overhear these things."

"Yes," Enli said, trying to sound as if this were a new idea to her.

"If you hear such things, Pek Brimmidin, you must share reality with me as head of this household, so I may know what my guests require."

"Oh, yes!"

Pek Voratur leaned forward. "It may be that sometimes you overhear things when the Terrans do not know you hear them. This, too, is reality you should share with me."

Enli nodded.

"But Pek Brimmidin—Enli—here is a very important point.

You need not share reality about what you tell me with the Terrans themselves. No, don't look shocked, girl. Remember, the Terrans are not of World. The servants of the First Flower have not yet declared them real . . . and *that*, you know, is a reality we do not share with them until we are sure they possess souls. So neither need you share with them that you report to me what they say to each other. There, now, does that help you understand?"

"I don't—"

"Your head hurts. I can see it in your eyes. Poor Enli. But would you like to be a gardener, Enli, and share reality with me?"

"Yes, I—"

"Good. Then it is a bargain. May your flowers bloom in glorious profusion."

"M-may your garden please your ancestors," Enli stammered.

"You will begin as gardening assistant to Pek Sikorski tomorrow. I will tell her myself. Good night, Enli."

"Good night," echoed the trader's son.

Enli could barely see as she made her way back to the servants' court. Pain lanced the flesh between her eyes, the tissue behind her eyes. No headpain had been this bad since . . . What had she done? Promised to inform on the Terrans to Hadjil Pek Voratur. Pek Sikorski would then ask her questions about the Voratur household which Enli would answer, a kind of informing on World. And every tenday she would report to Pek Nagredil and inform on her informing. How much could you twist shared reality until, like a wire of metal, it broke? And she, Enli, impaled on the sharp ends . . .

Oh, Tabor. Only for you.

Halfway through a deserted court, vertigo made her stomach heave. There were no lamps here. In the darkness she doubled over and puked. Oh, please, not on flowers, let there be no flowers below her *please* . . .

When the attack had passed, she stumbled to the personal room she shared with three other female servants. Sick with pain and nausea, Enli fumbled in her tunic for more of the government pills that would let her sleep.

FOUR

ORBITAL OBJECT #7

Another three hundred clicks," the pilot said, unnecessarily. Syree Johnson knew exactly where the object was, to the meter. But Captain Daniel Austen, whom she'd worked with before on Special Projects, was garrulous on the job. It made a strong contrast to his discretion off duty. He was a good soldier.

Not that any of them had had a Special Project like this before.

The planet called World had, the natives believed, seven moons, which they called by terse syllables: Ap, Lil, Cut, Obri, Ral, Sel, and Tas. Six were natural satellites. Tas was a captured artifact, almost as old as the planet itself.

The artifact, which the recon team had named Orbital Object #7, circled World in a lower orbit than the natural moons, averaging fewer than twenty-three hundred kilometers above the planet. To keep that low, it moved fast: six clicks per second, completing an orbit in 2.34 E-hours. From the planetary surface, its speed made it appear retrograde, moving from west to east. It also looked small. With a diameter of only four clicks, it barely subtended one-tenth degree of sky. Its orbit, fifty-four degrees out of the plane of the ecliptic, was roughly circular. The relative absence of micrometer impact craters suggested that the artifact had not been captured all that long ago, perhaps as recently as a hundred thousand E-years. It had a high albedo and matte finish, so there was no specular reflection. It did not rotate.

"One hundred fifty clicks," Austen said.

Syree stood suited; now she put on her helmet. Orbital Object #7 grew larger on the display, although not yet large enough to see the markings that had sent the recon team scurrying home.

Only one other object in the human universe carried those markings, and it was not human. Discovered fifty-three years ago in orbit beyond Neptune, it had opened the stars to man. And it, too, had at first looked like a small moon. But it had been a space tunnel, a wormhole transport point to a vast mappable net of usable tunnels. When a spaceship got itself laboriously out to Neptune and maneuvered inside Space Tunnel #1, it emerged elsewhere in the galaxy, directly outside a planetary system—and very near yet another space tunnel.

The discovery of Space Tunnel #1 had rocked the struggling solar civilization. Humanity was not only not alone, it owned an instantaneous superhighway.

More precisely, Mars owned it. The first alien artifact had been discovered and claimed by a Martian military explorer, the *Kettleman*. By the infant space-salvage laws, modeled on much older marine laws, Mars owned Space Tunnel #1. Screams of protest did not stand up in court. Nor was any physical challenge feasible; the balance of power was too risky, and no one wanted to blow up the tunnel in order to save it, assuming that was possible. In fact, Mars happened to be politically positioned well to be a keeper of the tunnel—not too powerful, not too weak, not too allied, not too isolationist. In addition, Earth's long series of ecological crises meant that she could not spare the resources to build the space cities which Mars already owned. The first legal, political, or belligerent challenges petered out. Mars owned Space Tunnel #1.

The first years were filled with triumphs and disasters. Experimentation proved that a ship—or any other object—put through a space tunnel for the first time went to wherever the directly previous ship had gone. A ship that had gone through a tunnel and then went through it from the other side was automatically returned to its starting point, no matter how many other ships had used the tunnel in the meantime. Somehow—that most operative word in human understanding of tunnel technology—the tunnel "remembered" where each individual ship had entered tunnel space. Since most (but not all) star systems had three or four tunnels clustered together, the result was an intricate, mappable network of visible nodes and invisible tunnels: an interstellar "Chutes and Ladders" comprised of all chutes.

All the tunnels led to planetary systems. Some were inhabited; most were not. New disciplines sprang up: xenobiology, interstellar treasure hunting, holomovies shot under pink or yellow skies. Serious thinkers pointed out that humankind was scarcely ready to colonize the stars, having solved none of its problems at home. Nobody listened. The rich flourished on the new investments; the poor remained poor; Earth went on lurching from one ecological tragedy to another. The exterran solar settlements, their dangerous first years over, became the escape of choice for those who could afford it. The smart money moved itself into space. Space offered glamour, offered cachet, offered profit.

Mars, until then just one more space colony in Earth's massive and dark penumbra, became the queen of interstellar travel. Any ship wanting to go to the stars had to go through her military and administrative checkpoints. Mars ruled the always-shaky Solar Alliance, which only existed because she said it did. Everybody else could either get down in the dust to her or stay home from the stars.

They got down in the dust, Luna and the Belt, the Confucian Hegemony and the Arab League, Io and Titan and even Syree's own United Atlantic Federation, with its proud history of independence and freedom. The people who had caused Runnymede and Bunker Hill and the Place de la Concorde got down in the dust, and sometimes they choked on it. That was too bad, thought Syree the soldier. You had to have law, and rules, and a chain of command.

She had been born the year the first ship went through Space Tunnel #1. She was three years old when the first alien civilization was discovered, stone-age hominids on a planet someone too-whimsically named Sally's Cupboard. Even as a child, Syree had not approved of whimsy, nor of slackers. She grew up in a UAF military family, the fifth generation of soldiers.

James L. Johnson, born in 1974, had died as an enlisted man in Bosnia, two weeks after the birth of the son he never saw. That son, Brian James Johnson, made an idol of his unknown father and got himself into West Point, graduating in 2021. Of his four daughters, two followed. Catherine died in combat. Emily James Johnson, Syree's formidable grandmother, rose to two-star general. Her son, Tam Johnson, also attended West Point, but by the time Syree was eighteen, things had changed. West Point had become the heavy-gravity training branch of the Solar Alliance Military Academy on Mars.

Mars had long recognized that since the space tunnels worked two ways, not all the alien civilizations that humans found would have to be preatomic.

They found the Fallers the year Syree received her doctorate in physics and her second-lieutenant's bars. The Fallers, too, had space travel within their own system. They had not known about their own space tunnel, that high-albedo, matte-finish artifact orbiting around their most distant planet, until humans arrived through it.

As the humans had twenty-five years earlier, the Fallers were thrust into becoming a starfaring race. They acted, however, as if they were still alone. They did not trade, they did not negotiate, they did not communicate. They settled a few other planets, and no humans were permitted on any of them.

Syree was a captain when the Fallers attacked Edge, a human settlement four tunnels away from the Faller home system. No one knew why they attacked. Attempts to establish dialogue with the Fallers had failed. Although they were carbon-based hominids, the enemy did not seem to spring from the same seed as the rest of the galaxy's sentient species. The product of an independent evolution, they appeared to humanity deeply strange, and deeply dangerous. Mars led the formation of the Solar Alliance Defense Council, with its broad military-law powers that many regarded as more dangerous than the Fallers themselves.

Syree was not concerned with the political or sociological shifts that the Fallers brought to human power bases. She was a soldier. What interested her was that the Fallers did not establish cooperative communication with humans because the Fallers chose instead to establish war.

The Solar Alliance Defense Council retaliated with an attack on the Faller home system itself, on the second moon of their fourth planet.

Syree Johnson distinguished herself in the skirmishes that followed, both for her brilliant analysis of captured alien weapons and, once when she was the ranking line officer left alive, for bravery. When the Fallers attacked Bolivar, a fledgling human mining colony on the high-gravity world of Vista Linda, Syree fought for the last time. She lost her left leg at the knee to a lasersweep, and the robomeds barely got her out before she bled to death.

They grew her a new leg, of course, from her own cells shaped over a dissolvable polymer scaffolding, with digital nerve-connection assistance. The leg took only a few weeks to grow, nourished on the skinless back of a permanently immobilized dog bred without an immune system. The dog was the problem. After her new leg was attached, Syree could not get the image of that dog out of her mind. She found she could not—*could not*—put her full weight on her left leg. No amount of rehab, physical or behavioral or verbal or neuropharmaceutical, helped. She could not make herself fully use her left leg.

Syree was deeply mortified by this failure of nerve, which was how she saw it. With every halting step, she heard Grandmother Emily's stern dictum: *A Johnson masters herself!* Syree reentered rehab, failed again, and retired from the army with twenty-one years active service.

She hated retirement. She regarded boredom as a moral failing, the mark of a mind insufficiently stocked to occupy itself. So she diligently read physics journals, making a hobby of the history of space-tunnel theory, such as it was.

It wasn't much.

After fifty years, science still knew almost nothing about how space tunnels actually worked. The physical objects, panels floating in space in the general shape of a doughnut, were completely impenetrable. The science was too alien. The best guess was that the panels created a field of macro-level object entanglement, analogous to the quantum entanglement that permitted one particle to affect its paired counterpart regardless of distance, thus eliminating any spatial dimension to the universe by treating it as a single point. But this was merely a guess. Achieving entanglement for an object the size of a warship—let alone *controlling* the phenomenon—violated so many cherished principles that the feuding in physics journals resembled gang warfare. Syree spent days studying the fulminations, doing the calculations, extending the premises behind the speculations.

She taught a class at the Academy.

She took more futile rehab.

She tried to get interested in gardening.

She was aware, every endless limping day, that half her life span remained.

When the call came about the *Zeus* mission to World, she had realized at once that high command wanted her not only for her knowledge of space tunnels but also for her retired status. The Fallers, it was rumored, might have human informants, drawn from those countries on and off Earth that were displeased with the Solar Alliance and its leader, Mars. Colonel Syree Johnson, retired, would arouse no interest if she took a berth on a minor scientific expedition. And she knew as much as anyone still living about how Space Tunnel #1 had been first approached, decoded, used. She was prepared to do the same for Orbital Object #7.

It grew larger on the shuttle display as Austen maneuvered his craft. Silent, cold, enticing.

"Match orbit as close as possible," she said.

"Matching orbit."

While Austen fine-tuned his position fifty meters behind the artifact, Syree put on her helmet, ran a last check on her suit and tether rings, picked up her bag of instruments.

"Leaving ship, Captain."

"Good luck, Colonel." He gave her his fine irreverent grin and tossed off a flamboyant salute.

Outside, Syree's jets carried her to Orbital Object #7. Then she floated next to it, touching it. At its equator, the surface was deeply indented in regular flowing patterns that made convenient handholds. She hitched herself to a groove and orbited with the artificial moon.

"Contact."

"Acknowledged."

Slowly Syree ran the fingers of her right glove over the metallic surface. Yes, it resembled the feel of the sparse markings on space tunnels. Computer analysis would confirm that the language was the same, and the Solar Alliance had a Rosetta stone for that.

She opened her instrument bag. A sudden absurd image came to her: an old-time country doctor, making a house call. This was no time for absurdities; perhaps she would increase her dosage of Contex, which increased mental concentration. For now, she banished the silly image by sheer will.

"Beginning detailed data scan. Testing reception."

"Receiving data," Austen said. "Colonel, the first-contact ceremony on World is beginning. You asked to be informed."

"Thank you. Record the ceremony, as per orders."

"Acknowledged."

She would watch the recording cube later. She would have to: Officially, contact with the natives was the only reason the *Zeus* was here. All ship personnel were required to remain current on World data, in case rescue intervention became necessary.

Which it wouldn't. Syree had read the recon reports. The natives had barely reached preindustrial; they even made bicycles manually, one by one. And they were unusually peaceful, with no known history of war. Otherwise the "social scientists"—there was an oxymoron—wouldn't bring human kids down there. The contact ceremony would consist of bowing and passing around flowers, and the xeno-team's eventual results would consist of one more report stuck in some academic library somewhere. None of it mattered, next to what orbited under Syree Johnson's fingers. She didn't yet know what it was, but she knew it could change radically the human/Faller balance of power.

As she worked her way completely around the sphere, twelve and a half clicks, a stream of data flowed silently through her instruments to the shuttle and from there to the computers on board the *Zeus*. It would take days to analyze all of it, but not the flowing script. The *Zeus* would have that in a few minutes.

She had barely completed circumnavigation when Austen said, "Incoming data."

"Relay."

Her first assistant, Major John Ombatu. "Markings on Orbital Object #7 decoded, Colonel. Ready to receive?"

"Ready to receive."

"Translation, using the Webbel-Grey translation model: 'unknown-word unknown-word small holding-together disruption device unknown-word stop strengths one, two, three, five, seven, eleven, thirteen, seventeen, nineteen.' End."

Syree said, "That's *it*, John? Three unknown words out of seven, plus a strength-calibration listing by primes?"

"Those old aliens were fond of primes, especially eleven. As you know."

Of course she knew. Space tunnels were all labeled in primes—to the extent anything was labeled at all. Without extensive markings on the floating panels, Webbel and Grey had actually had very little to go on in constructing their translation model. Syree guessed that "holding-together" came from one of the few repeated markings they did have, a warning that any mass above a certain limit would not go through a tunnel.

This had turned out to be true. The *Anaconda*, A *Thor*-class

cruiser, had been lost, along with nine hundred lives. The
cruiser had fit, tightly, inside Space Tunnel #1, but not inside
the unknown field that the tunnel was presumed to enclose.
The *Anaconda* had disappeared in a massive implosion, without debris or residual radiation. Intense experimentation determined that the same thing would happen to any object
which massed more than roughly one hundred thousand tons.
The *Anaconda,* Martian physicists decided, had had a
Schwarzschild radius—defined as the radius below which, if
you squeezed the mass, it would become a black hole—larger
than the tunnel's capacity to handle. From the disaster, xen-
olinguists had learned the meaning of the alien marking for
"disruption."

Now Syree pushed away her disappointment. She'd hoped
the translation would confirm that Orbital Object #7 was a
weapon. That possibility had not been ruled out. But it would
take a lot more data analysis before she could form a hypothesis to test.

Three ship-days later, she was no closer to understanding the
object.

Her team had performed every noninvasive test Syree could
think of, from the obvious spectral, sonic, and magnetic analyses to less reliable statistical simulations. The facts were
clear; there just weren't enough of them.

The artifact emitted no radiation of any kind, had no magnetic field, and no thermal gradations. The hull, 0.9765 cen-
timeters thick, was made mostly of an allotropic form of
carbon that resembled a known class of fullerenes but was
subtly different. The artifact contained no heavy metals, nothing with an atomic number above seventy-five. It massed
slightly less than a million tons. Inside was mostly hollow,
although unidentifiable structures were suspended inside
(how?) in an extremely complex but partial manner, without
direct connection to each other. These unknown but stable
structures appeared to be without any mass—an impossibility.
When the computer ran mathematical analyses, the suspen-

sions suggested a complicated web wherein each curve folded back on itself many times, a sort of multidimensional fractal. Computer breakdown further suggested a strange attractor, a region in which all sufficiently close trajectories were attracted in the limit, but in which arbitrarily close points over time became exponentially separated. Syree figured the Hausdorff dimension of the suggested fractal. It was 1.2, the same dimension as the galactic filling of the universe.

None of it added up to anything. None of it indicated what Orbital Object #7 might be *for*.

The only way to determine that was to activate it.

"What if it blows up the entire star system?" John Ombatu asked.

"It wouldn't have different strength settings if it was designed for a one-time, scorched-earth solution."

"Okay, what if it just blows up World?"

"Still a lot of different settings for that extreme a measure to happen at the lowest one."

Commander Peres said skeptically, "Are you sure you even know how to activate it?"

"Of course I'm not sure," Syree said. "But it seems to have double-button pressure points. A user must activate both buttons simultaneously, so they can't be set off accidentally by, say, a meteor hit."

The team fell silent. Syree could feel her own breath, loud in her chest. She waited.

"I think it's too great a risk," Ombatu said finally, and she knew something about him she had not known before.

"Do it," said Lieutenant Lucy Wu, the junior officer. "The Fallers took out that colony on New Rome just last week, remember. Six thousand dead. We haven't got that many off-system colonies left. If we don't risk anything here, where we don't even have a colony, we risk everything everywhere else."

Syree's thinking exactly. But she waited to hear from Daniel Austen and Canton Lee. She needed to know what her team was made of. Although the final decision rested with Peres. Syree was project head, but he commanded the *Zeus*; any decision potentially endangering the ship was his.

"Yes," Lee said.

"Yes," Austen said. "We're at *war*."

"All right," Peres said. "At the artifact's *lowest* setting."

Syree said, "I'll go out at oh-seven-hundred. Commander Peres, the *Zeus* should move to the other side of the planet, as shielded as she can be. Austen, you pilot the shuttle."

Her tone allowed for no further discussion. She didn't look at John Ombatu.

The most disciplined—or Disciplined—mind may wander under stress. Syree, experienced in combat, already knew this. So she was not surprised when she left the shuttle airlock and found herself thinking again of Grandmother Emily.

Emily James Johnson had seen action in Africa, in South America, and, shamefully, in the Resistance Rebellion when the United States joined the United Atlantic Federation. She married late and when Syree remembered her grandmother, she remembered her old. Frail, stooped, liver-spotted—she had stopped the cosmetic genemod treatments at eighty-five. But still stern. When Syree, about four, had a temper tantrum, Grandmother Emily had swatted her across the shoulders with her oak cane. "A Johnson masters herself! Remember that, Syree!"

Syree's mother had cried over the welts and given Syree a cookie. Syree looked at her mother with contempt. Even at four, she had known that Grandmother Johnson had been right to hit her, and that her mother was a soft weakling.

Floating toward Orbital Object #7, Syree regretted that contemptuous look of forty-odd years ago. Her mother had not deserved it. She was not a soldier, and Syree's father had married her for her soft sweetness. Syree could still see her, holding out the rejected cookie in one slim white-fingered hand, her first intolerance from a daughter to whom tolerance would be the hardest discipline, always.

Syree put her family out of her mind.

Orbital Object #7 was once again under her hand. She fastened the remote pressure device on the raised circle under the flowing script for "one." Quickly she swung along the hand-holds (tentacle holds? machine grips?). The flowing script on the opposite side of the artifact included identical raised circles. Over two thousand clicks below her, World turned under equatorial clouds. How did that sky look to the natives, who saw farther into the infrared than Syree but less far into the short-scattered blues?

However they see, let them go on doing it after I'm done. She fastened down the second pressure device.

"Remotes set," she said.

"Remotes set," Austen repeated in the shuttle. "Coming to pick you up."

"Don't," Syree said. "I'm staying out."

There was a long pause. "Colonel, that's not per plan."

"I'm staying out," she repeated. She didn't offer her explanation: that if the entire planet of civilians was at risk from whatever Orbital Object #7 delivered at force one, then so should she be. Either Austen understood or no amount of explanation would make him understand.

"Permission to remain," Austen said.

"Permission granted." Now she knew something else about Daniel Austen. Something worth knowing. "Back up a few hundred meters, Captain. Let's get two more perspectives."

"Affirmative."

There were, of course, instrument satellites covering the artifact activation from several different positions. The more, the better. Syree watched the shuttle maneuver into position. Austen said cheerfully, "Recording equipment activated. Ready when you are, Colonel."

"Stand by."

"Let the games begin!" Austen said, and she heard the jaunty laughter in his voice.

Syree jetted back from Orbital Object #7. At twenty meters, she activated both remote pressure devices.

For a long moment, nothing happened. The artifact didn't change at all. Then the *shuttle* began to glow. An eerie, deadly glow that brightened as she watched.

"Austen. What do the displays show?"

Silence.

"Austen. Come in, Captain Austen."

Silence.

"Daniel! Come in!"

Silence. The shuttle still glowed. Syree jetted toward it. After a hundred meters, her suit spoke urgently in prerecorded warning: "Radiation ahead. Do not advance. Three thousand rads. Twenty-eight hundred rads. Twenty-six hundred rads . . ."

Three thousand rads? And *decreasing*? That made no sense.

The only part that made sense was that Daniel Austen was now dying. And so was she.

Only she wasn't.

Aboard the *Zeus* the medtechs laved her thoroughly inside and out, frowning as they did it because no counters anywhere aboard ship showed that she'd taken any radiation. Austen had, and so had the shuttle. Robots went aboard and retrieved Austen, along with samples of everything aboard ship. By that time, the shuttle had stopped glowing.

The medtechs did what they could for him, knowing it was probably futile. They pumped the contents of his stomach and sent robotic scouring tubes down his esophagus, into his bronchial tree, up his rectum, into nose and ears and eyelids and urinary tract. They scrubbed his skin with chemicals, shaved off all hair, inserted an endotracheal tube because in a few hours he would need help breathing. They gave him a drug to make him sweat, attached an IV, hooked him to both invasive and skin monitors. Throughout, Austen said little except to make his official report. He knew.

By the next day, Austen was vomiting. The ulceration of his digestive tract had begun. Nothing had happened to Syree.

The team, plus Rafael Peres, met in her quarters to go over the data. Lieutenant Wu, Major Ombatu, Engineer Lee. Graphs and tables littered the table. Syree said, "Major, summarize what we have so far about the effect." That's what they were calling it: "the effect." Austen, she thought irrelevantly, would have come up with something better. *Let the games begin.* And his voice full of that jaunty laughter.

"The effect is a wave," Ombatu said, frowning, "emitted uniformly from Orbital Object #7 and traveling at the speed of light. It's subject to the inverse square law. We know that from the rads taken by each of the outlying instrument satellites. The wave seems to have caused primary radioactivity, with a rise time of several minutes. After it passes, secondary radiation remains, but—and this is the key—not uniformly. Some objects retrieved from the shuttle turned radioactive, and some did not."

"Why?" Peres said, frowning.

Syree said, "I have a hypothesis."

They all looked at her. She knew how momentous it was, what she was going to say. She picked up the lab report on the shuttle samples. "Look at the elements that went radioactive, and the ones that didn't. The titanium hull: no. The platinum in the life-support catalyst vials: yes. The iridium alloy in the pressure vessels for gas samples: yes. The lead in Captain Austen's pewter belt buckle: no. Mercury: yes. Gold: yes. Aluminum: no. Antimony: no. Iodine: no.

"Nothing below atomic weight seventy-five destabilized when the wave went through. And everything above did."

Lucy Wu said instantly, "Lead is above seventy-five."

"But with an extremely stable nucleus. That argues that the effect caused nuclear destabilization by weakening the binding energy of the nucleon."

Canton Lee blurted, "The effect *fucks* with the *strong force?*"

"I think so," Syree said.

Ombatu looked thoughtful. "Yes. That would explain why Syree wasn't affected. Her suit is made of a carbon composite, and the lighter molecules wouldn't be affected because the electromagnetic repulsion between protons isn't enough to overcome the reduced binding energy..." He went to the computer and started to key in equations.

Peres said, "So Captain Austen took the radiation not from

the wave itself, but from the radioactivity of the shuttle parts that the wave affects."

Lucy Wu said excitedly, "And when the wave passes, the nucleus restabilizes. But there's a rise time; the effect doesn't happen instantaneously, or vanish instantaneously. It takes several minutes."

"The *strong* force," Lee repeated. He seemed mesmerized. "What a weapon!"

Syree said, "And we only experienced it at force one. It goes up by primes to nineteen."

Peres said suddenly, "We have to secure it before the Fallers ever learn it exists."

"Agreed," Syree said. "But unfortunately the mass exceeds space tunnel capacity."

She watched them digest that. Any object that failed to pass through a space tunnel became a black hole. That was the theory, even though the initial mass wasn't large enough to form a black hole under normal circumstances, and even though no one had actually observed a black hole formed in this way. What had been observed and verified was the cutoff mass: one hundred thousand tons. Orbital Object #7 massed nine times that.

On the other hand, it had been made by the same beings who made the tunnels. Perhaps that would make a difference. Although, why would it?

Why wouldn't it?

Lucy Wu said, "Can we take the artifact apart? And reassemble it beyond Space Tunnel #438?"

Ombatu said, "Do you have any ideas how to do that safely, Lieutenant? Or how to do it all?"

Lucy Wu blushed and looked down at the floor.

Syree said crisply, "We need more data on the interior. Maybe those massless constructs are modular, even though we know the hull isn't."

Lee said, "I don't know how to determine that, ma'am. The design is so alien . . ."

"It will become less alien as we study it."

"Yes, ma'am," Lee said, but he sounded doubtful. So was

Syree. She just didn't see any other alternative, at least not as yet.

On the third day after the accident, Daniel Austen could no longer talk. The inside of his mouth, like his skull and body, had become a mass of oozing sores. By the fourth day his body had swelled so much from edema that he couldn't move, and only heavy doses of painkillers kept the pressure of the bed from being an agony. On the fifth day he died.

They buried him in space, with a small service in the chapel for the military officers and medtechs. In the space for "Religion" on Austen's service file, he had entered "None." Syree dumped the standard military funeral script for secular personnel. She had heard it too often, and it was too bland. It didn't fit Austen, with his constant ship chatter, his irreverence, his jaunty bravery. *Let the games begin.*

Instead she recited a poem from Kipling, one her grandmother had quoted often. The Johnsons were not ones for poetry, but Grandmother Emily had liked Kipling. *A soldier's poet*, she'd always said. Syree stood at the front of the tiny chapel, trying not to favor her left leg. She recited the Kipling as she remembered it, knowing the verses were not complete, knowing they were enough.

> " *'There was no one like him, Horse or Foot,*
> *Nor any of the guns I knew;*
> *And because it was so, why of course he went and died,*
> *Which is just what the best men do.*
>
> *"He was all that I had in the way of a friend,*
> *And I've had to find one new;*
> *But I'd give my pay and stripe for to get the beggar back,*
> *Which it's just too late to do.*
>
> *"Take him away! He's gone where the best men go ...'* "

After the brief service, Syree went to the small observation chamber of the *Zeus*. The bridge had sharper virtual displays, but she wanted to look out on space for real, not at a digital-ized simulation. Below her, World turned slowly, its single equatorial continent like a thick irregular belt around a fat civilian belly. But it wasn't World she observed. She waited impassively until Orbital Object #7 sped by, lower than the *Zeus*, dazzlingly bright from the sun's reflection off its high-albedo surface. Outlying instrument satellites monitored it constantly, of course, and their data were instantly available to Syree. But she wanted to see again, for herself, what had killed Daniel Austen.

It looked exactly the same.

FIVE

GOFKIT JEMLOE

The first major difficulty arose over flowers. Dr. Bazargan had anticipated it, but that made it no less awkward.

He stood with Ann in her laboratory, or what passed for a lab on World. It was a large, airy room of irregular shape, with curving walls and many arched windows opening onto gardens. By Terran standards, World was a generous planet: fertile, warm, seasonless, plentiful. Building materials abounded, so walls could be made wastefully irregular. Food abounded, so the relatively small population (why? unknown so far) could spend vast resources cultivating flowers. Not even the gardens of Isfahan, the ancient Iranian city where Bazargan had been born, had had gardens to compare with those on World.

Although Isfahan and World were closer than Bazargan had expected. Isfahan, the "Pearl of Persia" even now that it had become a museum city, also had curving doorways, arched windows overlooking elaborate gardens, pale walls (although on World they were lightest green rather than white). The saji tree outside Ann's window, with its fragrant pink blooms, might have been a flowering almond tree in the Maidan. The swooping designs painted on the lab floor would not have been out of place on an Iranian rug or tapestry. And although in an

Iranian "healer's" workplace the lab benches would not also be curved in parabolas, nor would the ceiling rise in a dome, the overall effect didn't feel particularly alien to Bazargan. Certainly not as alien as Argos City on Europa, where he had done graduate field work on the organisms living in hot springs below the ice. There, the people had looked like him and the environment had been exotic; here, the reverse was true.

Beyond the lab windows, Hadjil Pek Voratur strolled through the garden in all its curving glory. World averaged roughly the same received energy per square foot as Earth, but in a shifted spectrum. To human eyes, adaptable as they were, the landscape looked subtly off in a way difficult to define. Still, the Voratur gardens were staggeringly beautiful. Colors, scents, shapes—all perfectly balanced. Even the insects that fertilized the riotous blooms fit with the garden's serenity: They neither bit nor stung. "Lifegivers," the Worlders called them, and they fascinated the biologist in Ann Sikorski.

"They perch on my hand, my body, my legs, Ahmed—but never on my head. Never!"

"Are you sure?"

"No, not yet. I haven't run any experiments. But I've never seen them land on a Worlder's head, either—have you?"

"I haven't been watching, but I will," Bazargan replied, watching instead the native "assistant" assigned by Hadjil Voratur to Ann. Enli Pek Brimmidin. The girl was a spy, of course. To be expected.

Hadjil Voratur reached the lab doorway, his sleek bulk blocking nearly all of it. "Pek Bazargan," Voratur said, smiling. He held out a visitor's flower, orange and yellow striped petals. "I honor the flowers of your heart."

"Pek Voratur," Bazargan answered, plucking a hospitality flower from the pajal bush Ann kept by the door. "You are welcome to the flowers of your own house."

Voratur laughed. Worlders, Bazargan had discovered, possessed a multifaceted sense of humor. They appreciated whimsy, exaggeration, irony. Only social satire was alien to them; satire required distance from one's own social conventions, difficult in a biologically monocultural world.

"May your flowers also bloom, Pek Sikorski," Voratur said to Ann. "Although that is what I am here to talk about, alas."

Bazargan said, "That our flowers do not bloom for you."

"You knew this?" Voratur said in surprise, genuine or feigned. "That we would plant the seeds from your visitors' flowers and the seeds would fail to grow?"

"I knew," Bazargan said, "that such a skillful gardener and canny trader could not fail to do otherwise."

Voratur looked gratified; there was no higher compliment on World than "skillful gardener." Although the gratification, too, might have been feigned. Bazargan felt at home with this play of sham emotion. In Iran, it was a necessity of survival.

He was especially interested in how Voratur's playacting—if such it was—fit in with the concept of totally shared reality, without subterfuge. There were two possibilities. One was that everyone in the culture knew that playacting was a part of trading, which made even sham statements fully shared in their essence. The other hypothesis was that sham statements were permitted only with Terrans, who were outside the culture. Bazargan did not yet have enough evidence to choose.

Ann, he saw, was less comfortable with the trader's feigned innocence. She had grown up in the American middle provinces, where straightforwardness was a virtue.

Voratur said, "May I ask why the Terran flower seeds did not grow for us? Is Terran soil needed?"

"No," Bazargan said. "The seeds did not grow by design. We treated them specially." Every bloom brought down to World had been irradiated to sterility. "You see, Pek Voratur, these flowers do not grow naturally on World. Has it ever happened here that some very strong plant from, say, an outlying island has been brought to an inland village, planted, and perhaps completely taken over the flower bed?"

"Ah, I see," Voratur said. "You protect us from your beautiful flowers."

"From their unknown effects," Bazargan said, smiling. The trader had no idea how far that protection in fact extended. The human team had been thoroughly decontaminated, inside and out. Every necessary microbe that could be replaced by a genemod version unable to survive outside the human body, had been. No one was naive enough to think that World would remain untouched by the human presence, but the goal was to make that touch as delicate and smudge-free as possible.

Voratur appeared to consider. "Let me propose a different trade. You will give us fertile seeds of your slowest-growing, hardest-to-grow flowering plant, and I will undertake to grow it in a glassed garden, with World flowers, until we are sure it can do no harm."

Bazargan pretended to ponder. This had all been foreseen, and hydroponic geneticists aboard the *Zeus* had developed a genetically modified crimson rose with limited competitive ability. Also, it would produce only three generations. The fourth-generation germ-line recombination activated a terminator gene that flooded the seeds with biotoxins. However, it would be a while before Voratur discovered that his roses had turned sterile and the negotiations proceeded to the next round.

Bazargan said, "That is a possibility. But you spoke of a trade . . ."

"What would you like in return, Pek Bazargan?"

Ann looked sharply at Bazargan. He knew what she wanted.

"Pek Voratur," he said formally, "what I ask is ten minutes of time from you. In this ten minutes, we will put a metal hat on your head and a machine of ours will take a picture of your brain. That is all."

"A picture of my brain?" Voratur said, and this time Bazargan was sure his emotion was not feigned. Voratur's neck-fur ruffled in alarm, and his skull ridges creased into deep folds. "How can this be? The brain lies hidden from view inside the skull."

"Yes," Bazargan said, "but our hat can see through the skull. It will not hurt, it will not affect you in any way, and it will take only ten minutes. In return, we will give you seeds for flowers such as World has never seen."

Voratur hesitated. Ann held her breath; a Lagerfeld combined brain scan was a major tool in neurobiology. Bazargan saw the trader's greed war with the provincial's distaste.

Something else entirely won out.

"The soul lives in the brain," Voratur said reluctantly. "I cannot risk exposing my soul to something I do not understand. Perhaps if you gave me one of these hats to explore beforehand, or traded it to me . . ."

"Alas, I cannot do that," Bazargan said regretfully. He didn't need to say more. Voratur was an ideal alien contact; as a successful trader, he understood the limits of what one was willing to give away for free.

"Then I must refuse the brain picture and ask you to name another price for the flower seeds."

"Let me think about it," Bazargan said. That would give the Worlder time to think about it as well; he might change his mind. Although the recon team had run up against the same refusal. "Perhaps you could consult the servants of the First Flower."

"Perhaps, perhaps," Voratur said, although this would most likely not help Bazargan's suit. Whatever Voratur thought, the priests would also think. Shared reality.

Voratur added, "A bargain should be possible between us, Pek. You Terrans came to trade, did you not? The previous Terrans said, 'We will return for the manufactured item.' "

"They did?" Bazargan said, startled. He recovered himself. "Yes, of course. Terra is a noted trader among her neighbors."

"So we supposed," Voratur said, his eyes sharp in his fleshy face. "Tell me, Pek Bazargan, must this brain picture be of me? Would any Worlder do as well?"

"Yes," Bazargan said. Voratur nodded, made his farewells, and left. Was he considering one of the servants? Although he would only do so if the servant, the priests, and everyone else concurred. That was how World worked. But a servant might be paid enough to voluntarily take the risk. That, too, was how World worked.

"Do you think he will agree?" Ann asked, in English. "A Lagerfeld scan would be great!"

"I don't know if he will agree or not," Bazargan said, in World. He didn't like to exclude Ann's alien assistant when the girl was present. Nor to give Enli reason to report back to

Voratur that the Terrans were plotting in secret tongues, which might easily be construed as witchcraft. Priests everywhere could construe that.

Ann nodded; usually she remembered to speak World, even though hers was not as good as Bazargan's. This time excitement had gotten the better of her. "A brain picture," she said carefully, "will help us to choose an idea about the central question."

"Yes," Bazargan said. He understood her excitement. For Ann, the xenobiologist, the "central question" was the biomechanism of shared reality. Unlike Bazargan, she was convinced it was biological, and had formulated several hypotheses to explain it. A virus which, like neurosyphilis, overexcited one specific area of the brain. Or a condition like Tourette's syndrome, which increased excitatory transmitters only at specific sites. Or mutant peptides present only under pathological behavioral conditions, such as the tripeptide found in anorexia nervosa.

Bazargan added, only partly for the benefit of Enli, "Shared reality is a moral idea."

Ann again switched to English. "The relationship between affective and moral sensibility is always complicated."

Bazargan smiled. "I know."

"I meant cerebrally, in the frontal cortex."

"But I did not."

Ann laughed, her long plain face aglow, and turned back to her work. Bazargan's gaze snagged on Enli.

She bent closely over her bench, preparing thin sections of leaves for the atomic analyzer, as Ann had shown her. Unlike human hair, neckfur could not grow long enough to hide facial expressions. Enli's skull ridges were deeply creased; her lips were pulled slightly back over her teeth; her coarse neckfur stood out. The alien girl was terrified.

Of what? Enli hadn't looked like that when Bazargan had entered the room. He considered. If Enli's fear had started when Voratur asked whether anyone at all could be the subject of the brain scan, that was interesting. Not if her fear was only provincial fear of the unknown, but if it was due to something else . . . to what? Was Enli hiding something?

The lily seemed to menace me/ And showed its curved and quivering blade . . . Hāfez. Fourteenth century.

It was something to think about, along with everything else. World, with its complex ecology and even more complex society, was a fascinating planet. As were the natives, with their sophisticated sense of humor and finely honed acquisitiveness. Engaging, even. As long as you didn't trust them too far.

David Allen felt he had come home. World was what he'd been looking for his whole life.

True, the crelm house isolated him a bit; he saw much more of babies than of government, of teething schedules than of manhood rituals (if they existed). But so what? There was material here for a dozen major anthropological papers, and all of it was interesting. His gift for languages had paid off. He spoke World better even than Dr. Bazargan, or at least with a better accent, and each evening after the crelm house lay asleep David had hardly time enough to record all his observations and ideas about the day. When he returned to Princeton, he would be an instant star in the small, fierce, fiercely coveted world of xenoanthropology.

But it was more than the career opportunity that David loved about World. He wasn't, he told himself proudly, that shallow. World represented far more than journal articles. It represented no less than a chance for humanity to remake itself.

Thinking about this actually took his breath away. At night he lay in his "personal room," a combination of bedroom and private dining room, and shifted around on the uncomfortable pallet, unable to sleep. His mind raced, and his heart along with it. *Don't be grandiose,* he would tell himself; and, *In the morning be sure to adjust your Discipline for greater calm.* The admonitions didn't help. His mind still soared.

Shared reality was the key. There had never been a war on World. Not so much as a border skirmish. The Worlders he talked to, nannies and the other tutor, Colert Pek Gamolin, explained it all casually, as if he already knew it. Which he did, from the recon team, but that was not the same as seeing it in action. When two people were not in harmony, when they did not share the same beliefs and values and worldview, they got headpain. It was as simple as that. You cannot launch a war if it will cause you major pain, and it would, because the people you were slaughtering would not share your view that this was a good thing, and you couldn't help but know that. No, *feel* it, in the intimate cells of your brain, to the point of agony. So the plans for war could not even be made. And were not.

Unpremeditated murder still existed, of course. The time it took to smash someone over the head with whatever was handy was an eye blink, not enough to cause deterrent pain. You'd have the pain afterward, maybe . . . wouldn't you? He'd have to ask Colert Gamolin. Either way, the main idea was untouched.

Humans could end war.

All they had to do was figure out the physiological mechanism for shared reality, and then import it as a dominant gene into engineered human embryos. These genemod people would then cooperate with each other in shared reality. Cooperation was, in the long run, a more powerful evolutionary strategy than violence, once a species was high-tech. Those in shared reality would pass the successful strategy on to their children, until the solar system became the nonviolent paradise that World was.

Of course, Ann had told him that she didn't think the shared-reality mechanism was genetic. Both she and the earlier research team had had no trouble obtaining DNA samples from hair, blood, shed skin. The analyzers had reported only minor variations in a composite World genome from a composite human one: less than .005 percent. Just enough, Ann told David, to account for neckfur, skull ridges, other minor evolutionary differences. No, she'd admitted, she couldn't be *positive* that shared reality wasn't somehow scattered among those differences, or hidden in the junk DNA carried so copiously by both races. Being positive would require years more experimentation with equipment she didn't have. But she was pretty sure the differences were not genetic. Worlders were, after all, so fully compatible with humans that theoretically they could interbreed with fertile offspring. The differences were all superficial, and the DNA analyses were the closest match found yet among the kissing-cousin races that had, at one point, been moved light-years apart.

But, David had persisted, without further experimentation, she couldn't be *positive*. He said it so often that even patient Ann had finally snapped, "No! I can't be positive it's not genetic! And yes, if it is, it could in theory be spliced into human DNA! Now will you please stop pestering me?"

No more war. And the enormous economic costs of war diverted to peaceful pursuits, the real pursuits, of learning and loving and raising children (seventeen percent of children on Terra still died from disease, violence, or starvation).

Already it was happening, in a way, with Bonnie and Ben! The twins had taken to life on World with the same enthusiasm as David. Just today, they had toddled into the corner where David was telling stories, talking to the World six-year-olds to teach them English. The six-year-olds were actually more like three-and-a-half-year-olds in Earth years, of course; World's year included 213 rotations of the planet, each a little more than twenty-four hours. The children were adorable, sitting on their low kidney-shaped pillows with their tiny bald heads craning toward his picture screen, their hands cutting the air in excited curves. The story was David's own adaptation of "Peter Rabbit." Anything with flowers in it was always a success.

". . . and so Peter Pek Freb went *again* into Pek McGregor's garden and ate a flower!"

Three pairs of dark eyes went wide at such wickedness.

Into this literary moment Ben and Bonnie crashed, still unsteady walking, twice as large as Nafret and Uvi and Grenol. Ben gurgled and reached toward the carved wooden freb on David's lap. The toddler tripped and fell onto Uvi, his elbow giving her head a nasty crack. She wailed.

Ben thought it was a game. He laughed.

Nafret and Grenol had immediately starting stroking the crying Uvi, soothing and comforting. But at Ben's laugh, Nafret looked up, frowning. He looked again at Uvi, again at Ben, and he put his hand to the side of his head. His small mouth puckered.

The World tutor, Colert Gamolin, was instantly beside Nafret. He squatted down to the child's height and waited intently. Nafret continued to gaze from Ben to Uvi; tears formed in his eyes. Gamolin said gently, "Is the soil good today, Nafret?"

"My head hurts."

A grin spread across Gamolin's face: huge, delighted, relieved. He picked up Nafret and carried him outside, but not before directing his grin at David. Meanwhile, a nanny held Uvi, who had mostly stopped crying. David watched Ben.

The little boy looked puzzled. He stared at the sobbing Uvi in the nanny's lap. Then he picked up a toy from the floor, a soft stuffed cloud the children all liked, and lurched over to Uvi. Wordlessly, seriously, he held the toy out to her.

It was not the same, David knew. Human children as young as six months often developed empathy for another child's distress. Ben's sweet consoling gesture had none of the biological force of little Nafret's distress, and Ben could, unfortunately, quite easily be trained out of his empathy for the Other, and not so easily trained to keep it. *But it was evidence.* Evidence that the same evolutionary mechanism that existed in Worlders had at least a rudimentary hold in Terrans. If the basics were there, it would be even easier to genetically engineer such a closely related evolutionary path.

"No," Ann Sikorski had said, patience regained after the genetics argument. "Shared reality isn't a logical evolutionary strategy, David. It just isn't. I've run the computer simulations twice, according to the Dawkins equations, and that kind of rigid altruism can't overrun genetic selfishness as a winning strategy."

"But on World it *has,*" David pointed out, irrefutably.

"I know," Ann said. She pushed her lovely long hair back from her face, looking troubled. "For one thing, there apparently was no real competition from a strategy of genetic self-ishness, although I don't know why. Not yet. On every other planet, the sentients are competitive. There's something else going on here, but I don't know what. Not yet, anyway."

Biologists. Locked into their computer simulations, their evolutionary mathematics. David *knew* what was going on here. In fact, it was the same thing that already went on among enlightened humans, those who took the Discipline seriously, with its moral obligation to establish the optimum brain chemistry for the day's tasks. Neurotechnology was a responsibility to oneself *and* to others, a taking seriously of one's potential to be the best and most effective person possible. Weren't neurotechnology, genetic engineering, and World's shared reality all really aspects of the same thing: biological tools to make the best possible society?

Yes. They were.

David went outside. Nafret and Gamolin were walking around the flower beds, reciting the names of various blossoms. *Pajalib, rafirib, allabenirib.* Gamolin still wore his exalted expression, and he held the little boy's hand with increased tenderness. When the flower lesson was finished, the tutor sent Nafret back inside and turned to David.

"That is the first sign I have seen in Nafret, Pek Allen. I must tell Pek Voratur immediately. His son is becoming real."

"All flowers smell of sweetness and joy," David answered ritually. He couldn't help smiling. Gamolin's pleasure was infectious. But this was also a good opportunity to obtain information. "Is Nafret the usual age for becoming real on World?"

"He is slightly early." Gamolin's eyes widened. "Why? At what age do human children begin?"

"Later," Allen said. It was important to protect Bonnie and Ben. "About nine years old." That would be five years old on World.

"So late!"

"Yes. But Pek Gamolin, I would ask another question. If a child here should prove unreal . . . what is the World procedure?"

Gamolin's radiant smile faded. After a moment he said. "We try for as little pain as possible. In the past . . . but our distant ancestors could not smell flowers that had not yet grown, you know. Now we cut the throat. A quick, very sharp knife, when the not-child is asleep. They never suffer. And on Terra?"

David managed calm. "A different procedure. We . . . we use potions." Not a lie. The children of Earth with uncorrectable brain disorders were frequently given opiates. Although not to kill them. "May I ask what proportion of your offspring are . . . not-children?"

"Oh, very few," Gamolin said, cheerful again. "In fact, it is quite ridiculous how parents worry about it, when the chances are so small. Especially among the rich like Pek Voratur. A separate crelm house for those not yet declared real by the priests . . . it's silly, really. And I suspect that eventually reality will shift and crelm houses will disappear. Do the rich on Terra have them?"

"No."

"Well, there, you see. Your reality shifts are ahead of ours. Not that I didn't already know that from the Terran bicycles Pek Bazargan has given the household! What magnificent machines! Mine has exactly the curves of bleriodib, and it goes much faster than any bicycle I've ever owned."

"I'm glad you like it," David said. He didn't know what bleriodib were, and his usual keen interest in the language seemed to be missing today.

"I go now to inform Pek Voratur of Nafret's headpain," Gamolin said. "The priests will want to begin planning the ceremony. Till our flowers bloom together."

"Till our flowers bloom together," David said.

Now—irony, irony—he had a headache. Although it shouldn't affect him like this. He was an anthropologist. He knew that all societies had undesirable aspects, and many, even ones as culturally advanced as World, destroyed damaged infants. A six-year-old, however, was not an infant. If humans could be genetically engineered to feel physical distress in the presence of unshared reality, would they, too, destroy their own children? Was that the necessary price of peace?

No. It didn't have to be. Human geneticists, unlike World evolution, didn't have to rely on the harshness of natural selection, nor on the vagaries of genetic chance. They could tinker with the basic gene patterns, find a way around the problem of the severely brain-damaged. It might lie in other genes besides the ones for the shared-reality mechanism. It might be something easily modified.

And maybe the difficulty wasn't even genetic! Maybe it was just cultural. The priests that must declare little Nafret "real"— they held the power of life and death. And wasn't *that* a common pattern in human history! Greedy religious orders, wanting to keep power for themselves, using custom and myth and threats and murder to keep the people in line and then making them believe it was all for their own good so they wouldn't challenge the supremacy of the priesthood. Some political thinker of a few centuries ago had nailed it exactly: "Religion is the opiate of the people."

Well, if the killing of children was cultural, not biological, then it wouldn't even be a component of the human genetic adoption of "shared reality." So why was he, David Allen, feeling so upset about it?

That was the real problem, wasn't it? Not with the genetics, but with *him*. He was feeling pessimistic about a minor difficulty when he ought to feel jubilant about a major insight. Tomorrow he would make a significant adjustment to his Discipline. The implications of this were too big for petty mental stumblings.

He might have the means to save humanity from itself.

Whistling, he walked the beautiful gardens of the Voratur household, feeling hope bloom in him like a flower.

SIX

RAFKIT SELOE

Enli stood miserably before Pek Nagredil in his small cramped office in the government center. Outside the arched window, chill rain fell steadily on the high arches and curving courtyards of Rafkit Seloe.

"Pek Brimmidin, Reality and Atonement had hoped for more from you. Much more," Pek Nagredil said.

"I know," Enli said.

"You have a favored position in the Voratur household—direct assistant to one of the Terrans! You should have acquired all types of useful information. But what do you tell me? The Terrans expel disgusting bodily fluids from their noses. Their bladders empty on an average of six point four times daily. They do not have sex—we know that isn't true, from the Terrans who came previously. They—"

"What I said was that these Terrans make no sexual displays," Enli said wretchedly. Rain dripped off her clothing, her neckfur, her fingers, making puddles on the government floor.

"Don't interrupt. You tell me that the Terrans work steadily on plants and animals, like healers. That they are probably—'probably'!—observing World people whenever they can. That the Terran children play with World children in the Voratur crelm house. And that they have given flower seeds for 'rosib' to Pek Voratur, which the whole world already knows."

"I—"

"The only new piece of information you have told me is that Pek Bazargan asked to take a picture of Pek Voratur's brain inside his head, and that Pek Voratur naturally refused."

"They speak their strange Terran words when they're alone," Enli said. "Even though I listen, I can't understand."

"Then you had better find a way of learning Terran, or observing actions instead of speech. This is a pathetic informant report for five tendays."

"I'm sorry. I—"

"You should be able to learn Terran words. The informant assigned to the previous Terrans—an informant who, Pek Brimmidin, is now real!—learned the language. At least enough to be able to understand such overhearings as 'We will return for the manufactured item.' Don't you think you can do at least as well as that? You are intelligent, after all."

"But I—"

"You may go, Pek Brimmidin."

"But—"

"You may go."

Not even a polite wish for her future success. Enli turned and dripped her way outside. She mounted her wet bicycle and started back to Gofkit Jemloe through the cold rain.

"Please, Pek Sikorski . . ." Enli began.

"Yes, Enli? What is it?"

"Would you teach me to speak your words?"

Pek Sikorski looked surprised. Back at Gofkit Jemloe, dried off and rested, Enli had regained her confidence. Hadn't she succeeded at every other informant job? She could do whatever was necessary to succeed at this one, too.

Pek Sikorski said, "Why do you want to learn our words, Enli?" She did not speak as well as Pek Bazargan, and her accent was strange. Also, it looked to Enli as if Pek Sikorski was developing a flower sickness. Her nose dripped a little and her eyes had begun to turn red and swell. Trifalitib were just coming into bloom; Pek Sikorski was probably flower sick from that. Tabor had had it, a shame to him every time the lacy flowers came into season. . . . No, don't think about Tabor.

The odd thing was that Pek Sikorski didn't seem ashamed to have a flower sickness. She wasn't hiding in her room as rich women did, or keeping her head bent in atonement as working people did, or making ritual apologies to a trifalitib bed for her miserable failure to appreciate their glorious gift. She hadn't even braided her neckfur—headfur—in atonement braids. Her headfur looked the same as always, today caught on top of her skull in a shining loop.

Enli said, "I want to learn your words because I like learning things." Only yesterday Pek Sikorski had praised Enli for her neat job of preparing pieces of dead worm for the strange Terran machine, "gene sequencer." There were a number of these odd machines, all looking like sealed metal boxes with mouths that swallowed bits of dead things and never gave them back.

Pek Sikorski smiled, sneezed, and wiped her nose. She didn't even make the sign of atonement. "Well, Enli, I'll be glad to teach you Terran. Shall we start now?"

"Yes, please." Didn't the woman even care that she was offending a flower? What was wrong with these people?

"Let's start with the objects in this room, shall we? This is a *table*."

"*Table*," Enli repeated, tasting the strange word. Pressure began to bore between her eyes, but she was taking so many of the government pills that the pressure was small and far away. There was no other way that she could get through the day with these awful Terrans. Enli might not have had many facts to report to Pek Nagredil, but she had impressions.

"*Floor*," Pek Sikorski said, stooping to touch the floor. She sneezed again, without bowing her head.

"*Floor, floor, floor*," Enli said, not looking at her.

"*Wall*."

"*Wall, wall, wall. Floor, floor, floor. Table, table, table.*"

"Good. Here's an important one for you: *flower*." And Pek Sikorski actually touched a trifalit blossom from the bouquet on her table. *While* she had trifalit flower sickness!

Enli felt sick herself. So the Terrans weren't real after all. No one who was real could commit a sacrilege like that. Pek Sikorski should cry out with pain, crumple to the floor . . . she did no such thing. She greeted Pek Bazargan, who had just entered through the door.

"Good morning, Ann, Enli . . . May your gardens bloom always. Ann, you don't look too good. *Allergy*?" The last word was in their speech.

"Yes, it feels so," Pek Sikorski said ruefully, in World. "I haven't gotten around to taking an *antihistamine* yet. Enli asked to learn English, and we're having a lesson."

"Good," Pek Bazargan said, smiling at Enli. "May your flowers bloom in this endeavor. But, Ann, take that *antihistamine* now." His last sentence had a peculiar intensity.

Pek Sikorski said, "Oh. *Taboo*?" Another weird Terran word.

"Very much so."

"Excuse me." She left the workroom.

Pek Bazargan strolled toward Enli's *table* and inspected her work. "Very nice, Enli. I'm sure you're a great help to Ann."

"Thank you," Enli said.

"I saw you ride in yesterday on your bicycle, in the rain. You must have got very wet, riding on such a day."

"Yes," Enli said cautiously. Did he have some way, some unreal Terran way, of knowing where she'd gone? Was *he* an informant, too?

"I'd like to ask you a question, if I may. Your bicycle, like everyone else's, has a lock on it. Now, shared reality shifts over time, as we know, and I am very interested in that. So my question may sound strange, but please remember that shared reality on Terra, while of course shared, may have shifted a bit from World. Why do bicycles have locks, when stealing one would surely violate shared reality?"

Enli made her hands work steadily on the worm pieces. Here it was, then. Even Pek Nagredil would agree this was significant information. Yes, shared reality shifted, but not so much that it could lead to ignorance of such a basic concept. Pek Bazargan must be unreal to even ask it. And if he had asked it of anyone not on the government pills, it would have revealed such an unreality that the result would be smashing headpain . . . But he had asked it of Enli. Should she pretend pain? No, he didn't know the difference.

She said, as quietly as her hammering heart would allow, "Stealing does not violate shared reality. People will always take things they see and want and do not already have. That is just Worlder nature, and everyone knows it. It's shared."

"Ah," Pek Bazargan said, and there was something intense in his strange pale Terran eyes that Enli suddenly didn't like.

Was it possible that he had already known the answer to his own question? That he had asked it not to hear her reply, but to see if she could make it without headpain? Did he suspect already what *she* was?

Panic struck Enli. If that was so, if her informant status was ruined and she had failed . . . She fought to calm herself, to reveal nothing, while Pek Bazargan watched her from his alien eyes. It was a relief when Pek Sikorski returned.

Except—Pek Sikorski was no longer sneezing, red-eyed, nose-dripping.

That wasn't possible. The trifalit blossom still stood on the *table*. And trifalit fragrance filled the air: there was a lacy bed of it at the far end of the garden, beside the pool. Trifalitib would be in bloom for two more tendays, which was how long Tabor had always suffered, each day worse and deeper into atonement. But here stood Pek Sikorski, with no flower sickness.

I haven't gotten around to taking an antihistamine *yet.*

They had some potion that took away flower sickness, as the government pills took away headpain.

Enli's hand steadied on her worm knife. She was a good informant after all. She would have something important and unique to tell Pek Nagredil next tenday. Not to mention Pek Voratur.

"Well," Pek Sikorski said, "are you ready, Enli, for more Terran words?"

Enli nodded yes.

"Are you sure?" Pek Voratur said. "Completely sure?"

"Yes," Enli said. "I saw it. She had bad flower sickness for trifalitib, then she took an *antihistamine,* and she did not have any flower sickness at all."

Pek Voratur stood, crossed to the window, and looked out. Enli gave him time to think.

Pek Voratur's personal room was by far the grandest she'd ever stood in. The walls were covered with flat waxed flowers, every inch, their many colors faded by the wallers' art to muted, harmonious beauty. Arched windows faced a private court of pajalib, sajib, and rare yellow anitabib. Underfoot lay a thick carpet from Seuril Island, gold as grass, with one continuous intricate curve of black woven through it. The sleeping pallet had of course been removed, but breakfast bowls of dark oiled wood and heavy pewter trimmed with gold remained on the low curved table, along with a jumble of severely circular business letters.

Along the south wall stood the flower altar, the loveliest Enli had ever seen. Living wood had been trained to grow in those swooping curves, trained for years until the wood was harvested, polished, fitted with two silver vases. The vases held fresh bouquets in honor of the First Flower, the perfect bloom that had come down from the moon Obri and unfolded to create World. Between the two vases lay a flower remembrance for Pek Voratur's ancestors, and it, too, was the most beautiful thing of its kind. Delicate glass blown into looping tunnels, through which ran the quick silver-red liquid metal called flowersoul.

Enli looked away. Until she was once more real, flower altars were not for her. Especially not for her. *Tabor* . . .

Pek Voratur turned around. "We will go together to see Pek Bazargan."

"Me?" Enli said, confused. But then she understood. This

was not informing, but real, trader business. Reality must be shared. She nodded, hoping that Pek Voratur did not know she had hesitated, did not realize that for a moment she had forgotten that he, at least, was real.

"We will go now," Pek Voratur said, and plucked a pajal from his hospitality bush, while Enli looked away.

They found Pek Bazargan in his personal room, which was far less sumptuous than the household head's but far more so than Enli's shared chamber. Pek Bazargan was not alone. With him were Pek Allen, on a rare visit outside the crelm house, and the huge male Terran, Pek Gruber, whom Enli had not seen since her first day in the household. Pek Gruber looked sweaty, dirty, and very happy. He had obviously just arrived. A pack of distressingly square design still straddled his back, rising above his enormous shoulders. The three Terrans stood talking intently. She heard the words "Neury Mountains."

Pek Bazargan spotted Enli and Pek Voratur and picked a flower from his hospitality bush. "May your garden bloom, Pek Voratur."

"May your flowers please your ancestors, Pek Bazargan, Pek Allen. Pek Gruber, welcome back."

"Yes, our Pek Gruber has returned from his journey."

"With rocks," Pek Voratur said, and Enli knew he was laughing inside. Everyone thought Pek Gruber's passion for rocks was funny. Rocks!

"Wonderful rocks," Pek Gruber said. His World was accented with the soft slurring of the mountain people.

"The flowers of my heart rejoice for you," Pek Voratur said, still with that same inside laughter. Only Pek Bazargan smiled back. Once more Enli felt a stab of doubt. Pek Bazargan seemed to share reality so much more than the other Terrans . . . Was it possible that only he was real? But he also seemed to share reality with Pek Sikorski and Pek Allen and now Pek Gruber, so he couldn't be real . . .

Pek Voratur said, "I have thought about that picture of my brain, Pek Bazargan. Perhaps there is a way to bring a bargain to flower."

"What might that be?" Pek Bazargan said. Enli saw him

make a small motion with his hand, so small that even she might have missed it if she had not seen him make it often before, to Pek Sikorski. It meant, *Say nothing, I will talk for all of us.* A strange gesture.

Pek Voratur looked pointedly at the pillows heaped on the floor. Pek Bazargan apologized and everyone sat down, Pek Gruber finally shrugging out of his heavy pack. It fell with a heavy thunk. Rocks.

"Enli will join us," Pek Voratur said, and Enli, too, sat on a curving pillow, off to the side. Bazargan offered a plate of small cakes.

Pek Voratur began. "Enli Pek Brimmidin, as assistant to Pek Sikorski in her healer's chamber, naturally spends much time with Pek Sikorski. They share the day's reality. And of course Enli shares reality with my household, too. In this way I have come to hear of a curious thing. Is it not shared reality that Pek Sikorski had a flower sickness for trifalitib? And that she took a potion of Terran devising and the flower sickness disappeared, even though trifalitib are still in bloom?"

"It is shared reality," Pek Bazargan said.

"And this potion is called an *antihistamine*?"

"It is shared reality."

"Aaahhh," Pek Voratur said. "Then this is indeed a valuable potion."

Pek Bazargan said nothing, his dark gaze steady.

Pek Voratur changed from questioning learner to brisk businessman. "I would bring a bargain to flower between us for this potion, so that I might be the sole trader of it on World. Your *antihistamine* traded for a picture of my brain."

Pek Bazargan nibbled on a sweetcake. Giving himself time, Enli thought. These Terrans were indeed good traders. Eventually he said, "When we discussed this once before, Pek Voratur, you said to me that you could not risk exposing your brain, the home of the soul, to something you do not understand. Why has shared reality shifted?"

He knew immediately that he had made a mistake; Enli watched him watch Pek Voratur's astonishment. The answer itself was shared reality—Pek Bazargan should already *know* it. Pek Voratur's face shifted from astonishment to discomfort. The headpain was starting.

Pek Bazargan said quickly—too quickly, to Enli's alert ear—"I would hear you say it, Pek Voratur. It is better to have our shared reality shared aloud. Such is the custom on Terra."

Pek Voratur's face eased. Enli knew his thoughts: Speaking reality aloud versus not speaking aloud was only a small shift. Well within what was real, especially for a sophisticated trader, used to local shifts in reality. The headpain would now be receding behind Pek Voratur's eyes. But not behind hers. She could feel it, a storm raging just beyond the strong artificial seawall of the government pills.

"In the first months of life," began Pek Voratur, as if reciting a story on a village square, "we are all infants. We are buds, not yet real blooms. Buds are tender and must be protected. So, many parts of shared reality are withheld from children, just as direct rain and sun are withheld from the petals of buds, safe in their enfolding green.

"As we grow—Is this indeed how reality is shared on Terra, Pek Bazargan? With the obvious told, as if adults were children in the crelm house?"

"Yes," Pek Bazargan said.

"Very well. As we grow, more and more of reality is shared with us. But even as adults, we may need protection. Does a village family require that the old grandmother share the heavy lifting of logs? No. So the strong young men risk their backs so that the old may have shelter. The fisherwoman risks the sea that her family may eat. The mountain father risks his life to save his child from wandering into the Neury caves. Risk for the shared good is part of shared reality.

"If thousands, perhaps millions, could be freed from the shame of flower sickness, is that not a risk worth a brain picture of one man of World? Even if I do not understand it? The soul will always emerge triumphant from a risk on behalf of shared good, although it may not from a risk undertaken purely for profit. Nothing is more pleasing to the First Flower, and so nothing is more real, than a person who risks his life for others. Except, of course, the person who actually gives his life to save others—the special and adored joy of the First Flower, who bloomed and died to create World. There, I have told the shared reality aloud."

Pek Voratur smiled, although Enli could tell he still felt uncomfortable.

Pek Bazargan nodded. "I thank you. Now permit me to offer you flowers of learning."

Pek Voratur nodded graciously, accepting the subservient role of learner. This at least was familiar bargaining ground.

"World and Terra may share reality, but we do not share bodies. You have neckfur, we have headfur. You have dark eyes, some of us have light eyes. You can eat hanfruit, we cannot—if we try, we will become very sick."

"You have tried this?" Pek Voratur asked with interest.

"In a manner of speaking," Pek Bazargan answered, and what, Enli wondered, did *that* mean? But Pek Bazargan rushed on. "There may be many more differences deep inside our bodies, where we cannot see. If we trade for the *antihistamine* potion, World bodies may be made sick by it in ways we cannot foresee. Naturally, Terrans do not wish to cause you harm."

"May your flowers bloom," Pek Voratur said. He was frowning.

"May your garden bring joy," Pek Bazargan replied. "So, unfortunately, we cannot trade the *antihistamine* potion for the brain pictures. However, to trade water pipes that never rust, as once we discussed—"

"I will think on it," Pek Voratur said abruptly, rudely, and rose. "I will share reality with the servants of the First Flower. Come, Enli."

She scrambled up from her pillow, surprised at his loss of courtesy, of smoothness. Pek Voratur had even omitted farewell flowers!

Hurrying behind him across the courtyards of the great house, Enli realized the reason. Pek Voratur was furious. She had not, in her stay in the Voratur household, seen this before, but apparently it was not unknown. Servants, gardeners, even a houseguest from the capital took one look at Pek Voratur's face and disappeared into doorways, behind trellises, under an arched stone bridge spanning an ornamental stream.

Once more in his personal room, Pek Voratur turned to Enli. His voice, controlled as ever, made her neckfur rise.

"You will steal the *antihistamine* from Pek Sikorski's personal room and bring it to me. Tonight. Do we share reality, Pek Brimmidin?"

"We share reality," Enli got out. Then she managed, "But if it is dangerous to World bodies . . ."

"Shared good justifies the risk. For those Terrans to presume to decide that for me . . . for me! Enli"—abruptly his voice changed—"I begin to wonder if they are real at all."

Enli said nothing.

"Of course, that is for the servants of the First Flower to decide, not me. I don't envy the priests their task! But meanwhile, these presumptuous Terrans are guests in my household, and the *antihistamine* is certainly real enough. Steal it."

"I will. But . . . Pek Voratur . . . if I may ask . . . who will swallow it?" *And risk death,* she didn't say. Or need to.

"I, of course." Pek Voratur said. "Who else? I will."

SEVEN

GOFKIT JEMLOE

He's very angry," Dieter Gruber said, in English.

Ahmed Bazargan nodded. Voratur had indeed been angry. It was the first time Bazargan had seen the alien anything but smiling, affable, slippery as eels but manageable. Now Voratur had been touched at his core. That was dangerous.

"The problem is that girl, Enli," he said to the other two. "I think she may be—"

"The problem is the priests!" David Allen burst out. "Didn't you hear him say he was rushing off to consult with them? The priests have these wonderful people totally in thrall, almost certainly to keep themselves in power!"

Bazargan looked bleakly at Allen. The young man was fired up about something, hot with it, fevered to the soul. Just as clearly, he was not ready to discuss it fully with the whole team. Oh, the young. Always convinced their theories, no matter what the scientific discipline, would uproot everything that had gone before. Equally convinced that older, more established names were eternally on the prowl to claim credit that should be theirs. Not experienced enough as yet to know that the big leaps forward often started not with the heated vision but with the small anomaly. The seemingly inconsequential detail that didn't quite fit. Like Enli.

"If it weren't for the priests," Allen rushed on, his unlined face flushed, "no one would be declared 'unreal' and then killed. The physiological mechanism of shared reality would still exist, the headaches would still act as social restraints, the only thing that would change is that there might be slightly more divergence of thought between isolated regions as societal controls eased. That's not bad! And the whole populace would be released from fear that—"

"They are not a fearful people," Bazargan said, more sharply than he intended. Something about David Allen bothered him. Something more than rampant ego coupled with tedious insecurity. "However, I would be glad to listen to your theory later. Right now, I wish to hear Dieter's report. He has, after all, been gone several months."

An exaggeration, but it worked. Allen subsided.

"Much of what the recon team stated I merely reconfirmed," Gruber said in his accented English. His blue eyes shone. When Gruber was really excited, Bazargan knew, he lapsed into German. "But I also went deep into the Neury Mountains, which the first team didn't have time to do. *Lieber Gott,* it is amazing! The composition changes utterly. The mountains have not the same composition as the rest of the planetary surface. They're a jumble—some light volcanic rock, basalt and dacite and pumice and obsidian, riddled with radioactive elements with enormously long half-lives. Much more thorium and uranium than you'd expect. All this mixed up with the hard rock typical of deep-sea formations. I believe the Neury Mountains are the remains of an enormous asteroid hit sometime in the earliest geological ages."

"Interesting," Bazargan said. He could tell Gruber was not done, and that he would tell his story in his own way.

Allen was not so patient. "Well, what's so amazing about that?"

Gruber ignored him. "The asteroid probably hit on water, above a 'hot spot' where there was already underwater volcanic activity, with magma being forced up from the planet's core. That underwater impact caused the rock that was thrown up to be full of gas, forming all that pumice. Pumice may even have filled the entire strike basin, on top of the asteroid.

"Eventually, tectonic plate subduction lifted up the whole basin to form the Neury Mountains, *without* cutting it off from the initial hot-spot stresses. Volcanic rock erodes easily, and it was already porous, so what you ended up with is square mile after square mile of caverns. Interconnected caves with so much underground water, chimney holes, lava tunnels, and peculiar radiation that it's all combined to create entire underground ecologies, including some of the most amazing mutant flowers!"

Ann's face lit up. "The Neury Mountains are supposedly where the First Flower unfolded. The World creation myth. That's why the mountains are forbidden."

"The radiation might have something to do with that as well," Bazargan said dryly. "Dieter—"

"I took only thirty-two rads total," Gruber said, "and I had my suit. And no one saw me enter or leave the mountains, I am sure of it. But the radiation is the marvelous thing, Ahmed. I have never seen anything like it. In places, water or rocks of denser metals form natural shields, so that one cave may be perfectly safe and another beside it—or *under* it—may be lethal. And the niche ecologies created by that! Ann will be ecstatic."

"If she sees it," Bazargan said. "For now, there is enough to do here."

"Yes. But wait, there is more. Listen to this! In some exposed rock walls in the mountains, I found the thin layer of clay one would expect, yes, from a major asteroid impact. Dirt gets thrown into the air, blown all over, settles gradually. We have such a clay layer on Earth, from the asteroid impact sixty-five million years ago at the K/T boundary that—"

"Dieter, not too technical," Bazargan said. "Have mercy."

Gruber gave his great, belly-born laugh. "I get carried away, *ja*? But just look at this!"

From his pocket Gruber dug out a handful of dirt. He displayed it on his big dirt-seamed hands as if the dirt were diamonds. Peering closely, Bazargan saw tiny grains of something glassy mixed with the loose silt.

"Quartz!" Dieter roared. "Under my scope, the grains are all cracked and strained, like happens only with sudden great heat and pressure. Such as an asteroid impact!"

"Ah," Bazargan said. "Does the—" But there was no interrupting Gruber on a geological bender.

"The asteroid that made these is a marker. Below the clay-and-quartz layer all the fossils differ from above it."

Ann breathed, "Punctuated evolution . . ."

"*Ja!* The asteroid impact was a catastrophe for World—dust thrown up to block the sun, tidal waves, earthquakes. Life changes fast when catastrophe comes. Maybe this, Ann, is where the biology for the shared-reality mechanism evolved."

She said, "I need your data, Dieter. Now. I have to run the computer sims."

"Yes, of course, Frau Professor Flower. But may I wash first? I smell, I think?"

"Like a cesspool," Bazargan said, and Dieter laughed. Despite his other worries, Bazargan chuckled. It was good to see a scientist filled with the joy of discovery. This was, after all, why they were here. He must try to remember that in the midst of Voratur's anger and Allen's grandiose hyperenthusiasms and Enli's spying, which he was more and more sure she was doing on behalf of someone besides Voratur.

"Dieter, before you go," he said to Gruber, "what was your impression of the Worlders beyond Gofkit Jemloe? How did they react to you?"

"Pretty well, I think," Gruber said. "They had all heard of me, of course. Shared reality. I spoke little, and pretended I could not understand as much as I can. I thought that was the best way to avoid mistakes. I am not an anthropologist, you know, *Gott sei Dank*." He grinned mischievously at Ann. Allen, puerile prig, bridled.

"Also," Gruber continued, "to pretend not to understand is to encourage talk in your presence. In the inns and pel houses the Worlders seemed to regard us as simply traders from a place farther away than most. They were not threatened by us, not alarmed, not unaccepting. Merely curious. Of course, it was all recorded, and you can see whatever you want before I send the data to the *Zeus*."

"Yes," Bazargan said. "Go have your bath. Do you remember where your room is?"

"In this warren? No." Gruber laughed; Bazargan could see that the geologist's exuberance would be good leaven for this serious team. "I can find my way through the deep sacred caves of the Neury Mountains, but I cannot find my room in this winding house!"

"Show him the way, David," Bazargan said, thereby ridding himself of Allen's overheated theories about priestly self-interest. For now, anyway. He needed quiet. He had to think.

Allen, looking sulky, led Gruber away. Bazargan went into his personal room, closed the door, and pulled close the gauzy curtains over the arched windows. In the semidarkness scented with flowers, he sat down on a curving pillow to think how to best convince Hadjil Pek Voratur that Terrans were, despite the evidence Voratur must be accumulating, real.

It was vitally important that Voratur continue to believe that. In his weeks on World, Bazargan had accompanied Voratur to his cottage-industry "manufactures," to Rafkit Seloe, to friends' homes, on various business trips. Despite the obvious gag on asking questions—why would anyone ask if they already shared reality?—Bazargan had learned much. He was now familiar with the major government departments: Processions and Ceremonies, Taxes and Donations, Annals and Sunflashers, Roads and Bridges, Gardens and Wildlands. And the most powerful of the World compound-named departments: Reality and Atonement.

It was Reality and Atonement that determined who had committed transgressions against shared reality. It was Reality and Atonement that determined the punishment. For offenses severe enough to be declared unreal, that meant death. There were only a few types of exemption, none of which Bazargan understood as yet, although he suspected that the servant Enli might be one of them.

One thing was completely clear to Bazargan, as it had not

been clear to the hastily recalled recon team, and was not yet clear to his own small landing team. Reality and Atonement was almost surely turning its shared, cold eye on the Terrans. And if the Terrans were found to be unreal, they would die.

In one sense, then, young Allen was right. The priests—"servants of the First Flower," in their own eyes—with whom Voratur undoubtedly shared all the reality he experienced, were dangerous. But not to Worlders. To humans.

Of course, Bazargan could pull his team out. Radio the *Zeus,* call for the shuttle. But he wasn't going to do that. There was too much rich scientific knowledge to be gained on World, in too many different fields. Ironically, Voratur had said it best: *a risk on behalf of shared good.*

But now Bazargan had better come up with effective ways to convince Hadjil Pek Voratur that humans were not perverse illusions on his beautiful, flower-scented planet.

It was too much. They lacked balance: Bazargan, Gruber, even Ann, whom David Allen admired. Unbalanced, all of them: so immersed in their individual scientific disciplines that they couldn't see the big picture. Which was, for God's sake, unfolding right in front of them, in this ridiculous ceremony!

David shifted on his bench. It was raining, a soft warm rain that stopped none of the ceremonies in the main court of the Voratur household. Servants had spent the morning constructing canopies over the benches that ringed the court, set behind the flower beds and against household walls. Another canopy sheltered the dais built in the middle of the court over the reflecting pool. Toward that dais walked little Nafret, dressed in the briefest of tunics and a long, trailing cape woven of freshly picked flowers. Behind him—this was the part that rankled David—walked not his family but sixteen priests carrying mammoth bouquets of sacred blooms.

David shifted again on his bench. Bazargan looked at him, one slow sideways glance from those hooded dark eyes. David was careful not to fidget again.

But when you looked at it right, Bazargan's careful respect

for native customs was *part* of the problem. Yes, an anthropologist had to act neutral, had to fit in with the population he studied, or else he would be thrown out and couldn't study it at all. That was basic. But Bazargan went so much further. He thought—they all thought, the old men of the field—that their neutrality had to extend into their private beliefs. *Judge not.* No culture was better than another, no culture should be deemed in need of uplifting. Crap! It was the worst kind of moral laziness masquerading as cultural relativism.

Anthropology should be beyond that by now, David fumed, conscientiously not fidgeting on his bench. Anthropology had a duty to the peoples it served, both human and alien, to make life *better*. It was the same duty an individual had to himself, to create the best person he could be through the Discipline. You gave yourself whatever neuropharms your body lacked so that you could be free of chemical deficiencies and excesses, free for optimum functioning in the world. And a society, too, should be given whatever it needed for optimum function and freedom.

Which was not sixteen pompous priests solemnly deciding that they would let a little boy live.

Nafret looked scared, trailing his heavy and fragile cape of flowers. He climbed the two steps to the dais the way small children did: right foot on step one, left foot on step one, right foot up, left foot up. The priests followed. One of them—a big star in Reality and Atonement, no doubt—lifted Nafret onto a high, flower-covered chair at the center of the dais. Nafret looked frantically around, searching the benches for his mother or tutor. His gaze found David, who smiled encouragingly. The little boy still looked frightened.

The priests sat around the high throne in a circle, facing outward, and began to chant.

David's World, fluent as it was, still wasn't good enough to follow the archaic, highly inflected chant, but he knew it was the story of the First Flower, and that it would go on for at least an hour. After that would come the blessing that declared Nafret real, in which for the first, and last, time in his life unless he became a priest, Nafret would eat a flower. Then feasting and dancing inside the household, family and guests and servants alike, far into the night.

It might have been an initiation ceremony in any society, except that it was gentle, nonviolent, and based on a biological fact which was not puberty. Worlders pretty much ignored puberty. What mattered was sharing reality, getting discomfort or headpain when you were out of belief with your community, knowing empathy for others in the physical body, not merely as an abstract.

Becoming real.

A sudden longing hit David, as unexpected as it was sharp. To *know* you belonged, were accepted, were in synch with your fellows . . . When had he last had that? He had never had that. Certainly not from his father, who never hid his disappointment in David, nor his mother, too busy with her medical career to notice her only son. Nor anyone at Princeton . . .

Bazargan was giving him another sideways look. David returned his attention to the ceremony. Bazargan didn't really respect him, either, David knew. Bazargan thought David Campbell Allen III was too pampered, too young, too excitable, too ignorant. But in actuality it was Bazargan who was unworthy of respect: stodgy, narrow-visioned, hidebound.

David would show him. He'd show them all.

After the ceremony, Bazargan approached David as he stood talking to Colert Gamolin. "Pek Voratur would like to see us all in his personal room, David. Where's Dieter?"

"I don't know. What about?"

"He didn't say. You and Ann go ahead, and I'll find Dieter."

As they made their way through the laughing crowd, David said to Ann, "Do you know what this is about?"

She bit her lip. "I'm afraid I do. This morning I did inventory, and some antihistamine is missing from my room."

"Antihistamine? Who—"

"May your flowers bloom forever," Voratur boomed. He had come out to meet them. He was magnificently dressed in light, embroidered spidersilk, and his neckfur had been tied into a hundred small bunches decorated with tiny flowers. Voratur's broad flat face was flushed. Drinking a lot of pel, David guessed.

He smiled at the Worlder. "I rejoice in your blossoms on this happy day, Pek Voratur."

"Ah, we will do it for Bonnie and Ben one day, too. A wonderful flower ceremony!"

From a Worlder, it was an unbreakable promise. And not a cheap one; David estimated that today's feast cost Voratur half a year's revenue. Including, of course, huge payments to the parasitic priests. David managed to smile. "Thank you on behalf of Ben and Bonnie."

"Yes, Pek Voratur, thank you," Ann said, more warmly. "Your flowers gladden my heart!"

Bazargan came up to them, leading Dieter Gruber. Gruber had grumbled about losing a whole day of rock analysis to the flower ceremony, but now that he was here, he looked as if he was enjoying it more than the other humans. His face was as flushed as Voratur's, David noticed with disapproval. Although not with pel; Ann had vetoed the intoxicant for humans. "It won't actually cause physical damage," she'd said, "but each local brewery adds so many additives that I can't be sure of the net effect on our nervous system."

Gruber must have taken a fizzy he'd brought down from the ship. Or several fizzies. David didn't see how people could deliberately upset their brains like that. If he were a religious man, he'd call Gruber's condition a sacrilege.

"Pek Bazargan! Pek Gruber!" Voratur cried. "May your flowers bloom forever!"

"And yours, on this happy day," Bazargan said.

"Come in, come in." Voratur led them past his personal room, which was filled with select guests clustered around Alu Pek Voratur. Nafret sat miserably still in his clumsy cape while the other children darted in and out of the adults' legs, shrieking and laughing. Voratur took them into a small antechamber, the purpose of which David couldn't guess. It had painted walls, no windows, and no pillows or tables. In the middle was a high domed object of woven cloth stretched over thin struts of metal or wood. The dome hummed softly.

"I would like to bring a bargain to bloom between us," Voratur said, still flushed and smiling. But more focused, David thought. Voratur was not as drunk as he'd first thought.

Gruber was. "Anything in exchange for your firstborn daughter," he said, in English. Voratur ignored the rudeness of using words he did not understand. Bazargan gave Gruber a look so cold that Gruber, even in his current state, grew quiet.

Bazargan said, "What bargain is this, Pek Voratur?"

"The one we spoke of before. A picture of my brain for *antihistamine* to market."

Bazargan said calmly, "That antihistamine, some of it, was missing from Pek Sikorski's quarters this morning."

"No, not this morning," Voratur said. "Although perhaps you noticed it only this morning. But it was missing a tenday ago. I had it stolen."

Not a trace of guilt appeared on Voratur's face. The pel? Or because stealing for business advantage was a part of shared reality? Maybe both, David thought.

Bazargan said, still calm, "I see. But what I told you before, Pek Voratur, is still shared reality. The antihistamine may be dangerous to bodies on World. We cannot bring a bargain to bloom with the *antihistamine*."

"No, my friend," Voratur said cheerfully. "Reality has shifted, and I share reality now with you. The antihistamine is not dangerous to bodies on World. I know because I have eaten the *antihistamine*, and I am fine!"

Ann said quickly, "How long ago did you eat it?"

"Ten days ago, nine days ago, and the rest, a big bite, seven days ago. And I have a flower sickness, Pek Sikorski. To fakim. You notice my household grows no fakimib. I am fortunate that it is not a ritual blossom. But four days ago I rode to a friend's house and spent an afternoon in a garden of fakimib, and I was not sick. You notice that not once have I had to braid my neckfur in atonement. Your *antihistamine* is safe, Pek Sikorski, for Worlders. And it will make all of us very rich."

Ann looked at Bazargan. Obviously the two of them had already discussed what to do. Why was he, David, left out of these discussions so much? They said it was because he was relatively isolated in the crelm house. But they could walk over to the crelm house if they wanted to include him. Obviously, they didn't.

Another small resentment was added to the store David Allen was accumulating.

Bazargan said, "Pek Voratur. Hear me well, my friend. We still cannot bring a bargain to bloom with the *antihistamine*. I am sorry, but we cannot. This is why: Even on World, bodies differ. This is shared reality. You have flower sickness for fakimib. Another may have it for rafirib. Still another for pajalib or trifalitib. In the same way, one man may eat *antihistamine* and be cured of flower sickness. Another may eat it and become sick in another way. Another may die. It is *not* safe."

Voratur's smile vanished. He walked over to the domed object in the middle of the small closed room and stood beside it. "Then share this reality, Pek Bazargan. If World bodies differ so much from each other, Terran bodies must do so, too. Is this not shared reality?"

"Yes," Bazargan said.

"Yet one Terran, Pek Sikorski, takes the *antihistamine*. Why does she do so, if it is not safe because of different bodies? And if it is safe for one Terran, then it will be safe for one Worlder."

"No," Bazargan said. "Let me share this reality with you, Pek Voratur. On Terra there are . . . healers who make the *antihistamines*. Then our government tests it on many, many sick Terrans. In this way, we see how many are made sicker by the potion, and if any die. Only if none die and a very, very few are made sicker, does the potion come to bloom in a bargain for market."

"What government department makes this test?"

David saw Bazargan consider. Finally he said, "Reality and Atonement. The drug must be declared real."

Voratur nodded. It made sense to him. "Then we, too, will

have Reality and Atonement make a test. With many Worlders."

Ann said, "But Pek Voratur—"

"Enough," Voratur said, and now his voice was cold. "We will make these tests."

Ann looked helplessly at Bazargan.

"You cannot treat us like unreal children in the crelm house," Voratur said. "That is not sharing reality. We are not children. Do you share reality with us about the *antihistamines*, or do you not?"

David felt his throat seize up. Voratur was issuing an ultimatum. If the Terrans did not share reality, then the Terrans were not real. If they were not real . . . Suddenly he remembered the retarded little girl who had run up to him his first day on World, the unreal child he had mistakenly spoken to. What had happened to her?

He knew what must have happened to her.

Bazargan said, "You are right. Forgive me; I will braid my headfur in atonement. Yes, we share reality. Tomorrow I will send Pek Sikorski to the healers of your choice to show them how to make *antihistamines*, and to conduct the tests on many, many Worlders."

Immediately Voratur was again all smiles, all warm host, all jovial business partner. "Wonderful! May our flowers bloom together for a long time, and their fragrance rise to the clouds!"

"May our flowers bloom together forever," Bazargan said. To David he didn't look dejected, despite having lost. Well, Bazargan was an old politician, among other things. He would always sell out an ideal for a compromise.

Although David was elated over this particular compromise. They would get an actual Lagerfeld scan of a World brain! Along with the DNA and other data Ann already had, surely that would be enough to understand the biological mechanism that permitted shared reality. Perhaps even to duplicate it physiologically? He'd ask Ann. And then, with genetic engineering . . .

"When may Pek Sikorski take the brain picture?" David said.

"As soon as you like," Pek Voratur said expansively. "Tomorrow. But now I must return to my guests."

"The petals of your blossoms delight me," Bazargan said.

"I rejoice in the flowers of your heart," Voratur said. All at once he let out a great laugh and thumped on the dome beside him. The humming inside swelled to a strong buzz. *Lifegivers*, David realized, the small insect-equivalents that pollinated flowers. Come to think of it, he had seen no lifegivers at all during the long hours of Nafret's ceremony, no lifegivers buzzing annoyingly in front of guests' eyes or tickling their hands. How the hell had the Worlders gathered them all up?

"These small Worlders cause their own sickness in just a few people," Voratur boomed, "and that, too, we will heal with potions. And we will all be richer than Seuril Island!" Laughing, he thumped the dome again and went out the door, calling loudly for more pel.

The four humans looked at each other. Three, David realized in disgust. Gruber was asleep standing up, leaning against the painted wall. Asleep or passed out.

"You had no choice, Ahmed," Ann said, in English.

"No," Bazargan agreed. "I did not. Not unless I want to pull us out."

"Pull us *out*?" David said. "You mean, leave? Over an allergy medicine?"

"Over avoidable biological contamination of the planet," Bazargan said.

"You even considered leaving before we fully understand the shared reality mechanism? The biggest boon to humanity ever?"

"Not now, David," Ann said warningly. She watched Bazargan.

David subsided. But inside he seethed. The shortness of vision, the timidity of thought . . . What was *wrong* with these scientists? Were they that corrupted by the prissy stuffiness of publish-before-all?

Ann said, "There's just one thing I don't understand, Ahmed. Voratur accepted the idea of a clinical trial for antihistamines, a trial run by Reality and Atonement, before he even talked about it with the priests. Is that because he and the priests share reality so much that he already knows what they'll say?"

"Probably," Bazargan said. "But also because shared reality among the ruling classes, priests and heads of great households includes a complex system of 'gifts' that we would call bribes and kickbacks. I haven't unraveled it all yet; it's hard to do fieldwork when you can't ask many questions. But don't underestimate the priests, Ann. They hold enormous power on World, even though they can't maneuver outside shared reality."

"I don't underestimate the priests," David said. "I've said right along that they're deadly parasites!"

"That's not what I said," Bazargan answered, and though his tone was calm as ever, something in it made David fall quiet.

Ann and Bazargan left, both supporting Gruber to his room. David lingered, even though he knew he should go back to Nafret. He was, after all, one of the boy's two tutors. Under their temporary dome, the lifegivers buzzed angrily. Temporarily captive, temporarily kept from their true function.

But only temporarily.

EIGHT

ABOARD THE *ZEUS*

Syree Johnson and Rafael Peres waited in the docking bay as the light, enclosed gangway unfolded from the *Zeus* and extended toward the small ship seven meters away. Beside the *Zeus* the flyer looked like a kitten stalking a hippopotamus.

And "stalking" was the right word, Syree thought. If the flyer had brought good news, it would have given it by radio right after emerging from Space Tunnel #438. Instead, the flyer's pilot had merely notified the *Zeus* of its presence, which the *Zeus* already knew of. The instant anything emerged from the space tunnel, a beacon sent an encoded description to the *Zeus*. The flyer's request to approach and dock had taken fifty-six minutes to reach the *Zeus*, and the flyer itself had taken five E-days. Flyers traveled at 2.3 gees acceleration and deceleration. This was hard on their pilots, but the pilots, all young and fit hotshots, didn't care. The bodily strain was a point of pride. Thinking about this made Syree feel old.

"Gangway contact," the OOD said to Peres. "Locking . . . locking confirmed."

"Pressurize," Peres said.

"Yes, sir. Pressurizing."

Syree and Peres both wore full dress uniform. Going down

with all flags flying. If indeed they were going down, if this mission was being recalled. Syree didn't mind recall. She did mind not having accomplished what she came here to do.

"Airlock opening on the flyer, sir."

Another voice, over the intercom from the gangway. "Captain Llewellyn Jones of Flyer 583. Request permission to come aboard."

"Permission granted. Lieutenant, open the airlock."

"Opening airlock."

Jones came aboard, suited but carrying his helmet, walking with the carefully controlled steps of someone adjusting to a big gravitational change. But walking: another point of pilot pride. When you preferred jumping around the galaxy to any steady command, and you never knew from one hour to the next what you would be required to do, it was important to demonstrate control of yourself at all times. Fast, small, hard to detect, flyers were to warfare what operatives were to intelligence work.

Peres said, "Welcome aboard, Captain Jones."

"Thank you, sir."

"This is Colonel Johnson."

"Ma'am." Peres didn't need to give Syree's title, Team Commander for Special Project; it was obvious that Jones already knew who she was and what she was doing here. Or, rather, trying to do here.

"The mailsack for *Zeus* personnel is aboard my flyer," Jones said. "Download whenever you say. And I have a live-recipient-only message for Colonel Johnson from Headquarters."

"This way."

Peres led them to his quarters and activated a security shield. The room was now impervious to electronic detection of any type. If the bridge caught fire, a soldier would have to knock on the door to get Peres's attention.

"Do you want to desuit, Captain Jones?" Peres said.

"No, thank you, sir. I'm not going to be here that long. My message is actually an official inquiry for Colonel Johnson, from General Stefanak. The general wants to know what you've discovered, ma'am."

Syree had expected this. There was no way to send a message through a space tunnel unless it was carried by a physical object: a capsule, a probe, a person. The first two could carry questions and replies, but only people could ask the next questions, the ones that always arose from the reply. Jones was a human message capsule. That Stefanak had decided to send him told Syree that the war was not going well.

This particular space tunnel had not, as far as humans knew, yet been discovered by the Fallers. Sending a flyer through it increased the chance that it might be. Stefanak had done so anyway, which suggested great need on the other end.

"I've prepared a complete report to take to General Stefanak," Syree said, handing Jones the communication cube. "Let me also summarize for you. The artifact does indeed seem to be a weapon, and of a type we have never seen before. We have activated once, at lowest setting, to no damage to the *Zeus* or the planet but with destruction of a shuttle and one casualty, shuttle pilot Captain Daniel Austen. The artifact appears to emit a spherical wave that temporarily destabilizes nuclei of all elements with an atomic number above seventy-five."

Jones's eyes widened, his professional unflappability momentarily breached. But only momentarily. "And your current plans for the artifact, Colonel?"

"We've made extensive investigation with every means we could research, invent, or imagine," Syree said. "The information yielded has been either negligible or unuseful. There seems no way to get to the interior unless we cut it apart with the *Zeus*'s weapons, which may render it useless. Neither will the artifact go through the tunnel; the Schwarzschild radius is too large."

Jones waited.

"The options therefore appear to be limited. The weapon can in theory be towed toward the space tunnel, established there, and set with probes to destabilize anything coming through the tunnel that doesn't give off a preset alarm signal.

In that way it can be used to defend this star system. The star system can then be used as a secure base for military operations and storage."

Jones nodded. "I see. That might be useful, ma'am."

"Possibly. The one planet within Earth-class parameters is already well inhabited with sentients. However, reports from the scientific team on the surface indicate that the natives are very open to the concept of trade. Raw materials supply for our engineers is therefore a possibility. And, of course, this system could be used for secure stations and dry dock."

Again Jones nodded. "And the reports from the team planetside?"

"Included on your cube. They seem to be routine"—Syree hadn't actually viewed all of them—"concerned with the preindustrial native culture. Also with geological findings, and such. No evidence of any alien visitation, including Fallers, except for Orbital Object #7 itself. And the natives consider that to be just another moon."

"Yes, ma'am. Any other message for General Stefanak?"

Such as what? That Syree had failed in her mission to find a way for this invaluable discovery to turn the tide of war? The failure might be unavoidable, but failure it nonetheless was.

"No other message, Captain Jones."

Peres said, "What news of the war?"

"Complete official dispatches on your download, Commander. Unofficially, the news stinks." Jones suddenly looked much older, despite the juvenile diction. "The Fallies destroyed our military base on Camden before we even knew that they knew it was there. They also destroyed three more cruisers. The bastards won't tell us what they want, or why they want it, or negotiate at all. More and more it looks like all they want is to just wipe out humans completely. Pick us off on colonies first, weaken the fleet, and then eventually move in on the solar system."

The flyer pilot's tone was as crisp and even as always, but silence followed his words.

Peres broke it. "What else can we do for you, Captain?"

"Nothing. I'm on my way back as soon as the mail exchange is completed. Commander Peres, Colonel Johnson." He saluted, and Peres escorted him back to the docking bay.

Syree remained in Peres's quarters. On a shelf sat his bio-monitor. The commander of the *Zeus* was a follower of the Discipline, then. What mix of neuropharms did Peres call up in the morning? What was the optimum mix to face a day in which your mission was mostly futile, your reports were mostly negative, and your species was losing a war with a genocidal enemy no one could understand?

There had to be a way into Orbital Object #7. A way to dismantle it short of destroying it. To take it through the space tunnel into the human space on the other side, Caligula system. And then on through other tunnels, back to Sol. To reassemble it and set it guarding humanity's prime home instead of this gods-forsaken, three-miles-up-the-asshole-of-the-world planet where nobody lived except a species whose main interest in life was growing flowers.

There had to be a way.

NINE

GOFKIT JEMLOE

T his is Pek Renjamor," Voratur said expansively. It was the morning after the party—very early in the morning, Bazargan noted. However, Voratur looked fresh and eager. "Pek Renjamor is a healer. He also owns a manufactury of healing doses, which will be manufacturing your *antihistamines* for me."

Pek Ranjamor offered a hospitality flower. Bazargan, trying not to yawn, took it and smiled. The alien manufacturer made a comic contrast to Voratur: small, wrinkled, and silent.

Voratur boomed, "The sun shines this morning, and Pek Renjamor and I are ready, Pek Bazargan, to show you how we will find many people with flower sickness for any bloom you care to name. Already Pek Renjamor has healers in his manufactury prepared to duplicate whatever Pek Sikorski teaches him. We hope to begin the tests on World bodies by tonight."

Tonight? Pek Bazargan stifled another yawn. It was *very* early.

"Come, come," Voratur said. "I have your bicycle outside the gate, for the ride to Rafkit Seloe. We do not want to waste the sun. Or time!" He laughed, then grew solemn again. Somehow his round face lengthened. "We have just enough time to return here before the picture of my brain must be made."

"The brain picture is not dangerous, you know," Bazargan said.

"I know," Voratur answered, in tones of such dread that Bazargan went to put on his clothes and ride to Rafkit Seloe before the trader changed his mind.

Despite himself, he was impressed by the sunflasher station in the capital. It was amazingly simple. And amazingly fast.

The three men walked, puffing, up a steep hill outside Rafkit Seloe, and then climbed an even steeper set of winding stairs that curled around the outside of a slender tower. At the top sat a woman in a sunflasher tunic and enormous hat. Its brim extended two feet from her head, shading her from the bright orangy sun.

"Pek Bazargan, this is Pek Careber, sunflasher. One of the best, I must add—I always try to send messages while she's on duty here!"

The woman flushed with pleasure, then turned elaborately businesslike. "And what is your message today, Pek?"

"We need people with flower sickness to pajalib, mittib, or jelitib, to be paid for work with healers. Here, I have written it out. Pek Bazargan, watch this, now. She is very, very fast. And completely accurate."

Bazargan wrenched himself away from the view. World lay spread at his feet, lush and beautiful. From this height the land was a colorful mosaic spreading away from the neat center whiteness of Rafkit Seloe. In all directions lay small trim villages, white roads, green or yellow or orange fields, darker woods. And everywhere was riotous patches of flowers: in gardens, in parks, by roadsides, even in the middle of crop fields where no Terran farmer would ever plant them. Crimson, cobalt, lemon, apricot, scarlet, turquoise, mauve, emerald, damask. Never had Bazargan been so aware of the many gorgeous words for color, or of the primacy of flowers on World.

"Watch, please, Pek Bazargan."

He watched. The sunflasher tilted a large mirror to the east.

An answering flash came from a tower Bazargan couldn't see. The sunflasher nodded and began to rapidly tilt the mirror this way and that, consulting the paper Bazargan had given her, and pausing every so often for confirming flashes.

Bazargan said, "How far apart are the towers?"

Voratur answered him. "They average seven cellib."

About thirty kilometers. The circumference of World was thirty-six thousand kilometers, with its principal landmass conveniently girdling the equator. The towers, Voratur had told him, were constantly staffed on all sunny days. Assume that an emergency message took half a minute to flash, and then was immediately flashed on to the next tower. If the weather cooperated, a message could travel halfway around World, from dawn to sunset, in about ten Earth-hours. And then another ten for the other hemisphere. Undoubtedly there were branch towers as well, off the straight equatorial line. And the ubiquitous bicycle messengers for remote villages.

Voratur's message didn't need to circumflash the globe. But theoretically, at least, a really desperate message could reach everyone on this "backward" planet in a single Earth day.

Despite himself, Bazargan was impressed. And, of course, messages would be instantly believed; nobody had to be talked into anything. Shared reality would therefore make for enormously fast mobilization. Although it also made for pretty slow inventiveness. The culture lacked truly maverick thinkers. Although sentient long before any species on Terra, World had yet to invent the steam engine.

"There," Voratur said with satisfaction, after the sunflasher translated some answering flashes from the distant tower. "Pek Renjamor, you will have about forty people with flower sicknesses reporting to you at sunset."

"Ah," said Renjamor, practically the first word he'd spoken. The syllable held deep satisfaction.

"Now," Voratur said to Bazargan, "I am ready for the picture of my brain."

* * *

By the time Bazargan bathed after the hot bicycle ride back to Gofkit Jemloe, made his way across the gardens, and knocked on the open archway of Ann's lab, she already had the Lagerfeld scan set up.

Like all the team's advanced equipment, the Lagerfeld was usually kept locked in a featureless, impenetrable metal box. Worlders understood that Terrans had many "objects from manufacturies" which they did not choose to trade. This caused no problem. Too pragmatic to consider the science equipment "magic," Worlders were also too commercial to show much interest in that which didn't seem to lead to any profit. That attitude explained their own lack of scientists, with the exception of healers. Still, the lockboxes could only be opened by DNA ID, could not be moved without setting off major alarms, and gave off homing signals detectable by orbital probes that could, in turn, beam the location back to the team's comlinks. Bazargan trusted commercial pragmatism only so far.

Voratur, fatter than Bazargan, was resting after his ride to the sunflasher tower. He'd told Bazargan to expect him at Pek Sikorski's "shortly." Before the alien arrived, Bazargan had several things he wanted to discuss with the team biologist. "Good morning, Ann."

"Good morning, Ahmed. May your flowers bloom in profusion," Ann said in World.

Then Bazargan saw Enli, sitting quietly on a round pillow in the corner. Irritation pricked him. He was careful not to let it show. "May your flowers bloom, Ann, Enli. Enli, Pek Sikorski and I have many things to discuss."

The ugly girl—Bazargan was developing an eye for World standards of beauty—rose obediently. "I will return, then, Pek Sikorski, when Pek Voratur arrives."

"Fine," Ann said with a smile.

Bazargan watched Enli leave, cross the courtyard, and disappear behind a curving wall. That path, he knew, wound back around several buildings to end up at the thick, hollow wall surrounding the Voratur compound. Was it possible . . .

"Ann," he said in English, "how much English has Enli learned?"

"Not much," Ann said. "We have working lessons several times a day, but she just doesn't seem to pick it up."

"Could she be pretending, and actually understand more than she pretends?"

"I don't think so, Ahmed. After all, that would cause her a whopping headache."

"Yes, of course," Bazargan said. "Forget it. I see you're eager for this experiment."

"That doesn't begin to describe it." Ann laughed. "Even so, I'm not as eager as David. He's coming from the crelm house for the scan. Not Dieter, though."

"I'm not surprised. Undoubtedly Dieter is still sleeping off yesterday's party, snuggled next to a bag of his precious rocks."

Ann laughed again. Not a pretty woman, but appealing. Bazargan approved of her trim body, shining blond topknot, expressive eyes. But Bazargan took his marriage vows seriously, as did his wife Batul, waiting for him in Iran. The seriousness was helped along by the standard dose for fieldwork of sex suppressants, the only neuropharm Bazargan used. The whole team took sex suppressants. It removed potential complications.

Ann had set up the Lagerfeld scanner on a bench that formed a perfect parabola, although Worlders didn't call it that. She had already run the diagnostics. The square, boxy lines of the Lagerfeld, with its softly glowing display screen, looked odd to Bazargan, after so many weeks of World's preferred curves. It was astonishing how quickly one's own culture looked alien on an alien world, while the alien became the norm. No wonder young Allen was getting so carried away.

"David is part of what I want to talk to you about," Bazargan said. "I'm concerned about him."

"I am, too, I have to admit. Has he explained to you his theory that the shared-reality mechanism, once we understand it, could be incorporated into the human genome?"

"Yes. I told him—quoting you—that the mechanism is most likely not genetic. And even if it is, and if it can be spliced in, it still would not change humanity. If you made the genemod voluntary, all you'd produce is a small number of peace fanatics who couldn't stand to interact with the rest of humanity. If you made it involuntary, you'd get either the worst tyranny the solar system has ever had, or else a systemwide civil war. And the current political structure doesn't allow for either. He seemed not to understand the political aspects at all."

Ann frowned. "He has the idea that if a small, initially isolated colony did splice it into all their offspring, they would have such a winning evolutionary strategy that bit by bit other groups would have to join them or lose out to natural selection. But the Dawkins equations say just the opposite, Ahmed. I ran the sims for him. No matter how you define 'small initial population,' the ability for individual deception always wins out genetically over inability to cheat in any major way."

Bazargan said, "Do you know the poet Sadi? Let me try to translate . . .

" 'Human beings are like parts of a body, created from
the same essence,
When one part is hurt and in pain the others cannot
remain in peace and be quiet.
If the misery of others leaves you indifferent and with no
feelings of sorrow,
You cannot be called a human being.' "

Ann stared at him. Bazargan suddenly felt foolish. He hadn't meant to defend David Allen, who was thinking like a genuine fool. Nor had he meant to quote poetry to an appealing young woman who was not his wife. It must be due to World, with its constant scent of perfume, its lush ripe gardens . . .

"May your flowers flourish and bloom!" said Hadjil Voratur from the archway. He was early.

Bazargan felt relief. "May your garden please your ancestors, Pek Voratur."

Hospitality flowers were exchanged. With Pek Voratur were his wife Alu, looking anxious, a woman in the flowered tunic of a priest, and the silent Pek Renjamor. All four crowded into Ann's lab, followed by Enli. Of course. The girl was like a burr. Bazargan still wasn't sure whom she worked for, and was still puzzled over how she could be working secretly for anyone, given shared reality. Wouldn't it give her horrible hcadpain?

Maybe they'd all know more after the Lagerfeld scan.

Pek Voratur made the introductions. His jovial gaze swept around the lab, pausing at the Lagerfeld scanner on the curving table. It was obvious he considered it unnecessarily ugly but was too polite to say so.

"Pek Sikorski," Voratur said, "I was hoping to see the *antihistamines* ready for us. As I already told Pek Bazargan, Pek Renjamor has healers in his manufactury prepared to duplicate whatever you teach him. We hope to begin the tests on Worlder bodies by tonight."

Ann said, "I'm sorry, Pek Voratur. I was busy arranging for your brain picture. As soon as we have finished that, I will prepare the first batch of *antihistamines*, and Pek Renjamor may watch me do it."

Voratur nodded, satisfied. Alu Pek Voratur plucked at her neckfur. "The brain picture is not dangerous?"

"No, no," Ann said. "Not at all. Well, let's begin. Pek Voratur, if you will sit here . . ."

The trader settled his bulk on a large pillow, his back to the low table holding the scanner. Ann settled the helmet on his head. It adjusted itself to fit snugly over his scalp, neck, and forehead, leaving his face clear. This was not Bazargan's field of knowledge, but he knew that hundreds of minute electrodes were sliding into place on Voratur's bald head and through his neckfur. Tiny needles carrying their own anesthetic would also sample blood, cerebralspinal fluid, even sweat. But the most useful data would come from the MOSS component of the Lagerfeld.

MOSS—Multilayer Organ Structure Scan—delivered almost neuron-by-neuron detail of the brain in action. Which cells were activated, which neurotransmitters were released, which neuron-firing patterns emerged. Receptor-cell docking, transmitter reuptake, enzyme cascades, substance breakdown and by-products . . . MOSS captured it all, analyzed the data in multiple ways, and delivered equations and formulae to explain them. It did everything but synthesize pills and put labels on the body. Without MOSS data, medicine would still be in the Dark Ages.

Bazargan had had his first Lagerfeld scan at eighteen, when he was ready to begin the Discipline. The MOSS data provided the base for his personal mixture, the fingerprint ID showing where his brain worked optimally, where it was biochemically deficient. Every adolescent who could afford it then spent the next few years learning to monitor himself in all the subjective ways that supplemented the MOSS base, and to mix the neuropharms that would best boost that day's planned performance.

Bazargan hadn't cared for the whole process. He'd done it while at college and graduate school; there was no other way to stay competitive with the other students. But in the long years since, he'd mostly skipped morning neuropharms, except in unusual circumstances. He knew this was irrational. How to reasonably object to artificiality, when all of anthropology spotlighted how artificial all cultural institutions actually were? Nonetheless, Bazargan felt a faint distaste for the enthusiastic use of neuropharms. Or perhaps it was not distaste but pride. His base MOSS profile had been in the ninety-eighth percentile for personality stability.

Alu Voratur laughed uneasily at her husband. "Flower of my heart, you look like a beetle in that . . . thing. A beetle with a smooth hard green head!"

Voratur waved a plump hand negligently. "Yes, yes. But it will not harm me once it begins."

"It has already begun, Pek Voratur," Ann said. She watched the display intently. Graphs flickered past, meaningless to Bazargan.

Immediately the priest, the healer, the Voraturs, and Enli began to chant. No signal had been given that Bazargan could see; they just all plunged in simultaneously. Shared reality.

"Please, softer!" Ann said in English, caught herself, and repeated it in World. "We'll need to ask you some questions, Pek Voratur . . . there. We have a base reading."

The chanting quieted to a low, rocking singsong. Flowers figured prominently. After another moment, Bazargan recognized it. A ritual blessing for a person engaged in any risky activity, such as climbing down a cliff after birds' eggs. Bazargan smiled.

"I am going to show you objects and ask you different questions to see how the picture of your brain changes, Pek Voratur," Ann said in her careful World. "Would you please smell this flower?"

"With pleasure," Pek Voratur said. His voice was heartily cheerful as always, but Bazargan saw the neckfur below the helmet collar stir. This could not be easy for someone who seldom encountered anything not already long established in his, and everybody else's, reality. Worlders possessed strange courage.

"Thank you," Ann said. "Now will you think of your children? . . . Good. Now think about having a terrible accident, falling off your bicycle and breaking your back . . . Yes. Now think of a wonderful success with bringing the *antihistamines* to market . . ."

The session wore on. Voratur sweated, although the room was not hot. Alu Voratur frowned, fluttering anxiety giving way to a sterner concern. The chanting grew louder. Just when Bazargan feared the tension would be too much, Ann said, "We're finished. Thank you, Pek Voratur."

She removed the helmet and Voratur sprang up like a bounced ball.

"Good, good, no difficulty at all!" Voratur said. Sweat shone on his flushed face, and he blinked several times. Bazargan guessed that Voratur had the mother of all headaches. Discreetly Bazargan moved to stand in front of the Lagerfeld scanner, blocking it from view.

"We thank you, Pek Voratur. Now Pek Sikorski will show you how to prepare the *antihistamines.*"

"Yes, yes, but show Pek Renjamor, he's the healer."

"Come, flower of my heart, and lie down," Voratur's wife said.

"No need, no need, dearest bloom." But he let her lead him away. At the archway, however, he turned back. "First, a gift. Enli!"

The girl rose from her corner pillow and left the room. She, too, Bazargan noticed, was unusually flushed. Another headache? In a moment she returned, her arms full of pink roses.

Bazargan stood very still. Those roses should not exist. He had fulfilled his bargain with Voratur, replacing the irradiated sterile roses with viable seeds, all for red roses. The rosebushes had grown—through two flowerings. Then the lethal gene had kicked in, preventing further germination. That should have been the end of Terran roses—of any color—on World. But here were fresh pink roses, presumably the result of sophisticated manual cross-pollination with some white flower whose appearance genes were recessive. How had the gardeners managed that? And were these pink hybrids fertile?

Ann looked as startled as Bazargan felt. But after a moment she moved forward, said the right ritual thank-you's. It was very incorrect to ever inquire directly about the breeding methods of gift flowers. It would be like inquiring about one's host's sex life. Bazargan would have to wait to find out how the pink roses had been created.

"Your flowers bloom in my heart," Voratur said, with considerable emphasis. Then his wife led him away.

Ann put the roses in a vase and immediately turned to the healer and the priest waiting for instruction. And, of course, Enli.

Bazargan moved toward the vase and rubbed one pink petal. It slid under his fingers, living velvet, releasing thick perfume. He was back in his mother's walled garden in Isfahan. He was a small boy lifted up by his *laleh,* that patient servant who was half nanny and half bodyguard, to smell his mother's per-

fect, genetically enhanced roses blooming among the pome-
granates and almond trees.

Roses now existed on World. There would be no removing
them. Nor antihistamines. The idea that you could bring cultural change to World without bringing biological change was
wholly bogus. Not to a place like World, where the sentients
were as acquisitive as Medici.

Now it was Bazargan who had a headache. He pushed it
aside and sat down to watch Ann work, herself watched cease-
lessly by the girl Enli.

By the next day Ann had analyzed the Lagerfeld scan. She
had stayed up all night to do it, Bazargan suspected, after a
day spent teaching basic lab techniques to the World healer,
Renjamor. Ann's face had the peculiar combination of exhaustion and elation that comes with the biggest, best results.
Despite his increasing worries about their position on World,
Bazargan let himself yield to the charm of that look.

"We got it," David Allen kept saying. He was as excited as
Ann, after his initial sulkiness at having missed the scan session itself. "We got the son-of-a-bitch pinned, dissected, labeled!"

"Let Ann tell it," Dieter Gruber said. The geologist had
recovered from his drunken celebration of his own finds in the
Neury Mountains. "But, Ann, have pity for us nonbiologists,
yes?"

"Yes," Ann said. "But understand, this is only a preliminary
analysis. Very far, David, from a wholly labeled, pinned, and
dissected son-of-a-bitch."

David grinned. Bazargan settled himself more firmly on his
pillow. They were meeting in Bazargan's personal room,
which was filled with the scent of something in the garden
that had just come into bloom. The pillow had lovely curves,
but they were not the same curves Bazargan's body had. He
shifted again.

"The Lagerfeld shows a brain structure completely consistent with ours, as we'd already guessed," Ann said. "Whoever

'seeded' the galaxy with hominid life-forms did so fairly late. There are only minor deviations from our brain development among Worlders, Candiotes, Atvarians, and Blickers, and nothing that doesn't fit with probable evolutionary development to a point nine five confidence level. The Fallers, of course, are a different case."

"As far as we can tell," Gruber said. Xenobiologists had dissected dead Fallers, but no live ones. They did not permit themselves to be taken alive.

"Yes," Ann agreed. "Voratur's brain shows only two major divergences from ours. One is in some of the hormones related to digestion—you *do* all know that the body is thrifty, it often uses the same substances as hormones in the body and transmitters in the nervous system?"

"No," Gruber said.

"Yes," Bazargan said.

"It doesn't matter!" David Allen said. "Go on!"

"The digestive-hormone differences are presumably related to the differing diet on World. There's some overlap, which is why we're able to digest some of their food. It also suggests that they could metabolize some, but not all, of ours. The other difference is of course the shared-reality mechanism."

Ann stopped, licked her lips once, unfocused her eyes, and ran a hand over her hair. Bazargan recognized the signs of a scientist trying to figure out how to simplify the hopelessly technical for the benefit of the hopelessly ignorant.

"Let me start with the basics," Ann finally said. "The brain is both electrical and chemical. The electrical comes first. *Something* starts millions of neurons firing simultaneously in many different parts of the brain. That something might be an external stimulus: a physical sight or sound or smell or sensation. It might also be internal, like a memory or an intention. Or it might be a combination, like when I asked Voratur to think about something that never physically happened: falling off his bike and breaking his back. The accident is imaginary, but the sound of my voice using linguistic symbols is physical.

"Whatever the stimulus, it starts neurons firing in rhythm, including a particular high-frequency firing called 'synchronized gamma oscillation.' It lasts for only about a quarter of a second, but the synchronization of oscillations in separated parts of the brain is what lets people think of thoughts as a coherent whole. A 'thought' is really millions of separate electrical impulses in different brain areas—sensory areas, motor areas, memory, emotion centers, all that. But because of the gamma-oscillation synchronization, the person *experiences* the thought as a single, horrifying, painful image of falling off a bicycle and breaking his back. It's the pattern of the firings that's important, at a macro-level. You all still with me?"

"Yes," Bazargan said. "Go on."

"Okay." More lip-licking, eye-unfocusing. "Here's what happens at the chemical level. On each nerve, the moving electrical impulse creates a moving toroidal electrical field, with the nerve as axis. The moving field reaches the nerve end, where there's a very small space between that nerve end and the beginning of the next."

"The synapse," Gruber said, clearly proud of himself.

Ann smiled. "I'm making it too simple, aren't I?"

"Even for a dumb geologist, Frau Professor," Gruber said, and there was a teasing note in his voice that made David Allen glance at him sharply and frown.

Ann continued. "Anyway, at the end of all nerve spines are structures called 'paracrystalline presynaptic grids.' They look like tiny, tiny rigid lattices inside a tiny pyramid. In the interstices of each grid are thirty to forty little balloons called vesicles, and inside *those* is a supply of a chemical neurotransmitter. Some grids hold dopamine, some serotonin, some the peptides that inhibit pain, and on and on . . . everything your biomonitor mixes up for your morning Discipline, David."

Bazargan saw Allen nod, pleased at Ann's attention.

"So the electrical nerve impulse reaches the presynaptic grid, with all its waiting balloons of neurotransmitters, and the electrical impulse causes an influx of calcium ions that makes one—and only one—balloon get released into the synapse. That in turn starts the nerve on the other side of the synapse to fire, setting off its balloons of transmitters, and so on. You get a chemical cascade, and the chemicals do everything you expect chemicals in the body to do. Break down energy for action. Stimulate motor cells. Affect blood flow. Get the adrenaline flowing or the emotions hopping or whatever. All this so far we understand pretty well.

"But understanding the parts doesn't mean we understand the brain as a whole. The whole is somehow greater than the sum of its parts."

Bazargan said dryly, "Rather like a culture taken as a whole."

"Too subtle for me," Gruber said.

"Which is why you should stick to rocks," David Allen muttered.

Bazargan felt impatience. Gruber was nowhere near as dumb as he pretended, and Allen nowhere near as combative. They were both showing off. For Ann?

He suddenly wondered if all of his team were taking sex suppressants after all.

Ann continued. "Here's one aspect of the brain we *don't* understand. When that electrical impulse hits the presynaptic grid, it has a measurable, constant voltage, the same voltage across all neurons. *But*—sometimes it causes a release of neurotransmitters and sometimes it doesn't. The probability of release varies from point seventeen to point sixty-two, depending on the kind of neuron. And no one really knows why."

Gruber said, "Just how small is this grid? Are we down to the single-atom level here?"

"Yes, and that's one of the problems. With the calcium ion trigger, we're close to quantum level. Research is difficult because measurement affects the outcome. One theory says that so do mental events."

"I don't understand what you mean," Bazargan said.

"All right. Briefly—I *am* getting to Voratur's brain scan, really!—what happens seems to be this. You think of something unconnected with any immediate external stimuli. For instance, you're alone in your room in the dark, and you think of someone you left on Earth. A loved one. Suddenly you can see her in your mind's eye, even smell her. Your whole body reacts physically. But what started that cascade? A memory with no identifiable energy source in your brain, without even a single location. It's just a pattern of scattered neural configurations. We call that a 'mental event.' But this nonphysical event started a whole chain of electrical firings that triggered—some of the time!—a whole chain of neurotransmitter balloons.

"How does that happen? Why do presynaptic grids release balloons sometimes but not other times, when the voltage is the same? What's going on at the atomic level? We just don't know."

The "basics" had gone on long enough for Bazargan. He said, "But Ann . . . how does this all apply to Voratur's brain? What is that second big difference you mentioned between his brain and ours?"

She smiled. "I'm getting carried away, right?"

"No!" Allen said explosively. "It's good to see a scientist who doesn't treat hard data like a comedy routine." He scowled at Gruber, who didn't notice.

"Voratur's brain," Bazargan reminded patiently.

"Yes. All right. All the cerebral structures are identical to ours. Evoked emotions follow the same neural pathways as ours. Gamma oscillation matches ours. So does neural voltage, neurotransmitter composition, and all other process trackings. The only real difference the Lagerfeld scan showed was greater activity in both the ventral anterior cingulate and in the nucleus accumbens."

Allen said eagerly, "What are they?"

"The anterior cingulate is a little structure behind the bridge of the nose that—"

"That's where shared-reality headpain is!" Allen crowed.

"Yes. But the anterior cingulate isn't causing the headaches. I mean, it *is*, in that it's causing the release of pain-inducing transmitters. But the anterior cingulate only coordinates information from many different brain areas. For instance, it's one of the few cerebral structures connected directly to the hypothalamus, which initiates response to stress. But—and let me be clear on this—the anterior cingulate is *not* the seat of the shared-reality mechanism. It's only a switchboard for processing it. The cingulate just sets off cascades of stress transmitters when reality is not shared, or pleasure transmitters when it is."

"So where is the source of this shared reality?" Gruber said.

"That's just it—there isn't one! In Worlders' presynaptic grids, different amounts of neurotransmitters are being released than in human brains. But the input to cause the release—the voltage of neural firings—is exactly the same! Same input, same processors, different output. It makes no sense."

Bazargan said diffidently, "And of course you've ruled out pathogens, environmental toxins, dietary diff—"

"Yes, of course I have." It was rare for Ann to be curt. "All those would have showed up on the Lagerfeld."

Gruber grinned. "A mystery, yes? Factor X. A spiritual radio wave, an invisible personal download?"

Allen said coolly, "Don't be ridiculous."

"Don't be premature," Bazargan said to Ann. "You've gained an astonishing amount of data, Ann. In time you may be able to put it all together."

She smiled tiredly. "I want it now. It just doesn't add up. And look! That's another thing!"

"What's another thing?" Bazargan said.

"This 'lifegiver,' " Ann answered, and now he saw the small pseudo-insect on her bare shoulder, just short of her tunic strap. Windows were always open on World. The lifegiver folded its transparent wings and settled onto Ann's skin, gripping with tiny suckers. Its yellow body was faintly luminescent.

Ann said, "This is as close as they'll ever get to anyone's head. Human, Worlder—they won't ever perch on anybody's head. I was hoping the Lagerfeld scan would show some logical reason why, something about the electrical field generated by the brain, maybe, set alongside a lifegiver field. But no, nothing."

"Another mystery," Bazargan said, "at least for now. But let's focus instead on what we did learn. The Worlder headache when 'shared reality' is violated . . . it's a real, physiological, documentable phenomenon?"

"Oh, yes," Ann said. "Although remember that even in humans, the relationship between emotional physiology and moral judgment is complex. Consider the sociopath. He performs amoral acts, such as casual murder, because he has no feeling whatsoever for his victim. Worlders are just the opposite. They have what we would consider an excess of relationship between their physiology and their moral sense. It's partly learned behavior, in that children are heavily socialized about how to react to their feelings of repulsion and pain when people say things that violate cultural mores. But the repulsion and pain are real and documentable. Shared reality has a solid physiological basis."

"An evolutionary advancement," David said. "The next step in hominid moral growth!"

Ann said quickly, "I did *not* say that."

"But your findings imply it."

"No, David, they don't. I'm discussing the biology, not making evaluative judgments."

Allen frowned; Bazargan saw that to him the two were identical. But all the boy said was, "The real question is, can we duplicate the physiological process in humans? Physiological processes are based on proteins, and proteins are genetically encoded. We should be able to splice in the relevant DNA."

"Do *what*?" Gruber said, and Bazargan realized this was the first time the geologist had heard David's nutty theory.

Ann said wearily, "David, I told you before. There are no significant genetic differences. Whatever's happening in the Worlders' brains is happening with the same input and equipment as ours. Which is why I don't understand such a different result."

David didn't answer. Instead he looked meditatively out through the arched window. Bazargan knew, as clearly as if the boy had spoken aloud, that he had rejected what Ann had just said. He didn't believe that shared reality wasn't tied to a clear, undiscovered genetic sequence. He wanted there to be a stretch of DNA code that could be snipped out and spliced into the human genome. And because he wanted it so badly, he believed it must exist.

Very dangerous thinking. And not only to Allen himself.

After a long moment, Allen said, "How can we learn more? If you assume that DNA *is* the key, then what's the next step?"

Ann finally lost all patience. "Dissect a Worlder brain, cut out shared reality, and hardwire it into our own skulls!"

Bazargan stepped in. He said soothingly, "Ann, what else do we need to know today? Anything else you want to tell us about the Lagerfeld?"

"I don't know . . . oh, yes . . . no, that's not important. But . . . wait . . . no . . ."

"You're exhausted, my dear," Bazargan said. But it was Gruber who took action.

"Come on, Annie," he said, pulling her up from her pillow, putting an arm around her for support. "When did you eat last, *Liebchen*?"

"I don't remember. Yesterday morning? I'm all right, it was just a passing faintness."

"A good reason to eat and sleep," Gruber said. " 'Bye, guys."

He led Ann through the archway toward her rooms, his arm still around her waist. David looked after them, frowning. "What gives him the right to make decisions for her?"

"Perhaps she does," Bazargan said, and instantly regretted it. The boy couldn't help being irritating, no more than a gnat could help stinging. Bazargan was supposed to be above being bothered by gnats.

"Please excuse me, David, I think I'm feeling tired myself. This was a useful session, wasn't it? Does what Ann was saying fit well with your notes on child development in the crelm house?"

"It fits perfectly."

"Good. We all learn more every day. Now, if you'll excuse me."

David got up and left, only a trace of sulkiness around his mouth. Bazargan drew the light curtains across the archways of his room. He had a headache himself, he found.

He wasn't in the mood to appreciate that his headache, too, in its own way, came from disjoints in perceived reality.

Philoctētēs, a celebrated hero of the Trojan War, had both a magic bow that never missed its mark and an oozing, never-healing snakebite that caused him constant pain. The one was the price of the other. Cure the wound and the marksmanship was destroyed.

But was shared reality, with its elimination of ever being truly separate, the wound or the bow?

David Allen was sure of the answer. Ahmed Bazargan was not.

He swallowed a pill for his headache and unrolled his sleeping pallet. In a later version of the Philoctētēs myth, he remembered, Philoctētēs was cured of his snakebite. That was the trouble with these old stories. They mutated over time. You ended up never knowing what to believe.

Bazargan lay down in the dim room and waited for his headache to pass.

TEN

RAFKIT SELOE

Y ou're sure that's what you heard," Pek Nagredil said.

"Yes," Enli said.

"Wait here." He disappeared through an archway, leaving Enli standing in his cluttered office, trying to sort out exactly what she was sure of and what she was not.

The Terrans could do that to you.

It was not raining this time. On every one of Enli's other trips to Rafkit Seloe, it seemed to her, it had been raining. Today brilliant sunlight washed through the open windows, bathing everything in soft orange. Ralibib had just come into bloom, and the heavy perfume of the tiny white blossoms, hundreds on each branch, hung on the air. Beneath the ralib bushes, the allabenirib were just finishing. Soon the gardeners would cut the stems back to the ground, readying the plants for their next blooming.

In the Voratur gardens, a bed of allabenirib had been dug up to make room for Terran rosib.

Enli reached into an inner pocket of her tunic and took another headpain pill. She was using ten or twelve a day now. Pek Nagredil had told her no more than eight, but eight couldn't keep the pain at bay. If only this job would be over! Soon, let it be soon . . .

When the job was over, the Terrans would die. Because of what she'd overheard, Enli would be the instrument of their death, just as she had been of Tabor's. Pek Sikorski, who had been so kind to her. Pek Gruber, whom she hardly knew—was it right to judge those one hardly knew? No priest from Reality and Atonement would ever do so; reality judges were always from the local government, familiar with local personalities and circumstances. Pek Bazargan, with his calm, steady face. Pek Allen, certainly crazy but so loving with the children, World and Terran both. And the Terran children, those beautiful small buds . . .

Enli squeezed her eyes tightly shut. Another pill? No, she couldn't, she'd already taken three in just a few minutes, any more would put her to sleep. She couldn't sleep, she had to make her report. Her head felt so heavy on her neck, the inside of her skull so heavy . . .

"Pek Brimmidin."

Enli opened her eyes. Pek Nagredil was back with two others, a healer and a priest. Enli tried to bow, stumbled, almost fell over. The servant of the First Flower grasped her arm and led her to a pillow. "Sit down, Pek Brimmidin. Would you like a cup of water?"

"I—"

"Bring her pel," the priest said to Pek Nagredil, who did, looking startled. "Here, drink it all."

The pel warmed her a little, dulled her headache a little. Made it at least possible to go on. The pel and the firm warmth of the priest's hand on her arm.

"Now, little blossom," he said kindly, "tell us what you have learned of these Terrans."

Enli took one more swallow of pel. "They. . . . they took a picture of Pek Voratur's brain."

"Yes, so we know," the priest said. "And we know about the *rosib,* and about Pek Renjamor's manufactury and testing of *antihistamines,* so you needn't go over that again. In fact, Pek Renjamor has made the first batch of antihistamines and forty people are taking it now, did you know that? All seem cured of their flower sicknesses. The sicknesses were various, although of course mostly to ralibib, since that is the bloom the First Flower blesses us with in this season . . ." He went on in his soothing kind voice, talking of nothing and everything, giving Enli a chance to collect herself.

When she had, the priest said, "But there is something more, I think, Pek Brimmidin. Something our other informant has not told us. Perhaps something you learned because you understand the Terran words so much better than any of us."

"Yes," Enli said. She felt her courage returning, flowing back along her veins with the pel. "Yes."

"It is dangerous?"

"Yes!"

The priest composed his hands in the New Bud pose. "Then I am ready to hear it."

"The Terrans . . . they . . ."

"Speak, little flower." The kindness was still there, but also a note of command.

Enli said, "They want to cut open the heads of Worlders and take out shared reality, so that it may be put with hard wires into their own heads!"

Pek Nagredil's eyes widened. On his face Enli saw the signs of swift pain: the stretched skin around the eyes, the clenched mouth. The healer put both hands to his forehead. Only the servant of the First Flower controlled his headpain, although above his neckfur his skull ridges throbbed. He said, "This is not possible."

"Of course not!" the healer cried. "But to even think of it . . . to be able to think of it! They *must* be unreal!"

"Wait," the priest said. "Pek Brimmidin, you are sure you heard this? From which Terran?"

"First from Pek Allen," Enli said. Now that the terrible reality had been shared, she felt her own headache recede slightly. But only slightly. "Then five days ago, all of them discussed it together. I was in the secret place inside the garden wall, which Pek Voratur showed me. It has thin plates for listening to the guest rooms. Of course, everyone knows that traders do such things, but . . ." Again Enli faltered. But did the Terrans know? If not, that was in itself further proof that they did not share reality. But if they did know, why had they let her overhear their terrible plans?

"Drink a few more swallows of pel, little blossom."

Enli did as the priest said, draining her cup.

"Now continue."

"The Terrans were discussing Pek Voratur's brain picture. Pek Allen asked if Pek Sikorski had learned enough from the picture to put shared reality into Terrans with hard wires. She said no. She said first she—"

"Wait," Pek Nagredil said. "I must ask something. You understand Terran much better than anyone else on World, Enli. But did you understand *all* the words the Terrans used? Every one?"

Enli waved her hands. "I thought of that, Pek Nagredil. Over and over. And some of their words were strange to me. But not so many that I could not understand their meaning. And one word I know very well. Pek Sikorski and I use it all the time in her work. It is . . . is *dissect*. It means to cut up a plant or animal to learn about it. Pek Sikorski said . . . she said . . ."

The three others waited: the healer and the government official plainly in dread, their mild stolid faces twisted. Only the priest sat calmly, his face filled with sorrow.

Enli said, "Pek Sikorski told the others she must *dissect* a Worlder brain to get the shared reality into Terran skulls."

The healer cried out. Pek Nagredil briefly closed his eyes, then reached into his waist pouch for a pill. Enli recognized it as the same one she herself was living on these days. Oh, if this job could only be over . . .

The healer said violently, "Then that proves it. They are most certainly unreal!"

"Wait," the priest said, and everyone fell silent.

Minutes crept by. Enli felt drowsiness steal over her. So she had taken too many pills. Or maybe it was the pel. Or maybe just the relief of sharing reality with these good people . . . her people . . . Tabor had said once . . .

A hand shook her. "Not just yet, Pek Brimmidin," the servant of the First Flower said gently. "A few more questions before you sleep. No, no atonement is necessary, just answer a few more questions. What is the Terran word for floor?"

Enli gave the word.

"For brain?"

She answered.

"For justice? . . . For reality? . . . For the sole cultivation of a private meditation garden?"

"There is no word for that in Terran."

"Is there no word, or have you perhaps not learned the word?"

"I don't know," Enli said.

"What is the word for a child who has not yet achieved the sharing of reality?"

"*Infant,* I think."

"Are you sure? Completely sure?"

"No," Enli said.

"How about the word for a bud open enough to see its color but not yet the shape of its petals?"

The priest went on for twenty or twenty-five more words, asking for the Terran for each. Some Enli knew; many she did not. Her struggle to stay awake made her sit bolt upright on the pillow. Finally she dug her nails into the soft flesh under her upper arm. The priest saw her.

"That's enough, little blossom." He turned to Pek Nagredil and the healer. "She knows much Terran, but there are un-budded places in her knowledge. It is possible, therefore, that she misunderstood what they said. I will certainly tell the High Council what she has reported, but I will not say for certain that it is knowledge in full bloom. The Terran question remains still unanswered."

Slowly Pek Nagredil and the healer nodded. Some of the strain left their faces. They thought the same. Reality had been shared.

Even with *her,* Enli thought, and warmth flooded her. Oh, it was so good to be part of reality again, to know as the others knew, to share the truth of the world instead of holding secrets alone in the dark. Her whole body responded to that good feeling, relaxing and letting go. Oh, so good . . . If only Tabor were here . . .

"Sleep, little blossom," a kind voice said, and warm hands eased her to a lying position on the wide pillow. She felt a blanket laid over her, heard the murmur of voices like the steady low music at a village dance . . . the cookfires burning bright and the children laughing in the warm perfumed twilight . . .

Enli was asleep. She didn't hear the government messenger rush into Pek Nagredil's office, so agitated he did not even bring a hospitality flower. She didn't hear him say that one of Pek Renjamor's volunteers had collapsed and died minutes after being given an *antihistamine*. She didn't hear the servant of the First Flower begin the chant for the soul of the dead, walking its blossom-strewn path to rejoin its ancestors.

Nonetheless, the chant filled her dreams.

ELEVEN

GOFKIT JEMLOE

Once again, they had left him out. David didn't hear about the Worlder's fatal allergic reaction to the antihistamine until Ann, Bazargan, and the increasingly detestable Dieter Gruber had already discussed it among themselves and decided what to do. Without including David. Was he or was he not a member of this team?

To make it worse, it was *Gruber* who told him the decision. Gruber, who hadn't even been at Voratur's Lagerfeld scan because he'd been so careless of his own mind that he'd gotten blind-shit drunk at Nafret's flower ceremony. Now the geologist had just strolled into the crelm house, looking around him with an amused expression on his face. Yes, amused. Smug. Superior. Because David worked with living children, while Gruber worked with dead rooks? The geologist probably thought David was a kitty-boy, not fully a man. And that was the person Ann had chosen to sleep with, probably . . .

Stop. Wait. He was getting angry, and there was no reason to get this angry. He needed to adjust his neuropharms again. More serotonin, more activators for the left prefrontal cortex, more cortisol blockers.

"David?" Gruber said in English. "Are you listening to me?"

"Of course I'm listening," David snapped. "You said one of Renjamor's beta-test subjects died of an allergic reaction to Ann's antihistamine."

"Yes. The funeral, or whatever they call it, is at noon. Ahmed wants us all to be ready to walk there with the rest of the household about an hour earlier. Full dress uniform."

"It's called a 'farewell burning,' Dieter. Not a 'funeral'. "

"My World isn't nearly as good as yours," Gruber said, unruffled. He gazed around the crelm house. Nafret, of course, had moved to the Voratur family court, now that he was fully real. The remaining children, including Bonnie and Ben, were playing some riotous game in the play corner David had set up. On World, toys for children were always miniatures of objects from the adult world: dolls, carved wooden bicycles with tiny wooden figures to ride them, dishes and farm animals and, of course, flowers. To these David had added something new, abstract forms such as painted wooden blocks, interlocking plastic spheres, free-form inflatable balloons tough as steel and large as the kids themselves. All these had bewildered World adults. What were they *for*? they asked David. What were they supposed to *be*?

But after sharing the reality of the strange, nonfunctional toys with everyone, it seemed, in the entire village, a consensus had emerged as if it had always existed. The Terran playthings were harmless, if eccentric. Worlders asked only that the rectangular wooden blocks, which Ben and Bonnie's mother had brought with her on the *Zeus,* be altered. They were too ugly for children. It wasn't good for small brains to play with ugly objects. So David had a household carpenter saw and sand the blocks into circles, kidneys, parabolas, swooping curves that no longer piled neatly on top of one another but did create much more interesting towers to build up and knock down.

From the beginning, the World children had loved them. Their unabashed imaginative reaction, turning the small blocks into wild animals and the large balloons into mountains, amazed the adults. David had made reams of notes on the presocialized infant imagination. He planned a major paper when he returned to Mars.

Now three of the children, Uvi and Grenol and the irrepressible Ben, tumbled over the balloons, shrieking and laughing. The point of the game, insofar as it had one, seemed to be to try to land on another child. Colert Gamolin, David's fellow tutor, watched indulgently that the play didn't become too rough. Bonnie, thoughtfully inspecting a free-form bright yellow block, lay on her back in the center of the room, having her diaper changed by an ancient nursemaid who had probably cared for three generations of World babies. The woman, fat and comfortable, was Bonnie's favorite.

Gruber surveyed all this activity with indulgence. David wasn't in the mood for indulgence.

He said, "The farewell burning shouldn't be happening at all! Didn't Bazargan even try to get permission for an autopsy on the Worlder? This is a perfect opportunity to examine the effect of a fatal biochemical reaction on a Worlder brain, and maybe learn more about the shared-reality mechanism!"

Now he had Gruber's full attention. "You must be funning, David."

"I'm not 'funning'! Please don't patronize me!"

Gruber studied him. "I'm not patronizing you at all. But you must realize that the situation does not lend itself to violating their death customs. Even *I* realize that, and Ann keeps telling me I'm insensitive as a vacuum."

It was said with a smile, but David didn't accept the conciliation. What was it, after all, but more patronization? Plus a not-so-subtle flaunting of Gruber's relationship with Ann. But David forced himself to calm

"Look, Dieter, I know there's a death ceremony prohibition on autopsy. I'm the anthropologist, remember? But this is unique opportunity. Bazargan could tell Voratur that the autopsy was necessary to find out . . . oh, I don't know . . . something crucial about the antihistamines to make them work over the long term in Worlders' brains. Ann could help him invent something. And think what we might learn about the shared-reality mechanism!"

Dieter's gaze grew more intense. "You want Ahmed and Ann to lie to Voratur? Aren't you the one who admires shared reality because it eliminates lies?"

David felt himself flush. "This is different! The potential gains are so enormous, so . . . so unprecedented . . ."

He was floundering. Damn, in front of Gruber, too. David wasn't at all sorry when Bonnie, diapering completed, toddled up to him and clutched his legs.

"Hello, sweetheart," David said in English.

She answered him in World, holding up a red circular wooden blocks. "Mine flower."

David bent to her level. "No, Bonnie. That is not a flower." It was the only prohibition with the abstract toys that the Worlders insisted on. They were never flowers. Only flower toys were flowers.

"Mine flower!" Her small pink mouth set in stubborn lines.

Gently David pried the block from her fingers. He picked up a flower toy from the floor, a stuffed and intricately sewn allabenir, and handed it to her. "This is a flower, sweetheart," he said in World.

The child looked at the wooden block in his hand. Keeping his face stern, David moved the hand behind his back. With the other hand he offered her the stuffed allabenir. After a moment's hesitation, she took it. Her mouth relaxed.

"Mine flower."

"Yes, that's Bonnie's flower. What a pretty flower!"

Bonnie nodded and toddled away to offer the flower to her beloved nursemaid. David stood.

"They make no distinction between World and human," Gruber observed.

"Of course not," David said. "That's the *point*. Dieter, an autopsy would—"

"It's impossible, David. Give it up."

"Damn it, nobody here even *sees* the potential that World offers to the whole human race!"

"Nobody but you," Gruber said, smiling. "See you at the funeral procession." He left before David could even offer him a farewell flower. And Bonnie was watching. Damn it, didn't the man even know that mimicry was how children learned, and that adults had an obligation to be consistent in what kids were supposed to mimic?

"Pek Allen," the old nursemaid said, coming up to him. "Do your flowers bloom in good soil?" She meant, was he feeling all right? David looked at the kindly old face, neckfur gray and sparse, and his anger at Gruber drained away. Desolation took its place. He couldn't get any of them, his own people, to see. Either they were blind or he was.

"The soil is poor today," he said to Pek Fasinil, and tried to smile. Always David was courteous to Worlders.

"You must go lie down, Pek Allen." She nodded three or four times, a vigorous old woman too sure of her worth and her place to fear giving him orders. "Go now."

"I will. May your flowers bloom and flourish."

"May your flowers bloom," she said, and waddled toward a child who had fallen off a huge inflated balloon and started to wail.

David went to his personal room and closed the archway curtains. He unlocked his biomonitor from its safebox and set it on the low, free-form table. Settling on a comfortable pillow, he stuck his finger inside the machine. When the display lit, David's eyes widened.

No wonder he was feeling so irritable! The hormone and transmitter mix was almost in the red range of the graph for calmness, security, nonimpulsiveness. *Plus,* the sex-suppressant dose was only doing a borderline job of damping desire. That probably accounted for his jealousy of Ann and Gruber. Although not completely. Why an intelligent and kind woman like Ann Sikorski would want a Neanderthal like the tunnel-visioned Gruber . . .

There. Those thoughts proved the dose's inadequacy.

David reset the controls for a supplementary neuropharm mixture to be injected now, with a revised daily mix starting tomorrow morning. Again he stuck his finger into the machine to receive the injection. Even as he relocked the biomonitor into its safebox, he could feel the neuropharm calming him down. Complete bodily adjustment to major neurotransmitter changes took about a week, of course, but the computer recognized that and added quick-acting calming agents in the meantime.

Already he was feeling much better. He could attend the farewell burning with appropriate tranquillity, since apparently it was going to take place. And maybe another Worlder would die from the antihistamine trials. Not, of course, that David wished anyone to die! But if anyone did, an autopsy should be performed. David would have time to work on Ann about that, now that he knew the possibility existed.

All problems had solutions. You just had to approach them in the right spirit, with all possible help from modern technology. After all, that was what technology was for.

The farewell burning was the most moving ceremony Ahmed Bazargan had ever seen.

He was a little surprised at himself. He had attended so many funerals in his life, beginning with his father's when Ahmed had been twelve years old. At first those proceedings had filled him with fear: his mother wailing and tearing at her hair; his father's body borne by his own soldiers on a plain wooden pier toward its elaborate tomb; the endless eulogy in the mosque jammed with the odorous bodies of too many men. But then the twelve-year-old Ahmed had felt come over him a kind of detachment, an uncoupling from felt grief like the uncoupling of DNA as it prepared to replicate and so preserve itself. In all the funerals in all the years afterward, that detachment had come, making him an observer and not a participant. The funeral of his mother, of his friends, of his colleagues. The detachment would even be there, Bazargan suspected, if someday he must attend the funeral of his wife, Batul, patiently awaiting his return to Earth. Detachment was what would get him through.

But not here, at this funeral, in this alien land. Ahmed Bazargan had not even known the dead woman. But he felt his heart move for her, and searched for the reason why.

It wasn't the funeral procession itself, which from the point of view of a jaded anthropologist was pretty ordinary, except perhaps for the excess of flowers. The mourners walked first, moving slowly in lockstep toward the Gofkit Jemloe communal pyre. The color of mourning on World was black, but not for the Earthly reasons of night, the underworld, etc. Black was the only color flowers could not be; black buds absorbed too much heat to live. They died before they opened. So no gardener on World had bred black flowers, and the family members shuffling and chanting past Bazargan were each wrapped in a thin cloak of deep black.

Behind them came the priests, led by the local representative of the order of the First Flower. Or so Bazargan thought of it, although he knew that Worlders thought differently. The servants of the First Flower were divided not into "orders" but into some structure more nebulous, something the Terran anthropologists had not yet unraveled, except that it was somehow connected with the Neury Mountains. The priests wore flowered robes adorned with tiny glass vases, each stocked with a living blossom in special water.

Next came the entire village, also covered in black. As they drag-stepped past, the four Terrans joined the throng. World funerals were a shared event, and that meant everyone shared who possibly could. Bazargan saw an old man with a broken leg carried in a makeshift litter by four strapping young people. Children old enough to have had a flower ceremony walked solemnly beside their mothers.

Finally, almost as an afterthought, came the deceased. The unwashed body rode on an ordinary two-wheeled farm cart, pulled by two kin. The corpse was hard to see, being almost buried under huge mounds of flowers, every type currently in bloom anywhere within miles.

When everyone except the corpse reached the burning fire, they formed a huge circle around it, leaving only a narrow lane through which the cart was pulled. The pullers brought it to the very edge of the fire. A low ripple ran over the Worlders.

Then came the part that Bazargan had seen before, at the funeral he had attended with Voratur, but which was new to

Ann, Dieter, and David. The cart was tipped forward. The wood had been highly waxed; the body slid effortlessly into the flame, mostly hidden by flowers. And everyone in the entire crowd, the grieving and the old and the halt and the lame, simultaneously threw off their thin black robes and shouted loud enough to wake the dead.

It was a shout of pure joy. The dead woman was returning to her ancestors.

The Worlders chanted and sang. Under their black capes they all wore brilliantly colored short robes sewn, festooned, entwined that morning with fresh flowers. Each bloom represented some facet of the wearer's relationship with the soul now so jubilantly released to the spirit world, where every flower bloomed forever.

"Mein Gott," Dieter said, smiling. Bazargan could barely hear him above the incredible din. Ann looked stunned, but she also smiled. Only David looked as if he were fighting off a desire to jump up and lecture the deluded villagers on their worship of death and the priests who controlled it. Which he probably was.

Bazargan turned away from the boy. The funeral still affected him. Not with grief, or with the joy the Worlders obviously shared, but with some other emotion he couldn't quite pin down. What was it?

The body was nearly burned by now; the fire must use fuels that reached enormous temperatures. Dieter would know. There was no smell of burning flesh. Probably the priests knew some oil, some plant compound, that either masked or eliminated the odor. Was Ann investigating this? Bazargan made a mental note to ask her.

But no amount of intellectualizing masked his mild, agreeable, but very real emotion. And now, as the villagers began to dance to the thin high sweetness of pipes and strings, Bazargan knew what his emotion was. Admiration.

This was the first funeral he had ever attended which had the quality he admired most: balance. Between the grief of separation and the joy of eternity. Between secular and religious. Between, literally, life and death. It didn't matter that the Worlders' belief in a spirit existence with fulfilled ancestors was not Bazargan's belief. What he admired was the dignity of those beliefs, and what moved him was the dignity in a death ceremony in which no women tore out their hair by its living roots, no relatives fought over the will, no politicians maneuvered for the power left behind by the dead—or assassinated—corpse. Death on World was, in a curious sense, pure. Stripped to its balanced essence: fire, ashes, flowers.

Bazargan glanced at Ann, solemn in full dress uniform. No—not quite. None of them wore their swords. Bazargan remembered the tiny contretemps with Syree Johnson aboard the *Zeus* and smiled at Ann, wanting to share the memory. But she was looking at Dieter. Watching them both, Bazargan missed the beginning of the disruption of the dancing.

Someone in the back of the circle was shouting, pushing forward. Then two people, five, a small group. At first Bazargan couldn't distinguish the words. When he could, they didn't at first make sense, because their content was so unexpected. It was like hearing soccer fans at a wedding.

"Death on the unreal Terrans!"

"The Terrans that killed Pek Aslor!"

"Unreal! Unreal!"

Bazargan heard, in a shocking moment of whimsy, *Unclean, unclean!* Philosophical lepers? Then his anthropological antennae took over.

One of the protesters pushed through the huge dense circle to Bazargan's right. It was a young man, neckfur glossy with youth, carrying what could only be a club. The young alien seemed surprised to have emerged from the thickly packed crowd so close to his quarry. He took a step backward, caught himself, and clutched his club more tightly.

"Death on unreal Terrans!"

Now the people around him had begun to put hands to heads, to screw up faces in the unmistakable signs of headpain. The young man seemed to feel it, too; his forehead wrinkled and Bazargan saw in his eyes the unmistakable signs of pain from unshared perceptions. What had Ann said—pain-inducing neurotransmitters set off by the anterior cingulate. The mind punishing itself.

Two more young people pushed through the crowd to stand beside the first. The three glanced at each other and seemed to gain strength from their common purpose.

"Kill the Terrans who killed Pek Aslor!"

"The Terrans are unreal!"

The crowd stood as fixed as Ann's specimens, except for their wrinkled skull ridges. No one seemed able to do anything. Bazargan guessed that they were stunned by the unprecedented. How could seven or eight—the number of protesters seemed to be no more than that—not share the reality that the Terrans' status was not yet decided? It wasn't possible. It was happening. It couldn't be happening.

It was happening.

The first, brashest protester raised his club toward Bazargan.

Instantly David Allen pushed Bazargan behind him. Allen was pale but not threatening. A complicated emotion flashed through Bazargan: resentment that David Allen thought he, Bazargan, needed protecting; amusement at the same idea; recognition of Allen's bravery; irritation at its histrionics. Before he could step around Allen, a servant of the First Flower stood beside the protester with the club.

"Young twig," the priest said in a controlled voice, "the Terrans are not declared unreal by Reality and Atonement. That is shared reality."

The protester swung to face the priest in her flowered robe. Something shifted behind the young man's eyes, something Bazargan caught only in profile. Then the boy nodded.

"That is shared reality," he agreed.

The priest looked at the other protesters. One by one, they nodded, murmuring, "That is shared reality."

Bazargan watched, fascinated. It was not capitulation, not the biological submission of the lesser members of the pack to an alpha member. Nor was it the cunning sham submission of the rebel biding his time. The protesters said, "It is shared reality," with almost casual conviction, as a human might announce, "It's raining outside." The crowd around nodded, not in relief or triumph at a defused problem, but with the same unarguable but casual acceptance. And then the music started again and everyone, including the protesters, resumed dancing.

"*Mein Gott,*" Dieter said. "Come, Ann, let us dance."

"Yes," Bazargan said. He was more shaken than he wanted to admit. But he turned to the nearest group and joined the dance.

Only David Allen did not dance again. He stood staring after the servant of the First Flower, who had herself resumed dancing as if nothing had ever happened to stop her. Allen watched her for a long time, and Bazargan hoped the Worlders were not yet adept enough at human expressions to interpret his.

"I don't know what more evidence he needs," David said. "My God, what does it take to convince Bazargan? Sky holos? A vision on the road to Damascus?"

He and Ann stood in the garden outside her quarters. Dieter Gruber was probably inside; David didn't really care. In fact, it would be better. Let Gruber overhear. Maybe the geologist could convince her better than David could. Although why an intelligent woman like Ann needed convincing, why she couldn't just see what was right in front of her . . .

God, she looked wonderful tonight. Not beautiful, maybe, the way those rich genemod dollies on Mars were beautiful, but vital and alive. The farewell burning had ended at dusk, as was customary, and everyone had returned to the village, many full of pel. The Terrans, under Bazargan's orders, had not drunk at all. But in the light of three Worlder moons Ann looked flushed, fair long hair loose on her shoulders, pupils dilated in their clear blue irises.

"David," Ann said gently, "Ahmed knows what he's doing. He's walking a very fine line, you know. Sooner or later Reality and Atonement will come to a decision about whether we're real. If the decision is yes—and Ahmed is doing everything he can to swing it that way—we want to have good relations with the priests, so our work can continue. If it's no, we have to be ready to pull off World at a moment's notice. Are you—"

"Yes, yes, I can leave in thirty seconds. My notes are prepared. God, Ann, you treat me like a child. I *know* everything you just said. But there's a larger point here. These people are virtually enslaved by their priesthood! You saw what happened. A riot was averted by just a single sentence from a self-proclaimed way-high-up-there tin-god type. Granted that her word saved our hides—this time. She could just as easily have pushed the crowd the other way. It's holding that kind of power at all that's scary, not today's specific decision. Worlders are gentle, good people. They're not killers . . . you *saw* that in the speed that kid backed down and started dancing again, for God's sake. He didn't want to hurt anybody. It's the priests who organized the whole concept of killing whoever they decide is 'unreal,' as a means to hang on to their power. It's a classic ploy in homogenous rural societies. Why doesn't Bazargan know that?"

"I'm sure he does," Ann said wearily. "But it's nearly midnight, David. I'm not really in the mood to debate anthropology with you."

"But *you* must see—"

"Good night, David."

He leaned over and kissed her.

Ann neither pulled away nor responded. She stood unmoving, even though the kiss was not passionate—credit the sex suppressants with that. When he finished she said quietly, "Don't do that again, David."

"Ann, I love you."

"No, you don't. You—"

"You're treating me like a child again!"

"You're acting like one. Think, David—you know what this is. Your training covered it. It's a fieldwork infatuation growing out of isolation and danger. I'm fifteen years older than you and—"

"And is that what you and Dieter Gruber have? A fieldwork infatuation growing out of isolation and danger?"

"Good night, David." She went through her curtained archway.

He thought of storming after her and having it all out—there were no real doors inside a World household, excepting the gates in the outer wall. But the thought that Gruber might be inside, laughing . . . Oh, God, why had he kissed Ann? He had opened himself up to Gruber's scorn, and probably now Ann would put up a barrier between them, or worse, tell Bazargan . . . Shame flooded him.

His neuropharms needed adjusting. Again.

That's what he would do. Stumbling back to his own rooms, he planned carefully. A mixture that would make him impervious to any amusement on their part. Dampen down all vulnerable emotions, increase brashness and aggression . . .

Why had he kissed her? Why? Stupid, stupid . . .

Someone moved behind a tree, across the garden. A dark shape. David stood still, peering through the gloom. One of the protesters, maybe, his courage rekindled by distance from his tyrannical priests . . .

The figure moved again. It was the servant girl, Enli.

David's shame returned. Now he was jerking at shadows. Definitely, a better neuropharm mix was called for. Tomorrow morning, a fresh start.

"May your blossoms unfold in peace, Enli," he called. The girl started, and he felt a little better as he crossed the scented moonlit garden.

TWELVE

ABOARD THE *ZEUS*

The alarm sounded when Syree was in the sonic shower. *Battle stations.*

In three seconds she floated, naked, by the intercom. "Colonel Johnson here, what is it?"

Executive Officer Debra Puchalla answered from the bridge. "Something emerged from the tunnel, ma'am. A Faller skeeter. It's headed this way at top speed."

"I'm on my way."

But not very fast. Skeeters, the Faller equivalent of flyers, traveled at about one and a half the top pilot-sustainable acceleration of the human version, arguing that Fallers had a much sturdier biology than that of humans. Syree was less interested in the biology than the technology, but so far no one had captured a Faller skeeter to reverse-engineer it. The Fallers blew them up instead. But even at its top speed, this skeeter would need a few days to reach World from Space Tunnel #438. Also, by all intelligence data, skeeter firing range was considerably less than the *Zeus*'s maximum. This was a crisis, but not one that was going to advance instantly.

Commander Peres reached the bridge before Syree. She stood quietly, weight on her right leg, as he issued orders. Her mission gave her power to determine the *Zeus*'s actions under ordinary circumstances, but not during acts of war. Peres was in charge now.

When he finished, she said, "Did they destroy the probes?"

"First thing," Peres said, which she'd expected. Most likely the Fallers had emerged blind through the new space tunnel they'd just discovered. They had then detected both marker probes, which had already detected them and sent full data toward the *Zeus*. Immediately the enemy had blown up the probes, which of course they'd recognized as human. In their place, Syree would have done the same thing.

In their place, her next act would be to send a data missile back through the space tunnel to wherever this skeeter had come from, to alert their command of human presence in this new system. Either that or pop back through themselves, report in for orders, and return through the space tunnel. Although if that had been the scenario, more than one skeeter would now be hurtling toward the *Zeus*. It all depended on how far away reinforcements were from the Faller side of the space tunnel. It was possible that the skeeter *had* gone back and this was a different, better-equipped ship from the original intruder. With the marker probes destroyed, Peres couldn't be sure either way.

Peres turned to her. "We're moving toward the enemy, Dr. Johnson. I'd rather engage them as far from the planet as possible. The shuttle can leave now to pick up your people planetside and still catch us well before the engagement. Or your team can remain below. Your call."

Syree had expected this. "I want to talk with Dr. Bazargan."

"Certainly. But we need a decision now."

"I understand. Do you have any reason to suspect that the enemy knows about Orbital Object #7?"

"No. But neither do we know that they don't know."

"Protection of the artifact is a major military objective, Commander."

Peres looked at her hard. "I'm aware of that, Dr. Johnson. But it does not outrank engagement with the enemy."

"No."

"Commander . . ." The exec, with a military question. Syree

moved away. Peres was making it as clear as possible that despite her experience, this command was his. She moved to a far corner of the bridge and activated her comlink.

Each member of the planetside team had a personal comlink sewn under the skin for emergencies, but removing it was unpleasant. The official comlink was held by Bazargan, who answered Syree's signal almost immediately. "Ahmed Bazargan here."

"This is Colonel Johnson, Doctor. Are you alone?"

"Dr. Sikorski is with me. No one else." He sounded wary, as well he might. Bazargan had struck Syree as a solid type, for a civilian.

She said crisply, "The *Zeus* is engaged in a military action. A Faller ship has emerged from the space tunnel and is advancing at all possible speed toward your planet. The *Zeus* will engage as far out as possible, and is presently leaving orbit. We can send the shuttle for your team if you so choose. If yes, you will be aboard the *Zeus* for the engagement. If not, and if the *Zeus* is destroyed, you will be marooned on the planet in what will then be Faller-controlled space, at least temporarily. The decision is yours, but it must be made now."

A brief silence, then Bazargan said, "I understand." His voice remained steady.

She heard Bazargan say, "Ann?" Sikorski's murmur wasn't intelligible. Then Bazargan said, "Dr. Gruber and Mr. Allen are not available for consultation, Colonel. Dr. Sikorski and I agree. The team will stay. Please inform us of the . . . the military outcome."

"Of course," Syree said, and didn't add that no information meant no *Zeus*. Bazargan was smart enough to figure that out.

After a moment he added, "Is there anything else?"

Syree wondered suddenly if he suspected about the artifact. His tone held a curious significance. But no . . . Bazargan was merely an anthropologist. No one would have briefed him, and security on this project had been as tight as she'd ever seen.

Of course, she could choose to tell him now. It was possible the planet personnel might be in danger from more than the

Fallers. Swiftly she reviewed the options, then made her decision.

"No, nothing else. Good luck, Doctor."

"And to you," Bazargan said quietly.

Syree was glad to have that out of the way. Now she could consider the real question: the artifact. The Fallers might or might not already know it existed. If they did, they undoubtedly wanted it. It was Syree's job to make sure they didn't get it.

The detonators were already fixed on the surface of the artifact, that matte surface that nothing thus far had been able to penetrate. The detonators would penetrate it, all right. They would vaporize it, set the planet's reddish skies aglow with the light of shattered atoms. Commander Peres controlled the remote signal, although it would also go off automatically if the Zeus was blown up.

Then nobody would have the artifact.

What would be the effect on the planet turning serenely below? Nobody knew. The wave of induced strong-force tampering that had killed Captain Austen was the only time the artifact had been "used," however inadvertently. And that use had only been at the artifact's weakest strength setting. If it blew up, it might or might not emit its wave at full force. Whatever that was. How great an effect it would have on the planet below was anybody's guess. So was the location of Bazargan's people at the time: directly in the wave's path, partly shielded by the planet, a hundred eighty degrees on the other side. It wasn't worth warning Bazargan, risking the Fallers learning anything about the artifact, when the gain to the planet team was so uncertain.

She told Peres that the civilians below were staying.

"Skeeter within range," the gunner said. He was a big rangy enlisted man named Sloane.

Peres said to the exec, "Ms. Puchalla? Any communication from the skeeter?"

Syree snorted inwardly. When had the Fallers ever communicated? She watched the tracking displays on the bridge of the *Zeus,* where technically she shouldn't be during a military engagement. But her status on board ship was so anomalous that she and Peres had avoided discussing it. She suspected she had more battle experience than he did. But he was the commander, and she was Special Projects, and it was easier to proceed with tacit acceptance that she would observe everything and interfere with nothing.

The skeeter's presence identified itself by everything but sight: thermal signature, mass, radiation emission. It was making no effort to hide.

"No communications from the skeeter, sir," Puchalla said.

"Fire."

"Firing," Sloane said.

The beam of protons accelerated to relativistic speeds shot out from the *Zeus,* a deadly arrow of particles. Syree could clearly see it on the display. See it shoot forward across empty space, hone in on the skeeter . . . and then *go through it.*

The skeeter still showed a clear thermal signature, still moving forward toward the *Zeus.*

Syree caught her breath. What she had just seen wasn't possible. Where had the beam gone? Why wasn't the skeeter vaporized?

"Jesus J. Christ," the big gunner said. His hand had gone slack at his side. The officers shot each other incredulous glances.

"Fire again," Peres said in a high, tight voice.

Again the beam shot out from the *Zeus,* met the skeeter, and went through it.

Syree's cloned leg gave way. She put a hand on the bulkhead to steady herself. The familiar hard, cool metal cleared her mind.

"They have a shield of some kind!" the gunner blurted.

"No, not a shield," Peres said, in that same altered voice. "The beam went *through* them. Dr. Johnson?"

Everyone on the bridge jerked around to look at her, even the helmsman, whose eyes should not have left the displays in front of her. Syree's mind raced, circled . . . and settled on the only explanation possible. Even though it made her mind circle even more.

"Display the readings of the beam just before it hit the skeeter," Syree said, and no one corrected her to point out that the beam had never hit. The gunner brought up the data. For just a second he leapt into reality—young, downy-faced, probably his first tour of duty, his Nordic-blue irises wide in eyeballs traced with delicate red capillaries. Then she forgot him again in the data on the screen.

Yes. It wasn't possible. But it was happening.

"It's not a shield," she said rapidly to Peres. "It's a . . . we don't have a word for it. They've altered the wave function of the proton beam, making its phase complex just before it hits." *How?* In God's name, how?

Peres said, "Explain it so I can understand, Dr. Johnson."

She looked at the officers and the two crewmen, gunner and helmsman. Probably nobody had the physics to understand. Christ, *she* didn't understand. But it had happened. The skeeter still sped toward them, but its firing range was only about half the *Zeus*'s. It couldn't fire on them for a while yet. Unless, of course, it had new weaponry as well as new defensive technology.

"Dr. Johnson?"

"Sorry, Commander. Let me try to explain. Our proton beam, of course, is a stream of particles moving at a large fraction of light speed. But as you know, a beam of particles can also be considered a wave, with the properties of waves, including amplitude and phase. The firing beam is both a wave and a stream of particles until the moment it is . . . is observed. The target of any weapon system is a sort of observer. The firing beam acts on the skeeter and so resolves itself into a particle beam. Only this time it didn't." The equations rose into her mind, and she pushed them aside. Peres was not a physicist.

"Why didn't it?" Peres demanded.

"The observer—that's the skeeter—kept the firing beam as a *wave*. It altered the phase to a complexity that doesn't interact with ordinary matter. So the beam went through the skeeter. In terms of the necessary observer, the skeeter chose not to observe the beam and so not to resolve its duality."

" 'Chose not to observe it?' " the exec said. "What the hell does that mean?"

Syree looked at her. If this were her command, Puchalla would not get away with that tone. "Just what I said. Chose not to observe it. By altering the phase of the wave aspect to high complexity, the firing beam became unreal for ordinary matter."

"Unreal?" Sloane said, although he should not have spoken unless addressed by an officer.

"Yes, Mr. Sloane. Unreal. Not in our reality."

The gunner laughed. The harsh, hysterical sound seemed to echo in the silence on the bridge. Peres said, "Mr. Sloane, you are relieved of duty. Ms. Puchalla, summon Mr. Sloane's replacement to the bridge. Dr. Johnson, do you have any idea whether this Faller ability to alter the wave phase of the firing beam can be used as an offensive weapon?"

"No way I can see," Syree said. "But if they can do this, it's not possible to predict what else they can or can't do."

Peres stared at the display. "I understand." The skeeter sped toward them across the star system's inner space.

The *Zeus* fired on the skeeter five times more over the next two days, gauging the effect of distance on the Faller wave-phase alterer. The clumsy name was Peres's; it seemed as much as he could, or would, grasp of the physics behind the Faller defenses. None of the five firings affected the skeeter at all. Nor did it fire back at the *Zeus*.

That scared Syree more than the alterer itself.

Clearly the Fallers were not interested in engaging the *Zeus*. The odds would have been against them, but usually Faller ships, even skeeters, fired anyway. Not this one. So why had they come?

The only other thing of possible interest to the enemy in this remote, primitive system had to be Orbital Object #7.

As the hours scraped past, grating everyone's nerves, Syree

became more sure. The skeeter flew past the *Zeus* and kept on going. The *Zeus* turned and pursued, helplessly, unable to stop the Fallers but only to trail behind and see what they did. Observers themselves, now.

"Dr. Johnson?"

"The orbital calculations are clear enough," Syree said. "They're doing a fly-by of the inhabited planet. Data-gathering. No point to that unless they suspected there was something interesting enough to gather data about."

The project team met in Peres's quarters. Peres, Canton Lee, John Ombatu, Lucy Wu. Peres had included his two ranking officers as well, Puchalla and Kertesz. The artifact mission had always been on a need-to-know basis; evidently Peres had decided his exec and third officer needed to know. Syree briefed the two, who looked grim at having not been told sooner.

They also, like everyone else, looked like hell. Unshaven and, from the smell in the cabin, largely unwashed. Ship's time was twenty-two hours. Everybody had stopped following normal day-night routines. The lights didn't dim, and battle stations were maintained constantly. The officers slept in snatches and woke already grabbing for their clothes, afraid they'd missed something in the few hours of fitful sleep. All this tension, and nothing actually happened. The skeeter flew toward World, the *Zeus* trailed behind. The inactivity made it all worse.

Syree had boosted her daily neuropharm mixture for greater serotonin, balolin, and substance J. But she didn't dare up the dopamine or fight-and-flight complex until there was something to actually do. Too rich a mixture too soon would just burn the body out. She assumed the others were doing the same.

Peres said to her, "What, in your opinion, can the Fallies do to the artifact?"

Syree picked up the printouts of her calculations, even though they'd make no sense to anybody but her. "They can fire on it, of course. A proton beam would probably vaporize the artifact. Probably. Or they can just observe it, gathering whatever data they can. Other than that, I don't see what the enemy can do to the object."

She didn't add, *After all, we couldn't do anything to it, and we've had months.* Everyone was hyperaware of that already.

Lee shifted on his chair. "Colonel, we once worked out that the *Zeus* could tow the artifact toward the space tunnel. Could the skeeter tow it?"

Syree had thought of that. "I don't think so, Canton. We haven't ever had the chance to reverse-engineer a skeeter, of course. But the best I can do with the equations says that the skeeter can't stop without impairing the effect of their wave-phase alterer. Not only does the firing beam have to be moving for the defense to be effective, but the skeeter has to have a certain minimum velocity as well. They're barely above it now."

Peres said, "But they're already out of our firing range. If they reach the artifact and stop long enough to secure the artifact, all the Fallers would have to worry about is automatic guns in orbit. And we already know they can detect and destroy everything we have in that line."

"Yes," Syree said. She felt light-headed. How long since she'd eaten anything? Better eat soon. "But the equations say that yanking the artifact out of orbit and then getting back up to sufficient velocity would slow them down so much that the *Zeus* would get within firing range before they left World."

"So they can't tow the artifact," Puchalla said.

"If your equations are right," Peres said.

Syree agreed. "If my equations are right."

"And even if they did tow it," argued Syree's assistant John Ombatu, "what good would it do them? We know the artifact's mass is too high to go through the tunnel. And we've been trying and trying to separate it into components ourselves, and nothing's worked. So why should they be able to do that?"

"Why should they be able to make a wave-phase alterer?" Peres said. "Christ, I'm tired. So where are we?"

No one answered. They knew where they were: trailing an enemy skeeter like debris behind a comet. Trailing and waiting. In another few days they still wouldn't have done anything useful, most likely, but at least they'd have some answers to useful questions. Such as: Were the Fallers merely going to look at the artifact, confirming the existence of the second known object from the race that had established the space tunnels? Were the Fallers going to blow it up? Were the Fallers, perhaps, going to blow up the *Zeus* by means of yet more unsuspected technology? Blow up the planet?

"There's something else that has to be said." Peres looked as if he knew they had already thought of this, which of course they had. "Anything else could come through the space tunnel at any time. Faller battleships, whatever. Just because it's been a few days and nothing's appeared, doesn't mean anything won't."

One by one, the people crammed into the tiny, malodorous room nodded.

"Anything else?" Peres said. "No? Okay, then now we wait. Deb, you've got the conn."

Puchalla nodded. Syree stood to leave, steadying herself on her right leg. She was going to grab a few hours' sleep. Or at least try to.

The hardest thing, always, was to do nothing.

Six hours later, the skeeter changed course. Without slowing down, it made a close swoop past Orbital Object #7. Syree and her project team, plus Peres and his battle team, crowded the bridge of the *Zeus* to watch the skeeter's graceful fly-by. It never slowed. The skeeter then took off back toward the space tunnel, with whatever data it had taken, to lead to whatever action the Faller high command chose next.

"All right," Peres said, after a long, long silence. "Now we know what they're after."

THIRTEEN

GOFKIT JEMLOE

Enli rode back to Gofkit Jemloe feeling better than she had in a ten of tendays. How sweet had been the sleep in Pek Nagredil's office! Wrapped in the warmth of shared reality with the high priest of the First Flower, Enli had slept for hours. When she awoke, it was dark outside, yet Pek Nagredil was still there.

"Let the flowers of your heart be still, Pek Brimmidin," he had said quietly. "A message has been sent to Gofkit Jemloe. The Voratur household will not expect you until tomorrow."

"But—"

"Let your flowers rest quietly. Here, this soup is still hot."

She hadn't expected to feel so hungry. Greedily she slurped all the soup. Pek Nagredil silently refilled her bowl, and she ate all of that, too. He poured her a glass of pel, moving around the gloomy office lit only by the moonlight streaming through the arched windows. There were few oil lamps in Rafkit Seloe. No one worked in the capital city after dark.

"Have you eaten enough?"

"Yes. Thank you, Pek Nagredil."

He pulled a pillow close to hers, his back to the window. He was a dark silhouette in a halo of graying neckfur, a middle-aged middle official who had not had, nor taken, time to decently comb his fur.

"Enli, I would ask you some questions."

He had never called her by her child-name before.

"The servant of the First Flower could not stay. Reality and Atonement meets tonight to discuss the Terrans, as I'm sure you surmised. But our priest is very concerned about you. The job of informant is supposed to allow the unreal to earn back their souls by service to shared reality. It is not supposed to destroy the soul itself. Now look at you. You are so thin. You jump at noises. Your eyes water at questions. You fall asleep here as if into death. So I must ask you, Enli. Is being informant to the Terrans too much for your soul?"

"I—"

Pek Nagredil held up his hand. "Wait. If it is, I can excuse you, on word of the servant of the First Flower. Another job of informant can be found for you to finish your atonement. You already know, of course, that we have other informants in the Voratur household, watching the Terrans. Two of them, now. Neither is placed as you are, working so closely with Pek Sikorski. Neither can provide us with as much information as you can. But if the price is to destroy you, the price is too large. So you must choose, Enli. Do you wish a different informant job?"

Enli swallowed the rest of the pel in her cup. Its warmth spread through her body. To get away from the horrible headpain of the Voratur household . . . But this was her job. Her atonement. She was doing it for Tabor, so that he might be set free to join their ancestors. Set free with the same joy as the woman who died from *antihistamines* had been sped toward her ancestors. That was the reality she shared now with Tabor.

And with Pek Nagredil.

And with the servant of the First Flower who had been so kind to her.

And even with the Terrans. After what she herself had reported about taking shared reality out of the skulls of Worlders and putting them with wires into Terrans . . . even now she flinched, thinking of it. After that report, undoubtedly the Terrans would be found unreal. But they hadn't been *yet*. That was reality, and she shared it with the peculiar aliens. Enli might have heard the Terrans wrong, the priest had said. And perhaps she had. Pek Sikorski, so kind to her always . . .

She said to Pek Nagredil, "I will stay in the Voratur household, informing on the Terrans."

Pek Nagredil nodded. He had expected that answer, of course. They shared the reality of the situation.

"You may sleep here tonight, Pek Brimmidin."

"May your flowers bloom throughout the night."

"May your flowers bloom throughout the night."

Pek Nagredil left, mounting his bicycle and pedaling down the deserted streets of Rafkit Seloe. Enli, to her own surprise, had returned to sleep almost immediately, despite the long refreshing sleep she'd already had. At dawn she pedaled out of the capital, washed herself in a cool pond, and ate breakfast at a travelers' house.

Now she rode by fields of crops in various stages of growth or harvest, each field bordered by its patron wildflower. The sun rose steadily, and Enli watched with pleasure as the livelier flowers turned their faces to follow the warm red ball in the clear sky. At the gates of the Voratur household, she dismounted and wheeled her bicycle directly to Pek Sikorski's rooms.

"Enli. I missed you this morning," Pek Sikorski said, in Terran. "You're looking very well."

"The soil is rich today, Pek Sikorski. May your flowers bloom." Enli spoke World; she wasn't sure why.

"May your flowers bloom," Pek Sikorski said, in World. She did not look as if her soil were rich today. Her peculiar headfur was uncombed and her tunic soiled. The lab benches were covered with the Terran machines, out of their ugly square boxes, and with bits of the various plants and animals that Pek Sikorski put into them.

"Can I help plant your soil?"

Pek Sikorski smiled. "Thank you, Enli. But neither of us

can plant this soil, I'm afraid. There's a big piece of information missing."

Enli suddenly knew that Pek Sikorski was talking about Pek Voratur's brain picture. About taking pieces of Pek Voratur's shared reality out of his skull and . . .

Enli's head began to hurt. She had taken no government pills this morning; for the first time since coming to the Voratur household, she hadn't needed them. It had felt so good not to need them. But now the horror was sliding back into her skull, the unthinkable violation of shared reality that the Terrans contemplated . . . if they did in fact contemplate it . . .

She had to know. Now. While she was feeling strong again, feeling her real self again, before she could again be laid low by the disjoints with shared reality that the Terrans scattered around them like pollen, wherever they went.

"Pek Sikorski," Enli said, and now she had switched to Terran, because there must be no mistaken meaning this time. "Pek Sikorski, will you take parts of Pek Voratur's shared reality out of his skull and put it inside a Terran skull?"

Pek Sikorski turned, her face astonished. "Do what?"

Enli repeated it slowly and carefully. She no longer cared if she revealed how good her Terran really was. "Will you take parts of Pek Voratur's shared reality out of his skull and put it inside a Terran skull? With hard wires?"

"Hard wires . . . oh, my God. 'Hard-wired.' "

Pek Sikorski's mouth made a round red O. Her eyes, that strange pale noncolor, went almost as round. The two women stared at each other across the lab bench crowded with alien machinery and World greenery.

"Enli . . . what did you hear? What do you think it means?"

Enli didn't know how to answer. All she could do was repeat the question a third time. "Will you take parts of Pek Voratur's shared reality out of his skull? To put it inside a Terran skull?"

"No! My God, no! Listen, Enli, we aren't going to harm any Worlder. We aren't going to take anything out of any Worlder skull. What you heard was a crazy idea of Pek Allen's to try to make Terran babies have—"

She stopped. Have what? Enli wondered. Shared reality? But that would mean they *didn't* have it now.

"Have many different bits closer to Worlders' when they're born," Pek Sikorski said firmly. "That's what 'hard-wired' means. For instance, you are 'hard-wired' to have neckfur, and we are not."

Neckfur. The Terrans only wanted to acquire *neckfur*. And why not? They must know how ugly they looked without it.

"Neckfur," Enli said, and so much joy was rising in her, nectar in the flowers of her heart, that she scarcely noticed Pek Sikorski look away. Neckfur!

"And other hard-wired qualities," Pek Sikorski said, in a muffled voice. "But Enli—when did your English become so good?"

Again the two women stared at each other. After a long moment, Pek Sikorski smiled sadly. "It seems there's much we don't know about each other."

"But we share reality!" Enli blurted out. She couldn't help herself. It must be real!

"Oh, yes," Pek Sikorski said, and now there were Terran shades in her voice that Enli did not understand. "We certainly do occupy the same reality."

It was an odd way of putting it, even in Terran. And Pek Sikorski looked at her oddly, too: intently, as if she knew that Enli was not sharing all of her own reality.

Which, of course, she wasn't.

The headpain suddenly stabbed Enli so hard she cried out. The room blurred. This was what she got for not taking the pills . . . Enli put her hands over her eyes. The light, the light, it hurt so . . .

"What is it? Enli?" Pek Sikorski's hands on her, cool and concerned, helping her sit down.

Enli shoved the hands away. Fumbling in her pocket, she finally found the pills and pushed a handful of them into her mouth. Bit by bit the room reappeared around her as the headache receded reluctantly, a beast withdrawn temporarily into the shadows.

Pek Sikorski reappeared as well, a rumpled woman sitting

beside her on the polished floor, holding Enli's hand.

"All right, Enli," Pek Sikorski said softly. "Tell me what that attack was."

Enli only shook her head. The motion hurt.

"It happened when I said, 'We certainly do occupy the same reality.' Because you know we don't. That was an unshared-reality attack inside your brain, the largest I've ever seen. Enli, who are you?"

The beast drew out from the shadows. Enli's hand closed on more pills.

"What do those pills do? Enli? My God—they damp down the headaches. So you can tolerate not sharing reality. But Worlders believe . . . Enli, who are you?"

Enli swallowed two more pills. How many was that? She mustn't take any more, it was too dangerous.

"I'm making it worse, aren't I? I'm sorry, Enli. Don't talk if you don't want to."

Pek Sikorski put her arms around Enli. Enli, startled, jerked away, but the motion made the beast lunge, jaws open. Slowly, moving as carefully as if her head were blown glass, Enli leaned against Pek Sikorski. The Terran arms felt so warm, so strong. No one had touched Enli since Tabor's death.

Tabor . . .

Pek Sikorski said softly, "Even when we try to do no harm, harm happens, doesn't it? Not even specifically because we're Terran. Just because we're all people."

Enli said, "My brother is dead because of me."

Immediately she regretted it. The words had just slipped out, because of the firm kindness of Pek Sikorski's arms. Because of the headpain. Because the words were reality, and it had gone unshared so long. So long.

"I'm sorry, Enli. But I'm sure that whatever happened, it wasn't your intention that he die."

Enli untangled herself from Pek Sikorski's arms. With difficulty, she got to her feet. She stood looking down at Pek Sikorski, who apparently did not understand what she had just revealed. Pek Sikorski turned her tired, concerned, kind face up to Enli.

Pek Sikorski did not realize—did not *know*—that reality was not a matter of intention. Reality was a matter of fact.

Pek Sikorski really did not know that most basic thing.

"No, Ann," Enli said. "It was not my intention that Tabor die."

"Stay here and lie down for a bit—"

"I must go to my personal room and sleep."

That was a lie, of course, but in the face of all the larger ones, it hardly mattered.

She found Pek Voratur in his business room, set close by the household's front gate. He was not alone. A gardener stood beside him, carrying a basket of roots, the knees of his tunic dirty from kneeling. He was an old, small man with yellowed neckfur and a mild face, one of tens of undergardeners who moved constantly around the flower beds of the various courts, a man nobody would look at twice. The instant Enli saw him she knew he was another of Pek Voratur's household informants.

"I would make a report, Pek Voratur," Enli said.

"So it would seem," Pek Voratur said. His sleek jowled face and shining skull both creased harshly. "And not just to me. You're a government informant, Pek Brimmidin."

"Yes."

"You're unreal."

Enli said nothing. There was no need.

"And I was not told."

"It is not customary to tell anyone near an informant that the unreal person is unreal. The strain is too great."

"But not if you have those pills you just took. What are they? Did the Terrans give them to you?"

The old man said, his voice as unremarkable as the rest of him, "She had them in her tunic."

"So they are from Reality and Atonement? Pills to make the pain of not sharing in reality become bearable. Such a thing exists?"

"I will leave your household now, Pek Voratur," Enli said.

It was what she had been coming to tell him anyway. Pek Sikorski would certainly tell Pek Bazargan about Enli's attack and her pills, and Pek Bazargan was the Terran who understood World the best. Once he realized that Enli was unreal, he would have told Pek Voratur. They shared that much reality. Enli had heard them do it, all those nights listening behind the walls.

"No, Enli. I think you will not leave."

Even the old man looked startled. Pek Voratur dismissed him with a wave of his hand, and the man scuttled from the room.

"Let me see the pills."

"No," Enli said. For a sudden moment she saw him trying to take the pills by force. But of course he would not do that. Pek Voratur was real.

"But I'm right? They are from Reality and Atonement, to make it possible to do your job?"

"Yes."

"I see."

But it was Enli who saw: the unmistakable signs of pain behind Pek Voratur's skull. She was too much unreality, just standing here.

"Pek Brimmidin," he said formally, "I will think on this. Go now. Do not leave my household. I wish to consult a priest."

"Yes," Enli said.

"Go."

No farewell flower blessing. Of course not. He knew what she was.

She stumbled in shame across the blooming, scented courtyards, answering no one's greeting. In the personal room she shared with three other women servants, she fell on her pallet. The beast slavered close, but sleep came closer. Sleep again? Yes, she'd taken too many pills. Sleep . . .

As it came, she wished it were death.

FOURTEEN

GOFKIT JEMLOE

In the middle of the night, Bazargan's comlink gave the emergency signal for the second time since he'd come to World.

Immediately he jerked upright on his pallet and fumbled to light the oil lamp. Someone wanted his instant attention. That meant that at least the *Zeus* still existed. "Ahmed Bazargan here!"

Syree Johnson's calm, flat voice said, "Dr. Bazargan. Colonel Johnson here. I'm sorry to tell you that we have a further emergency on the *Zeus* which will also affect you. The Faller craft returned back through the space tunnel, but we expect a larger deployment to reappear eventually."

"I see. You want us aboard. But we already said—"

"No. The situation is more complex than that." Johnson's voice had not changed, but nonetheless Bazargan felt his body stiffening in the darkness.

"Dr. Bazargan, the *Zeus* has a military mission in this star system beyond merely escorting your scientific expedition. One of this planet's moons, 'Tas,' is not a natural body but an alien artifact, of the same origin as the space tunnels. It appears to be a powerful weapon. The Fallers want it, and so do we. In the time until their ships reappear, the *Zeus* will tow this artifact to the space tunnel and attempt to take it through."

"A moon? You're going to move a *moon*?"

"We are going to try. The only alternative is to blow it up, and if the Faller fleet appears before we reach the tunnel, we'll do that instead. The reason—"

"Why wasn't I told this at the start of the expedition?"

"Knowledge was on a military need-to-know basis," Johnson said coolly. "You had no need to know."

"But the—"

"I don't have much time for this call, Dr. Bazargan. Please listen. Whether we take the artifact through the space tunnel or must resort to blowing it up, there may be consequences to the planet. That's the reason I'm telling you now. The artifact emits a spherical wave that temporarily destabilizes elements with an atomic number greater than seventy-five. Such elements will emit radiation for an unspecified period of time. We have already lost one person to the lowest possible setting of this wave effect. Future emissions may occur with much greater disruptive force. You are being told now so that you may remove your personnel to a relatively safe area. Whether, and how, you also warn the natives is left to your discretion."

"What . . . when . . ." Bazargan scrambled for his meager knowledge of physics. *Destabilizes elements with an atomic number greater than seventy-five . . .* what did that include?

"We don't know when," Johnson cut in. "That's what I've been telling you. I'm assured that you have someone with you who can understand the implications—Dr. Gruber. The rest is up to you. Good luck."

The comlink went dead.

Bazargan reopened the link, his hand shaking. The *Zeus* didn't reply.

In the gloom Bazargan stood up and walked to the window. Only once before in his life had he been this angry, and then he had acted so rashly that years had been spent recouping his losses. Right now he didn't have years. He breathed deeply and struggled for control.

They had not even told him. His team at risk—the entire planet at risk—and the bastards had not even seen fit to let him know of this possibility. Despite his record, his reputation, his scientific standing . . .

In the deep places of the heart, two forces, fire and water, struggle together . . . Ferdausi. Tenth century.

They had used him as a cover for a covert military operation, used all of World as a cover, put an entire planet at risk . . .

The scent of flowers reached him. *The lily seemed to menace me, and showed its curved and quivering blade* . . . Hafiz. Fourteenth century.

Johnson had given him sixty seconds of her precious time, given it curtly and with no apology, leaving him to clean up the mess this would make of World-human relationships, not to mention the complete end of the anthropological project, blown up now as completely as the so-called "artifact" . . .

Crush not the ant who stores the golden grain:/ He lives with pleasure and will die with pain . . . Sadi. Century forgotten, at least for the moment.

Gradually he grew calmer. At some point, his hand holding back the loose window curtain and his senses flooded with night, he realized that he could mix a neuropharm to calm himself. No, better this way. The Persian poets were more reliable.

Flowers bloom every night/ Blossom in the sky,/ Peace in the infinities;/ At peace am I . . . Rūmī. Deep breath.

Thirteenth century. Deep breath.

He went to wake the others.

"Tell me again, Dieter," Ann said. In the glow from a single oil lamp in the middle of the lab floor, her skin looked pale, almost translucent. Bazargan had brought David Allen from the crelm house, guessing that Dieter and Ann would be together. One less movement through the dark gardens to attract attention before they were ready for it. Only one moon shone in the sky, low enough to be obscured by buildings and trees.

Dieter, hastily dressed in a tunic that looked as if it had lain three weeks in his field pack, shifted on his pillow. Stress deepened his German accent. "I can go only by what Ahmed says that Johnson said. If a wave disrupting nuclear stability really does hit with any force, and if it really does affect anything over atomic number seventy-five, then all sorts of things will go radioactive. If it is temporary—she did say 'temporary,' Ahmed? *Ja?*"

"Yes. Can that be?"

"Not with anything we know how to do. But we didn't know how to make space tunnels, either. So if it is so, all sorts of things will emit alpha radiation. Iridium, platinum, gold . . . everything above seventy-five? Ahmed, did she mention lead? It is so stable!"

"No. I don't think so. I'm not sure."

"Call the bitch back and ask!" David blurted. They had already had to calm him down once.

"We've tried calling. The *Zeus* doesn't answer. Now be quiet, David," Bazargan said.

"I won't be quiet! They've fucked us over completely, don't you get that? Now everyone on World might die!"

"No, no," Ann soothed. "That won't happen. In the first place, only half the landmass will be facing any wave that comes at a given time—maybe rock stops it. It could be. Also, living bodies would not be majorly affected by what Dieter is describing. I hope. Even if the wave comes at all, which it may not."

"So we just sit here with our heads up our asses and hope it doesn't come? And let half of World fry, but that's okay because it's only half?"

Bazargan stood. The bright curving pillows of World were low; on his feet he towered a meter over David. "I said to be quiet, and you chose not to listen. If you are not quiet now, you will be ejected from this meeting. By force, if necessary."

David stood, too. "You wouldn't do it."

"Yes," Bazargan said. "I would."

The two men faced each other. Shadows danced on the walls. Gruber stood and moved beside Bazargan.

David laughed. "So that's how it is, huh? All right, I guess

Syree Johnson isn't the only martinet on this expedition." He sat down.

Bazargan sat, too, in no way acknowledging his victory. After a moment Gruber followed his lead.

Bazargan said, "We must warn World. No other choice is morally justifiable. We must tell them exactly what will happen, and when, and why."

"We don't know what or when," Ann pointed out. "Will Dr. Johnson even tell you before she blows up that moon? Which one is it, again?"

"Tas," Bazargan said. "I'll try to make sure she is. Does." It had been a long, long time since his English had failed; perhaps he should have taken a supplemental neuropharm after all. Instead he breathed deeply, arranging his thoughts as precisely as he could.

"I will keep calling until I get a commitment from the *Zeus* to notify us just before they either detonate Tas or try to move it through the space tunnel, which—"

"Madness," Dieter muttered. "The mass is *too great*."

"—lies, after all, almost six days away, if Dieter's calculations are right. Of course, if the *Zeus* doesn't reply, or if the Fallers just appear and blow up Tas themselves, then the *Zeus*'s warning won't come in time. So perhaps it is best that we warn the natives of what might happen even before we know for certain that it will."

"Yes. 'No other choice is morally justifiable,' " David mocked. His young, handsome face twisted in bitterness. But Bazargan had run out of patience with youthful disillusionment.

"Dieter, you must list everything that must be removed from all villages and from Rafkit Seloe. Or would it be better to have the natives remove themselves?"

Gruber considered. "I don't know how long they'd have to be away, and most of their actual building materials aren't going to be affected by the wave effect . . . On the other hand, if the nuclei affected drop much below seventy-five in atomic numbers . . ."

"Then living bodies will be affected and we'll all die anyway," Ann said.

Bazargan said, "Then make your list, Dieter. Now. In the morning we will all go together to Pek Voratur, as our host, and ask him to take us to the Office of Emergency Aid in Rafkit Seloe. Yes, I think that's best."

Ann said quietly, "They will be angry with us. What sort of retaliation can we expect?"

Bazargan said quietly, "They might declare us unreal, of course. But I hope not. It will take a while to summon the High Council and make the decision. By that time I hope to have convinced everyone necessary that we are sharing reality as soon as it shifted for us. That's why going to Voratur tomorrow is absolutely necessary. Any delay will be seen as unsharing."

Ann said, "I think then that we had best go right now. Dieter can make his list afterward."

In the lamplit gloom, Bazargan saw Gruber nod slowly. After a moment, David Allen followed.

"All right, then," Bazargan said. "We'll go now." And then, rising out of some deeply buried childhood belief, the words surprising even himself: "And may Allah be with us."

Gruber grinned.

Enli stirred in her sleep, then came fully awake in the darkness.

Her personal room was absolutely dark, and absolutely still. How was that possible? She should hear Udla and Kenthu and Essli breathing in their sleep. Kenthu snored . . . where was Kenthu's nasal music, out of tune as a rusty flute? Where was the window, where the moonlight?

Something moved against a far wall.

Quietly Enli rolled off her pallet and across the floor. She had been good at this as a child, so good that Ano and Tabor had never known where she was. When she reached the middle of the room, or what she judged to be the middle, she stopped. Whoever moved around the perimeter would expect her to move the other way, against the safety of the wall.

She could see a little more now. The curtain had been drawn across the arched window, but a slim line of very faint moonlight shone around one end. Opposite the window the moving shape had stopped at the four wooden chests that held the serving women's personal possessions. A lid squeaked weakly as the shape opened it. The small chests stood close together; Enli couldn't distinguish which one he had. But if it opened, it was slovenly Udla's. The other three kept their chests locked.

Now Enli could see that the floor was bare of all but her own pallet. Essli, Udla, and Kenthu had not even come home to sleep. Relief washed through her; at least they had not been hurt.

Who was the intruder? A petty thief? How did he get into the Voratur household?

The lid of Udla's chest squeaked close. The shape tried the other three wooden chests and found them locked.

He—she?—made no sound. But he moved unerringly through the dense gloom to the place where Enli always unrolled her pallet. In another minute, he would discover she wasn't there.

Enli didn't wait. She pushed off hard from elbow and knee, not trying to be silent, and sprang toward the intruder. Surprise was her ally. She tackled the dark shape and brought it down.

If it was a strong man, she would be overpowered.

It wasn't a strong man. Enli straddled him, pinning both his arms to the floor. Her skin had scraped across a rough beard, but the room was too dark to see who he was. Then he spoke.

"Please, Pek Brimmidin . . . don't hurt me!"

The old man, Pek Voratur's other informant. Of course. Enli had refused to turn the government pills over to Pek Voratur, so he had sent his other informant to steal them. She should have expected it.

"I'm not going to hurt you, you old dustbin! But you won't find the pills. They're not here."

"Oooohhh, don't hurt me so. I'm very old."

Enli loosened her grip. Standing, she turned to the archway

to draw back the curtain. She wanted to see the man's face. Stealing, of course, was not a violation of shared reality; everyone half expected it. Pek Voratur would never have taken the pills from her by force. He was real; the real did not violate the ultimate reality of another's physical being. But of course he would try to get them anyway; they would make valuable trade goods. And this old thief was already unreal, or he wouldn't be an informant. Enli wanted to see his face in the light. She had told him the truth about storing the pills elsewhere at night, but she wanted to share face-to-face reality with the thief so he would not ransack her room again and again, disturbing Udla and Kenthu and Essli.

Enli grasped the window curtain in her fingers and pulled. Something hard slammed into the small of her back.

. . . And this old thief was already unreal, or he wouldn't be an informant . . .

Informants could kill. She, Enli, had.

"Where are they?" he snarled.

The pain was astonishing. It danced up her spine, down her legs. It crushed everything under its ruthless feet. She couldn't move, couldn't see, couldn't speak. There was nothing but pain.

"Where *are* they, Pek?"

She whimpered and spasmed on the floor, unable to answer. He said something that might have been *Dung* or *Do it* or even *Help us*. Then Enli felt the unthinkable, the truly unreal . . . a knife slide into her skin, her flesh, her living side. Everything disappeared,

By the time the four Terrans had made their way across the dark gardens to Pek Voratur's personal rooms, Bazargan had regained his composure. Well, perhaps not composure. One could hardly be composed bringing news of possible mass destruction to one's alien hosts. But at least Bazargan again felt a superficial calm.

In the master of the household's personal garden, Ann whispered, "Ahmed, wait for Dieter."

Bazargan turned. "Dieter? Where did he go? I thought he was with us."

"He will be. He just went to his own room for some rock samples. He wants to show Voratur exactly what will go unstable when the wave effect hits."

It seemed to Bazargan that the show-and-tell could have waited until after the first announcement, but Gruber had already left. The others had no choice but to wait for him, shivering slightly. It lacked a few hours until dawn. Another moon was in the process of rising; Bazargan didn't know which one. The glowing light rose above the dark bulk of the household wall. One of the larger, slower-moving moons: Ral, or perhaps Cut. Not Tas, which was being towed toward Space Tunnel #438. Through the cold pale light drifted the fragrance of unseen flowers.

Not a nightingale but knows/ In the rosebud sleeps the rose . . . Hafiz. Not since Bazargan was a boy had anyplace evoked so much Persian poetry in his mind. It was the flowers, the architecture, the courtyards.

It was the Byzantine situation.

The inability to accomplish anything without complications, intrigue, night plotting. All the reasons the young Bazargan had hated Iran, and loved it. All the reasons he had chosen to study abroad, and had ended up studying anthropology, the opportunity to experience other groups' night plotting rather than one's own. And so coming to this night garden that smelled like Isfahan.

"I am here," Gruber said, materializing beside Bazargan. Gruber had taken the time to dress in warm clothing. He carried a large bag of his beloved rocks.

"Show time," Ann said, and Bazargan saw again that side of her usually hidden, the bravado that was counterpoint to her gentleness. "Let's go in."

They each plucked a flower from the hospitality bushes, and Bazargan tinkled the announcement chains.

*   *   *

Pek Voratur's personal servant led them into the personal room. The servant had drawn the outer curtain to the garden, blinking in sleepy astonishment, fumbling to light a lamp. Then the man had vanished into the inner rooms, from which had come an annoyed exclamation, a female whisper, and more lamps. Finally Pek Voratur had emerged alone, letting the heavy curtain fall between him and Alu. The stout Worlder scowled; his neckfur stuck up in stiff ridges around his jowls.

"Pek Voratur, my flowers wilt in shame at awakening you like this," Bazargan said, "but it is an emergency. We have just learned that reality has shifted and we must share it with you immediately."

Voratur's face changed from annoyance to the trader's alert calculation. "May your flowers bloom, Pek Bazargan. What reality has shifted?"

No invitation to sit. The servant hovered respectfully against the wall; Voratur had not chosen to send him away. There was no choice but to plunge ahead.

Bazargan said, "Our large flying boat has called us from space. There is a danger to World and all on it. A strange weapon"—he used the World word for "thing causing an explosion or forest fire"—"has been discovered circling your world. Terrans are trying to . . . to keep it from exploding, much as frelbark explodes when tossed into a fire. But this explosion may—I say 'may,' because we don't know for certain—affect World in very strange ways. As soon as the Terrans on our ship told us about this, we came to share reality with you. You must take us to the Office of Emergency Aid. The whole planet will need to prepare."

Voratur looked bewildered. With one fat hand he swiped at his unruly neckfur, then seemed to forget it. "A weapon circling World? What weapon? Whose weapon?"

"We don't know," Bazargan said truthfully. "It's very old. It has been in orbit around World for a long, long time."

"And it will explode? How—"

"*May* explode."

"—do you know?"

"Our priests aboard ship are examining the weapon. This is

what they think. We must go to the Office of Emergency Aid so that the planet can prepare."

"Prepare how?" Voratur seemed more bewildered than ever.

"We will explain. It's complicated, Pek Voratur. But reality is shared, and it's possible no one on World will be harmed at all." Possible, yes. But how likely?

"What . . . what is this weapon that you have discovered called?"

Bazargan thought rapidly. Worlders were keen sky observers; they would soon notice that Tas, fastest-moving of the two low-orbit moons, was not scurrying as usual across the sky. "The weapon is the moon Tas, which is not a moon. It is a hollow metal ball."

"A hollow metal ball! The moon is the moon!"

"No. I'm afraid it is not."

Bazargan watched as Voratur struggled with the idea. "But it . . . all right, it is a hollow metal ball. A weapon. Very old. Not Terran and not World. And it may explode."

"Yes, Pek Voratur. It may explode."

"I don't understand any of this!"

David Allen said sympathetically, "It *is* hard to understand, Pek. We Terrans do not understand all the behavior of Tas. But we do know that it is a manufactured item."

Voratur froze.

What, Bazargan thought frantically, *what does that word mean to him? What's happening now . . . ?*

" 'Manufactured item,' " Voratur repeated. "Tas is the manufactured item. 'We will come back for the manufactured item,' your traders said the first time. We thought you meant for the items made in our manufactures. But you meant Tas. You came back for Tas."

"Pek—"

"You *knew*. You knew it was not a moon but a weapon. You knew nearly a year ago, and you did not share the reality."

"No," Bazargan said swiftly. "No, no. We have just learned this. Our people in orbit have just told us—"

He saw his mistake. Too late.

"They knew," Voratur said. "Terrans in space knew. And they did not share reality with you, with others *of their own kind* . . ."

Voratur's face changed. The headpain must be blinding, Bazargan thought. Blinding, thrusting, stabbing. But not so much that Voratur could not think, could not draw the inevitable conclusion. People who could violate reality *with their own kind* . . . Terrans were not real. Proof positive, proof not even requiring the wisdom of a High Council. A World child could see it. He, Bazargan, had to act fast, or they were all dead.

Voratur and Gruber acted faster.

"Unreal!" Voratur said to the servant by the archway. "Call the household!" The man ducked through the curtain. Gruber was already bending over his sack of rocks, but by the time he came up holding a tunable laser gun, the servant had vanished not only from the room but from the outer courtyard.

"*Verdammt!* Pek Voratur, lie facedown on the floor, please." Bazargan heard his own voice sounding tired. "Not necessary, Dieter. They don't do it that way." And indeed Voratur was already looking through the Terrans, past the empty space they did not occupy. They were unreal.

"What?" Gruber said. "That servant will tell the household we are unreal!"

"I'm sure he already has. And if Pek Voratur were strong enough to attack four adults, he would destroy us. But he is not, and so we simply do not exist. We are unreal."

"But the household altogether is strong enough to attack us, *ja*? So we will leave. Ann, follow me, then you, Ahmed, then—David? David!"

Bazargan turned. David Allen stood stiffly, brittle as glass. And Bazargan realized.

And if Pek Voratur were strong enough to attack four adults, he would destroy us . . .

Bonnie. Ben.

"David, wait!" But Bazargan was already too late. Allen flew across the courtyard, stumbling in his haste, trampling a bed of allabenirib in his headlong dash to the crelm house.

"Oh, my dear God," Ann whispered.

"They've only had a few minutes . . ." Bazargan said, and found that he didn't believe it. A few minutes could be enough. When you had absolute moral certainty on your side, a few minutes could be more than enough.

"Stay together," Gruber ordered. He led them to the crelm house, following David Allen's crashing path. With each courtyard they passed, the sky lightened, the flowers unfolded, and the household of Voratur boiled from its buildings, only to catch sight of the three Terrans and freeze into ice.

A gardener caught Bazargan's gaze and turned his back.

A woman rushed from the wash house, her face bursting with the horror of the news that the Terrans were unreal. She saw them actually in her own garden, shrieked, and then went blank, with that curious glazed blankness that refused to see. Her hands went to her head.

Another woman hurried past them, eyes straight ahead, carrying reality in the hunch of her shoulders. How fast could shared reality travel on World? At the speed of speech, since to utter the words was to verify them, to have them believed. All were one in reality.

All, now, but the humans.

Bazargan, Ann, and Gruber had not yet reached the crelm house when they heard David Allen's anguished cry.

"No, no, no," Ann whispered over and over, meaninglessly.

Bonnie and Ben had been taken into the play garden, away from the real children. Whoever had cut their small throats was already gone, but it didn't matter who it had been. It could have been anyone. They all shared the same mind.

Bonnie wore a yellow nightdress, the same color as her hair. Ben had already been dressed for the day; children awoke very early. He wore a World tunic, red. The blood showed less than on Bonnie's nightdress. David keened over the small bodies, his shoulders shaking.

Ann put a hand on him. "David . . . David. Come on, David. You can't help them, and we have to leave."

Allen jumped up and whirled on her, fists clenched. If it had been Gruber, Bazargan saw, Allen would have slugged him. But not Ann.

"You can't help them, dearest," she said again. "Come on. Before the household organizes an attack."

He let her take his hand and lead him away.

"Stay together," Gruber said. "The closest gate is through the servants' court. This way." Holding the gun, he led them past rushing people, who is their frantic communicative haste to tell each other the humans did not exist, acted exactly as if the four humans did not exist.

FIFTEEN

THE NEURY MOUNTAINS

Enli woke with the light.

Cold. The light was cold. No, she was cold. The old man, the unreal informant, had stabbed her. Of course he had; he was unreal. The unreal could kill. He had killed her.

She was unreal. But she had not killed him.

Cold. She was so cold.

She lay still on the floor of her personal room. Sticky dark stuff held her to the floor. No, she could crawl. Her blood wasn't that sticky.

So cold.

She must tell Pek Voratur. He was real. He would not use an informant who could kill. He would make the old man go away from the household. She must tell Pek Voratur.

Tabor had been this cold, lying in his own blood at the foot of the flower altar. So beautiful the altar had been, covered in rafirib and adkinib and red Terran rosib . . . no, no, no, the Terran rosib had come to World much later . . . Tabor. Cold.

She must tell Pek Voratur. Only then could she live to set Tabor free.

Enli pulled herself across the floor. Another arm's length to the archway. Her vision blurred. She kept on going. Now she had reached the curtain. She crawled under it, cold. The floor under her changed from icy tiles to icy garden stone.

Morning. Barely morning. Oh, Tabor . . .

Someone shrieked. Not in her court, in another. Why were people shrieking in the orderly Voratur household this early in the morning? It wasn't because of her; she hadn't seen anyone yet. It wasn't because of Tabor; he was far away, dead at the foot of the flowered altar . . .

"Enli! Oh, my God, Enli!"

Pek Sikorski. But that made no sense. Why would Pek Sikorski be in a servants' courtyard at dawn, when it was so cold . . . ?

"Enli. Can you hear me?"

She was being rolled over. Pek Sikorski bent over her.

"Y-yes, P-P-Pek . . ."

"She's alive. Stabbed. And blood on the back of her head . . . Dieter, I need my medkit."

"It's here," another voice said, and Enli realized they were speaking Terran, not World.

"You knew," Bazargan said. So he was here, too, in a servants' courtyard at dawn. So strange.

So cold.

"You knew how Voratur would react, and that's why you had the gun, Dieter. And the medkit. And whatever else is in that bag."

"No, of course I didn't know. Who can know what these Worlders will do, Ahmed? But I thought to prepare, and it's a good thing, *ja*? Ann, you cannot take time to do that."

"It's Enli," Pek Sikorski said, which was strange because Enli already knew who she was. Didn't the others?

"But Ann—"

"Don't you see?" Pek Sikorski's voice scaled upward. "She must have been knifed because of us. Because of her close association with us. Like . . . like . . ."

"Ssshhhh, Ann."

"She's coming with us. She's not that badly hurt; it looks worse than it is."

"Ann, consider—"

"I'll carry her," said yet another voice, and it was Pek Allen's, only it wasn't.

Pek Sikorski put something on Enli's skin, something warm, and the pain went away. Just like that—the pain went away. Enli felt herself being lifted, and caught a glimpse of Pek Allen's face looming over hers. Some people ran past her in the garden, but never looked in her direction.

"She'll be out cold in a minute," someone said.

There was only time to say, "Bring Tabor," and then warmth spread over her and she smiled and it didn't matter that nothing made any sense.

She and Tabor danced on the village green, between the cookfires, with the other young people. Old Pek Raumul played the pipes. They danced as they danced every night in Gofkit Shamloe, among the dinners cooking and the children racing in and out and the shared reality warm and heavy as perfume. Only it wasn't every night. It was the night she and Tabor left the green and went down to the river among the pajalib and Tabor said, "There are hard wires on brains floating down the river—you better give me the government pills," and then the old man stabbed him in the side with a Terran rose.

"It's another twenty kilometers," Tabor said, only it wasn't Tabor at all, it was a Terran voice, speaking Terran words. "I wish we had the bicycles."

Enli opened her eyes. She lay on open ground, under moons and stars. The stars looked pure and sharp, very far away. Cold night air brushed her cheeks, but the rest of her felt warm under some impossibly light blanket that seemed to generate its own heat. Nothing hurt—not her torso, nor the back of her head. Instead her whole body felt strangely buoyant, as if she floated on unseen water. Nearby the four Terrans sat under similar blankets around a small glowing cone of light such as Enli had never before seen or imagined.

"Do you think they're coming after us?" Pek Sikorski.

"Not till morning," Pek Bazargan's deep voice said. "I

would guess that Voratur will want to share this reality with the priests."

"Priests. They're the cause of this!"

"No, David," Pek Bazargan said. "We're the cause of this. Our own people on the *Zeus*. We should have been informed of every facet of this mission at the beginning. That's the only way we could have made a better judgment of what to tell the Worlders."

"And what would you have told them?" Pek Gruber challenged. "The alien weapon was a military secret. You could not have said anything anyway."

"Fuck military secrets!" Pek Allen said.

"*You* would think so," Pek Gruber said.

"Stop it." Pek Sikorski, as stern as Enli had ever heard her. "We can't afford to quarrel. David, Dieter, you know that."

Pek Bazargan said, "We need to plan, and then to sleep. A few hours only. Then keep walking, to reach the mountains as soon as possible, so we won't have to fight off anyone sent from Reality and Atonement. By now, news of us is starting on its way around World." He thought of the sunflashers on their efficient towers. "I don't want to have to kill any Worlders."

"Not even the priests that slaughtered Bonnie and Ben?" Pek Allen said bitterly. "Not even the so-called religious, power-mad Worlders that could cut the throats of babies while they lay sleeping in their . . . their . . ." The voice faltered. Then Pek Allen stood up and stalked off into the darkness.

"Asshole," Pek Gruber said. "Does he think he's helping by fighting with us? Or by getting lost alone out there?"

"He won't go far," Pek Sikorski said. "This is worst for him, Dieter. He took care of those babies every single day."

"I know," Pek Gruber said, more quietly. "Look—Enli is awake."

Then Pek Sikorski was leaning over her, putting things against her forehead, her side. "How do you feel, Enli?"

Enli said, "You are unreal. All of you are unreal."

Pek Bazargan spoke over Pek Sikorski's shoulder, not in Terran but in World. "And so are you, Enli. Aren't you?"

"Yes," Enli said, and it was a relief made somehow possible because of the strange buoyancy of her body.

"Is it because of us?" Bazargan again.

"No," Enli said. "It is because of Tabor. My brother."

"Ahmed," Pek Sikorski said, "she's drugged. Don't ask her questions now, it's not fair."

"One question I must ask. Enli, we are going to the Neury Mountains. There are many reasons, but one is so that your people will not follow us inside to destroy us. Do you want us to take you with us, or to leave you here for Worlders to find? If you aren't unreal because of us, then perhaps you are best left here to continue with . . . with whatever arrangements you had made with Reality and Atonement."

Best left here. Continue with Reality and Atonement. Was that possible? Reality and Atonement had made her an informant, but not one who killed, as the old-man informant had tried to kill her. Did she and the unreal old man thus share the same reality? Or the same unreality? Did she share either with the Terrans, who were all so unreal that their own people had told them truth was not true?

Were there, then, many realities? But how could that be? How could people exist if that were true, living separately in different realities, isolated and alone?

It was the aloneness, then, that was real.

Her head didn't hurt. Here she was, Enli Pek Brimmidin, lying under the cold stars and thinking the unthinkable, and her head did not hurt. That must be because of the drugs the Terrans had given her. All of this was because of the Terrans, who had brought the new reality, or unreality, into the old, and so shattered the World. If they had not come, she would have served out her term as an informant, been declared once more real, and been allowed to release Tabor to join their ancestors. All these different realities, these isolations that carved and severed people apart and left them writhing alone, had happened because of the Terrans.

She hated them.

She did not hate them. They were her reality.

"Don't push her, Ahmed," Pek Sikorski said in her gentle,

kind, unreal voice. "You'll give her a headache. Enli, sleep now, and you can decide afterward if you want to come with us."

As if sleep, the little peaceful sojourn with one's ancestors, would ever be possible for her again.

Pek Sikorski adjusted the warming blanket over Enli, tucking it under her toes, pulling it up to her chin. She was like a mother fussing over a child: like Ano with small Fentil. But it was Pek Bazargan who leaned close to her ear and said, "I'm sorry, Enli. This was not the way it was supposed to be."

Bazargan swiped his hand across his forehead. He was sweating, even though the night air was cold. They were none of them used to this much walking, this fast. The muscles of his calves ached.

"How much farther, Dieter?" he asked.

Gruber sat close to Ann beside the powercone. "Another twelve or thirteen kilometers. We can cover that by noon, if we start at dawn."

"Even carrying Enli?"

"I think so. But, Ahmed, if they come after us it will be on bicycles, and we can't outdistance those."

"I don't think they will start out until daylight, and with luck we'll just outpace them," Bazargan said. "Now we need to sleep, but first tell me exactly what you packed in that emergency sack."

Gruber grinned. He was in the best physical shape of the tour of them and, Bazargan suspected, had the most relish for physical danger. A good person to have along if you got into a spot like the one they were in now. "Four s-suits—I didn't know we'd have Enli along."

"Of course not." Bazargan glanced at the sleeping alien. Any of their s-suits would fit her, but that would leave someone else without one. At the moment Enli lay wrapped in the thermal sheet Dieter had also brought, warm in its self-generating heat. But the Neury Mountains were highly radioactive, and nothing but an s-suit would protect against that.

"The power cone, some p-torches, thermal sheet, gun," Dieter went on. "The food powders you just ate—"

"How much?"

"Supplies for four for about a week. If we're careful. Ann's medkit, my portable geologue, some simple spelunking tools. That's about it."

"No wonder that pack weighs so much."

"Survival's heavy. But I'm getting point nine gee to help carry it." Gruber grinned again.

Something moved beyond the circle of light from the powercone. David Allen, returning from his solitary sulk. Barzagan watched him stretch out on the ground without speaking, face turned away from his colleagues, and pretend to go to sleep.

"In the mountains," Gruber said, acting as if Allen didn't exist, "the comlink may not work. Depends on how deep the rock cover is at any given point."

"We'll try to radio again before we go in," Bazargan said.

"Why? To tell them what? Unless the *Zeus* wins out over both the Fallers and that moon they're playing with, nobody's coming back for us."

"Then," Bazargan said quietly, "we'd better hope the *Zeus* wins."

The Neury Mountains rose abruptly from the plain. They had trudged for the last two hours down a long gentle slope and then up a steeper one, and at the top of the rise Bazargan got his first good look at their uncertain refuge. Panting, sweating, the four humans and Enli paused to stare at the home of the First Flower, whose unfolding petals had created World.

The mountains looked, Bazargan thought, as if a manic child had drawn them: uneven, jagged in places and rounded in others, broken at their bases into rifts, passages, humps like a paintpen gone wild. They were covered with the ubiquitous lush "grass" of World, dotted with the equally ubiquitous wildflowers, here grown more stringy in the rockier soil. Great outbreaks of gray rock splotched the foliage.

"They look like regular mountains," Ann said.

"Relatively new, geologically," Gruber answered. "This was all underwater in the last major geologic age. Tectonic plate subduction lifted the whole basin millions of years ago. But wait until you see inside." His tone was enthusiastic.

"Enli," Bazargan said, "can you walk farther?"

"Yes," the girl said. Ann had drugged her; she felt no pain. But that must mean she wasn't feeling her own exhaustion, either, or at least not until she fell asleep on her feet. She'd already done that once, falling to the ground and further bruising her head. After that David and Gruber had taken turns carrying her for a while, but she had proved heavy even for their young strength. Bazargan, feeling his age on this long forced march, had not even attempted it.

"But this is . . . is . . ."

"Yes, Enli?" Ann said.

"This is forbidden. The mountains. We cannot go in."

Ann took Enli's arm and drew her gently forward. Enli resisted.

Suddenly David Allen spoke, the first words he'd uttered since his outburst last night. "People just came over that low ridge behind us."

Bazargan whirled around. Ten or fifteen Worlders strode purposefully in pursuit, no more than a kilometer behind.

"Let us move," Gruber said, with his unflagging energy, and took Enli's arm from Ann. Gruber pulled Enli along, half running, at a pace the others were forced to match.

After a few minutes, Bazargan looked back. The Worlders were gaining.

"Faster," Gruber said, and broke into a run, pulling Enli along with him. To Bazargan's surprise, she was able to keep up. They had underestimated her toughness.

But not his own. Bazargan felt his chest ache as he ran along behind the young people. Ache, and then burn. He couldn't keep this up very long. His heart . . .

"You . . . you go on," he gasped, doubled over. "Use . . . my suit . . . Enli . . ."

"Come on, Ahmed," Dieter Gruber said mercilessly. "It's not that far now."

It looked very far to Bazargan. Pain crawled leisurely through his chest and legs, making itself at home. His vision blurred. His heart, his heart . . .

Gruber dropped Enli's arm and grabbed Ahmed's. In that strong grip—what the hell had Gruber's parents done to his genome, anyway?—Bazargan stumbled and ran, stumbled and lurched, every gasping breath a torture. Stumble, breathe, stumble, he couldn't breathe, stop please stop—

"They've stopped," David Allen said, and Dieter let go of Bazargan's arm. He fell into a heap, all consciousness focused on the exquisite pain in every rib, every fiber of his chest. Breathe, pain, breathe . . .

"Just catch your breath a bit, Ahmed," Gruber said, and the bastard wasn't even gasping.

When he could stand, hands still supporting himself on his bent knees, Bazargan looked around. They had passed the first of many huge fallen boulders littering the ground before the mountain's abrupt rise. Evidently the boulder was a marker of some sort; their pursuers had stopped a quarter kilometer behind, milling around in what looked like consternation. As Bazargan watched, wheezing and panting, the aliens again started forward, all together. Shared reality.

"*Scheisse!*" Gruber said. "We must go deeper in."

"No," Enli said, but she didn't struggle when David Allen picked her up bodily and carried her forward.

They reached the base of the towering gray rock and moved along it, Gruber muttering, "Here, here, soon . . ." Bazargan saw the alien death squad—that's what it must be—swing around to parallel their path. And draw closer.

They were armed with spears.

Ahmed had never seen these before. There was no hunting on World; the diet was mostly vegetable, supplemented by meat from animals long domesticated into docile herds. Predators had been eliminated millennia ago. Vermin were handled by poisons created by the healers. Worlders seldom killed each other, and then only in moments of passion or for unreality, and then knives were used. Where had the spears come from?

Bazargan lagged behind the others, still panting. A spear sailed past his head and hit the gray rock.

"Down!" Ann cried, grabbing his hand and yanking. Bazargan fell to his knees, scraping them. A smear of blood followed him as he scuttled forward, a wheezing crab, behind the others. They clung to the base of the enormous cliff face, now shielded by fallen boulders, now exposed. Bazargan saw a second spear narrowly miss Gruber, in the lead.

"*Ja!*" he cried. "Here!" And vanished into the mountain.

Bazargan scuttled forward. Ann was disappearing now, only her scratched and bleeding legs visible. Bazargan saw the hole. No more than a meter high, it was overgrown with grass and scrub. David Allen shoved Enli through the plants, into the rock. Then, to Bazargan's surprise, Allen crouched behind an inadequate boulder and waved Bazargan on.

It was not a time to argue precedence. Bazargan squeezed through. A moment later, Allen followed.

Bazargan had never liked tunnels. This one was a little more than a meter high, barely enough to crawl through, and nearly dark. The five of them were stuffed into the narrow space like sausages in a casing. The hair on the back of Bazargan's neck lifted. Something light crawled over his arm; he tried to shake it off.

"It gets better," Gruber called from up front. "Follow me."

As if there were a choice! Bazargan crawled forward, trying to calm his ragged breathing, telling himself it was due solely to his frantic running. The tunnel grew darker. The old irrational fear came back to him, crushing him . . . He would get stuck, unable to move forward or back, buried alive as millions of tons of rock settled onto his body, compressing his flesh and bones . . .

Breathe deeply. Focus on a still quiet spot in the mind. Breathe—

"Almost there," Gruber called cheerfully.

Bazargan could see nothing. He crawled blindly over jagged rock, until the tunnel turned again and he could see the faint outline of Enli's rear end. He followed it until it disappeared and the light suddenly brightened. Bazargan crawled faster. *Breathe . . . breathe . . .* Then he was out.

He emerged into a cavern the size of his personal room at the Voratur household, lit by a tall chimney through the rock. In the gray half-light Bazargan could see another tunnel, mercifully larger, branching from the cave's far end. The five people, the pupils of their eyes enormous, looked at the irregular walls, the second tunnel, each other.

"Enli," Ann said urgently in World, "is there any chance your . . . the people will follow us in here?"

Enli shook her head mutely. She seemed unable to speak.

"When I explored the mountains before," Gruber said in English, "I went a short way into a lot of these tunnels, and a long way into two. This wasn't one of them, but the whole system is basically homogenous."

"Tell us what to expect," Ann said. She smiled. "Briefly, Dieter."

"Yes. Well. A million years ago all this was underwater, in a shallow basin. The asteroid impact penetrated deep enough to hit magma, and the eruption of rock was full of gas. That's why you have so much pumice—this light and porous rock here." He picked up a stone from the cavern floor and held it out to them. Bazargan could see that it was shot with holes.

"Eventually," Gruber continued, "tectonic plate subduction raised the whole basin into mountains. The mountains still rested on—or maybe they drifted slowly toward—a hot spot in the crust. There was extensive volcanic activity, creating lava tunnels like the one we're standing in. We're still over the hot spot, which is why there are underground hot-water springs. And over time the soft pumice eroded by water and wind into more caves and chimneys and tunnels. Plus, of course, the whole system is radioactive."

"How radioactive?" David Allen demanded.

"Varies with location."

Bazargan straightened. It was time for him to resume command. "We have four suits to handle radioactivity, and five people. I suggest we rotate suits and keep a careful eye on how many rads everyone is accumulating. Enli, put this on, please."

He peeled off his s-suit. Enli looked at him dumbly. The drugs Ann had given her were probably wearing off.

"Do it, please," Bazargan said in World, and Enli responded to his tone as he had intended. Clumsily she pulled the thin flexible suit up over her legs and torso, onto her arms. Ann showed her how to fasten it, and pulled out the porous, inflatable helmet from the pocket.

Gruber said, "We don't need helmets here."

"Good," Bazargan answered. "If I stand directly under that rock chimney, can I raise the *Zeus* on the transmitter?"

Gruber squinted at the weak shaft of light. "No. But farther in, you can."

Allen said, "*Farther* in?"

"Yes. Come. But this time we will have light." Gruber took the p-torch from his pack, turned it on, and started forward. The rest followed him into the second tunnel, all of them but Enli stooping to fit. First Ann, limping slightly, her face calm. Enli, dazed, looking ridiculous with her tangled mousy neckfur sticking out over the neck of the s-suit. Allen, glaring at the walls. And Bazargan in the rear, steeling himself for another tunnel.

This one wasn't as cramped as the first one, but it was darker. Gruber's light didn't seem to illuminate much for Bazargan, at the end of the hunched procession. "Hold hands," Gruber called. Bazargan felt David Allen's hand grasp his own. Allen's fingers trembled slightly, and this, paradoxically, steadied Bazargan.

The tunnel went on, it seemed, for kilometers. Bazargan's shoulders began to ache from stooping. A few times he thought he heard water somewhere behind the dark walls of rock. Once a few pebbles fell from the ceiling, and his heart leapt into his mouth. *Erosion*, Gruber had said. *Soft rock*.

Gradually he became aware that he was climbing. The tunnel angled upward. It also grew smaller. Just as Bazargan was beginning to feel panic push at his mind, the tunnel turned abruptly and suddenly he could see the others in front of him, a shuffling stooped line clinging to each other's hands like worn-out elephants. Then Gruber was through, and Ann, and Bazargan heard her gasp.

He emerged into an open basin about twenty meters in diameter. Rock overhung the south side, but the north was open to the equatorial sun. In the center of the basin a spring bubbled up from the rock. The light, vertical in the open and diffused under the overhang, illuminated dozens of species of flowers of every color.

Ann darted forward. Bazargan flexed his knees, rolled his aching shoulders. He followed Ann, but Gruber abruptly pushed him back.

"Wait, Ahmed. The count is high here. Too high!"

Radiation. And now that Bazargan looked more closely at the flowers, he saw that many of them had mutated. A pajal bush with elongated leaves instead of the usual rounded clusters. A blue vekifir lying on the ground, too heavy for its spindly stalk. A monstrous huge red-brown flower like coagulated blood, one side bulging and the other stunted.

"The radiation source is the spring," Gruber said, frowning. "But . . . never mind. Ahmed, you can raise the *Zeus* from here, I think."

Bazargan moved another cautious step away from the rock face and pulled the comlink from his pocket. He felt curiously naked, the only one without an s-suit. It was like those dreams in which everyone else at a scientific conference is clothed and he stood nude, trying to give a presentation.

"*Zeus,* this is Dr. Bazargan. Respond, please."

"Colonel Johnson here. Yes, Doctor?"

"We'd like an update on what's happening out there," Bazargan said, not without harshness. Why did Syree Johnson think he was calling?

He knew the answer: Johnson wasn't thinking about the team planetside at all.

"We are towing the artifact toward Space Tunnel 438," Johnson said crisply. "No sign of enemy craft. No change in status."

"But there has been a change down here," Bazargan said,

even more harshly. "The natives have declared humans unreal and have tried to kill us. They did kill Ben and Bonnie Mason. The rest of us have fled to the Neury Mountains, where we are now. We cannot leave them without being hunted again. Food is limited. We tried to raise you last night to tell you all this, but you didn't answer. Can you send a shuttle for us?"

"Negative, Doctor," Johnson said. "Not without decelerating for shuttle launch, which would be counter to our military mission. If you—" A burst of unintelligble static.

"What? What was that?" Bazargan said.

More static. Then nothing.

Bazargan, Gruber, and Ann looked at each other. David Allen smacked his fist into his hand and stalked off, scowling. Enli looked uncertainly after him, and then at Ann.

"Something is happening up there," Gruber said.

"I think," Bazargan said quietly, "that we had best assume the worst. Dieter, if the artifact—Tas—emits that wave effect that destabilizes atoms, are we sufficiently protected if we stay right here?"

"No. Too open. But rock is a good insulator. If we go deeper inside, we will be. Provided we avoid areas of high radioactivity."

"Do you know how to get to a safe place from here?"

Gruber shook his head. "No. I came this far on my first trip, to this basin, then went back the way we came. But we can't do that. Even if the Worlders have gone away, it's a long distance outside to the next opening I explored. We would be exposed far too long. To both villagers and the wave effect, if it comes."

"So we go on," Bazargan said. "Are there openings under that overhang?"

"We will find out," Gruber said. "Circle around the spring against the wall, Ahmed, to that tunnel there. Stay away from the spring. Ann, you must leave those plants."

"I'm taking specimens with me," she said.

This time Bazargan went second, behind Gruber, which gave him much more benefit from Gruber's torch. The comfort of this was balanced by the tunnel's unknowns. Bazargan discovered that he was walking with every muscle clenched against rockfall or crevice, and consciously made himself relax. Remember Iqbāl of Lahore, that zealous reformer: *Upon what manner man is bound to man/ That tale's a thread, the end whereof is lost/ Beyond unraveling*. Bazargan smiled grimly.

The tunnel turned steeply downward. "No loose rock," Gruber said, "but we don't want to go too deep. Still, we will try for a small while."

"All right," said Bazargan, a man bound to man beyond unraveling.

They moved in silence for what seemed a long time. Occasionally the tunnel narrowed, but not unbearably. Occasionally it widened, so that it was almost a cavern in itself, long and narrow. Frequently Bazargan heard water, although he saw no more of it. Once Gruber stopped to shine his torch on the wall.

"Look, everyone. See that thin layer of clay there? That's from the time of the asteroid impact." The layer wavered along. the wall, rising and falling in the patterns of rock uplift, a mute curving testimony to global disaster.

Longer silent walk, steeper incline. Bazargan began to sweat. How deep were they going? Perhaps they should go back, look for another opening . . . Gruber had said the rock would shield them from the wave effect that Syree Johnson might let loose on the world. Shielding would do no good if they ended buried alive.

In front of Bazargan, Gruber abruptly disappeared.

"Dieter! Are you all right?"

A long moment, then Gruber's voice from somewhere below. "*Ja*. It is all right, just an incline. Not too steep. You can slide down on your asses. There are ways back up from here."

He shone the torch back along the slide, and Bazargan saw a fairly smooth incline of perhaps thirty degrees. He sighed, sat on the blanket he carried, and slid down with no more than a single sharp jolt to his tailbone as it went over an unyielding stone. At the bottom he stood and moved away for Enli to follow him.

He and Gruber stood in a large dark cavern illuminated only by Gruber's torch, which was pointed the other way. In the gloom Bazargan could see stalactites and stalagmites like large double teeth. Water dripped from the ends of the canines. Sweat dripped from Bazargan, who was unprotected by the temperature-modulating suit.

"Something is not right here," Gruber muttered, studying a display strapped to his thick wrist.

"What isn't right?" Bazargan asked, but before Gruber could answer, Enli came down the rock slide, an s-suited alien, neckfur flapping, eyes wide and terrified. But the girl made no protest, only picked herself up and moved away from the bottom of the slide as Ann rushed down it.

"What is not right?" Bazargan repeated. The words came out slowly. Something was wrong with his head; it felt muffled in soggy wool. Fatigue, most likely.

Allen slid down the rock, graceful and scowling.

"The geothermal gradient," Gruber said, and his voice sounded as muffled to Bazargan as his own. A headache was starting just behind Bazargan's eyes. Fatigue, anxiety, hunger. They had not stopped to eat since last night.

"What about the . . . the gradient?"

Gruber frowned at his wrist display. "It gets hotter as we go deeper, ja. That is normal. Even separating out the effects of magma, naturally occurring radioactivity heats the rocks. Small amounts of radioactivity here—you are not in too much danger, Ahmed—even on Earth. The rock holds the heat, it is an excellent insulator. But as you go deeper, the rate of temperature rise should decrease, since most radioactivity is near the surface. But here, the rate of temperature increase is *rising*."

It was an effort to follow this. From the depths of his headache Bazargan summoned the expected query. "Why?"

Gruber shrugged. "This is not Earth."

"A genius among us," David Allen said, and for a second anger flared in Gruber's blue eyes. It died away, replaced by the same lethargy Bazargan felt.

He made himself speak. "Lead on, Dieter."

Gruber shuffled forward, shining his light toward the opposite side of the cave. Multiple openings fringed the distant wall. Gruber started up one.

"Pek Bazargan," Enli said, walking behind him, "we should not go this way."

It took Bazargan a minute to assimilate what she'd said, or even that she'd spoken at all.

"Why not? Dieter, wait."

Dieter shuffled to a halt, turned ponderously to shine his torch on the people behind him.

Enli said something in World. After a moment she repeated it in English. Her voice was too quick, too sharp. "The other way goes up. You said it gets too hot deeper. We must go up!"

Up. Yes, that was right. Enli was right. They must go up; Dieter said they must go up.

The humans huddled in confusion.

"Up!" Enli said.

Up. Yes, that was right. Enli was right. They must go up; Dieter said they must go up.

His head hurt, Bazargan thought.

They must go up.

Someone seized his hand and put in Ann's. Enli. She forced all their hands together, squeezed past them to the back of the line, and pulled. The train of humans shuffled after her, heading up.

But then they were back in the caves with stalactites. Bazargan blinked. Wasn't that down? Weren't they supposed to go up?

He couldn't remember.

Enli was pulling them along, into a different tunnel. She had the torch, somehow; she was in the lead, somehow. They lurched somnambulently along in the gloom. Bazargan didn't know how long; perhaps he was asleep. He felt asleep, dreaming, a long dream of stumbling along stone paths, some even and some rough, some wet and some dry, climbing, always climbing . . .

Time went by.

More time went by.

All at once, something happened.

His neck snapped . . . No, his *head* snapped. Something inside it abruptly gave way and he could think again. It was like the cracking of a shell around his skull.

"What . . . what?"

All four humans looked equally dazed. Enli watched them with anxious eyes. Finally she said, "The soil was very poor. For all of you."

"A field of some type," Dieter said, consulting his displays. "Only it doesn't register here . . . except that the rate of geothermal rise is now decreasing!"

Ann said excitedly, "A field that affects thought . . . but Dieter, it has to be electromagnetic!"

"No. Not according to my displays," Dieter said. "But, Ahmed, while we were . . . were like that, you took another seventy rads."

Bazargan said, "What's my total?"

"One hundred ten."

Not good. He would be sick in a day or two, although not fatally, even without medical help. Still, it would be very unpleasant, and it would probably shorten his life in the long run.

David Allen was stripping off his s-suit. "Here, Doctor, take mine."

"I . . . thank you." Why not? They had agreed to rotate suits, and Allen was the youngest team member.

"You are all right here, David," Gruber said. "Comparatively. Listen, I hear water."

"Down that tunnel," Ann said.

"Wait here." Gruber passed out smaller p-torches and disappeared with the big one. The others waited. They stood in a cave the size of a small bedroom, barely large enough to let Bazargan control his breathing, given that the cavern lay under tons of rock. But the floor was dry and reasonably level, and in the light from his torch Bazargan could see an equally smooth, rounded ceiling. One of Dieter's emptied lava deposits, perhaps. In the gloom Bazargan heard the others breathing:

Ann slightly fast, from the climbing. Enli slower. And David Allen, ragged and quick.

The boy should not be that exhausted from the climb. Bazargan's muscles all ached, and his stomach grumbled, but his heart wasn't racing and he had a generation on Allen. So what was bothering David?

Ann said, "If it wasn't an electromagnetic field, what the hell *was* it?" No one answered. Bazargan pulled on Allen's ssuit and felt it mold itself to his different contours.

Gruber returned, lugging an expando full of water. Expandos folded flat and weighed almost nothing, but at a touch they formed tough, impermeable bags shaped by thin flexible struts almost impossible to break. Every s-suit carried a few.

"The water's good," Gruber said. I suggest we camp here— eat and drink and sleep. It's as good as anywhere else."

The suggestion was welcome. They prepared the tasteless, nutritious food powders with Gruber's water, drank deeply of more water—it tasted metallic and warm—and arranged themselves to sleep.

Bazargan lay listening to Gruber and Ann argue softly.

"Our *thinking* was affected," Ann said. "And Enli's wasn't. She was the only one functioning normally. That suggests only a few possibilities. An odorless gas that retarded our brain functions but not hers, and I can't imagine what that could be chemically. A pheromone to which she's adapted but we're not—except that the tunnel was too dark and dry for any sort of vegetation. Well, maybe not any. Or an electromagnetic field."

"It wasn't an electromagnetic field," Gruber said, "or the display would have caught it. There might be dark-adapted fungi emitting pheromones."

"For what purpose? Why would they evolve? Surely conscious thought can't be an evolutionary threat to fungi growing a half kilometer underground!"

"Not likely," Gruber said grudgingly. "All right, then, the odorless gas. But Ann, I am more puzzled by the increase in rate of geothermal gradient as we descended and the decrease as we climbed. That is opposite to normal. And if the rate of increase changed at that same constant, it would melt all rock at about thirty kilometers down, and nothing indicates that's true here."

"So what do you think controls the gradient?"

"I can think of nothing."

"Me neither. Only an electromagnetic field."

"Ann, I told you . . ."

Eventually they stopped arguing and Bazargan heard their breathing grow even and deep. Enli's was already regular, but she was an alien; impossible to know if she was really asleep. The last thing Bazargan heard as he drifted off, the smell of damp stone earthy in his nostrils, was David Allen's breathing. Quick, ragged, agitated, as if, for Allen, sleep had been murdered along with poor little Bonnie and Ben Mason.

SIXTEEN

EN ROUTE TO SPACE TUNNEL #438

A conclusion is just the place where you got tired of thinking.

Syree tried to keep on thinking, even though the towing operation was proceeding without a glitch. She stood on the crowded bridge considering possibilities, contingencies, feasible disasters.

"Acceleration one gee, speed eight point eight clicks per second," the helmsman said.

"Continue acceleration," Peres answered.

"Acceleration continuing."

Someone behind Syree let out a long low whistle between clenched teeth.

By now every person on the *Zeus* knew the ship's covert mission. It was impossible not to know. The *Zeus* had dropped from geosynchronous orbit to twenty-three hundred clicks above the planet. Carefully the *Zeus* had matched the orbit of World's smallest and fastest "moon," Orbital Object #7. That moon now stood jammed up against the front of the *Zeus*, its bulk filling the viewscreen like a huge gray peeled grape. The *Zeus* wasn't towing the artifact as much as unceremoniously shoving it out of orbit and into space. That shove took everything the ship had.

"Acceleration one gee, speed ten point six clicks per second." The helmsman had been instructed to announce every three minutes.

"Continue acceleration."

"Acceleration continuing."

Orbital Object #7 was roughly eighteen times the mass of the *Zeus,* which was capable of twenty gees at maximum power. Nobody used maximum power for more than a few moments of evasive action, because nobody wanted to crush all the humans aboard into pulpy jelly. But to accelerate an object eighteen times as big as you are at a rate of one gee, you needed eighteen times one-gee power. Syree could feel the *Zeus* straining around her. She felt it in her bones, in the vibration in her head. How much more, then, must Peres, her commander, feel it.

Peres said, "Stability report."

"Maintaining stability."

The Zeus had to target its shove at the artifact's exact center of mass. Electromagnetic stabilization helped, of course; Syree had induced the field across the surface of the object. Thank God it was a conductor. She couldn't imagine this operation succeeding if it weren't.

"Acceleration one gee, speed twelve point four clicks per second."

"Continue acceleration."

"Acceleration continuing."

The farther the ship shoved the object out of orbit, the easier the shoving would be. The inverse square law was on their side. The *Zeus* would accelerate all the way to the space tunnel, rather than beginning deceleration halfway. This would cut the transport time to five days, seventeen hours, three minutes. It also meant that when the artifact sailed into the space tunnel, it would be moving at four thousand eight hundred clicks per second. Nothing had ever flown into a space tunnel moving that fast. No one knew what would happen when it did. But then, no one knew a lot of things about this desperate operation.

Behind Syree, someone coughed, then coughed again.

"Clear the bridge!" Peres snapped. So he felt the strain, too. Officers left, reluctantly. Syree stayed where she was. An image came to her, from an old training film: a submarine way below its depth, the bolts forced out of its cracking hull by water pressure. One had flown into the head of the helmsman, his crushed skull accidentally caught on film to horrify generations of cadets.

Her comlink beeped. "Yes?"

"*Zeus,* this is Dr. Bazargan. Respond, please."

"Colonel Johnson on the *Zeus.* Yes, Doctor?"

"We'd like an update on what's happening out there," Bazargan said. To Syree his voice sounded uncharacteristically harsh.

"We are towing the artifact toward Space Tunnel #438," she said crisply. "No sign of enemy craft. No change in status."

The helmsman said, "Acceleration one gee, speed fourteen point one clicks per second."

"Continue acceleration."

"Acceleration continuing."

"But there has been a change down here," Bazargan said, even more harshly. "The natives have declared humans unreal and have tried to kill us. They did kill Ben and Bonnie Mason. The rest of us have fled to the Neury Mountains, where we are now. We cannot leave them without being hunted again. Food is limited. We tried to raise you last night to tell you all this, but you didn't answer. Can you send a shuttle for us?"

A shuttle? Didn't these so-called scientists understand the first thing about the physics that governed their lives?

"Negative, Doctor," Johnson said. "Not without decelerating for shuttle launch, which would be counter to our military mission. If you—" The ship jolted hard enough to knock the comlink out of her hand.

"What the hell was that?" Major Canton Lee said, picking himself off the deck.

The helmsman said shakily, "I don't know. The . . . the artifact pushed back!"

Syree studied the displays. Nothing unusual. She questioned

the helmsman, but all he could say was that the displays blinked for a moment and the artifact shuddered. Now it had stopped.

"Acceleration reading!" Peres snapped.

"Acceleration one gee, speed fifteen point eight clicks per second."

"Continue acceleration."

"Acceleration continuing."

It did, evenly, as if nothing had happened. Peres said to Syree, "Don't use your comlink again, Colonel."

"Commander, there's no way the signal from or to the planet could have affected the—"

"Are you positive about that, Colonel? Do you really understand the physics of this thing so completely that you can say positively what does and does not affect it?"

Syree was silent.

"Acceleration one gee, speed sixteen point five clicks per second," the helmsman said, returning to standard orders.

"Continue acceleration."

"Acceleration continuing."

Syree deactivated the comlink and put it in her pocket. On the viewscreen Orbital Object #7, nine hundred thousand tons of featureless gray sphere, moved ponderously from its orbit toward Space Tunnel #438, over a billion klicks away across empty space.

What had made the artifact shudder like that? She didn't believe it was the comlink. No, something had switched on inside the enigmatic sphere, perhaps as an automatic reflex to passing a set velocity. Or to moving a set distance away from the planet. Or to something else they couldn't guess.

But what had switched on? And to what future effect?

SEVENTEEN

THE NEURY MOUNTAINS

David woke first. For a terrified moment he didn't know where he was. The utter blackness, the hardness below his back, the smell of stone . . . the cave.

He turned his torch on low, shining upward. The curiously polished rock of the ceiling emerged, flecked with shiny specks. Mica? Gold? Who cared?

Nobody would look at the real gold on World. Nobody but him. And maybe Enli.

He sat up, peering at the sleeping alien. She had saved all their lives yesterday, leading them past that place that disrupted their thinking, that made David feel . . . But he didn't want to think about that. Think about Enli. She had courage, and brains. And like all the Worlders, she was *good*. A good person. Evolution made her that way. The shared-reality mechanism made this stocky sleeping being with the tangled drab neckfur so far superior to his own kind that David was ashamed to be human. Worlders could not lie in any meaningful way, could not torture, could not kill—

But Worlders had killed Bonnie and Ben.

A dull grinding began in the back of David's head, and for a panicked minute he thought it was the return of whatever had attacked them yesterday in the deep tunnel. But no, he could still think. Worlders had killed the children. Worlders had killed—

"Pek Allen," Enli whispered. "Wake up! Your dreams wilt you!"

She sat beside him, blinking, one hand on his arm. David seized the hand eagerly, felt it, ran his thumb over the tough skin covering thin bones. Enli tried to pull her hand away, but he grasped it harder. This hand kill children? Hands like these, life-saving hands, child-tending hands? Colert Gamolin's hands? Or little Nafret's, in a few years? How could it have happened that way?

"Pek Allen, please . . . let me go!"

The answer came to David in a burst of sound and color, replacing the grinding in his head. It felt like that: sound and color, with the beautiful inevitability of sunrise and birdsong. *It hadn't happened that way.*

"Pek Allen . . ."

"I'm sorry, Enli," David said, letting go of her hand. He tried to make his voice reassuring. The poor thing was scared. Of course she was— she couldn't see what he could, put together what he could. She was good, and courageous, and, above all, moral, but her people did not yet have the vision and insight and knowledge of his. It was in the combination that the answer would lie. The answer, the salvation. The sum greater than its parts.

If it hadn't happened that way in the crelm house, how had it happened? What had really killed Ben and Bonnie? What had—

"Pek Allen, do you need your doses? Your morning doses?"

It took him a minute to realize what Enli meant. Her concerned voice, soft in the half darkness, a living thing amid the dead stone. She meant his morning neuropharm mixture. How did she know he followed the Discipline? She must have seen Ann do it; she spent most of her time with Ann.

"No, Enli, I'm fine," he whispered back, but the whispering was wasted because there was that dumb bull Gruber waking everybody up, *crash crash,* no manners, typical.

"Ahmed, are you awake? Ann, here is enough water for

breakfast, I think, but if not I'll get more. And we should try again to raise the *Zeus* somewhere open. Here, the food powders . . ."

Gruber and Ann stirred the powders into water and passed them out in expandocups. Protein, fat, and carbs in ideal proportions, mixed with dehydrated fiber and an appetite suppressant to stay hunger pangs. Plus vitamins and flavoring, the latter usually inadequate. But David drank his without tasting it. His mind raced, and his hand stayed protectively close to Enli. Worlders were *good*. So what had really happened in the crelm house?

One thing was certain: None of the other humans would be able to help him learn the answer. Gruber, oxlike in his plodding conventionality, knowing nothing but dead rocks. Bazargan, the consummate politician, willing to believe—or act as if he believed—whatever was expedient to the situation. Even Ann, sweet-natured as she was, had too limited a knowledge of the language, was too absorbed in her plant biology, had too limited a worldview.

It was up to him, David Campbell Allen, to discover what had really happened in the crelm house. And not only that. He saw it now, whole, the larger picture Bazargan had so determinedly tried to cloud for him. It was up to David Campbell Allen to override Bazargan, to reestablish this mission on World, so that eventually the two genetic stocks, human and World, could be rejoined. Humanity—no, that was the wrong word, the joining would produce something greater than humanity. That greater entity would become whole. Healed. Able to share reality as Worlders did, able to control reality as technological man did. Complete, at last. Restored, and shining, and healed.

That, and no less, was his mission.

A deep peace filled David. He squeezed Enli's hand once more, then stood and stretched. At his full height, his fingers brushed the top of the cave, smooth and burnished as glass. Looking down, he found the seated Bazargan watching him, empty expando in hand. Bazargan wore David's discarded s-suit. Fitting. David smiled at him. Not even Bazargan could bother him now. Bazargan was merely a middle-aged administrator. He, David Allen Campbell, was beyond Bazargan, above him. Beyond irritation at Gruber, beyond jealousy over Ann. He was the selected one, the means to heal the sentient universe.

Him.

"Are you all right, David?" Bazargan asked quietly.

"Of course."

There was a little pause before Gruber said, "Then if we are all ready, let's go. We need a place above ground to raise the *Zeus* and find out what the hell is happening."

"Enli," Pek Bazargan said to her in a low voice, "what was Pek Allen talking to you about this morning?"

They had been walking only a short time, and the tunnel clearly led upward. But it was not as smooth as yesterday's tunnels. Pek Allen, without one of the strange Terran suits, walked directly behind Pek Gruber. Then came Pek Sikorski, Enli, and Pek Bazargan. There was no way Pek Allen could hear what the head of his household had just asked.

"His dreams wilted him," Enli answered. "I woke him." Who, she wondered, complained in Pek Allen's dreams? Did the unreal Terrans have their own unreal dead wander and moan through dreams? The thought made her head hurt.

She had no government pills left.

Pek Bazargan said, "Did he say what his dream was about?"

No, he—" A sudden stab in her gut made her stop.

"Enli? What is it?"

Another pain, flooding her gut, overwhelming the pain in her head. Hurriedly Enli fumbled at the close-fitting suit.

"What? Tell me!"

"Diarrhea," she said in World, working faster to strip off the constricting suit. From Pek Bazargan's face, it was clear he didn't know the word. Enli didn't know it in Terran. She said, "Loose bowels like smelly water . . . Oh!" It hurt.

To her surprise, Pek Bazargan looked embarrassed. Why?

Diarrhea was normal, was part of shared reality. His embarrassment must be because he was unreal.

Now the pain in her head outweighed even the one in her gut.

"Dieter, wait," Pek Bazargan called. "Enli has . . . a personal problem."

He walked quickly away from her, along the tunnel after the others. Enli turned off her light and squatted. Until now everyone had used a designated alcove or side tunnel for this, but there were no alcoves or side tunnels here. The smell was terrible. Enli hoped they would not have to retrace their steps for any reason. And then she could hope nothing, overtaken by a wave of nausea. Her bowels were being torn loose inside her body. She gasped.

"Enli, it's Ann." She shone her light obliquely on the tunnel wall, rather than on Enli. "Do you need help?"

"No, I . . . I'm all right."

"We'll wait for you around the bend in the tunnel."

It took Enli a long time, and the bout left her weak. Leaning against the tunnel wall, she finally lurched after the others. Her legs felt watery, and she carried her Terran suit, afraid of another attack.

"Enli?" Pek Allen said softly. The males held scarves of thin cloth over their mouths and noses.

"I'm . . . all right."

"No, you're not," said Pek Sikorski, the healer. "Come, lean on me. Dieter's instruments say there's a larger cavern ahead."

"Don't . . . talk," Enli pleaded, too exhausted to even say *please*. But if Pek Sikorski—any of them—said anything to violate shared reality and make her head ache again . . . Her gut twisted once more.

"I won't talk, Enli. Come on, dear. Go slow."

They hobbled forward, Enli leaning on the Terran. The alien, unreal, kind Terran female, whose arms felt warm on Enli's cold, suitless skin. Enli let all thought melt, puddle formlessly into Pek Sikorski's warmth.

Until the tunnel abruptly ended.

"Verdammt," Pek Gruber muttered. "The display indicated . . . Wait, here it is."

He shone his powerful torch upward. Just above the height of their heads, the light showed a narrow opening about the width and height of a man's shoulders. Gruber jumped, angling his torch into it. He landed unevenly on the broken rock of the tunnel floor and crashed sideways into the wall.

"Dieter!"

"I'm fine, Ann," he said crossly, rubbing his shoulder. "But that's the connection to the next cave, I'm afraid. I don't think it's very long, but I can't be sure; the radiation affects the instrument."

"How much radiation?" Pek Bazargan said.

"Not too much . . . yet. Still, Enli should put on her suit now."

Enli shook her head. She feared another attack of diarrhea.

Pek Gruber said, "I think first I should see how long the tunnel is, and how wide. This may be the worst piece. David, if you will."

Pek Allen stepped forward. He had said nothing as they walked, but now Enli could see his face. He was smiling. In the weird shadows reflected off the cave wall, his smile looked exultant, as if he had just had a great triumph of some sort. What sort? It made no sense, these Terrans made no sense, of course not what did she expect, they were unreal . . .

"Steady, Enli," Pek Sikorski said, "I'm here," and once more the kindness brought Enli back from the brink, anchoring her before she fell into the abyss.

Pek Allen cupped his hands, Pek Gruber stepped into them, and the younger human threw Pek Gruber upward. He shoved his body into the opening. For a moment Enli thought his shoulders were too wide, but as the four others stood below him, shadowy in their lesser torches, Pek Gruber's body wriggled forward like a fish until his torso disappeared. Then his legs, his feet . . . He had wriggled into the rock.

No one spoke until Pek Sikorski whispered, "If he gets stuck . . ."

"He's an experienced spelunker," Pek Allen said, and his

exultant voice matched his exultant smile. "But if he gets stuck, I'll go in and pull him out. Easy!"

Pek Bazargan turned to look hard at Pek Allen.

Time crawled by. No one spoke. Pek Sikorski pulled Enli to sit down, and Pek Bazargan joined them. Only Pek Allen stayed standing, smiling, his eyes blinking rapidly.

"*Ja!*" Finally a shout came from the tunnel, muffled by stone. More minutes, and Pek Gruber's face reappeared at the high opening, dirty and grinning. "You must see to believe it! Come, it is not so long a tunnel. Not even seventy yards. And not much tighter than this."

Pek Allen demanded, "See what?"

"I won't tell you, but it's wonderful. And a space beyond open to the sky. With more water." More and more of him protruded from the opening: head, shoulders, torso, hips, until Enli thought he surely must topple forward and fall to the tunnel floor. But Pek Allen reached out, Pek Gruber embraced him, and Pek Gruber was drawn out of stone like a plug from a pel bottle.

"Ann, you first. Then Ahmed and Enli. David and I can help get you up, and we will come last."

Pek Sikorski said, "Enli is still sick, I think. It's the protein powders. Her system apparently can't handle them. But I thought she needed to eat something, and took the gamble. Only—"

"Enli," Pek Allen said, kneeling in front of her, "are you sick still? More diarrhea?" He used the World word; unlike the others, he knew it. Of course, he had worked in the crelm house, with babies. She nodded at him.

"Would you rather wait until the sickness passes?"

"I'll wait with her," Pek Sikorski said.

"You can't," Pek Allen said, and Enli wondered briefly why Pek Bazargan wasn't giving the orders. "You couldn't get her back through that high hole."

"Yes, I could," Pek Sikorski said, flushing slightly. "You underestimate my strength, David."

"Ann," Pek Bazargan began, just as Pek Gruber said impatiently, "It isn't—"

"I am not staying here," Enli said loudly, in World. These Terrans, they acted as if she were a child. She was not a child; she was the only real person here. And she was not staying in this dark cramped place when there was a larger place beyond open to the sky. Diarrhea or not. Although now that she had spoken up, the attack in her gut actually seemed to be subsiding.

For a moment all the Terrans stared at her from their light, depthless eyes. Then Pek Gruber nodded. "Enli may choose for herself. Like the rest of us."

Did he have any idea how alien he sounded, how unreal? One did not choose reality; it simply *was*. Once again pain stabbed her head.

"You are hurting her, Dieter," Pek Bazargan said quietly. "Just start the lifting."

Pek Gruber cupped his hands. Pek Sikorski was thrown up to the hole, caught the edge of rock, and began to wiggle forward until her feet disappeared. Enli stood and pulled on the suit she had peeled off before.

"Ahmed," Pek Gruber said.

"I can't."

Pek Gruber and Pek Allen turned to look at him. Pek Bazargan was very pale, even for a Terran, and his face sweated. Enli could see the bare skin of his neck, where there should have been fur, pulse rapidly.

"I have . . . difficulties with tunnels. I've managed so far, but that opening is so small . . . trapped in rock. I can't." He shuddered violently.

It was the first time Enli had ever seen Pek Bazargan show weakness. Apparently also for the Terrans. Pek Gruber frowned. Pek Allen once again got that strange, exultant smile, and he rose forward on his toes. Enli had never seen anyone do that before: rock themselves higher, then drop, again and again.

"I'm sorry," Pek Bazargan whispered. "I can't."

"Then stay here," Pek Allen said easily. "We'll come back for you the way we came, from the outside, after we finish in these mountains and this conspiracy is finally finished."

" *'Conspiracy'?* " Enli didn't know the Terran word.

"There is no conspiracy, David," Pek Gruber snapped. "Ahmed, you *are* coming. We need you to raise the *Zeus*. And—"

"You can take the—"

"—you're going through if David and I have to stuff you by force into that tunnel."

Pek Allen stopped rocking on his toes. His smile broadened, changed, until Enli had to look away. Pek Allen *wanted* to stuff Pek Bazargan by force into the tunnel. He would enjoy it. Pek Bazargan looked bleakly from one Terran to the other.

"You mean it, Dieter."

"I mean it. I know you, Ahmed. I know you are not a coward."

Bazargan, pale and sweating, smiled. "I am too old to be shamed by a young man's dare, Dieter."

"Nonetheless, you are going."

Pek Gruber was like a *tumban*, Enli thought. She had seen one once, in a traveling zoo. The stupid, tough-hided animal began walking in a straight line, eating leaves as it went, and nothing could make it turn aside. It plodded through swamps, through thorns, through the smoking embers of fire. There were people like that on World; her sister's husband's sister was like that. And so was Pek Gruber, this unreal Terran.

Who had seemed increasingly real to her, Enli Pek Brimmidin.

He was not much different from Ano's marriage-sister.

This time she expected the sharp hard pain in her skull. She was even braced against it, she discovered, although not by nearly enough. Through a shaking blur she watched Pek Bazargan step shakily onto Pek Gruber's cupped hands, falter, try again. On the second throw he caught the edge of the rock. For a long time he hung there, head and enough torso to balance himself inside the tunnel, buttocks and legs and feet dangling helplessly. The feet flailed. Pek Bazargan was trying to back out. Pek Allen sprang upward and shoved the buttocks, hard.

"David, *verdammt*—be careful of him!"

"Conspirators don't deserve care," said Pek Allen, with vicious glee. Pek Gruber clenched his fists, stopped, looked at the high tunnel. Pek Bazargan's flailing feet disappeared slowly into the hole.

"Enli," Pek Allen said, and for a moment fear swamped her stabbing headpain. Would he stuff her in like that? But Pek Allen was gentle, cupping his hands and raising her carefully, while Pek Gruber steadied her. Enli's bowels gave a sudden lurch but then settled down. She caught the edge of rock and began to wriggle forward.

The headpain, she discovered, was gone. It had vanished when Pek Allen's cupped palms had cradled the bottom of her feet, and Pek Gruber's big, calloused hands had steadied her hips. Pek Gruber was a *tumban*, and the blooms in Pek Allen's mind grew crazily. Pek Bazargan was a coward. Pek Sikorski, kind as she was, was capable of violating reality. They were all capable of violating reality, even among themselves (how?). But they were here, solid as the warmth of hands under her feet, and each had a soul, however weird and strange. They acted like people—thought and argued and planted and reaped and gardened each other, unlike those poor empty children who must be destroyed because they were unreal. Those children did not nurture anyone, or feud with anyone, or hope for anything, or plan for anyone else. The Terrans did all these people things. Enli had *seen* them do all these people things. She had groped her way through shadowy tunnels with them, felt their individual souls bump and caress and pierce her own—in ways the priests had not.

Enli pulled herself along the hard stone. She was an informant. Very well, she had informed herself. Gathered information and looked at it hard and there it was, unwelcome and inescapable as the decay of a flower.

The Terrans were real.

EIGHTEEN

EN ROUTE TO SPACE
TUNNEL #438

Three days and two hours out toward the space tunnel. Two days and fifteen hours left to go.

Syree had hardly slept, even though no glitch had developed in the arduous process of moving Orbital Object #7. They hadn't yet covered even a third of the distance. Velocity had now reached two thousand six hundred klicks per second. Still Syree found herself silently urging—*faster, faster*—a pointless emotional exercise. The *Zeus* was delivering all the power she could.

The ship had not shaken apart, although she was severely strained. If she could keep it up for another two days and fifteen hours, they could cut power and let inertia carry Orbital Object #7 through the space tunnel at 4,873 clicks per second.

If, of course, Orbital Object #7 would go through at all.

Syree had, for lack of anything else to do, run the equations dozens of ways, with dozens of variables, hopeful estimates, downright fudge factors. If the capacity of this particular space tunnel varied by only three percent from all the other space tunnels . . . if the standard capacity estimate by Martian engineers was off by only two percent . . . if the mass of the artifact was four percent less than they'd determined . . .

None of it made any real difference. Any mass had an associated Schwarzschild radius, defined as the radius below which, if you squeezed the object enough, it would become a black hole. That was what had happened to the *Anaconda* fifty-three years ago. It was what would happen to the artifact as well. Unless the equations had a loophole in them that human physicists didn't know about.

Loopholes existed. Otherwise, the Fallers could not have constructed their wave-phase alterer. And humans knew so very little about the artifact, which had been constructed by the same vanished beings who had created the space tunnels. Probably. So maybe it was possible that Orbital Object #7 would go through Entrypoint #438 when another object of equal mass but different origin would be compressed to a tiny black hole.

But not according to the equations.

At least if Orbital Object #7 was destroyed, the Fallers wouldn't get it. And there was that small chance of an unaccounted-for variable that would send the artifact careening out the other side.

"Communication signal from the *Hermes,* sir," said Lee, seated in front of his displays on the bridge.

"Play communication," Peres said. Everyone on the bridge paused to listen.

The *Hermes,* the *Zeus*'s tiny flyer, should be rapidly approaching the tunnel, eight hundred and fifty million clicks ahead of the *Zeus.* The flyer pilot, Lieutenant Amalie Schuyler, had been punishing herself with far too many gees in order to reach the tunnel this far in advance of the parent ship. Whatever she had to say had been forty-seven minutes getting to the *Zeus.*

"Hello, Commander," she said, and Syree recognized in Lieutenant Schuyler's labored voice the sound of a human body that could not take much more. "By the time you get this, I should be through the tunnel. It's less than a minute ahead of me now. No problems with the flight, no sign of the enemy. Instructions for Caligula Command understood and unchanged. Good luck to you all back there. Out."

Lee grinned at Syree. *So far, so good.* And by now Amalie

was safe in human-held Caligula space, beyond the tunnel. Caligula system was a military outpost; it kept a manned flyer in constant orbit around its side of the space tunnel. Lieutenant Schuyler would report to the flyer pilot, who would then relay the information to Caligula Command in plenty of time to act on it.

"All plans in order," Peres said to the bridge at large. His voice held less satisfaction than Amalie Schuyler's. The *Zeus*'s part of "all plans" was considerably more ambiguous than was the *Hermes*'.

By flying through Space Tunnel #438, the *Hermes* had assured that the next tunnel-virgin object would also materialize in Caligula space. That might be the artifact, but neither Syree nor Peres really believed it. The Fallers understood the habits of space tunnels as well as humans did (maybe better, given the new wave-phase alterer). Sooner or later—probably sooner—a Faller craft would emerge from the space tunnel. It would then go back through, so that whatever sailed into the tunnel after it would end up in Faller, not human, space.

The *Hermes* carried orders designed to keep that from happening. Syree had calculated the *Zeus*-cum-artifact's velocity, time, and distance out to the eighth decimal. If nothing disturbed the towing operation, the artifact would zoom into Space Tunnel #438 two days, fifteen hours, fifty-seven minutes, and three seconds from now, at 14: 37 hours ship time. Five minutes before that, per Lieutenant Schuyler's instructions, a flyer would dart from Caligula space into the tunnel, to emerge in this star system. It would then immediately dart back, "paving" the way for the artifact to follow it.

The Fallers might well anticipate this maneuver, of course. They had proven good strategists in the past. Thus, a second human flyer would also dart in and out from Caligula space four minutes after the first one, and only sixty seconds before the artifact reached the tunnel.

"Sixty seconds?" Peres had said, when Syree showed him her calculations. "Can we cut it that close, Colonel?"

"Yes," Syree said, with more confidence than she felt. The

numbers were solid, but reality had a way of intruding variables not in the numbers. She did not say this.

"So we detach the artifact at the last minute," Peres had said, "and it goes through into Caligula space. Then what?"

But to that, there had been no real answer. Lieutenant Schuyler had been briefed to warn Caligula Command that they might receive an invaluable alien weapon. Or a tiny black hole, perhaps traveling at 4,873 clicks per second. Or a powerful wave that destabilized nuclei of elements with an atomic number above seventy-five. Or nothing at all.

Meanwhile, key officers lived on the bridge, sleeping in chairs, unwashed and unsmiling. And all the while the great gray sphere filled the viewscreen, blotting out the stars.

"Lunch, sir." A soldier from the galley crew, carrying a large covered tray. Hot fragrant odors drifted through the bridge. The crewman set down the tray and uncovered it.

"Thank you," Peres said. "Dismissed."

Lee picked up a hot sandwich and took a big bite. Syree made herself eat another one. She couldn't have told what it was, except fuel.

Major Ombatu, whose spirits had evidently not been lifted by the *Hermes* message, said irritably, "I can't eat with that smell in here. Somebody needs to wash."

"Shut up, Ombatu."

"Don't," Ombatu said evenly, "tell me what to do, Lee."

They looked at each other in contempt, the pointless contempt of people together too long, under too great a strain, who nonetheless needed each other. Everyone needed to wash. No one wanted to leave the bridge long enough, even though nothing untoward had happened.

And then, seven hours later, it did.

Executive Officer Debra Puchalla had the conn. She said to Peres, who was lying down but not sleeping on a recliner in a corner of the bridge, "Sir! Object has just emerged from Space Tunnel #438 . . . getting a signature . . . it's a skeeter."

"Fallers," Peres said. "Direction?"

"Toward us . . . wait . . . second object emerged. Getting a signature . . . a Faller warship."

Peres and Syree both moved to the displays. The two enemy crafts, dots on a screen, were diverging. The skeeter hung motionless near the space tunnel, ready to dart back through. The warship began to move toward the *Zeus*. Undoubtedly the Fallers had identified the *Zeus*'s signature and had found it (surprise!) to have increased in mass by a factor of nineteen. The enemy now knew what the humans were doing. Their next step would be to prevent the *Zeus* from doing it.

"Commander," Puchalla said, "change in enemy direction. Skeeter is retreating . . . moving closer to the space tunnel . . . there, she's gone through."

"Heading back to Faller space to report," Peres said. Of course, Syree knew that what he'd meant to say was that the skeeter had already disappeared into the tunnel forty-three minutes ago. All their information was old, limited by c. As the space tunnels themselves somehow were not.

Puchalla said, "Enemy warship advancing. Enemy acceleration is two gee . . . present distance seven hundred eighty million and—"

"Turn off ship drive," Peres said.

Syree said swiftly, "Wait, Commander." The *Zeus* was an ant laboring along under a carefully balanced cantaloupe, but she couldn't allow the cantaloupe to be dropped just yet. "One moment, please!"

"Belay that last," Peres said to Puchalla. He swiveled to fully face Syree. "Dr. Johnson?"

The title said volumes; Peres was reminding her she was a project specialist here, not a line officer. She nodded. "Commander, I would guess you want to turn off the drive and detach the artifact. Let it sail on its trajectory to the space tunnel without us, so the *Zeus* is free to fight. But if you detach now, the artifact will be traveling at . . . just one moment . . ."

Furiously she keyed in the data, ran the equation. "If you detach now, the artifact will continue at our present velocity, two thousand eight hundred sixty clicks per second. Instead of the four thousand eight hundred seventy-three it will reach if the *Zeus* continues to accelerate it. At the reduced speed, the artifact will take another . . . just a second . . . another four days, fifteen hours to get to space tunnel. But *if* we can keep accelerating it as long as possible, we can cut the time it will take by a multiple factor."

"Dr. Johnson, we're under attack!"

"Not yet. The skeeter has gone. And when we get within the warship's firing range—even allowing for a comfortable margin for the unknown—we can detach the artifact. Just not yet. Even one more hour of acceleration will boost its velocity by another thirty-six clicks per second. With ten hours, we could get it up to three thousand two hundred sixteen clicks a second. And still give us time to detach and maneuver. To detonate, if that's what you choose."

Peres was silent. Considering? Syree rushed on.

"And remember, our flyers will come through at the designated time. The smaller the time interval between our flyers' appearances and the artifact's hitting the tunnel, the less chance of another Faller craft emerging and diverting the artifact to enemy space. To keep that time interval short, we have to keep accelerating the artifact as long as possible."

Peres scowled. "Do you really think the Fallers, now that they're here, will allow that to happen? They'll fire on the artifact just before it goes into the space tunnel, if they have to. They'll blow it up."

"They might try. But we don't really *know* what will happen between now and then. Until we do, continuing to accelerate the artifact loses us nothing and gains us shortened time for the Fallers to do anything more to us. And if we're attached to the artifact, and they want it, they're less likely to attack us, at least until we're much closer to the space tunnel and they see they have no choice. And at that point, of course, we've also moved the detonators on the artifact a lot closer to the enemy ship."

Peres looked thoughtful. "If we detonate just minutes before the artifact reaches the space tunnel . . . if we do that, can we get the Faller ship in the same detonation?"

"Depends on how close they stay to the space tunnel. But

it's at least a possibility. One we don't have if we detach and detonate now."

Peres considered. Syree held her breath.

"All right," he finally said. "We'll continue acceleration. For now, anyway. Unless the situation changes."

"Thank you, sir," Syree said, swallowing her pride. His decision, and she knew she must acknowledge that or risk looking like someone trying to jump the chain of command.

"Helsman, continue course and acceleration."

"Continuing acceleration."

"Ms. Puchalla, arm all weapon systems. Crew to battle stations."

"All weapon systems arming."

The *Zeus* was a retrofitted military cruiser, supposedly on a scientific mission. Syree doubted that under any circumstances could her weapons match those of a Faller warship. But right now her attention was fastened on Orbital Object #7. She had saved it, at least for some unknown stretch of time. Throughout the *Zeus,* battle-station Klaxons sounded.

"Weapon status."

"All weapon systems armed and ready. Enemy speed change . . . wait . . . he's decelerating, Commander . . . hard deceleration . . . stationary position. Enemy position: two hundred clicks from Space Tunnel #438, ninety degrees lateral to trajectory of artifact."

Almost eight hundred million kilometers apart, the two ships tracked each other. Their data was forty-three minutes old, but it served for cat-and-mouse. The cat stationary by the hole, the mouse moving faster and faster. And carrying a cantaloupe. Syree repressed her own mental image; Grandmother Emily would not have approved.

Peres said, "Dr. Johnson, calculate time and position of detonation of the artifact for maximum effect on the Faller warship, assuming it does not change position, and also assuming the artifact continues to be accelerated by the Zeus until we're a hundred clicks outside known enemy firing range."

"Yes, sir." Syree began the calculations.

Keep moving. One of the oldest of military dicta. Keep moving, stay out of easy range of the enemy, be prepared for changes in the enemy's tactics.

But in this case, Syree thought, the enemy had no reason to change tactics. Unless they suspected the artifact was rigged to detonate, which they might or might not suspect. If they did, probably they would let the artifact get only so close to the space tunnel before they attacked. But how close was that?

No way to know until the Faller ship moved.

And until it did, Orbital Object #7, formerly the planetary moon Tas, continued to be shoved along through space. Still intact, and still up for grabs.

NINETEEN

IN THE NEURY MOUNTAINS

The rock closed around him, suffocating him.

Bazargan could feel it in his throat, his lungs. He couldn't breathe. The cold smell of damp stone choked him, as all around him the relentless rock crushed his body to pulp . . .

Bazargan squeezed his eyes shut and stopped wriggling forward. He couldn't do this. Already his shoulders touched both rough sides of the tunnel, and ahead the passage grew even narrower. *He couldn't do this*. Rock was choking him, crushing him, and he would die here. He couldn't make himself move forward. Wave after wave of nausea swept him, and his heart hammered so hard it felt close to bursting. Sweat, unnaturally cold, streamed into his eyes.

He couldn't do this. He was going into shock, and he would die here.

Frantically he stabbed through his mind, looking for something—anything—to save himself. Could thoughts stop your body from going into shock? He had no neuropharms to stave off shock, he seldom used neuropharms, it was people like David Allen who relied on them. Americans, used to the easy, the luxurious. He was Iranian, he didn't need neuropharms, he needed . . .

What? He was going to die here. He couldn't do this. Something—anything—to grasp on to—

Give never the wine bowl from thy hand,/ Nor loose thy grasp on the rose's stem . . .

The rose's stem! Behind closed eyelids Bazargan pictured that stem, reached for it with cold fingers scrabbling on cold rock.

He couldn't remember the rest of the poem. Hafiz, the greatest of the Persian lyric poets, and Bazargan couldn't remember the poem. But the rose itself was still there, hold the rose . . . There were other poems . . .

How sweet the gale of morning breathes!/ Sweet news of my delight he brings . . .

Breathe in the gale of morning. Fresh air, sweet, smelling of flowers and dew . . .

News that the rose will soon approach/ the tuneful bird of night he brings—

Hold the rose. Smell it, stroke the silky petal, hear the nightingale sing high and sharp and sweet.

Ahmed Bazargan's heart slowed, a small slowing, but perceptible. The clammy coldness pressing on his body eased slightly. He was not in a crushing tunnel with tons of rock above him, he was in a morning garden. Birds sang. Roses released clouds of scent as he bent over them.

. . . odor to the rose-bud's veil, and jasmine's mantle white, he brings . . .

Jasmine. Yes. The long slender leaves, the white fragrant flowers.

Bazargan advanced through the garden. Leisurely, drinking in every morning moment, every scent and smell and sound. Pomegranate, rose, jasmine, almond. The garden sown of poetry was the most vivid and solid he had ever known, each drop of dew etched in crystal, every petal glowing with bright color. He advanced through this garden picking the flowers, holding them with warm living fingers: Mind the thorns, place the white lilies beside the red roses and savor the velvety contrast, breathe deeply of the glorious perfumes . . .

With every fiber of his being, blind to any other reality,

Ahmed Bazargan created the garden. And got himself through the tunnel.

"Ahmed! Ahmed!"

Slowly he came to. He sat with his back to stone. Ann bent over him, a small metal instrument at his heart. Behind her crowded Dieter and David and Enli. David's tunic was torn to shreds and blood smeared his shoulders. Of course—he had scraped through that narrow space without a suit.

Ann said, "You fainted, at the end of the tunnel. Do you remember?"

He didn't. Ann nodded, reassured by whatever she saw on her miniature display. "You seem all right now. No headache? Nausea? Coldness?"

"I'm not in shock."

"No, you're not. And you're here, that's the important thing. We're all here."

"Look!" Dieter said, and stepped aside so he no longer blocked Bazargan's view. David Allen had already turned away, looking disdainful. His tunic back fluttered in bloody ribbons. Gruber switched on his powerful torch, and Bazargan gasped. He staggered to his feet.

They stood in Aladdin's cave, in a bey's treasure room. Jewels sparkled on the cave ceiling, on the walls, in heaps on the floor. As Bazargan's dazzled eyes adjusted to the bright light, he saw that the jewels were millions of gold crystals. Spattered among them were glowing flakes of pure gold as big as thumbnails. Gold nuggets glittered on the floor. Piles of white quartz sand glowed like spun glass.

"It's a vug," Dieter said happily. "Although I've never heard of one this big."

"A what?" Bazargan said. The cavern must be twenty feet high, twenty-five feet in radius.

"A vug. Actually, it's the inside of a geode. There must have been the caldera of a volcano right here once. The gold precipitates out from circulating water heated by magma."

Bazargan touched a wall. Gold flaked over his fingers like shining rain.

"It's incredible."

"Is it not?" Gruber said, swinging his torch proprietarily around the walls.

"You don't understand me," Bazargan said. "I mean, it is incredible that this has been here—how long, Dieter?"

"Hundreds of thousands of years."

"—and no one of World has ever explored it, come here, mined the gold."

Allen said scornfully, "Gold is not a monetary standard on World."

"No," Bazargan answered. "But it is used in jewelry and other decoration. This could have made—could still make—someone very wealthy."

"No," Ann said. "No trader would violate the sacred mountains by coming here, or taking anything away."

Enli nodded. "I am the only Worlder who will ever see this."

She said it with a new authority that made them all turn to study her. Small, squat, her drab neckfur matted and dusted with stone powder, Enli gazed calmly at the sparkling forbidden heart of her planet's beliefs. In the silence Bazargan suddenly became aware of water dripping somewhere.

"Enli," Ann said, "are you all right? Do you have headpain?"

"Yes," Enli said clearly. "I do. But I am all right."

Something had happened to this alien girl. Bazargan could not imagine what.

David Allen said, not bothering to hide his contempt, "Worlders know they have a far greater treasure than shiny stones."

Gruber turned to geological matters. "The radioactivity isn't too pronounced here. You should be all right, David, without a suit. But the rate of thermal gradient has decreased. I still don't understand this. The rate should increase as we go higher, decrease as we descend. And it is the opposite." He frowned at his wrist display.

Bazargan said, "Tell me again why that should happen."

"On every planet we've surveyed, there is very slow radioactivity in the rock near the surface. The disintegration produces small amounts of heat, which accumulates over millions of years—rock is an excellent insulator, you know. But this rate of temperature rise decreases as you descend, since there is not much radioactivity in the deeper layers. But not here."

Ann said, "Does that mean there is something radioactive buried in these mountains?"

"Possibly," Dieter said. "But it would have to be very large to generate such a rate increase. Or very unusual."

"But," Bazargan said—the expression on Dieter's face told him this was important, even though Bazargan would rather get on with more immediate concerns—"don't we already know that the Neury Mountains are unusually radioactive? Dr. Johnson said something about neutrino flow from here, back on the *Zeus* . . ."

"Yes. But not so localized as this must be in order to cause this sort of thermal effect. There is something very small but very powerful radiating in these mountains, and doing it so unevenly . . . Some of the variation is due to the different insulating properties of the rock. You have so much here: light basalt and heavy granite, pahoehoe flows and aa flows, all a chronological jumble."

"Well, then—"

"But not all due to difference in rock composition, no. Not all. And the distribution of radioactivity, too—it is very strange."

"Yes," Bazargan said. "If you say so. But now we must move on, Dieter."

The geologist continued to frown at his display, calling up different combinations of data. Bazargan sighed inwardly. He still felt shaky and light-headed and very, very tired. Around him the gorgeous golden cavern sparkled like something from a fairy tale, but all four humans in it looked like what they were: misplaced, battered, and desperate.

David Allen stood at the far edge of the vug, talking quietly to Enli. Bazargan couldn't see her face, but he saw David's.

His upper lip twitched convulsively, in contrast to his strange, omnipresent smile and the angry slant of his eyebrows. The bloody tatters of his shirt made him look like some maimed harlequin.

"Dieter," Ann said, "Ahmed wants us to go. You said there was an open space to raise the *Zeus*? And water, so we can eat?"

Reluctantly, Gruber put away his data and led them on. The next tunnel, Bazargan was grateful to see, was tall enough to stand up in. But the bottom quickly became full of cold water covering broken, slippery rocks. Twice Bazargan slipped, soaking himself. His suit kept him warm enough, but he was so tired. The tunnel seemed to go on forever.

Something living slithered away from him in the water.

Here? Inside a mountain? But then the tunnel turned at almost a ninety-degree angle and abruptly they were out.

He stood under a heavy overhang of rock in what looked at first like another cavern. But as his eyes adjusted, Bazargan saw that instead it was another high, open rift in the mountains, larger than the last one. Almost a hidden upland valley. Stars glowed in a clear night sky.

Night again. He had lost track of time.

Gruber swept his torch over the small valley. The dark low shapes of vegetation dotted the ground. He led them between shoulder-high bushes to a small waterfall tumbling out of rock wall.

"We can camp here," Gruber said, "after I test the water. Look, the overhang here is much drier, and there are dry alcoves under it. David, it is your turn for my suit, I think, although the radiation is not bad here."

David Allen's eyes blazed. "I don't want your stinking suit! Do you think I don't know what you're up to, you bastard?" He stalked off in the darkness.

Gruber said, with heavy sarcasm, "And what am I supposed to be up to now?"

"Nothing," Bazargan said wearily. "No, Ann, don't go after him. Let's just make camp and call the *Zeus*."

Gruber, still angry, said, "What is his problem, anyway?"

Unexpectedly, Ann answered. Her voice was somber. "Grandiose paranoid schizophrenia, I think. David's daily Discipline mix was pretty heavy, and now he's without it."

"Grandiose paranoid schizophrenia?" Gruber said. "You mean he thinks he's Napoleon and we're all out to assassinate him?"

Bazargan couldn't summon a smile. "Not quite that bad. But Ann is right. Enli, what was he talking with you about in the golden cavern?"

The little alien said, "About the headpain of unshared reality. Whether I have it now."

Bazargan had to know. "And do you?"

"Yes. But different. Shared reality has shifted. Reality is different now."

She spoke quietly, but a little silence followed her words. Ann put her hand on Enli's shoulder. Gruber, immune to nuance, burst out, "How the hell did Allen get on this expedition in the first place?"

His father arranged it for him, Bazargan thought but didn't say. Germans understood more than Americans about the obligations of family, but not much more. Bazargan was so tired. But he pulled out the official comlink while they were in the open.

The *Zeus* did not answer.

"All right," Gruber said, "let's make camp. Over there is— Enli? What is it? What's the matter?"

That Gruber noticed someone else's emotional state made Bazargan turn quickly. Enli stood at the edge of the circle of Gruber's torchlight, her face turned up to the sky. "The moon . . . the moon is *leaving*."

In the sky just above the towering rock, one of World's moons moved. It took Bazargan a moment to realize that this was one of the "fast-blooming" moons—didn't it usually cross the sky every few hours? Yes. And it moved so fast it was retrograde. Now it stood almost still except for an almost imperceptible inching in the direction of the zenith.

"The artifact," Gruber said.

"Tas," Enli said, dazed. "Tas is leaving us."

"The Terrans in the big flying boat are moving it out of orbit," Gruber told her, with what he probably thought was great sensitivity. "You remember, we told Voratur. You were there."

Enli didn't answer. That night—only two days ago?—burned Bazargan's mind. Ben, Bonnie, the blood on the yellow nightdress . . . he'd pushed it out of his mind. But that never worked for long.

Ann said in her imperfect World, "Enli, I have no doses like government pills, but I can to give you something to sleep, to escape the headpain that way."

Enli said, "I'm not in pain." Then, tearing her eyes away from the sky, "Here I'm not in headpain. No headpain. Not since the littlest tunnel."

Even in the gloom, Bazargan could see Ann's eyes sharpen. "No pain? None?"

"None," Enli said. "It is different now."

"*Why* is it different? Why, Enli?"

Enli repeated her earlier words, "Shared reality is different now," but Ann apparently found that inadequate. She turned swiftly to Gruber. "Dieter?"

He already had out his handheld. "*Lieber Gott!* Look at this!"

"At what?" Bazargan said.

"The radioactivity—it has ceased. It was detectable earlier, but now—" He began walking around the rocky valley with his handheld, taking the torch with him. Bazargan, Ann, and Enli waited in the dark. It seemed to Bazargan that the moon was moving faster now, although perhaps that was just his imagination.

David still brooded somewhere out there in the darkness, pacing and twitching. *Grandiose paranoid schizophrenia. Masked by the Discipline, until now.*

The prices we end up paying for the technology that forms us.

Gruber returned. "Listen, Ann. The geothermal distribution makes a toroidal pattern. You know, like a doughnut, with an empty center. The thickest part graphs to where we all blanked out yesterday and couldn't think, except Enli. And now we're in the very center of the distribution."

"I don't understand," Ann said.

Bazargan said, "You mean the heat distribution and the . . . the thinking disruptions are related? When we couldn't think clearly, *and* now when Enli has no shared-reality mechanism?"

"Yes," Gruber said. "According to the data."

"That's not possible," Ann said reasonably. "Dieter, did you check for a second field, an electromagnetic one, perhaps generated by the first field?"

"Yes, yes. It is not electromagnetic. I don't know what this is. There is nothing like it in nature. Or not in nature! It is more like . . . like a hurricane. A still eye, then wind force increasing in strength and area, then decreasing again."

Bazargan, no physicist even when not exhausted, struggled to follow Gruber's thoughts. "A hurricane. But not winds. What does this force *do*? I mean, how?"

"I don't know. I don't know at all."

Ann burst out, "If only I had my Lagerfeld equipment! If only I could scan all of our brains at various places! Dieter, do you think—"

Gruber wasn't listening. He keyed rapidly on his handheld, studied the results, and walked off. In a few minutes he was back.

"The center. It *is* there, whatever it is."

"Where?"

"Underground, straight down from here. About a quarter kilometer down."

Relief filled Bazargan. A quarter kilometer was too deep for Gruber to start digging with a forked stick. But then Gruber said, "There are so many passages downward. But how to find the right one?"

"No," Bazargan said, surprising himself with the force and loudness of the word. "No, Dieter. Lateral tunnels are one thing. Spelunking down chutes and chimneys—I know how dangerous that is. And you don't have the right equipment. We can't afford to lose you."

"Ahmed, this thing down there is another artifact. Like the

space tunnels, like Tas. It's been there since before these mountains thrust up from the seabed, and it's still generating a type of field with totally new properties. This is the greatest potential discovery of the century . . . We must go investigate!"

"No. Eventually, perhaps, with an expedition equipped for drilling and spelunking, and after the proper permissions are worked out with both the Solar Alliance and Rafkit Seloe. Syree Johnson—"

"Damn Syree Johnson! This is mine!"

"This is World's," Bazargan said, and hoped Enli's English was not yet good enough to follow the debate. "Haven't we already done enough to World? We don't even know if the other artifact, Tas, is going to emit some sort of force that turns the whole planet into a radioactive morgue."

Gruber looked at Bazargan for a long time. Finally he nodded somberly. "You're right. We cannot bring a huge equipped drilling expedition to a place sacred to the Worlders."

Bazargan looked at him sharply—it just did not sound like Gruber—but before he could answer, Enli said, "Obri was the home of the First Flower, before she came down to unfold her petals and create World. Now the Neury Mountains are the home of her soul. If you dig up the mountains, the soul of the First Flower will wilt. And World will wilt with Her."

Ann said reassuringly, "No one will dig up the Neury Mountains, Enli."

"Yes," Enli said, and it was impossible to tell from her voice what the alien meant. Her reality was not theirs.

Something large crashed into an unseen bush. Bazargan said quickly, "Don't tell David about the toroidal field. Or the new artifact, or . . . anything. Not in his present state."

Ann and Gruber nodded. Again, Bazargan could not tell what Enli thought. Then David was with them.

"The *Zeus*?" he demanded.

"She doesn't answer," Bazargan said.

David nodded curtly. "Then make camp now. It's driest and most sheltered over here. Follow me."

"Meine Gott," Gruber said, "he acts like a general ordering around slaves."

"Let it go," Bazargan warned.

They unrolled their blankets at the back of a dry alcovelike crevice, about fifteen feet into the rock. Gruber left one of the smaller torches turned on: enough to see by, not too much to waste power. Dry now, warmed by his s-suit, fed with the water-expanded food powders, Bazargan tried to sleep. It should have been easy; he was exhausted. But his mind whirled.

Unknown forces. Underground, in the sky. The force of the Fallers against the *Zeus,* of Syree Johnson's "wave effect" against the Worlders, of David's unmedicated mind against itself. The force of Enli's religious faith, of her shared-reality mechanism, of whatever new reality was disrupting it. What did Enli make of that? Wasn't truth changed irrevocably for her now? She had gone into the Neury Mountains, and had not died. She had kept close to unreal persons, and her headaches had mysteriously ceased. She had seen Terrans, her intellectual and technological superiors, reduced to helpless zombies whom she had to lead by the hand. So much Enli had believed before had been proven untrue.

The untrue, Bazargan knew, was not always valueless. Not even when it was completely ungrounded in physical reality. It was the untruth of the morning garden that had gotten him through the tunnel.

Consider religious faith, an untruth the solar system had mostly outgrown. While it had lasted, while it had been believed, it had provided an alternate set of values to the ones rewarded by Darwinian reality. The world now rewarded push, shrewdness, money, power, single-mindedness, gregarious self-advancement. Religions—most of them, anyway—had promoted self-effacement, sacrifice, restraint. It had haloed in emotional glory the quiet life of duty, the sacrificial life of service to family, the altruistic life that did not wield money or power. From this everyone had benefited. The quiet wife and mother, the humble workman who could dedicate his work to his gods, the peacemaker who did not accumulate power but sought to defuse it. They could, thanks to their faith, measure themselves by something other than the pomp and fame celebrated by the world. When faith went, it was as if half of a balance had been sheared off.

How much of a balance were they shearing off for Enli? For all of World?

Assuming World survived human Darwinian reality at all.

Amid such troubled thoughts, Bazargan finally slept. When he awoke, the wide mouth of their cave showed daylight. He rose creaking—hard rock on old bones—and blinked sleepily. Abruptly he came fully awake.

Only Ann slept beside the glowing torch. Dieter Gruber, David Allen, and Enli were all gone.

He didn't find them anywhere in the small upland valley. Bazargan risked shouting. No one answered. He woke Ann, then took the torch and made himself go back through the half-submerged tunnel to the vug, thinking they might have gone to scrape gold off the walls . . . but Enli would not scrape gold off the sacred home of the First Flower. Gruber might have gone to collect samples, but he would not have taken Enli with him, let alone David. David had expressed contempt for mere gold.

They were not in the vug.

When he returned, wet and shaken, Ann waited for him at the tunnel entrance. Her hair hung lank around her drawn face. Bluish circles smudged the skin under her eyes.

"I inventoried the supplies," she told Bazargan. "They left us some of the food powder, one small torch, an expando for water, my medkit, and all the blankets. But . . ."

"But what?"

"They took Dieter's geology equipment, of course. But they also took his gun."

"The gun," Bazargan repeated stupidly.

"The one we didn't know he had. That he used to get us out of the Voratur household."

"Yes," Bazargan said wearily. *When faith went, it was as if half of a balance had been sheared off.* "I remember. The gun. But who has it, and for what?"

TWENTY

IN THE NEURY MOUNTAINS

Enli prepared herself to die, with rejoicing that she tried not to let Pek Allen see.

He had woken her in the sheltered cave, where she lay asleep in her strange Terran suit beside Pek Sikorski. So close was Ann that Enli could feel the woman's soft breath on her own cheek. But Ann had not stirred when Pek Allen leaned over Enli to put his lips to her ear and the *gun*—there was no World word—to her neck. "Come with me, Enli. Quietly. Now."

She had risen silently and moved with him out of the cave. Pek Bazargan and Pek Sikorski slept deeply. Enli didn't see Pek Gruber; he must be farther back. She and Pek Allen padded beyond the circle of light thrown by the torch, groped through the gloom beyond, and emerged into the deeper blackness of a starless night in the tiny mountain valley. The air smelled of coming rain. Pek Allen switched on his own torch, much less powerful than Pek Gruber's big one, and led her by the hand around the valley's perimeter to the tunnel leading to the vug. Only when they were inside did he speak to her again.

"Don't be frightened, Enli. I would never ever hurt you."

Enli nodded. She wasn't frightened. Whether Pek Allen

killed her, or she died in whatever plan he was trying to carry out, didn't matter. The important thing was that she was going to die here. Here, beyond the reach of the priests that would imprison her in chemicals and glass and so prevent her from rejoining her ancestors. Here, deep in the forbidden mountains, her body would decay and so release her soul, and Enli would rejoin her ancestors. It was a great gift Pek Allen was giving her.

Of course, there was still Tabor, imprisoned in chemicals and glass at Ano's house. But once Enli was safe in the spirit world, perhaps she could work to free Tabor from there. Such things were not unknown. Send dreams to the priests, trouble Ano's sleep (poor Ano), do what great and unknown things would be within her new powers, and their ancestors'. Yes, Pek Allen was Enli's savior, and her gratitude ran deep.

"You must see," Pek Allen went on, in his fluent World, "what's happening here. Of course you do, you can share reality. The others *can't*. Bazargan, Dieter, even Ann—you see that, of course. They're limited, narrow-visioned, evil. Yes, evil, Enli, like the bad unreal that disturb dreams. I've come to realize that. Bazargan in particular. He's in on the priests' conspiracy to keep human and Worlder from ever becoming one. He wants to prevent that so that together he and the priests can rule World!"

Enli nodded again. She didn't know the Terran word *evil*, but it didn't matter. Pek Allen was clearly crazed. The soil of his mind had soured, and the blooms growing from it were twisted and misshapen. Just looking at him, one would know that even though he had been real yesterday, something had happened to him during this dreamlike trip through the home of the First Flower. The muscles of his Terran face twitched, and his strangely lit eyes burned. Like a fire, his whole body gave off heat, consuming itself. Enli revised her thinking yet again. Whatever the other Terrans might be, David Pek Allen was the most unreal person Enli had ever seen.

She wondered why she didn't have a headpain near him. Because she didn't. Perhaps it was a gift from the First Flower, here in the home of Her soul. Enli could think of no other explanation.

"But I'm on to them," Pek Allen said. "They won't win. The shared-reality mechanism belongs to us all, and it's up to me to see it is given to all. There's no one else, Enli—you see that, of course. It was all fated. I didn't choose to become the savior of my race and yours—I was chosen. To refuse to act now *would* be evil. What was it that Earthman said once? 'For evil to triumph, all that is required is that good men do nothing.' No! Whatever my father thinks of me!"

He was mixing World and Terran words now. Enli breathed deeply. If he killed her here, maybe Pek Bazargan would carry her body out to Rafkit Seloe. It was the kind of thing Pek Bazargan would do: a responsible, head-of-household thing. Then the priests would imprison her, unreal forever. She must not let Pek Allen kill her here.

She put a hand on his arm. "We should start now."

His eyes blazed even brighter. "Yes! You do see! I knew you would! Follow me, Enli. Don't be afraid."

Torch glowing, he led her into the tunnel, still knee-deep in water. Enli sloshed through, sticking close to Pek Allen. Her Terran suit and boots kept her warm, but Pek Allen, suitless, must be chilled to his lungs. He didn't act chilled. He pushed forward, sometimes falling, scrambling again to his feet, talking the whole time. To her? To himself? He didn't seem able to stop.

"People are afraid to act in favor of truth. Not because it's dangerous, no. Because they're afraid of looking like fools, choosing the wrong side, risking their status, failing . . . oh, a thousand things! Rotten cowardly things . . . it's only when someone is willing to act, willing to do right, willing to risk failure . . . *I* won't fail. I can't. History is on my side, the triumph of the bold idea in the long run . . . all through history! Galileo . . . Humility, Enli. That's what I feel. It's an honor to be the one chosen to do this, I didn't ask for the honor, my God what my father will know about me when he hears—but that's not the reason. Never! Someone must act for truth and salvation . . . conspiracy to gain power, the most despicable of

ends . . . at the expense of peace and shared reality! My God!
What people *are* . . ."

They came to the vug. Enli shook the water off her boots.
Pek Allen swung the torch upward to shine on the ceiling.
Gold glittered and sparkled. Gold surrounded the human,
standing there dripping and raving, his twitching face on fire
with unreality. Enli looked away.

But Pek Allen must not kill her here, either. Bazargan would
too easily find her body. It must happen somewhere she could
decay without disturbance.

"Can you do it, Enli? Can you go through that narrow tunnel again, can you? Here, take the torch, you're going first,
can you do it?"

Why did she not have headpain enough to cleave her skull?
Why?

"I can do it."

"Of course you can. I'll be right behind you. Here, go
ahead, don't be afraid, you can do it, we can do whatever
needs to be done, the strength comes from somewhere have
you noticed that when the need is crucial enough I didn't ask
to be chosen—"

It was a relief to wiggle into the narrow tunnel and cut off
his voice.

Enli dragged herself forward on her elbows, protected by
the tough suit. The torch lit the narrow walls and rough rock
ceiling. Shorter than she remembered, the tunnel ended high
in the rock wall. A stink drifted toward her.

Just beyond here was the place she'd had diarrhea from the
Terran food powders. They'd have to go back that way, and
Terrans always acted strangely around shit. Well, Pek Allen
could hardly act more strangely than he already was.

Enli had eaten nothing since the food powders. Her belly
rumbled as she emerged, headfirst, from the tiny tunnel. Let
it rumble. Soon enough it would be still.

Return to her ancestors! If she did it by her own hand, of
course, they would reject her completely, never allow her into
the spirit world. But it would not be by her own hand. Unlike
Tabor, lying dead at the foot of a flower altar—an almost

unthinkable blasphemy in itself. Dead by his own hand, because he and she had loved too much, more than brother and
sister should ever think of doing . . . Even now she could remember the touch of his hands on the secret places of her
body . . .

No headpain. *Why not?*

Enli pushed herself out from the rock wall as far as her
waist. She shone the torch downward, looking for a handhold.
Below her to her right an irregular boulder jutted from the
wall. By grasping it as she wriggled the rest of the way free,
she broke her fall slightly, although the hard stone still bruised
her through the untorn suit.

A moment later Pek Allen shot out of the tunnel and spilled
heavily to the floor. He staggered to his feet and grinned at
her. Blood poured from his wide shoulders, suitless, and from
one cheek. It stained his lips so that tiny flecks flew off as he
talked. He didn't seem to notice.

"So far, so good! Come on, Enli, we can do it, we're almost
out!"

They were nowhere near almost out. Pek Allen grabbed her
hand, reclaimed his torch, and strode down the rough tunnel,
slipping and lurching and talking, talking, talking. He didn't
seem to even notice the odor of shit, nor the shit itself when
they walked right through it.

They came to another cave, small and irregularly shaped,
with two tunnels branching off it. No, Enli thought as Pek
Allen swept his torch across the walls . . . three tunnels. His
voice didn't falter.

"This is the right one, Enli, where Dieter took us before.
We came this way, I'm sure of it, come on! Who knows how
long before that demented Colonel Johnson explodes the alien
weapon in the moon? . . . explodes the moon! My God! She's
in on the conspiracy, of course, she'll share in the power with
Bazargan and the filthy priests, rulers of a whole world some
people need that crave it it's like a sickness in their blood,
Enli, but even so—come on! This is the right tunnel!"

Enli knew it was not.

She thought rapidly. If they went down the wrong tunnel,

they might both die—she when this crazed Terran turned on her and killed her, he if he could not find his way back. His might be a horrible death, from starvation or injury. But if Pek Allen did find his way out of the mountains, he would be killed by the first people to recognize him, which would be the first people who saw him. By now everyone on World would have shared reality about the Terrans.

Pek Allen would be killed swiftly and without pain, but afterward his body would be imprisoned in chemicals and glass and prevented from returning to his own ancestors. (Did Terrans have ancestors? Of course, they must.) On the other hand, if Pek Allen starved to death inside the Neury Mountains, his body, like hers, could release his soul. If he had one. Did he?

The other Terrans did. No matter what the priests said, Pek Bazargan and Pek Gruber and Pek Sikorski, gentle Ann, were real. And so perhaps even the deranged soul of Pek Allen might return to reality, by the sweetness of the First Flower, if the twisted vessel of his mind were allowed to release it naturally.

"Enli! Can't you hear me? This is the right tunnel!"

"Yes, Pek Allen," she said. "It is."

TWENTY-ONE

IN THE NEURY MOUNTAINS

Bazargan and Ann waited in the upland valley. For what, they weren't sure, but it seemed the best of their limited options.

They had discussed following the three runaways. But follow *where*? On the other side of the vug was the body-wide high tunnel; Bazargan knew he could not wiggle through it a second time. He just couldn't. He and Ann decided not to separate: too dangerous. A number of tunnels seemed to branch off their small valley, but there was no way to know where they led, or which one the others might have taken, or why. So they mixed food powders and fetched water, and then Ann gathered more plant samples and Bazargan tried, without success, to raise the *Zeus*.

"Ann, tell me what you know about grandiose paranoid schizophrenia."

Ann waved an insect away from her hand. They sat on the ground just beyond the overhang, Ann's samples spread on a blanket in front of her. "Not much, I'm afraid. A lot of mental diseases have yielded to biochemical analysis and cure, but not the delusional ones. We can alleviate symptoms, but we can't remedy the chemical causes of schizophrenia the way we can for simpler disorders like depression or anxiety. The neurological origins of schizophrenia are too multiple."

"Do you think David is delusional?"

Ann answered slowly. Her fair hair fell in greasy lanks around her scratched and smudged face. "Yes, I do. But I don't know to what extent. If I could test his blood for phenylethylanine . . . David hasn't talked to us much in the last few days, you know. He was holding it all in, everything about the twins' murder and Colonel Johnson's lies and whatever affected our brains when we passed through this field Dieter keeps talking about. But I don't know if he'll hold it in indefinitely."

"Do you think David's condition was affected by Dieter's 'field'? Any more than the rest of us?"

"Yes. Although I don't know why. Any more than I know why Enli is suddenly able to tolerate such big jolts to her conception of reality. She should be having crippling headaches, nausea, even shock. And all of a sudden she's not."

"Ann, you know Dieter better than any of us. Where do you think he took David and Enli?"

"You're assuming he took them, rather than David taking them. At gunpoint."

Bazargan shifted on the hard ground. "No, I'm not. I thought of that. But they've been gone at least twelve hours by now. Dieter is strong, and smart, and far more experienced in this environment than David. If David was fool enough to take Dieter prisoner, I can't believe Dieter would stay a prisoner. Not if he's unfettered enough to go spelunking."

"Then why didn't Enli scream or something? None of it makes sense. I don't . . . Did you see that?"

"See what?" Bazargan hadn't seen anything but more insects. Lifegivers, Worlders called them, the pollinators of their precious flowers. The swarm had stopped bothering Ann and moved to Bazargan, buzzing around his unsuited hands.

"The lifegivers," Ann said. "You swatted that one away from your hand. It flew up toward your face and almost landed on your cheek. There—that one *is* on your cheek!"

"So? They don't sting."

"They never land on anyone's head. Never. Not humans,

not Worlders. I noticed it in Gofkit Jemloe and asked Voratur and Enli both. Lifegivers never land on anyone's head. Look, there's another one on your forehead!"

"Let's move," Bazargan said. The lifegivers didn't sting, but they did tickle.

"No. If you don't mind, just wait here a bit more . . . There's another one. On me. I can feel it."

"What are you thinking, Ann?"

"I'm not sure yet. But they land on heads here and they don't anywhere else on World . . . It has to be because we're in the center of Dieter's field. Or rather, we're in the eye of the hurricane where the field isn't operating. That's the only thing different about this valley and the vug from the rest of the places we've seen!"

Bazargan sat up straighter. "Do you think Enli's lack of headaches are connected with this eye of the field, too?"

"How can I know? But they're all brain phenomena."

Bazargan tried to digest it all. Biochemistry wasn't his field; culture was. He only knew about brains working in concert to create societies. Also, he felt nauseated and cold, too cold for someone wearing an s-suit.

Gruber had warned him that he'd taken too many rads coming through the tunnels.

Ann hadn't noticed his weariness. She was too excited. "Ahmed, if this 'field' *is* affecting Enli's shared-reality mechanism and our thinking processes and even the course of David's schizophrenia, then it's not biochemical. Even some mysterious unseen gas or pollen or whatever couldn't produce such diverse biochemical effects. You're talking entirely different centers of the brain, utilizing entirely different cascades of neurochems. I just don't believe it."

Bazargan nodded. He felt weak.

"And Dieter swears there's no peculiar electromagnetic field. Of any kind. Although how he can be so sure of that . . . But if he's right, and this isn't a biochemical phenomenon, nor an electromagnetic one, then what is it? Heat gradients that mild don't affect the brain. What's left? Unless—Dieter!"

Gruber walked toward them, so filthy with mud and rock

dust that Bazargan didn't know how Ann had even known it was him and not David Allen. She jumped up and threw herself into his arms, such an un-Ann demonstration that for the first time Bazargan realized how deeply she cared for Gruber.

"I'm back," Gruber said, disentangling himself from Ann's embrace. His mud and soot had rubbed off on her suit as well. "Ahmed, don't scold. Not until you hear what I have found. *Ach,* it is stupendous! Call the others to hear!"

"Others?" Bazargan said, knowing he sounded stupid. "David and Enli? Aren't they with you?"

"With me? No, of course not. I left you all sleeping late last night, and went to find the tunnels down to the buried source of this field—where are David and Enli?"

"Gone," Ann said somberly. "With your gun, Dieter."

Dieter, uncharacteristically, said nothing. No one was acting in character, Bazargan thought tiredly. Not even himself. He didn't want to hear about Gruber's expedition, which Bazargan had forbidden. He wanted only to sleep.

"All right," Dieter said. "I will try to find them. But first I must sleep. And before that I must tell you what I have found. You will need to decide, Ahmed, what and how much to tell Syree Johnson."

"We still can't raise the *Zeus,*" Ann said.

"Has Tas gone overhead today?"

"No," Ann said. "We watched particularly. Whatever happened up there, they succeeded in taking the moon away."

"They had better be careful what they do with it," Gruber said. "Because I think the thing underground here is another piece of whatever Tas was before it became a moon."

The tunnel twisted but it didn't narrow. Enli and David could walk upright most of the time. As far as Enli could tell, they were headed downward, although in places there were abrupt turns upward. Sometimes they heard water; sometimes they waded through it. Parts of the tunnel ceiling had collapsed, and several times they had to climb over boulders or pick their way through rubble. Pek Allen didn't appear to notice—how could that be? This route looked nothing like the one through which Pek Gruber had led them into the mountains. Pek Allen was lost in his own private garden, talking and talking and talking.

"All people are capable of moral choices, Enli, they are, they are. But most people don't make them. They live their pathetic little lives from habit, or for convenience, or to impress others, or for immediate pleasure—it's true! They're like the story of the farm boy who enlists in a passing army—do you know this story? No, of course not, it's a human story and you don't have armies on World or war or—he enlists in a passing army because the crops have failed and the army offers hot food and a bedroll and a place to go, and he doesn't even know who the army is fighting or why—he doesn't even know, Enli! And he doesn't care! He may fight well, and develop admirable loyalty to his comrades, and even become a hero, but none of it is a moral choice, he's not on the side of 'good' or the side of 'evil,' he's in a no-man's land in between, a sort of spiritual limbo, it's an old story on Earth and on Mars, too, but it never ends, Enli, it never ends, to do anything different takes not only courage—the farm boy may have that—but vision, too, it takes . . ."

Enli didn't understand many of the Terran words. She stumbled on behind Pek Allen, noting in the light of his torch how many times the tunnels branched, then branched again. They would never find their way back. Here she would die, and decay, and release her soul to join her ancestors. And so would Pek Allen, too, if the First Flower so chose.

". . . savior of both races, no not such ridiculous idea or maybe it is but from such ridiculous ideas grow greatness and . . ."

How long had they been in the tunnels? A day and night? They had stopped so that Enli could sleep, but she hadn't eaten anything. Did Pek Allen sleep? She didn't think so. Nor eat, either. He seemed unable to do either, nor to sit still, nor to stop long enough to let them both die. And he wouldn't let Enli die, either. He pulled her along, talking and talking, and she stumbled behind in weariness and hunger until all sense of time and direction were lost.

Somewhere in this gray unending confusion, Enli's suit started to speak. She shrieked, and then recognized the words. Pek Bazargan's suit had spoken them once before.

"Stop. This area registers sixty rads. Leave this area now. You are in danger. Stop. You have taken . . ."

"Put on your helmet, Enli!" Pek Allen said.

She stared at him, not understanding. He had spoken in Terran. He reached toward her and grabbed something soft and shapeless from a pocket she didn't know her suit had. He pressed it and it became a rigid clear bowl that he turned upside down and jammed on her head. Enli stood passive; might as well die of suffocation as by murder. He sealed gloves on her hands, did something to the place where her boots joined the legs of her suit.

"There! You're safe now."

"But"—to her surprise, the words emerged through the clear bowl on her head—"what is the danger? And you . . ."

Pek Allen smiled. In the upcast light from his torch, standing with bleeding face and arms in the rags of his shirt, he looked like nothing Enli had ever seen or could imagine. His hands twitched, making the torch throw shifting shadows from the cave walls.

"The danger, Enli, is radiation. The special sickness of the Neury Mountains—you know about it?"

"Yes." She understood now. "But then you—without a suit . . ." She was being stupid again. They were both going to die here, anyway.

Pek Allen laughed, a horrible sound that echoed down the tunnel. "Oh, no, not me! Don't you understand? I'm immune! All saviors are above disease and sickness, even when we look like we're succumbing. It's the reward, and the glory, of doing what no one else will do, for the good of humanity. Yours, mine—come on!"

He grabbed her hand and pulled her, stumbling, deeper into the tunnel. Her suit continued to speak. "Stop. This area registers one hundred eighty rads. Leave this area now. You are in danger. Stop. This area registers two hundred thirty rads. Leave . . ."

"Come on!" Pek Allen shouted. The tunnel, widening now, echoed back: *On on on on.*

They were running. Enli felt herself grow warm—wasn't the suit supposed to stop that? It must be very hot here. The torch, carried by Pek Allen, wavered wildly as he ran, the beam of light hitting now the wall, now the rocky ceiling, now Pek Allen's bare bloody back. Sweat poured off him, a waterfall.

"Stop. This area registers seven hundred sixty rads. Leave this area now. You are in danger. Stop. You have taken . . ."

"Come on, Enli!" *Li li li li.*

She fell. He jerked her upright, almost tearing her arm from its socket, and kept on running.

"Almost there!" *There there there.*

Where?

"Stop. This area registers one thousand four hundred rads. Leave this area now. You are in danger. Stop. You have taken . . ."

A final steep incline. They both fell down it, landing in a heap on a bed of rocks. Instantly Pek Allen clambered to his feet, grinning. One arm hung limply at his side: broken. He didn't appear to notice.

"Look! The cleansing fire!"

Enli got up slowly. Her suit still lectured her about the sickness of the sacred mountains. Inside it, she sweated so much she thought she might pass out. They stood in a small chamber ankle-deep with water. The heat was enormous, stifling. And the walls glowed.

"Stop. This area registers three thousand six hundred rads. Leave this area . . ."

Pek Allen switched off his torch. The walls still glowed, with an eerie cold light that made Enli suddenly shudder. She sat down and prepared to die.

"No, no, not you," Pek Allen said, switching his torch back on. "You're not the savior, poor child. And you certainly don't need cleansing—not a Worlder! You aren't farm boys who enlist! Come on!"

Running again, splashing across the hot small cave, out another tunnel, another, another, twisting and turning through rock grayer and denser than before. And not glowing.

"Stop. This area registers one thousand sixty rads. Leave this area now. You are in danger. Stop. You have taken . . ."

She couldn't breathe. Her lungs shrieked, a solid mass of pain.

"Stop. This area registers nine hundred rads. Leave this area now. You are in danger. Stop . . ."

Her vision blurred. It must be that, because she thought she saw something else streak past them in the widening tunnel, some animal. A freb. But that would mean they were close to the outside . . .

"Stop. This area registers one hundred ten rads. Leave this area now. You are in danger. Stop . . ."

More running. Finally, Enli fell and could not get up.

"This area is not radioactive." The suit fell silent.

She gasped in great painful whoops, unable to catch wind, unable to see. Pain burned along each muscle, inside each bone. Slowly it receded, a long ebbing tide, and her vision cleared.

Light. She saw dim gray light, unlike the bright yellow shadow-making light of the torch.

Pek Allen must have pulled the clear bowl from off her head. She lay on an uneven stone floor, rock at her head and feet. And somewhere ahead, daylight.

Her vision cleared more, and Enli saw Pek Allen standing above her, straddling her limp body with his long legs, in protection. Or something. He gazed straight at the end of the tunnel.

"We're out, Enli." His voice had changed again. Now it was quiet, not raving. And yet there was a tone in it that made her think that Pek Allen's mind was even more twisted than before.

"We're out, and there's a village out there. A World village.

Now I can do the work I must do, and that you must help me with."

And Enli was engulfed in pain again. Not muscles this time, not bone, not lungs. The familiar pain was in her head, between her eyes, looking up at Pek Allen. For a while in the Neury Mountains it had gone, but now it was back: the head-pain of unshared reality. Of being with someone who was unreal.

It was back.

"Let's go," Pek Allen said, in World, and pulled Enli to her feet.

TWENTY-TWO

EN ROUTE TO SPACE
TUNNEL #438

The Faller warship remained stationary, hanging in space two hundred clicks from the tunnel, ninety degrees lateral to the trajectory of the *Zeus*. "A spider, waiting for the fly," Major Ombatu muttered. Syree ignored him.

The *Zeus*, a heavily laboring fly, continued to shove its burden forward. Orbital Object #7 accelerated serenely. The *Zeus* officers and Special Project team, less serenely, stayed on the bridge, talking little, sleeping less. Syree knew her gray fog of fatigue was dangerous. It slowed her thinking, her reaction times. But each time she slept, dreams awoke her.

She was four, in her grandmother's kitchen, listening to Emily James Johnson recite the family soldiers who had died honorably in combat. Corporal James L. Johnson, in Bosnia. Catherine Syree Johnson, in Argentina. Tam Wells Johnson, on Mars. *A Johnson masters herself, Syree. Remember that.*

She was on Bolivar, losing her leg. *Medbot! Medbot here!* someone yelled, and she realized dimly, gladly, that it wasn't herself.

She was inside Orbital Object #7, learning its secrets, relishing every moment, when it announced that it was going to blow up. *No, you have to accelerate more!* Syree cried in panic. *We haven't reached grandmother's house yet!*

"Acceleration one gee, speed 4,732 clicks per hour."

"Continue acceleration."

"Acceleration continuing."

The helmsman and Peres. Syree shook herself fully awake. How long had she been dozing this time? How close were they? She checked the displays, rubbing sleep-crust from her eyes.

She'd been asleep in her chair for four hours. The *Zeus* had carried the artifact over a billion clicks away from its planetary orbit. In another six hours, they'd reach Space Tunnel #438.

Lee said, "Commander, change in enemy position. Faller warship is moving toward the space tunnel. Twenty clicks . . . thirty . . . forty . . ."

"It's decided on engagement," Puchalla said. "Whether or not we hold the artifact."

"No," Syree answered swiftly. "They won't do that. They have every reason to want that artifact to sail on through the space tunnel into their space. They won't fire on us until after we detach."

". . . fifty clicks . . . sixty . . ."

Peres swiveled to stare at Syree. "You can't know that for sure, Dr. Johnson. The enemy may well anticipate our flyer maneuver and make sure the space tunnel opens on *their* space. We discussed this. Under no conditions can this vessel allow the Fallers to fire on us without any attempt at evasive maneuvers, first fire, or retaliatory fire. That is unacceptable. This is, first and foremost, a war."

"Yes, sir," Syree said. "But consider, sir, that our second flyer is going to come through the tunnel at the very last moment. Assume we don't detach until then. We can detach and fire simultaneously."

". . . eighty clicks . . . ninety . . ."

"That won't work now," Peres said. "The Faller ship is maneuvering to position herself *between* us and the tunnel. As soon as the enemy sees our first flyer emerge and then dart back, the Fallers will fire on the artifact—with us still attached—to prevent it from going through. Or, if they're still close enough, they'll just go through themselves ahead of the artifact to reconfigure the space tunnel. We can't fire on them if the artifact is in the way. And then the artifact will emerge in their space after them."

"That warship can't move that fast," Syree said. "They could beat the first flyer back through the tunnel, maybe, but not the second. Look . . . they've stopped moving now. The warship is stationary again . . . Mr. Lee, how far away is the enemy vessel from the tunnel entrance?"

"Still two hundred clicks, ma'am, but now on our direct trajectory."

"Look, the numbers work," Syree insisted. "Our first flyer comes through today at fourteen thirty-two hours. It darts right back again. At that time—if we don't detach now—we're five minutes from impact and traveling at . . . just a minute . . . at four thousand eight hundred sixty clicks per second." No mention of fudge factors or loopholes now. "We detach then, Commander, and remember that the *Zeus* is also traveling at four thousand eight hundred sixty clicks. That's *fast*, Commander."

"We have evidence that Faller weapons can track at that velocity. And we'd be in their range."

"Yes. But that high speed isn't as easy to track. And they'll be disoriented for some brief interval, deciding whether to fire on us, fire on the artifact, or try to beat it to the space tunnel. We gain at least a few seconds by surprise, to fire first."

Peres frowned. "Can the enemy beat the artifact through the tunnel? The enemy could see the first flyer come through and try to get to the tunnel before the artifact, without firing at all. Can it do that, in five minutes, from two hundred clicks out?"

Syree said reluctantly, "Unfortunately, yes. To cross two hundred clicks in five minutes—yes, the warship can do that easily. *But*—our second flyer comes through four minutes later from Caligula space. If the warship goes through after the first flyer appears, it will never even realize that the second one changed the tunnel destination yet again. If the warship doesn't go through after our first flyer because it's engaged with us, even if it wins the engagement it wouldn't have time to beat the second flyer back through the tunnel. It would have to cross two hundred clicks in sixty seconds, plus losing a few seconds to making the decision. It can't do that."

"Not even as a kamikaze run? What gee would they need to get to the tunnel in sixty seconds?"

"Eleven point three. It would be a kamikaze run. But I don't think they'd make it. It would take a few seconds to engage their drive. And we'd be firing on them anyway. As soon as we detach, we could swerve sharply to give us a clear shot at them without hitting the artifact. They'll have to either take evasive action or maneuver to return fire."

"True," Percs said. "And, of course, we can always detonate the artifact and use that as a weapon to get the Fallies, if we have to."

Syree nodded. Detonation was a last resort. She hoped that Peres thought so, too. She said, "If we detach at five minutes, we also have time to get farther away from the detonation blast ourselves. We'll be moving really fast, Commander. But I have to say this: I mean we'll be a safe distance away from the shock wave from our own blasters. I don't know what kind of wave an explosion of the artifact itself could generate."

So don't blow it up, she meant. Peres heard her meaning. All he said, however, was, "Understood. Ms. Puchalla?"

The executive officer said, "I see no problem with waiting until t-minus-five-minutes to detach. We're not in their firing range until then anyway, so its not like we're avoiding engagement."

"Agreed," Peres said. "All right. Helmsman, continue acceleration."

"Continuing acceleration."

"Mr. Lee, keep your eyes glued—and I mean glued—to that enemy position."

"Yes, sir."

The *Zeus* sped forward, gaining velocity every second, toward whatever the enemy or the artifact or the space tunnel chose to do next.

TWENTY-THREE

IN THE NEURY MOUNTAINS

Ann and Bazargan listened as the dirt-encrusted Gruber excitedly, with much arm-waving, explained what he had found deep under the Neury Mountains. Bazargan knew this was important: perhaps the most important explanation he'd heard since landing on World. But he couldn't concentrate. He hadn't been exposed to that many rads, and his radiation sickness wasn't bad enough to kill a person. But it could make a person feel pretty sick, especially a person who hadn't eaten much, hadn't slept much, had pushed his terrified way through miles of dank unhealthy underground tunnels in some strange force field that only Gruber was utterly convinced existed.

"I tried several tunnels until I found one with a deep chimney, no more than five hundred meters from here. Still in the dead eye of the field, according to my handheld. I had pitons and ropes, and—"

"You took a terrible chance," Ann said. "You might have been killed." In her filthy face her blue eyes were fascinated, reproachful, admiring, all at once. You had to still be young, Bazargan thought, to manage that combination. His bones ached from the marrow outward.

"*Ja,*" Gruber agreed cheerfully. "But I wasn't. The chimney terminated in another set of lava tunnels, smooth, supported by much older granite plinths . . . an unusual structure. I tried all the tunnels, carefully marking my way, until I found it. Came to it. Discovered it!"

"What?" Ann said. "What?"

"A small cave. No more than four meters' diameter, if it had been regularly shaped enough for a diameter, which it wasn't. A pockmark in the rock. And on the floor, the projecting curve of a metal sphere. Only a small part of it—a very small part. Most is encased in rock. I did what quick tests I could. The age of the rock melt close around it matches the age of the clay layer deposited when something crashed into the prehistoric ocean basin and formed these tunnels. Before the land all rose again into the mountains."

"The original asteroid," Ann breathed.

"Not an asteroid! This is an artifact, manufactured. Perhaps twenty-five-meter radius, judging from the curvature. The surface seems to be some allotropic form of carbon, something like fullerenes. I couldn't tell more than that, with the equipment I had. Except for one crucial thing—Ahmed, are you awake?"

"Yes," Bazargan said.

Ann turned from her rapt fascination with Gruber to look at Bazargan. He saw the moment she registered how awful he looked. Comprehension swept her dirty features. "You're sick, Ahmed. The radiation sickness."

"Yes. But I . . . didn't take too many . . . rads. I'll recover." He turned his head barely in time to vomit on the ground and not on her.

Between them, they carried him back into the cave, made a bed of the blankets. Gruber set his powerful torch for heat and positioned it on the ground to bathe Bazargan's shivering body. "I should have been watching for this," Ann said in self-reproach. "There's always a lag between exposure and onset of symptoms, and with everything else going on . . . Ahmed, you have to sweat, and you mustn't get dehydrated. Drink this." She brought him water, slightly muddy-tasting, from the valley stream. He drank what he could.

"I don't have the equipment to lave you internally," she said in frustration. "But I'm going to scrub what I can . . . Now, don't go modest on me, Ahmed. You're an anthropologist."

And anthropologists are better at being the observers than the subjects, Bazargan wanted to say, but couldn't. His throat was closing up.

Gruber and Ann scrubbed him with water and small harsh stones. They cut his hair as close as possible, made him vomit again, gave him an enema. Bazargan endured each indignity, knowing they were right, hating his own weakness.

When they were done and he lay in the cave, wrapped in blankets, Ann and Gruber returned instantly to the topic of Gruber's find. Bazargan listened as well as he could.

"The buried artifact measures as the exact center of the field, Ann. Of the toroidal distribution. I have kept careful track of the data, everywhere we've gone in these mountains since we first entered. Recorded it all, plus my data from the first visit. The thermal gradient whose rate increases as you go deeper, instead of decreasing . . . it should decrease because most radioactive rocks lie near the surface, generating heat that the rock traps for millions of years. But not here, because the *source* of radiation is that artifact. But not a normal source, and that's why the thermal distribution and radioactive distribution are out of phase. Listen, Ahmed, you must hear this, too—it is the greatest discovery here. By far!"

More arm-waving. Gruber, usually sardonic, was now at a pitch of idealistic enthusiasm that Bazargan could only observe with weary wonder.

"Radiation strength normally decreases according to the inverse square law. The closer you are to the source, the more rads. But here, the radiation does not even exist right up close to the source. It comes into being weakly at about a quarter kilometer away, then increases rapidly, then drops away rapidly. I haven't worked out the equations yet. We skirted the very top edge of it, I think, when Ahmed was without a suit and took the rads that make him sick now."

"I follow you," Ann said.

"Then follow this, it is key. The buried artifact does *not* emit radiation as such. It emits some sort of field that *causes* the substances around it to go radioactive, and also causes the thermal gradient. There is a lag, a rise time before the field takes effect, which accounts for the dead 'eye' we are in now. But the main effect—that's exactly what Dr. Johnson said the moon that they're moving, Tas, can do out in space!"

Ann let her hand rise, then fall again. She said, dazed, "Do you think this was another moon once, identical to Tas, whose orbit decayed?"

"Not identical, *nein*. Because Syree Johnson said the wave effect out in space was spherical. This one is a flattened toroid. But from my data, it seems that the generated field in turn generates, or strengthens, or somehow affects a much bigger field that envelops the entire planet. And this one is not radioactive. It's not electromagnetic at all. And it is not thermal."

"Dieter . . . while you were gone . . . Ahmed and I were speculating—"

"Let me finish first. This strange secondary field—although for all I know, it's the primary field and the other is secondary!—but anyway, it, too, has the dead 'eye' that we are in now. A hole directly surrounding the source. So all I can do is speculate from my previous data. The second field blankets the surface of the planet, increasing abruptly as you climb up from the surface, then decreasing again. It—"

"How high up?" Ann demanded, stridently for her. She clutched Dieter's arm. *"How high up?"*

He stared at her. "I'm not sure."

"Estimate!"

"The field seems to be densest about a half kilometer up."

"And where were we when we all blanked out, except Enli, in the tunnels? At what altitude?"

Bazargan, lying helplessly in his blankets, watched Dieter's face change. *"Mein Gott*—yes! We were that high above sea level, the only time we were . . . the tunnels go up and down. We were in the densest part of the field when that blank stupid patch took us . . . but not Enli . . . Ann, what is it? What were you and Ahmed speculating? Ahmed, are you hearing this?"

Neither of them waited for Bazargan's answer. Ann said, "It *is* just speculation, Dieter. But here it is. Your planetwide field isn't electromagnetic. It isn't radioactive—even from the Zeus we could pick up that radioactive activity is concentrated in the Neury Mountains, not evenly distributed over World."

"Yes. From the neutrino flow. Go on."

"The field is not biochemical: pheromones or anything like that. I'm convinced of it. Yet it affects the brain. Ours when we entered a section of its greatest density. Enli's ever since we've been in your 'dead eye'—I don't know if you noticed, but she's had no unshared-reality headaches while we've been in the eye. Possibly David's brain, too, in that his instability is much worse the last five days, although to be fair, that could be mostly from trauma plus withdrawal from the Discipline."

"So you—"

"Wait. There's one more piece. The lifegivers—you know, the insectlike pollinators—never land on a Worlder or human head outside these mountains. Never. But here in the valley, in your dead eye of the field, they do."

"They do? So?"

"So I think they're sensitive to your secondary unknown field, too. And I think the field acts specifically on certain kinds of living tissue. Because that tissue *evolved* interacting with the field. It acts on neural tissue in the brain."

Gruber shifted on the ground and frowned. "No, it cannot be. The brain is biochemical and electromagnetic. And I have just spent much time telling you this is neither."

"The brain is biochemical and electromagnetic, yes. Consciousness is a pattern of neural firings, a synchrony in the gamma oscillation. But there are new discoveries in biochemistry that haven't been popularized yet. Support evidence for a theory once considered radical, but less so each year, as we learn more. Do you know what a paracrystalline vesicular grid is, Dieter?"

"No," said Gruber, the geologist.

"I explained it to you once before, when we all discussed Voratur's Lagerfeld scan, remember? Never mind. Basically, you have billions of vesicular grids in your brain. They're found at the ends of nerve synapses. They control how much neurotransmitter is released with each nerve impulse, which in turn affects everything you think and feel. Paracrystalline vesicular grids are very small. They operate according to the laws of quantum physics, Dieter, not classical physics. They can cause quantum events *outside* their energy barrier, because part of their quantum probability field lies there. More and more, it looks like that's how consciousness affects the brain. Through altering its probability field. There's no other way for a purely mental event, such as deciding to get up from your chair, to produce an effect in the material world without violating the law of conservation of energy."

"Wait, wait," Dieter said. "I have not slept last night, I am very tired. Are you saying that the brain operates through a probability field?"

"Only partly. Electromagnetic nerve firings and biochemical events are also there, of course. But neurotransmitter release, caused by quantum events—*and* their associated probability field—is the basis for electric and chemical brain happenings."

"A probability field," Gruber said wonderingly. "In all brains? Yours, mine, Worlders'?"

"If the theory is right."

"And the buried artifact generates its own probability field. That affects everyone's brain on World. Steadily outside the Neury Mountains, erratically inside, depending on where in the toroidal distribution you walk through it. Our brains reacted differently from Enli's because her race evolved here and ours didn't . . . Ann! The probability field would have begun affecting World when the artifact hit the ocean on prehistoric World! It could account for the differing evolution of human and World brains, and solve your difficulty about why shared reality prevailed here when the equations say it's not a winning genetic strategy!"

"Yeeeesssss," Ann said. She sounded dazed. "Dieter, I need to think about all this. I need to—"

"More!" Dieter shouted. "If you bring in quantum mechanics, you bring in the possibility of quantum entanglement!"

"Of what?" Ann said.

"Entanglement! If two electrons are entangled, doing something to one will instantaneously affect the other, even if it's at the far end of the universe. Space and time separations don't matter. Scientists think it might be the theory behind the space tunnels, although we have no clue about the engineering. But if the buried artifact and Tas are somehow entangled . . . if both use probability fields . . ."

Ann seemed to have forgotten that she'd refused any more speculation. "And the brain uses probability, too. Human neurotransmitter release is probabilistic, so it's logical that Worlder brains work the same way. But if this probability field of yours exerted some sort of effect on neurotransmitter release, selectively favoring some grids over others, and it did so over a long period of time, an evolutionary span of time . . . that could be what shaped the shared-reality mechanism, Dieter. It could explain why the biology shows no difference between human and World brains, and yet the difference exists. It's in the frequency of probabilistic events. No wonder it didn't show up on a Lagerfeld."

"*Mein Gott*, it all ties together!"

"We need someone who knows more physics, though. Someone like Syree Johnson." Ann's voice changed. "Dieter, if we die here, no one will ever know all this."

He put his arm around her. "We won't die here, *Liebchen*."

"You can't know that."

He didn't answer. He'd fallen asleep, sitting slumped on the ground, a filthy exhausted elated lump.

Ann eased him onto his back. She checked on Bazargan, also asleep. Then she took Dieter's handheld, activated it, and began to make notes as rapidly as she could speak. Outside the cave the sky grew darker with thick clouds, and after a while it began to rain.

TWENTY-FOUR

GOFKIT RABLOE

Enli let Pek Allen pull her to her feet. She still gasped from their wild trip through caves and tunnels. But over the pain in her lungs and the unshared-reality pain in her head, an angry thought formed.

They had not died in the hidden spaces of the Neury Mountains after all.

And because they had not, the twisted blooms of Pek Allen's crazed mind would drag them to find Worlders, so he could "save" them. The Worlders would of course kill both Pek Allen and Enli. The priests would imprison their bodies in chemicals and glass, to prevent their returning to their ancestors and polluting the world of spirits. Enli and Tabor would remain unreal forever.

She tried to pull her hand free from Pek Allen's grasp, but he was too strong. Bloody, bruised, one arm limp by his side, fresh from the special sickness of the Neury Mountains (even her Terran suit had shrieked as much!), Pek Allen was still strong. The strength of a terrible unreality.

"Look, Enli. A village."

They stood at the edge of a tunnel leading out of the mountains. A steep incline of broken rock led to a ledge below, then another incline, less rocky and with some scrubby bushes. Beyond that lay fields and, in the distance, the smoking chimneys of houses, their roofs glistening in the rain.

"Pek Allen—"

"Don't falter now, Enli. The time to act is here. And who knows how much longer that bitch Syree Johnson will give us until she blows up her weapon and irradiates World?"

He spoke in World, but two of the words were Terran: *bitch* and *irradiates*. Enli was beyond caring what they meant. Her head ached with his unreality. Her belly mourned herself and Tabor. Even so, some small part of her desolate brain noted that Pek Allen had stopped raving. He spoke calmly, rationally, as if he could actually do what he said.

"Come on, Enli. Not much longer now. First, take off that s-suit. Do it! All right, now come with me."

They stumbled forward through the steady rain. The lush fields were food crops, but beyond them, around the houses, lay flower beds. Enli looked her last, hungrily, at the flowers. Pajalib, jelitib, blue trifalitib in a lacy cloud. Bright small mittib. Fragrant ralibib, vekifirib in the shade. Sajib, of the waxy pink blossoms big as her hand. All the flowers that were the glory of World.

The village was largely deserted, its breakfast cookfires in the square banked under their neat metal protectors, its houses closed. Everyone must be off harvesting zeli fruit. This was the season for it, even in the rain; the fruit would not wait. In such a small rural settlement, even the priest would help harvest. Still, there would be a few people left behind the wet doors. The very old watching the smallest young, the ill, the people with flower sickness for cariltcf blooms, which always were planted near zeli fruit.

Pek Allen stopped in the middle of the village green, surrounded by its ring of cookfire hearths. "Hello! People of World! I come with an important message from the First Flower!"

Enli closed her eyes, then opened them. Moments, perhaps, left to live. *Oh, Tabor ...*

"People of World! I come with an important message from the First Flower!"

A wooden door opened. A very old woman, bent with the seasons, peered out. When she glimpsed Enli and the huge bloody Terran, her face melted into horror and she slammed the door.

"People of World! I come with an important message from the First Flower!"

Another door opened. A man strode out, young and strong. Undoubtedly excused from the harvest for flower sickness; his neckfur was braided in atonement. He carried a long knife.

The young man wasted no words. He rushed toward them and thrust the knife at Pek Allen's chest.

Pek Allen grabbed the man with his good arm. To Enli the movement looked easy, almost inevitable, as if Pek Allen's rock-battered body had lived its whole life for this moment. He took the knife away from the man, threw him to the ground, and stood over him with a small metal machine, oddly shaped. It was, she realized suddenly from remembered Terran conversation, Pek Gruber's *gun*. Rain dripped off the end of it. Pek Allen did something and the *gun* made a shrill noise. Yet when her ears stopped hurting, the thing had not exploded, but lay still in his hand, and a wooden bowl left carelessly on the green had been sliced into useless pieces.

"Listen, Pek," he said in World, "I am David Pek Allen, Terran. You know that. Reality and Atonement has declared me unreal. But I come to warn you of something terrible that will happen to World soon, perhaps today. A shift in shared reality. You must listen to me.

"You know that Tas has gone. The other Terrans stole it. You know this. What you do not know is that the unreal Terrans will send a sickness from the Neury Mountains, like the sickness that is already there, but much stronger. It will sicken people a little. But it will sicken things—cooking pots, jewelry, flower remembrances—very much. These things will become as dangerous as the Neury Mountains themselves. You must warn people of this shift in shared reality."

The young man pinned on the ground turned his head away from the sliced wooden bowl and spat on Pek Allen's feet.

"Enli," Pek Allen said, "go into the house there, where the

old woman slammed the door. Bring me the child that's in there."

Enli started. But, yes, of course there would be a child in the house . . . the old woman wasn't infirm enough to have missed the harvest otherwise. She would have ridden on the back of a farm cart, helped prepare the noon meal, been a part of the shared fun.

"Enli! Go now!"

Enli didn't move.

Pek Allen's eyes slid in her direction, back toward the man on the ground. "If you don't go, Enli, I will have to kill this man. There is a whole world at stake here. Don't make me do that."

The flowers of his brain were *that* twisted! She hadn't known.

Enli walked to the house. The door was barred from the inside. Enli broke the glass in the window and called through the hole. "Open up, Pek, or this crazed brain out here will explode the house. With you and the child in it. I am sorry, but it is so."

The pain in her head almost blinded her. Was she really doing this? She, Enli Pek Brimmidin, at the bidding of an unreal madman?

The door opened. Enli walked in—how normal! to walk into a house through an open door, to share that simple reality—and spoke quietly to the old woman. "Go out the back door. Tell the child not to make any noise. Go down that little hill, keeping the house between you and the Terran, and hide in the vegetable garden."

The old woman simply stared at her. Not because Enli was unreal, but because the woman was terrified into stupidity. In the corner a cupboard door moved slightly. At least the hidden child was old enough to stay quiet.

"Go now!" Enli said, trying to sound like Pek Bazargan when he gave orders to her. Even so, she was faintly surprised when the woman obeyed.

Enli turned and walked back outside. "There is no child, Pek Allen. I looked."

He glanced briefly at her face. "You *lie*." The word was Terran; but the meaning obvious: to not share reality, but something else. Now he would kill her with the *gun*. It might as well be now. Enli closed her eyes.

Someone screamed.

But she still lived. Still stood in the rain. And when she opened her eyes, even though there had been no shrill deafening noise, the young man on the ground lay writhing and moaning and clutching his leg.

"It is only hurt a little," Pek Allen said, in that same strong voice. "So you don't hurt me before I give my message. You will recover fine, Pek. Enli, come."

She followed him dumbly. She couldn't think what else to do. Her head throbbed, and so how much worse must it be for the man on the ground? She had had time to see this unreality of Pek Allen's. The longer you saw unreality, Enli had discovered, the harder it was to tell the difference.

Her headache eased a little.

Pek Allen walked swiftly and unerringly to the vegetable garden and pulled out the cowering woman. A small girl clutched her around the neck, hiding her own face in her grandmother's bosom.

"Come out, old mother," Pek Allen said. "I will not hurt you. Or the child."

But he had to pull her from among the vegetables. "Listen, old mother. I am David Pek Allen, Terran. I bring a message from the First Flower in the Neury Mountains. Is there a healer in this village?"

The old woman, her scalp furrowed in pain, couldn't answer.

Pek Allen sighed. He reached for the little girl, which made the woman shriek and clutch harder. For a horrible moment Enli thought he would cut the child's throat with the knife he'd taken from the young man. Wasn't that what Worlders had done to the Terran children? But Pek Allen pulled the child free and held her gently. "Come, Enli."

The woman shrieked and wailed. The child screamed. Ignoring the noise, Pek Allen strode away, along the farm road.

Enli followed. What else could she do? If she could get the child away from him . . . but he still had the *gun*. And he was mad. She ran after him. The old woman, crying out incoherently, hobbled after Enli.

He walked so quickly that every few steps she had to run to keep up. The ground was muddy, but he didn't seem to notice, carrying the wailing child. The grandmother fell rapidly behind. When Enli turned to look over her shoulder, the old woman sat despairingly in the middle of the muddy road, her noise already blotted out by the falling rain.

After a while the little girl quieted, and then Enli, trotting painfully beside, heard Pek Allen singing in World. An old cradle song, tender and low. Learned in the Voratur crelm house, of course. He sang it twice, three times, and Enli saw the stiff little body in his arms slowly relax.

He wouldn't kill the child. Enli was sure of it. Which left only the question of when he would finally get around to killing her.

His song faltered. And then he stumbled, caught himself, went on. But she had seen. Pek Allen's strength, that artificial thing blooming from his madness, was waning. And then what? She could escape . . . but she could do that now, if she chose. He was weakening, and he held the child, and she could go. Where? There was nowhere to go.

This was her reality. All she could do was share it.

A farm cart rose into sight over a low hill, overladen with zeli fruit and harvesters. Two men pulled it and a woman walked beside, steadying the load. When they saw Pek Allen they stopped. When they saw the child in his arms, they started forward again, the wheels of the cart creaking with damp. Enli saw their faces emerge as individuals, horrified and in headpain.

"I am David Pek Allen, a Terran," Pek Allen said. "I bring an important message from the First Flower."

"Give me Estu," one of the men said in the soft slurred accent of the mountain villages, and with admirable calm. "Give her to me."

The child heard something in the man's familiar tone. Once more she started to wail.

"Listen to me," Pek Allen said, loud enough to be heard. "I come to warn you of something terrible that will happen to World soon, perhaps today. A shift in shared reality. You must listen to me.

"You know that Tas has gone. The other Terrans stole it, our fast-blooming moon. You know this. What you do not know is that the unreal Terrans will send a sickness from the Neury Mountains, like the sickness that is already there, but much stronger. It will sicken people a little. But it will sicken things—cooking pots, jewelry, flower remembrances—very much. These things will become as dangerous as the Neury Mountains themselves. You must warn everyone of this shift in shared reality."

"Give me Estu."

"This is Enli Pek Brimmidin. She will tell you that what I say is shared reality."

Enli looked at Pek Allen. Did he really think she believed him, or that these people would believe her, who had been declared unreal? He knew nothing about World, after all! Until now, his madness had made a crazed sense, like blossoms that grow twisted but at least grow toward the sun. But this . . . although Pek Gruber had said the same thing about the jewelry and flower remembrances, as well as a long list of other objects—and Pek Gruber was not mad. Did that mean that this object sickness might really come to World, just because Tas had been taken away?

Pek Allen was still talking. "You must take all these objects out of your houses and throw them away. Or you can leave your houses and stay in the root cellars until the sickness passes. It will not last long. I will tell you when it's safe. Share this reality, spread it all over World. I, David Pek Allen, say this to you to save you and your children."

He stumbled forward and handed Estu to the closest man. As the Worlder seized her, Enli heard Pek Allen say softly, "Be good, Bonnie. Be well."

The man retreated with the crying child. All three adults

backed away from the Terran and the unreal Enli, seemingly unsure what to do next. They should kill them both, of course. Everyone on World must share that reality. But these three were unarmed. Quiet people, unused to violations of their quiet reality. They looked at each other, and carefully didn't look at Enli, and she could feel their confusion and fear, could share it completely.

Pek Allen sagged sideways, took a step to recover himself, sagged again.

Suddenly she knew what to do.

Enli stepped toward the group, who instantly stepped back. She said, "He is dying. The unreal Terran is dying of sickness from the Neury Mountains. He was not sick inside the mountains. No one is sick inside the home of the First Flower. They become sick only when they leave."

That much, at least, was shared reality.

"But Pek Allen left the mountains anyway. To give you the message from the First Flower. And he is dying for it. Does that not show that he is real? Who but a real soul gives his life for another?"

The woman shrilled, "He is dying because he left the Neury Mountains, as all must die who leave them. He is not dying for us!"

"No. The First Flower uses him to send you a message that reality has shifted. Tas is gone. The sickness of . . . of manufactured objects will start soon. You must leave all the objects Pek Allen named and go into the root cellars for a little while."

The larger man started toward Enli, his fists clenched. He had resolved his confusion, or else her blasphemy had agitated his headpain more than he could bear. He picked up a heavy stick.

"What I say is shared reality," Enli said quickly. "Here is the sign of the First Flower in my words: I have been in the Neury Mountains, too. You know this. Yet I am not sick. Look at me! I am not sick!"

The man with the stick still moved toward Enli. Almost she could feel the blow on her head . . . she had wanted to die. But not like this. Their priest would put her in chemicals and glass, forever. Not like this!

"I am not sick!" she cried. Pek Allen reached a hand toward her, but it didn't connect. He stumbled again and this time didn't recover, falling sideways onto the road. It seemed to her that he fell very slowly, as if the reality of time had shifted along with everything else. The *gun* slipped from his hand into the mud.

"Wait, Riflit," the woman said. "She . . . she does not look sick."

Riflit growled something and kept coming.

"I said *wait*," the woman said, and a part of Enli's mind realized that she was his wife. *Wait,* the wifely tone said, *or you will regret it in a hundred different small ways for quite a while*.

Just so had Tabor ordered Enli to leave the flower altar so he could atone. Only, after that, there had been no more while.

Riflit stopped, scowling, his club still raised.

The woman said, "She really doesn't look sick. Do you think—"

"She is unreal!" said Riflit. "Reality and Atonement said she must die!"

"Then kill me!" Enli said swiftly. "I will die for my message, even as this Terran is dying. But the First Flower spared me the Neury Mountains sickness to give you this message. Share the reality of the message!"

The man holding Estu said, uncertainly and in evident headpain, "She's willing to die to have her message shared. Riflit . . . he's willing to die, too . . . Shared reality is greatest among those willing to give their lives for others . . ."

"Oh, I don't know!" cried the beleaguered Riflit. "I'm a farmer, not a priest!"

The woman stepped forward decisively. "Don't kill her. If she doesn't get Neury Mountain sickness, then it *is* a sign from the First Flower. *Has* to be. If she gets the sickness, then everything else she says is unreal, too. Then we'll kill her."

"You're not a priest, either, Imino!" Riflit snapped. But he lowered his club.

The man holding Estu said timidly, "If he and she both choose to die to give us this message . . . Dying for others makes shared reality bloom even in the unreal, my grandmother always said. And she *was* a priest."

Weariness overwhelmed Enli. She resisted it; she must not look sick. They would watch her closely, for any sign of weakness or sickness. She must look healthy.

Pek Allen vomited weakly.

Enli knelt over him, held his head, wiped his mouth when he was done. He smiled at her. The skin on his face had begun to redden, as if burned. When he opened his mouth to speak, she saw that his tongue had swollen.

"You are the real people, Enli."

"And you, David," she said, although later she would never be sure that she had really used his child-name.

"Tell them . . . how to save World . . . from us."

"Give him here, Pek," said the man who had been holding Estu, evidently the kindest of these Worlders. He lifted David Pek Allen and laid him atop the zeli fruit in the cart, where Estu already sat. Imino and the ferocious Riflit lifted the pull-bars at the front of the cart and slowly turned it around, and they all started back toward the harvest, where the people were, to start the sharing of this shifted reality with all of World.

TWENTY-FIVE

SPACE TUNNEL #438

Fourteen oh six hours by ship time. In twenty-six minutes, the first flyer would dart through Space Tunnel #438, then back again. The *Zeus* would detach the artifact and begin engaging the enemy. Four minutes later the second flyer would appear, and sixty seconds after that the artifact would sail into the tunnel. On the bridge the Special Project team and line officers sat silent, watching the displays. Tension prickled in the air like heat.

The Faller warship began to move.

"Shit," Lee said, breaking the silence. "Commander, change in enemy position. Faller warship accelerating directly toward us."

"Turn off ship's drive," Peres said. "Detach artifact."

"Turning off ship's drive," Lee said.

Syree ran the program on her handheld. She knew that this time there was no dissuading Peres; he would not burden the *Zeus* with the artifact if actual skirmishing was about to occur. The artifact was now on its own. Twenty-six minutes of acceleration lost. However, the artifact would hit the space tunnel only three point four seconds later than planned, which wasn't enough difference to matter. Unless someone blew it up first.

Ship's drive ceased, her thrusters came on to change course, and the artifact left the viewport of the *Zeus*.

Syree blinked. For over five days it had ridden there, a huge swollen Sisyphean burden, and now suddenly it was gone, dwindling visibly as the Zeus changed direction under Peres's orders, while the artifact continued on the original trajectory at 4,860 clicks per second. The vibration in Syree's head also ceased. She had become so accustomed to it that she didn't notice until it was gone. The *Zeus* was no longer straining to deliver twenty gees of thrust in order to gain one gee of acceleration. She was in free fall except for her lateral thrusters.

Twenty-five minutes till the first flyer came through the tunnel. Thirty minutes till the artifact would go through.

Syree corrected herself: *would try to go through*.

"Enemy vessel launching, sir!" Lee said. "A skeeter."

"What—"

"Skeeter flying straight for the space tunnel. Warship advancing toward us."

Frantically Syree keyed in data, but she already knew the answer. The skeeter was less than three hundred clicks from the tunnel. It would reach it far in advance of the artifact, which was still four and a half minutes away. When the first human flyer came through the tunnel, the skeeter would zap it. Then the skeeter itself would go through the space tunnel, changing its configuration so that the artifact would sail into Faller space.

Would the skeeter then stay on the other side of the tunnel? If it did, the second flyer would change the configuration back. Dart through, dart back to safety . . . the Faller warship would be too far away to reach the tunnel, even if it weren't busy with the *Zeus*. And the artifact would follow the second flyer into Caligula system space.

Yes.

But then Syree had another thought.

How long did the space tunnel "memory," if that was the term, hold true? Millennia? More? At some point, whoever made the artifact must have made it somewhere, at some point in space-time. Maybe that point was here, in this system. But maybe not. Maybe it *had* been manufactured elsewhere and brought here through this space tunnel. If so, would the space tunnel "remember" that, and return the artifact to whatever system it originally came from?

If so, both human and Faller maneuvering would go for nothing.

But it might go for nothing anyway. The mass of the artifact was too big to fit through a space tunnel.

Unless the human calculations were wrong. Unless there did exist that unknown variable, that fudge factor, that loophole.

Frustrated and helpless, all Syree could do was watch the displays. The artifact moved toward the space tunnel. The skeeter went into rapid acceleration around the tunnel. That made sense—the skeeter wanted the protection of its wave-phase alterer, which apparently needed very high velocity to function (why?). The Faller warship and the *Zeus* moved toward each other. Somewhere in Caligula system, fifty thousand light-years away and just on the other side of the tunnel, two flyers moved toward Space Tunnel #438. To find a skeeter waiting for them, a furious fast death they would never even see. Unless there *did* exist that unknown variable, that fudge factor, that loophole . . .

The outcome wasn't certain, she told herself. Not really. It was all a matter of probabilities.

TWENTY-SIX

IN THE NEURY MOUNTAINS

Dieter Gruber slept in the shallow cave for twenty hours straight. By the time Gruber woke, Bazargan felt better. He no longer vomited, and he could stand.

Ann said soberly, "I'm afraid there's still worse to come, Ahmed. With radiation sickness, the initial symptoms are often followed by a symptom-free period. But it doesn't last."

"I'll settle for symptom-free," Bazargan said dryly. He found he could get to his feet, although his knees still felt a bit watery. "I know I've probably got tissue damage, Ann, and genetic damage as well. Fortunately, I'm not planning on having any more children. Good morning, Dieter."

"Morning? Again?" Gruber sat up in the cave, blinking at its mouth. "How long was I asleep?"

"Twenty hours," Ann said. "It's actually afternoon."

"Ahmed?"

"I'm better," Bazargan said, half truthfully. Slowly he walked out of the cave. In the open space of the small upland valley, now flooded with sunlight, he pulled out the comlink and tried to raise the *Zeus*. Still nothing.

"Leave the link open," Gruber suggested, coming up behind him. "That way, if they've thought to leave their end open and contact resumes, we'll know it. We'll hear random noises on the *Zeus*."

"I intended to do so," Bazargan said quietly. Gruber, naturally, was unaware of the sarcasm. He stretched his massive forearms, yawned hugely, and laughed.

"I'm starved. Have we more protein powder, Ann? And I will wash in the stream. Making the scientific find of the century is dirty work!"

"Well, it's not a 'find' yet," Ann said. "Even if you're right and it generates some sort of probability field—"

"I'm right." Gruber grinned again.

"—which is responsible for the Worlders' shared reality, you don't know what will happen to it when Syree Johnson blows up Tas. If she does. And if Tas is somehow entangled with this buried thing."

Gruber stopped smiling. "You are right, of course. How much time remaining until those lunatics reach the space tunnel? By our best guess?"

Bazargan said, "Sometime today, I think. But we don't really know what's happening out there. Tas could already have been blown up, for all we know. Or gone through the space tunnel. Or anything."

Gruber accepted an expando of mixed protein powder from Ann. "Not gone through the space tunnel. It will not go. It is too big—I keep telling you this. Syree Johnson will try it, if she tries it at all, from total desperation."

Gruber drank his breakfast in one gulp. Ann said, "Tas didn't appear in the sky last night. After the clouds cleared, I checked, while you both were sleeping. I checked several times."

Bazargan said, "So the *Zeus* has at least moved Tas out of orbit. I think we better decide where we should be when it blows, if it blows. Dieter, is this cave still the best place?"

"Yes," Gruber said. "For you and Ann. But, Ahmed, I want to go back to the buried artifact. To see what happens there if its counterpart explodes a billion kilometers away. And if it emits Dr. Johnson's so-called 'wave effect.'"

Bazargan had expected this. He said mildly, "It's not a good idea, Dieter. You yourself said the descent down that one chimney was not easy. It's dangerous, isn't it?"

"Ahmed, anything worthwhile cannot be free of risks that—"

Ann said, "If you get killed going back there now, Dieter, there will be no one left who can explain to the Trans-Planetary University Funding Committee that digging out this artifact will be worth the expense and cultural disruption. Ahmed and I don't have the physics. You do, just barely. Without you, the buried artifact may well stay underground in the Neury Mountains for good."

She didn't look at Gruber as she said it; she stared across the tiny sunlit valley, her face carefully blank. But Bazargan saw the telltale twitch in the soft hollow of Ann's neck. She was gambling, to keep Gruber from yet another dangerous stunt. Bazargan smiled inwardly at the duplicity of women in love, and the secret smile seemed to him the first good thing that had happened in days. It gave him a peculiar and unexpected strength. Even as entire worlds were endangered, human connections endured.

He said soberly, "I'm afraid Ann is right, Dieter. If you die trying for a second look at the buried artifact, it will probably remain buried."

Gruber uttered what sounded like a blistering oath in German. He set off toward the stream, calling back over his shoulder, "I will wash now."

Bazargan weighed the cost of calling him back against the cost that the space artifact would blow in the brief time Gruber was immersed, exposed to the sky, in the very cold mountain water. He decided to let the geologist go. Perhaps it would help him cool his hot head.

"Come back inside, Ahmed," Ann said.

"Yes. But the comlink has to stay out here to keep possible contact with the *Zeus*. And I can't go too far inside, either, or I can't hear it." Assuming there was anything to hear.

Bazargan and Ann moved a few feet into the cave. Ann brought the blankets and arranged a makeshift couch. When Gruber rejoined them, he had put his s-suit back on. It, and he, looked marginally cleaner, a smeared gray instead of filthy and caked gray. Gruber's natural cheerfulness had returned. He set up various instruments from his pack both inside and outside the cave, then presented Ann with a gaudy red flower picked in the valley. "For you, *meine Blume*."

Ann smiled. Bazargan did not. He felt weak again, although not nauseated. "Sit down, Dieter. Sit down and tell me again what you think might happen to this buried 'probability field' if Tas blows."

"I have not the most blurry idea," Gruber said. "None. Really, Ahmed—until yesterday I did not know such a thing as a planetwide probability field could exist. Now you want me to say what it will do if a second artifact, a billion kilometers away, that may or may not be connected to the field, does or does not go through a space tunnel?"

"No speculations, even?"

"Sure, speculations. Why not? Tas will collapse into a black hole, its counterpart buried here will be forced by quantum mechanics to take the reverse state, and you and I and Ann will be inflated into gods. Able to control all probabilities. Walk through walls, align atoms, make love nonstop for days and days. Why not?"

Ann looked at Gruber with the mixture of exasperation and amusement with which mothers regard giddy small boys. Bazargan reminded himself that Gruber, too, had been under great strain.

"All right, Dieter. All right. We'll just wait."

"What else?" Gruber said, quiet now. "I know nothing about this situation, Ahmed. No one does. We all just sit and wait."

TWENTY-SEVEN

GOFKIT RABLOE

Y ou can't wait," David Pek Allen said to the priest bending over the farm cart. "Not even a minute."

How he hated talking to a priest! Enli thought. But talk he did, rasping out words around his swollen throat, looking as if he no longer knew what he said. Probably he did not. "Slimy, perverse, repulsive creature . . . you're only interested in using anything you can to get and keep power, aren't you? Even *this* situation! I wish I could kill you, rip you apart, you garbage . . . you exploitive *shit* . . ."

The priest gazed back at him, a mild, almost-middle-aged woman dressed in the rough clothes of a harvesting, bits of twigs and zeli fruit stuck to her tunic. She was heavily pregnant. Her bewildered brown eyes moved from the stricken human to Enli, the unreal Worlder. Enli saw the headpain that the sight of them cost her, that the whole situation cost her.

"The words have no meaning . . . ?"

"They are Terran words," Enli said. "I will say the World meaning for Pek Allen."

"Yes."

"He says the First Flower sent him and me as . . . as a message. That I have been in the Neury Mountains and am not dying, is a sign the message is indeed from the First Flower.

That Pek Allen is dying, in order to deliver the message that will save World, is a sign that he is real."

The priest nodded, her skull furrowed. She struggled, Enli saw, to understand. Not to accept—shared reality here was clear. Why else would a Terran die to save others, except that he shared the greater reality? There was no stronger proof. But nothing like this had ever happened in the quiet village of Gofkit Rabloe, nor anything like Pek Allen ever been seen.

He lay in obvious pain. Red dots had appeared on his face, his arms, his torso in its rock-torn rags. His swollen tongue was turning black, and bloody sputum flew from his peeling lips as he railed against the servant of the First Flower in a language she did not understand.

"You think I don't know what you are?" Pek Allen rasped. "Or who else is in on your little conspiracy? Bazargan, Voratur, that bitch Syree Johnson—" He tried to sit up on the cart, brandishing a clenched fist, but could not and sank back down on the zeli fruit.

Around the red dots, a slow burn flushed his skin, more than fever or rage. It looked, Enli thought, as if Pek Allen were being cooked alive, from the inside . . . Was that what the Neury Mountains did to people? But not to her, in the Terran s-suit he had given up to save Enli.

"You're all monsters, conspirators, vermin . . . *evil*. Keeping the power to oppress others—"

"He says," Enli told the priest in World, "to send word everywhere on World, immediately. To tell the nearest sun-flasher it is a great emergency. A terrible . . . sickness is coming from the sky. People must go into their root cellars and stay until told otherwise. Or they will die."

"Yes, die!" Pek Allen shrieked, in World this time. "All you conspirators should die! But you will not, because I will save you all, that's my burden, that's the reality . . ." He had subsided to muttering, and at some point had also subsided into Terran. Enli could no longer be sure of the difference. Nor could she be sure what, or how much, this simple rural priest, with her swollen belly and mild shocked brown eyes, actually understood.

More villagers crowded around the farm cart, drawn back from the harvest by the shared news. Each glanced at Pek Allen, recoiled in horror, and was hastily told by neighbors of the shift in reality. Each person then returned to the cart, skull furrowed in headpain, to stare at the Terran reality who was a gift from the First Flower.

Pek Allen found the strength to raise his right arm. He made a curious sign in the air, moving his hand down and then across. "Bless . . ." His eyes closed.

Not dead, Enli saw. But still cooking from inside.

The priest said in her soft mountain slur, "Pek Harit, Pek Villatir, and you, Unu . . . run to Gofkit Beslo. Pek Tarbif—"

Enli turned swiftly. "No, wait. There's more reality to share. The sickness will make certain objects dangerous. Turn them as deadly as the Neury Mountains themselves. No one must take any of these things with them into the root cellars. *No one.* The things are . . . Pek Allen?"

He had fainted, or fallen asleep, or gone into shock. His swollen lips cracked even as Enli watched, and began to bleed. She turned away, trying frantically to remember everything Pek Gruber had said.

"No one must bring any jewelry"—or had Pek Gruber said only gold jewelry? Enli couldn't remember, but it didn't matter—"no jewelry at all. No cooking pots. No flower honors, definitely no flower remembrances . . ." *That's mercury running around inside that ornamental glass,* Pek Gruber had said in Terran about the flower remembrances, which conveyed no meaning to Enli, but never mind that now. ". . . and . . . and no rocks that shine or sparkle in the dark. This is very important!"

"May your flowers bloom forever, Pek Brimmidin," the priest said.

"May your blossoms rejoice your soul," Enli answered, and the tired, middle-aged priest suddenly blurred in Enli's vision.

"All right," the woman said, still in that same tentative mild voice, but no one argued. This was shared reality. "You heard the items that must not go into the root cellars. Pek Harit, Pek Villatir, and you, Unu . . . run to Gofkit Besloe. Pek Tarbif, you have that fast new bicycle . . . go south on the main road as far as Pek Rafnil's, she'll get word to the sunflasher in Gofkit Amloe. You, Unja, bicycle to the Cannihifs' . . ."

Within a few minutes, she had her runners off. Within hours, Enli knew, the shifted reality of the sickness from the sky would be known all over World. Runners to tell runners, each one sending off many more, without question.

Nor did Enli question that all would obey. It was a message from the First Flower. It was shared reality.

The rain, which had never really stopped, suddenly fell harder. The little priest took Enli's arm. Enli saw that they were the only two left beside the cart. "I am Azi Pek Laridor, servant of the First Flower. Come with me, Pek Brimmidin. We will draw the cart to my house, and you and the . . . the Terran Pek can eat before we go to the root cellar. There is soup left from breakfast, I think, and the grandmother made bread yesterday. Come."

Enli followed her, stumbling along the muddy road toward rest and warmth.

TWENTY-EIGHT

SPACE TUNNEL #438

Fourteen thirty-one hours. The *Zeus* and the Faller warship closed in on each other from nine million clicks apart. The *Zeus* had once more turned on her main drive. Moving at the speed imparted by her long acceleration, she could have easily escaped the Faller warship, but that course was farthest from Peres's mind. This was war. He had swung the *Zeus* in a wide arc that would shortly bring the two ships within firing range of each other.

Fifty seconds left until the first flyer darted through Space Tunnel #438 from Caligula system.

Talk had resumed on the bridge of the *Zeus,* calm and impersonal talk. It was, Syree thought, as if each of them were a separate data terminal, efficiently connected, but with operating programs that did not touch.

The Faller skeeter orbited the tunnel at high velocity, less than thirty clicks from the nebulous panels that made up the tunnel's visible machinery.

Forty seconds.

Syree picked up her handheld. Once it was in her fingers, however, there was nothing to tell it. All the data about the artifact—everything they knew—was already stored in both the handheld and ship's library. Much of that data had also gone with the *Hermes* to Caligula command. So had every scrap of information about the Faller wave-phase alterer, about Space Tunnel #438, and even about the irrelevant anthropological expedition on the inhabited planet. There was no new information to add. But there was speculation.

Consider, for instance, the neutrino stream from the Neury Mountains, planetside. They had always disregarded that. It was probably some anomaly of radioactive rock distribution or planet formation . . . Syree was neither geologist nor cosmologist. And the neutrino stream was well within normal limits for radioactive rocks on a planet of this mass. Only its intense concentration in the Neury Mountains was peculiar. But since the radioactive field was purely local on the planet, having no effect whatsoever on the artifact or any other orbital object, Syree had left its exploration to the grinning, loutish-looking geologist on the landing team. Dr. Gruduer or Gruler, something like that. Radioactive rocks were not part of Syree's mission.

Thirty seconds.

But Orbital Object #7 emitted its wave effect by altering the binding energy of nuclei, which was of course the definition of radioactivity. Why hadn't someone made that connection before? Why hadn't Syree made it? She'd been too focused on the artifact itself, and on the time constraints in penetrating it before the enemy arrived. The constraints of war. They hampered thinking as well as action.

Two factors affected the stability of nuclei. The strong force attracted all protons and neutrons toward each other, while the electromagnetic force operated only between the protons in the nucleus and repelled them from each other. Since the strong force decreased more rapidly with separation distance than the electromagnetic force, for nuclei greater than a certain size, the strong force always "lost." Those nuclei did not have enough binding energy to hold them together, and were unstable. That much was so basic she seldom ever thought about it. It was just there, a given. Reality.

Twenty seconds.

But sometimes radiation was emitted from molecules despite the constraints of binding energy. Quantum events outside the energy barrier occurred all the time, although they could not of course be predicted or controlled. That was the nature of quantum theory, whose reality depended not on certainty but on probability. Part of a given nucleus's probability field always lay outside the expected range, so that, say, the emission of an alpha particle occurred despite the attractive strong force in the nucleus. The nucleus temporarily destabilized. In fact, one way to look at the wave effect of Orbital Object #7 was to say that it affected the theoretical probability fields of everything in its range. So normally stable atoms— or relatively stable, anyway—destabilized. That was what had killed Daniel Austen. An abnormal concentration of destabilized atoms . . .

Such as the neutrino detectors had identified in the Neury Mountains.

Ten seconds.

Syree sat frozen, for too long. Two seconds, three. No, it wasn't possible. Worse, you couldn't show if it was possible or not. The math didn't exist. The *theory* didn't exist. No one had ever identified, let alone created, a manipulatible probability field. But wasn't that what the new Faller wave-phase alterer came down to, in its essence? It manipulated the particle beam from the *Zeus* to keep it a wave whose path was never the one observed. In other words, the wave-phase alterer manipulated probability. But within a given field only, a field wrapped tightly around the skeeter, or else the fabric of spacetime itself might have been affected, including the node of it occupied by the *Zeus*. That hadn't happened.

Were the changes in probability caused by the radioactive "effect" emitted by Orbital Object #7 somehow linked to the improbable concentration of neutrinos coming from the Neury Mountains? If so, how? Was one or the other causal? Or were the artifact and the planetside neutrino source somehow "quantumly entangled," in whatever unknown way the two sides of a space tunnel were entangled to eliminate any spatial dimension between two points?

And if the artifact—once a planetary "moon"!—and the

Neury Mountains were macro-level entangled, how far did the field stretch? Orbital Object #7 had been moved over a billion clicks away from the Neury Mountains. Was it possible that anything done to one might still affect the other? Quantum entanglement was independent of distance.

"Flyer number one emerging from the space tunnel," Lee said crisply. "Commander—Oh, God . . ."

The flyer had emerged exactly on schedule, popping into existence as if newly created at that second. The next moment a beam shot out from the orbiting skeeter. The flyer disintegrated. The skeeter disappeared into the tunnel.

"Flyer destroyed," Lee said, and his voice faltered on the last syllable.

"Fire on the warship!" Peres said.

"Firing . . . a hit, sir. Range plus-five."

A plus-five hit would have inflicted barely minimal damage. The warship was barely in range, and Peres knew it. His order to fire, Syree thought, had been pure retaliatory instinct. A flyer pilot had just died. In his place she would have done the same thing.

Three minutes forty-one seconds until the second flyer appeared.

Peres stared at the artifact, racing toward the space tunnel circled by the waiting skeeter, which had darted back through. "Detonate," Peres said to Lee. "Now."

"No, wait!" Syree cried. She needed to think, to calculate— if the artifact *was* a probability field generator that could be manipulated, it had to be saved somehow, used somehow, it was too valuable to lose to the enemy—

"Detonating," Lee said, and Syree saw him key in the manual fail-safe commands.

Nothing happened.

The artifact continued to race at 4,860 clicks per second toward the space tunnel, now less than four minutes away.

"Damn it, I said detonate!" Peres said.

"I did! Repeating . . . repeating . . . it doesn't blow, commander. No, it does blow, the instruments say the explosives fired, but they didn't affect the artifact. And the residual radiation waves aren't there . . . aren't there *at all*. It's like the explosion happened and didn't happen at the same time . . . or the waves just went somewhere else!"

Outside the energy barrier, Syree thought. Into a different probability configuration. Another reality. The perfect defense.

Lee said, "One hundred fifty seconds until the second flyer emerges from the tunnel. Two hundred ten seconds until artifact reaches the tunnel . . . one hundred forty-five seconds . . ."

"Course change!" Peres said. "Dead on toward the tunnel, five gees acceleration, prepare to fire."

"Changing course. Accelerating . . ."

The frantic acceleration slammed Syree against her chair. A last effort on Peres's part to protect the second flyer. He could return later to attack the Faller warship, now actually closer to the tunnel than was the *Zeus,* thanks to the *Zeus*'s steep arcing. Now Peres's duty, as he saw it, was to fire on the skeeter, since he couldn't use the artifact to detonate it. Oh, Syree knew exactly how Peres was thinking. Maybe this skeeter, unlike that earlier one, wasn't equipped with the wave-phase alterer. Maybe Peres could take out the skeeter, saving the pilot's life *and* propelling the artifact into Caligula space. Peres was playing the wild card, hoping desperately to ride the long odds, the loophole, the unexpected probability.

Syree, crushed in her chair, gasped to breathe. They couldn't keep up five gees, of course, not without killing them all. But there were only ninety seconds left . . . eighty-five . . .

She couldn't speak. The force pressing on her lungs, her throat, choked off all air. But she could hear. Her comlink, sturdier than soft human tissues, came to life with a burst of static, followed by Bazargan's voice. When had the comlink come back on line? When the artifact failed to detonate? When the *Zeus* detached it? Earlier? There was no way to tell. And no way to respond; at this distance from Bazargan, the time lag was fifty-four minutes. All Syree could do was listen to words nearly an hour old.

"Dr. Johnson? Dr. Johnson? What's happening? Listen,

please, we've made a discovery here, buried in the Neury Mountains . . ."

The pressure on Syree's chest eased. Lee, or the overrides on the ship, had lessened the acceleration to save the crew. Syree felt her eyeballs burn and bulge outward, suddenly released from their fivefold weight.

Seventy seconds until the second flyer appeared.

". . . thinks it's some sort of probability field, and may be linked to Tas . . . to the artifact you're towing toward the space tunnel. Here is Dieter, he can explain much better than I . . ."

Syree tried to speak, couldn't. And there was nothing to say anyway.

Fifty seconds.

"Dr. Johnson, Dieter Gruber here. Are you there?"

On the display the Faller warship picked up speed, moving as fast as it could toward the space tunnel. Presumably to destroy the *Zeus* before it attacked the skeeter.

"*Scheiss,* what is wrong with me? They are an hour away at light speed, Ahmed, of course they don't answer."

Answer. No, Syree couldn't answer, perhaps not in this life. Too bad, really, she would have liked to work on this fascinating new problem, this probability field. Increasing the likelihood of nuclear emission only in specific ranges and among specific atoms . . . amazing. Unprecedented. Another reality.

"Fire," Peres said.

The proton beam shot out from the *Zeus* as the ship sped toward the space tunnel. Bruised, popping eyes tried desperately to focus on the displays. The beam hit the skeeter . . . and went through it.

No, Syree thought. Went through a different configuration of matter, with different probabilities of being "observed." "Detected." "Intercepted." And wasn't.

The skeeter dived for the tunnel, and within thirty seconds had disappeared into it.

In another ten seconds the skeeter was back.

The human flyer popped out of the space tunnel.

The waiting skeeter destroyed it. Then the skeeter flew once again into the tunnel.

"Firing on the artifact," Lee said, and Syree realized that she hadn't heard Peres give the command, although of course he must have. The detonators hadn't worked, but a proton beam from the *Zeus* . . . the probability was—

The beam shot out from the ship, crossed space at light speed, and hit the artifact. Nothing happened. Fourteen seconds later, Orbital Object #7 hit the invisible outer edges of Space Tunnel #438. A Schwarzschild radius is not a probable number. It does not sometimes exist, sometimes not. The mass of Orbital Object #7, too great to go through the tunnel, was collapsed and imploded, but not before whatever it housed sent a massive wave effect in all directions as it had been designed to do, a final defense when its attacker was too great for any other. It was a simple matter of the equations, without unknown variables, without loopholes, without fudge factors. Without anomalies lying outside the energy barrier.

Classical physics, not quantum physics, controlled the artifact's end.

The Faller warship, closer, caught the wave first. Syree saw it happen on the display. The enemy ship glowed, brighter and brighter, and then exploded like the trillions of tiny nuclear bombs it had become. The wave traveled at the speed of light, but as the destruction of Daniel Austen's shuttle had shown, it was also subject to the inverse square law. The *Zeus* was much farther away than the Faller ship had been. Maybe, Syree thought, far enough away that the wave will have spent itself . . . or if at maximum force it actually affected elements with an atomic number lower than seventy-five . . .

Her major regret was that she would, in all probability, never know what had really happened.

From her comlink Gruber's voice—that was his name, Gruber—said in disgust, "Ahmed, we cannot talk to them . . ."

No, because we're somewhere else, Syree thought, *or will be,* and actually felt her lips curve into a grin as the wave effect hit, so little diminished by distance that there was no perceptible lag before the *Zeus* exploded from selected nuclei outward and ceased to exist.

* * *

The wave raced outward in all directions.

Syree Johnson and her team of physicists had been right; at its lower settings, the wave effect from Orbital Object #7 obeyed the inverse square law. The weapon had been designed that way. Things that should be destroyed close up could therefore be taken care of, without undue damage to farther things that should not be destroyed.

Full-strength setting, however, was another matter. Full-strength was only activated by meeting a force that could destroy the entire weapon itself, and anything that could do that was very dangerous indeed. It must also be destroyed, no matter how far away it might be.

In fourteen minutes two seconds, the wave reached the nearest planet in the star system. Worlders, watching it wander through their sky, had named it Nimitri, "the sister blossom." A bleak, frozen, atmosphereless globe of rock, Nimitri was rich in iridium and platinum, with unusually large amounts of thorium and uranium. The nuclei of these deposits, plus those of every other element with more than seventy-five protons in the nucleus, destabilized. They underwent substantial increases in the probability that each nucleus would emit a radioactive particle at any given time. Radioactive decay accelerated dramatically.

When the phenomenon subsided, Nimitri was the most radioactive object in the system by a factor of twenty-nine—for the time being. However, there was no life on Nimitri to recognize this fact, or to be affected by it.

The wave effect sped on toward World.

TWENTY-NINE

IN THE NEURY MOUNTAINS

As the long afternoon wore on, Bazargan lay on the humans' collective blankets just inside the cave, while Gruber and Ann sat apart, talking in low voices. Bazargan could make out no words. On reflection, he decided he was glad of this. If they were discussing the coming wave effect, he felt too weak to follow what would undoubtedly be multiple complicated speculations. If, on the other hand, the pair were talking personally, Bazargan didn't want to hear.

What he must think about was what to do after the wave effect struck. He was still the leader of this sorry expedition, after all. A leader mildly cooked by radiation, of an expedition with two dead children, one team member missing and crazy, and one kidnapped alien, also missing and, by now, possibly also driven crazy by either the Terran lunatic or her own biology.

The ancient Persian poets didn't write verse that covered this situation. Unless, of course, you chose to stretch a situation. Sadi, for instance:

When the heart wanders, seeking endless change,
And from its own safe solitude does range,
Nor peace it finds, nor any virtue more ...

Certainly true enough! He'd left the safe solitude of academe for the field, and at the moment both peace and virtue seemed in very short supply.

Or—another thought—perhaps he, Ahmed Bazargan, had just become too old for fieldwork. As every anthropologist eventually did.

"Ahmed, what are you thinking?" asked Ann, the ever sensitive. Gruber looked around vaguely; undoubtedly in his theorizing he had forgotten that Bazargan was even there.

Bazargan said, "I was just planning what we should do after the wave effect passes. If we're still alive."

Gruber said, "We leave the mountains. Call the *Zeus*, find David, leave World, convince the authorities on Earth to send a properly equipped expedition to dig out the buried artifact."

"You make it sound so simple, Dieter."

"Well, no, not simple . . ."

Ann said, "We start by leaving the mountains, that much is true. Ahmed, you can't go back the way we came. You are too sick."

And too afraid to repeat that tiny tunnel. Bazargan was grateful to her for not saying it aloud.

"But," Ann continued, "Dieter thinks we can find another route, based on his explorations yesterday. He will go first, scout it, and return for us."

"Fine," Bazargan said. "But first—listen! The comlink!"

Static spewed from the comlink, left out in the open beyond the lip of the cave. Bazargan staggered to his feet and, supported by Gruber, lurched into the darkening afternoon. Ann bent to scoop up the link and hand it to him.

"Dr. Johnson? Dr. Johnson? What's happening? Listen, please, we've made a discovery here, buried in the Neury Mountains . . ." First things first. Bazargan had no idea how long anyone at the other end would listen. "Dr. Gruber thinks it's some sort of probability field, and may be linked to Tas . . . to the artifact you're towing toward the space tunnel. Here is Dieter, he can explain much better than I . . ."

Gruber seized the comlink. "Dr. Johnson, Dieter Gruber here. Are you there?"

No answer.

"*Scheiss*, what is wrong with me? They are an hour away at light speed, Ahmed, of course they don't answer."

"A billion clicks," Ann said, off to one side.

Finally Gruber said in disgust, "Ahmed, we cannot talk to them. Only make a report."

"Well, then, do so. And afterward leave the link open."

Bazargan returned with the blankets inside the cave. Ann and Gruber stayed outside, under the open sky. Bazargan watched them pass the comlink back and forth, each explaining what had been noted, discovered, conjectured. Bazargan, through a haze of weakness, caught only the occasional word. Lagerfeld scan. Probability field. Neurotransmitter exocytosis. Buried artifact. Space tunnel, toroidal field, beta decay . . .

Yes. He was too old for any more fieldwork.

He drifted into the fitful, unsatisfying sleep of the ill. Gruber woke him, calling back from the lip of the cave, "Ahmed! Ahmed! Syree Johnson spoke on the comlink. She said, 'Dr. Gruber, Syree Johnson here,' and then stopped. She——"

A roar: cataclysmic, explosive. It was so loud that the plastic comlink jumped on the valley floor. Bazargan heard the sound echo in the cave behind him, and a moment later echo again from the rock walls across the valley.

Then silence.

Finally Bazargan said quietly, "That was the *Zeus*, I think. All of them . . . dead . . ."

Gruber said, "Get back farther in the cave. Now. The wave effect also travels at c."

The three of them scuttled backward. Bazargan tried not to think what might happen if the wave caused a planetquake and the cave collapsed. But wouldn't that have happened simultaneously with the radio communication? No, Gruber had mentioned some sort of time lag . . .

They sank to the floor and waited.

Nothing happened.

Ann said finally, "I don't know what I expected, exactly . . . light, sound, action . . ."

"Look here," Gruber said. "My suit—all of our suits—they

are not registering increased radiation. If the wave effect were really destabilizing everything with an atomic number above seventy-five, the trace radiation in these rocks should jump . . . but nothing. *Nichts*."

"What does that mean?" Ann said.

"I must check my instruments." He got to his feet.

"Not yet," Bazargan said sharply. "Your instruments are all outside. If there is a lag effect, you'll be exposed. Wait here."

Reluctantly Gruber sat down again. Minutes passed. Finally he said, "Wait how long?"

Ann giggled. Both men stared at her. "I'm sorry," she said, sounding horrified at herself. "It's awful, I know . . . but all I can think of is my mother warning us not to go in swimming for an hour after we eat lunch!"

Bazargan's mother had told him that, too. Despite himself, he smiled.

"Well, I don't wait an hour!" Gruber said.

He didn't. Gruber stood decisively, shot a warning glance at Bazargan, and strode out of the cave.

In ten more minutes he was back. "I checked them all," he said, and even in the gloom Bazargan could read the bewilderment on his ruddy face. "All the instruments, all over the valley. No radiation increase, not of any kind, even near a small deposit of thorium! No thermal increase, no nothing! The wave didn't hit us!"

Bazargan said, "Maybe it weakened too much before it reached here."

"Possibly. The inverse square law . . . but there is something else!"

Ann said, "What, Dieter? You look . . . What is it?"

"The instruments, they are time-tagged. An hour ago there was a seismic wave originating a quarter kilometer underneath the valley. Too weak for us to notice, but definite, and coming from the artifact. An *hour ago*!"

Bazargan didn't understand. "So?"

"The seismic wave occurred exactly fifty-four minutes before Syree Johnson replied to us on comlink. Fifty-four minutes before the explosion! Do you see what that means?"

Bazargan, too weak to think clearly, didn't see. It was Ann who said, "The wave reached us fifty-four minutes before we heard the *Zeus* explode. The sound of the explosion—and of Colonel Johnson speaking—traveled at light speed. But the seismic activity set off by the buried artifact—*that* happened the same moment that Tas exploded."

"Instantaneous," Gruber agreed. "*Ach,* Ann, you do see—it means they were entangled! No space-time between them, like electrons in quantum entanglement. What it *could* mean . . . everything different from what we know. Everything changed."

"If it was an instantaneous increase in the probability field around World . . . But we have no idea how to be sure that's what happened. We don't even have any idea how to measure anything like a probability field. What units do you use? Not any ordinary ones. Your instruments showed nothing, except for a physical shifting of rock, and that's certainly a side effect of what happened. Whatever it was!"

"But then I cannot prove anything at all happened! Or that the buried artifact did anything!"

"Maybe it didn't. Maybe the seismic wave was coincidence."

"Coincidence! At the exact moment the *Zeus* blew up? No, no . . . the buried artifact was instantaneously affected when Tas exploded, or however it was destroyed. The buried artifact responded—it generated a probability field that neutralized any effect of the wave hitting World. Listen, *Liebchen*—radiation emission from nuclei is always a matter of probabilities. The emitted particle must tunnel through the energy barrier, and it can do that only because part of the probability field lies outside the barrier. So if the probability field blanketing World changed the probabilities of the wave-destabilizing nuclei . . . *But I cannot prove any of this!*"

It was a wail of intellectual despair.

Bazargan struggled to speak. "But we have one measure of the probability field . . . Ann said . . . the human brain."

Gruber said, "But my brain felt nothing different! Did yours? Yours!"

Bazargan and Ann shook their heads. But then Ann said, "Not the human brain, Ahmed. We're in the middle of this null zone in the field, remember? And our brain didn't evolve in this probability field, anyway. That's the whole point of why we can't 'share reality.' We need to see the effect of the wave, if it came, on *Worlders'* brains. On Enli."

"Yes!" Dieter said. "All right, Ahmed, can you travel? Let's go!"

Protest would be useless, Bazargan saw. And he wasn't going to get any fitter to travel in the very near future, anyway. No point in delay.

Ann said, "Shouldn't you find an easier way out first, Dieter? Make the trip as easy on Ahmed as possible."

"I know an easy way," Gruber said, unstoppable. "Mostly. Come on, Ahmed, I will carry you."

Bazargan got to his feet. He didn't want Gruber to carry him. But by leaning on both the geologist and Ann, Bazargan could hobble along without too much discomfort. Out of the Neury Mountains.

And into what? If the wave had affected the rest of World beyond Gruber's null zone, then there might be widespread physical havoc. If the wave—or the probability field possibly defending against it—had affected Worlder brains . . . then who knew *what* they would find beyond the mountains?

THIRTY

GOFKIT RABLOE

Having dispatched her fellow villagers to alert World, Azi Pek Laridor, servant of the First Flower, took Enli and Pek Allen to the village root cellar, which was communal, sturdy, and large. Enli had seen many like it in small farming villages. If larger villages ran out of food that could be preserved, Gofkit Rabloe was prepared to barter its surplus for "town sweets": fine cloth, bicycles, glass vessels, flower remembrances.

This root cellar was built into the side of a low hill. Azi pulled open the sloping wooden door. Most of the harvesters had gone as runners, but the old, young, and infirm were gathering up their necessary belongings to join Azi in the cellar. Enli saw them moving from the village square toward the hillside.

"Faauggh," Azi said. "Smells damp. We've had so much rain . . . But we build well, Enli. It's not too uncomfortable." She held up an oil lamp and led the way down, her gravid belly unbalancing her slightly on the three stone steps. The steps descended to a wooden platform that covered the entire floor, keeping it dry above the hard-packed dirt. The cellar smelled of loam and wood, mixed with the spicy lively odor of dried zeli fruit. Around the walls were crude wooden shelves packed with jars, crates, and vegetables. Wooden barrels dotted the floor, each marked with a family emblem. The barrels also served as tables for more oil lamps, which Azi lit, one by one. No attempt had been made to create beauty here; except for the round utilitarian barrels, all was straight lines and sharp angles. Yet there was a flower altar, to the right of the door.

Enli touched it. She had the right to do so, now that she was again real. Since it lived underground, the altar bore no living blooms. But on its carved stone sat a vase of dried trifalitib, their purple faded to a soft lavender, still wafting delicate scent over the altar. Beside it lay flower remembrance, memorial to the gardens of years past. This remembrance had obviously come from someplace other than Gofkit Rabloe. In the top chamber was more dried trifalitib—it must be the patron flower of Gofkit Rabloe. In the bottom chamber ran the quick bright liquid that World called *flowersoul* and Pek Gruber had called *mercury*.

"This will have to go outside, I'm afraid," Enli said to Azi. "Will you . . ."

"Yes, I must do it," agreed Azi, the priest. She finished lighting the lamps, her movements slowed by the curve of her belly. "But first let's get Pek Allen inside and comfortable. Here comes Pek Callin, first as usual. Nothing happens except that old woman hears about it first."

Enli looked up the steps, out the door. Hobbling toward her was the old woman Pek Allen had threatened, grandmother to Estu, the child that Pek Allen had stolen. Pek Callin led Estu by the hand. Both moved slowly, but determinedly. As they passed the farm cart on which Pek Allen lay, the old woman glanced at him, recoiled, and kept hobbling forward. But, Enli saw, it was a recoil at the way Pek Allen looked, battered and bleeding and cooked, rather than because Pek Allen had terrorized herself and her granddaughter. That was then; this was the present reality. Reality had shifted, and now Pek Allen was real, so of course the old woman accepted him. That was shared truth.

Enli understood. But she couldn't share, not fully. She knew too much more that the old woman did not, and never would. Enli was real, but nonetheless the fierce headpain, which had left her as she and Azi pulled the farm cart, returned between her eyes.

Azi was fussing around the root cellar. "Come in, come in, Udello, pick a corner before the others arrive. You brought blankets? Good, the ones here seem to have become a bit damp . . . What else did you bring? Enli will look, there are objects which will catch the sky sickness, you know, and that we don't want! But first let's get Pek Allen comfortable."

That didn't seem possible. Pek Allen was still asleep, but he stirred and cried out as the two women lifted him. Touching him, moving him, seemed to cause him horrible pain. But he bore it, eyes squeezed shut, without further noise as Enli and Azi settled him on a pile of tarps. They covered him with a dry blanket in the far corner of the root cellar.

"Water . . ."

"In this barrel," Azi said to Enli, and left to carry the flower remembrance reverently outside. Enli brought Pek Allen a dipper, but he could only drink a few drops. The rest dribbled across his reddening, charred-looking chin and neck, and seemed to cool it. Carefully Enli poured more drops over him.

He opened his eyes then, and Enli saw their bloody whites and filmed brown irises. The irises stared straight ahead, unseeing. He was blind.

More villagers appeared, including a few back from their running assignments. They all settled into the cellar while Azi kept count and Enli checked each person to make sure nothing had been brought into the cellar that had been on Pek Gruber's forbidden list. Some of the villagers grumbled at missing harvest light. Some looked frightened of this unknown sickness from the sky. Others took it as a religious occasion, this sign from the First Flower, and sat contemplating bouquets they brought inside with them. A few young people took advantage of the forced closeness to cuddle beside each other in gloomy corners, hands and thighs touching.

But no one protested, objected, refused. No one blamed Enli, or Azi, or Pek Allen. Everyone accepted that they must be here, now, for a short while, and so there was no dissent. It was shared reality.

"Nowhere . . . else . . . in the known . . . universe," Pek Allen gasped, and Enli had to lean close to catch the rasped words. Blood trickled from the corners of his mouth. "Enli . . . tell them."

"Tell them what?" Enli murmured back, but Pek Allen had again closed his eyes.

"Everyone's here," Azi announced, much later. "Close the door, Hertil."

A big muscular man with lush neckfur lowered the root cellar door. The light was barely diminished. Outside the ceaseless rain fell from dark clouds; inside, the oil lamps glowed cheerfully. To the odors of packed dirt, water, and dried zeli were now added the smell of too many bodies in too small a space. Enli breathed in deeply, and her headpain eased a little.

The villagers began to sing. No one started it, and at first two or three different songs competed, but everyone quickly settled into the same tune, a harvest chant. A version of it was sung in Enli's village, Gofkit Jemloe. A version of it was probably sung in every harvest village on World. Enli joined in the soft singing.

More songs, and then, again in unison, everyone fell silent. Azi said, speaking for them all, "Pek Allen? How long must we stay in here to be safe from the sky sickness?"

Tell them, Pek Allen had said. Enli answered in as strong a voice as she could, despite the pain it cost her. "We must stay here until there comes a sign from the First Flower."

Everyone nodded, then went back to singing, this time the oldest, most beloved songs: the flower lyrics.

Only Enli sat silent. She had said the first thing that came into her head, and it had been accepted as shared reality. She had said it because someone must say something, even if no one knew for certain what the reality actually was. And because the villagers—here and on the rest of World—could not stay underground forever. And because, looking at him during the softest and most melodious of the flower songs, Enli had seen that Pek Allen was dead.

Everyone but Enli fell asleep, at close to the same time. Enli thought it must be late afternoon, but in the root cellar there was no way to tell. Always before, Enli had been able to do what the others did: sleep when she chose to, when there was nothing else to do, when others slept around her. Not this time. Soft breathing rose and fell in the steady gloom of the oil lamps, and the comfortable odor of slumbering bodies filled her nostrils. But she could not share the reality of sleep with the others, even though she was again real.

She gazed at Pek Allen's dead face. How long did it take the bodies of Terrans to decay enough to release their souls? If they had souls, of course.

David Pek Allen had had a soul. Shared reality said so. And so did Enli's own brain.

Sitting beside him on the wooden floor, Enli considered what she should do next. Not what shared reality said to do: what *she* should do, even though this hiding in the root cellar was a shared thing.

Immediately the headpain started.

Enli found herself standing apart from the pain, watching it. Unseen by any living thing, her eyes widened. She had never done such a thing before: stand apart from a shared-reality headpain, as if it were not "she," but something else. But of course it was she. Then how could she be watching it, from the outside? There was no outside, there was only her brain, only reality . . .

The headpain grew abruptly worse. It wasn't as bad, she realized, as headpain she had felt when she'd been unreal. But now she was weak, hungry, frightened, and the pain was bad enough. Enli moaned softly and pressed her hands to her eyes. Wouldn't this ever end? She was real again, *damn it,* this wasn't supposed to happen when one was real . . . *damn it* was Terran, not World, the words had just slithered into her mind . . . into her head! Oh, her head!

All at once, the headpain stopped.

It didn't fade away. Instead, it disappeared instantly and completely, between one breath and the next. In its place, something happened to Enli's brain, something sent to her from outside her skull. Exultation filled her, a pure joy greater than anything she had ever known. Greater than any flower ceremony, greater than at a farewell burning, greater than her love for Tabor . . . Tabor! Who would now also be free, who would rejoin their ancestors, whom she would see again in the world of spirits!

Enli laughed aloud. In the dim root cellar, surrounded by sleeping farmers, she laughed like a child, like Fentil, and had no idea why. It wasn't because Tabor was free—that wasn't a new idea. Yet it *was* because Tabor was free, because she herself was free, because the World was full of flowers and the First Flower had just sent her a sign.

"What . . . did you speak?" Azi said sleepily, raising her head from the wooden floor. "I thought I heard you . . . I dreamed . . ."

The exultation was fading now, more slowly than it had come. In its ebbing, Enli smiled at the little round priest. "We can go out now, Azi. The sky sickness is over."

"You had a sign?"

"Yes. What did you dream?"

Azi blinked, looking confused. "I don't know. But it was wonderful. Wait . . . my sister was in it. And our old home, in Gofkit Kenloe. Oh, and a talking rock—something strange and unlikely!"

"Low probability."

"What?"

"Nothing. The word is Terran. We can go out now, Azi. Wake everyone."

Unquestioningly, Azi turned to do so. "Enli—Pek Allen is dead!"

"Yes," Enli said, "I know."

"May his soul rejoice in the flowers of his ancestors."

"May his garden bloom forever. Will you do the farewell burning?"

"Of course. Unja, wake up now, we can go out. Riflit, Unu, Pek Callin . . . wake up. Enli, may I ask you a question?"

Enli stood, looking down at Pek Allen. They would need flowers for the ceremony, and gathering them would delay the zeli harvest even more. Well, it couldn't be helped. "Yes, Azi?"

"We know now that Pek Allen is real. Are the other Terrans real, too? Pek Bazargan and Pek Sikorski and Pek Gruber? Has reality shifted about them, too?"

Even here, in remote Gofkit Rabloe, they knew the strange names. Enli reached down and pulled the edge of the blanket over Pek Allen's burned face.

"I don't know, Azi. The First Flower didn't tell me. That's a question for Reality and Atonement, still."

Azi nodded. "Of course. Unja, you lazy thing, wake up! It's time to go back out!"

THIRTY-ONE

GOFKIT RABLOE

Gruber was good at spelunking. Against all odds, he found a fairly direct way out of the Neury Mountains that was not too claustrophobic, nor too long, nor too wet. Bazargan was surprised, although he realized he shouldn't be. Gruber had not only knowledge but also enormous physical strength and an optimism that could focus itself within a narrow circumference. He was well suited to tunnels.

They emerged into evening woodland, the lush fast-growing woodland of World, under myriad green-purple leaves like sheltering hands. The sun had already set and the light was pearly and thin, looking curiously pure. Paths had been cut through the brush, as paths had been cut everywhere on this domesticated continent. Bazargan's nostrils filled with the delicious scents of evening. Day-blooming flowers closed and night-blooming ones opened, shy dapples of color in the cool shade.

Bazargan leaned on Gruber, Ann trailing gamely behind, carrying Gruber's pack. Despite lingering weakness, Bazargan found he could walk. Evidently he was still between the onset symptoms of radiation sickness and the debilitation yet to come.

"The forest won't be large," he said to Gruber, who nodded.

Forests on World never were. Small and numerous best supplied the woodland needs of World, so that all could have access to lumber and wildflowers. Bazargan, limping along, was grateful for World's shared generosity.

"Better I arm myself, then," Gruber said, which was not what Bazargan had had in mind. But the geologist was right. Humans were still outcasts, sinners, fit subjects for murder. Gruber transferred Bazargan's weight to Ann, then hunted up a thick branch to use as a club and began looking for a second one. David Allen, of course, had the gun. What had he done with it since he and Enli disappeared?

The answer could only be bad.

"Here comes someone," Ann said quickly. "Dieter?"

Gruber, branch in either hand, moved in front of the other two humans.

A Worlder, half hidden by trees, called, "Habkint? Is that you? Have you already heard?"

Gruber, his World less fluent than the others', whispered, "What does he say?"

"Habkint? We can all come out now, the sky sickness is past, but you must have already heard from—" The Worlder stopped dead.

He was young, just past adolescence, with golden curling neckfur and skull skin smooth as an egg. The golden fur lay matted with sweat; it darkened the armpits and chest of his rough tunic and beaded on his upper lip. He had been running, racing along in last light with the joyous strength of the young to spread the news, whatever it was, to whomever dwelt even farther away from a village than he did.

Bazargan said quickly in World, "The sky sickness is past? How do you know?"

"Word from . . . from Gofkit Rabloe . . ." the boy stammered. "You're Terran!"

Despite himself, Bazargan smiled. He saw that the smile registered the same moment as did the boy's headpain. The boy put one hand to his skull and ran back the way he had come, crashing into brush piled at the side of the cleared path and setting a flock of lifegivers swirling upward from a clump of yellow vekifirib.

Ann said grimly, "That answers that. I guess we're still unreal."

"In that case," Gruber said, "we go no farther. The villages are not safe for us. In fact, I think we must go back to the mountains, Ahmed. A little way in. They will not come to kill us there, and I can gather food from fields at night."

Ann said, "And David and Enli?"

Gruber remained silent.

After a moment Ann said heavily, "I think you're right, Dieter. We need to stay where Worlders won't track us. It isn't as if we can even make inquiries about David and Enli. No one would tell us anything. As far as we know, they're still inside the mountains somewhere. If not . . ." She didn't finish the sentence, but Bazargan did.

"If not, they're probably dead."

Ann looked away. Bazargan went on, as steadily as he could, wanting all three of them to face reality. "If we go into the mountains, it will be for how long? If we're unreal, we can't ever show ourselves to Worlders. The *Zeus* has been destroyed—Peres isn't going to ever send a shuttle for us. Especially not if the Fallers hold the system now. Do we just live like cavemen in the Neury Mountains, stealing food and drinking irradiated water until we die?"

"And what about the research?" Gruber asked. "If brains of Worlders are indeed the only documentable measure of the probability field, we must ask Enli what happened to her brain at the moment that Tas blew up."

Bazargan said irritably, "The research isn't our most immediate concern. Survival is. How long do you think we can hide in the caves?"

Gruber and Ann looked at each other. It was Ann who answered, but it might have been either one of them. Sometimes Bazargan forgot how young they were, with the hopefulness of youth. "As long as necessary, Ahmed. We stay in the caves as long as necessary."

Gruber added, "Who knows what will happen?"

Bazargan lacked the energy to argue. He didn't even know what he was arguing in favor of. They had no choice, unless they wished to commit group suicide. Or let themselves be murdered by Worlders.

"Let's go, then."

They turned back toward the mountains. Darkness fell fast on planets with little axial tilt. Already two of the moons were visible, Ap and Lil, or Cut and Ral, or Sel and Obri. But not Tas. Never again Tas.

Ann broke the silence. "Wait—I just realized something! Did you hear what that young messenger said? He said, 'We can all come out now, the sky sickness is past.' David or Enli, or both, must have gotten out and warned Worlders about the wave effect!"

"*Ja!*" Gruber said. "Do you think—"

The comlink shrilled.

Bazargan actually jumped; he'd forgotten he still carried it. The three humans stared wildly at each other. Ann whispered, "The *Zeus*? But how . . ."

Fumbling in his s-suit, Bazargan finally located the link and activated whatever message it had just recorded.

"Dr. Bazargan," said a voice in English but with a heavy, unplaceable accent, "this is Lieutenant Michihiko Gray on the flyer *Gnat*, attached to the battleship *Hachiya*, Solar Alliance Defense Council Base #32, Caligula system. I have just exited Space Tunnel #438 and am proceeding at all possible speed toward the inhabited planet, for the purpose of retrieving your party. At the moment this system is free of enemy craft, but please be advised that this state may or may not remain stable. This message will reach you in fifty-four minutes. My ETA is three days twenty hours. Reply discreetly, but with inclusions of your position coordinates on the planet, plus number of persons in your party. End message."

"Ha!" Gruber shouted. "They come for us! Ahmed, send our position."

"You do it," Bazargan said, overcome by another wave of weakness. Gruber seized the comlink and gave the data, finishing, "We are . . . Ahmed? Three? Four? Five?"

Five. Gruber must be thinking of Enli, if she was still alive. Her own people had declared her unreal. She was a failed informant. Would they murder her, then, unless the humans took her with them? But if Enli had already delivered her message, or David had, and she or he still lived . . . There was no way to know for sure what had happened.

Bazargan said, "Three or four or five."

"We are three or four or five, undetermined at this time." Gruber said. "Send probable landing time. And thank you."

Bazargan started wearily forward . . . all that long way to walk back into the mountains. But Gruber put a restraining hand on Bazargan's arm.

"Wait, Ahmed. Just another small minute. I must do this while we are still out from under rock cover."

In the falling gloom, the big man peeled down his s-suit and sat on the ground. Bazargan caught the brief glint of moonlight on the knife as Gruber sliced free the sewn flap of skin and removed the emergency comlink from his thigh. He didn't even wipe it free of blood before using it.

"David . . . David Allen. This is Dieter Gruber. Answer, please."

Silence. *It should have been I that did that,* Bazargan thought. But he had been too weary to think of it, too sick to carry it out. Wordlessly Ann knelt beside Gruber and swabbed meds on the gash on his leg.

"Ach, you don't answer, David. Then I will record."

Pointless, Bazargan thought. If David Allen wasn't answering, it was because he was dead. The Worlders had killed him. Proof that they had decided Terrans were, indeed, unreal.

But Gruber was not interested in facts. He went on from hope. "If you receive this message, David, answer on the planet-use frequency. Give your position. We will come for you if we must, or you can come to us. A flyer will rescue us all in three days, twenty hours. Bring Enli with you if she is in fatal danger here. We all think of you."

"That's all you can do, Dieter," Ann said softly.

"I know. We must go. Come, Ahmed, lean on me."

Bazargan did, although he would not have bet that Gruber

remembered he was there. Moving as quickly as possible along the darkening path, Gruber planned excitedly with Ann. "With orbital scanning equipment on the flyer, we have another chance to find David and Enli, *ja*? And then we can ask Enli in detail about what happened to her sense of shared reality when the wave effect hit World . . . maybe a Lagerfeld will even show some permanent, documentable brain effects. And an expedition can be formed to excavate the probability-field artifact from the mountains. Ann, an entire new era of science will begin, things we have only speculated about."

She answered in the same excited tone, but Bazargan lost her actual words. He was trying to picture what might have happened on World if David and Enli had indeed delivered their message about the "sky sickness." Word would have spread over the entire planet, efficiently delivered, unquestioned by any hearer, and the entire planet would have obeyed the call to safety. There was nowhere else in the known universe where such a reality could be possible. Nowhere.

And Enli . . . if Worlders did still consider her someone to be murdered, then the humans must take her with them. But in Caligula system, or on Earth or Mars or the Belt, surrounded by the permanently unreal, Enli's headpain would be terrible and unceasing. No shared reality for her at all; Bazargan wasn't even sure she could survive that. Although given a choice, perhaps Enli would prefer death on Caligula to death on World, because on Caligula her body could decay and she would, in her truth, have the chance to rejoin her ancestors.

But before that death, which could take years, Enli would live without sharing the reality of the human worlds. It would be for her a horrifying, completely discordant existence. Like putting a delicate blossom from a flower lyric into the scream of a shuttle launch.

Or like putting a human on World.

Ann and Gruber still foamed with enthusiasm. Bazargan didn't have the heart to tell them that none of it would come to pass. Any expedition to explore the buried artifact would have to get past the powerful political fact that humans were no longer welcome on World. An examination of Enli's brain, or even of her subjective memory, might indeed reveal that something had happened to her shared-reality mechanism when Tas had exploded. But it would be anecdotal evidence only, undocumentable and, by definition, unrepeatable. Therefore, not science.

And another truth must be recognized and shared as well. Even if poor David Allen's most grandiose fantasy came true and some geneticist could have found a way to genetically splice the shared-reality mechanism into the human genome, it would make no difference. Shared reality could develop nowhere else but on World, swathed in the probability-altering field of the buried artifact. Shared reality might be a true reality, but it was one closed to human beings.

The last of the sun's afterglow disappeared from the little forest. Gruber turned on his powerful torch, and it illuminated for the three humans a narrow, temporary path of light through the alien woods.

EPILOGUE

GOFKIT RABLOE

People had been arriving all day, usually in twos and threes, on bicycles and on foot and in farm carts. Some wore expensive tunics and shawls, but not very many. Except for the priests from Reality and Atonement, who had traveled from Rafkit Seloe, most of the people came from the rural villages near the Neury Mountains. These were the ones that had adopted this particular ceremony as their own. Enli saw Azi Pek Laridor arrive, pulling a small and dilapidated farm cart, Calit jumping up and down in the cart beside the new infant asleep in a basket. Azi looked dusty and hot and content. She set down her cart near the back of the small crowd, flexed her shoulders, and frowned at Calit. The child subsided, but not much.

Enli stood neither far nor near the flower altar. It was plain for an altar, a single bare curving slab of stone supported by three legs curved like trifalit stems. The flower beds surrounding the altar weren't spectacular, either, although the lush pajal bushes made a colorful display. Yellow and orange, the colors of hospitality. The Terrans were welcome to return to World.

Although, in three whole years, they had not.

A servant of the First Flower raised his arms, and the straggly crowd quieted. All together, they began to sing. First the harvest chants, then the flower lyrics, in the exact order they had been sung in the Gofkit Rabloe root cellar. From the corner of her eye, Enli saw little Calit begin to dance in the farm cart. Gently his mother stilled him.

"People of World," the priest began, when the singing had ended, "may your blossoms rejoice."

"May the flowers of your soul flourish forever," the crowd answered.

"We come here on this day to honor a messenger of the First Flower, David Pek Allen, who saved World from the sky sickness."

People nodded. Over the years Enli had heard rumors that shared reality now included doubts that the sky sickness had occurred at all. Certainly there had been no sign of it after everyone emerged from the root cellars. No sick animals, no wilted blossoms, no diseased cooking pots, as Pek Gruber had foretold and as happened when people ventured too far into the Neury Mountains. But no one dwelt seriously on the possibility that Pek Allen had played some sort of unfathomable alien trick. That the sky sickness had in fact occurred was now shared reality, not yet shifted into open disbelief. This was true, even though as each year passed, Pek Allen's sacrifice became a less important part of shared reality, with room for passing doubts. A minor ceremony, observed only in this one place.

The servant of the First Flower finished his speech and called for presentations. Those presenting stepped forward, one by one, and placed their offerings on the bare altar, murmuring flower blessings.

Estu, the child Pek Allen had abducted to force Gofkit Rabloe to hear him, offered a bouquet of wildflowers she had gathered herself. People smiled; an appropriate offering from a young girl.

Pek Callin, Estu's old grandmother, laid on the altar a woven wreath of rafirib, a work of art in its lovely curves. "Aaaaaahhhhhh," the crowd said appreciatively.

From Riflit Pek Lafir and his wife Imino, a loaf of fresh-baked bread.

From a man that Enli didn't recognize, a wooden carving of a mountain.

Azi came forward, leading the fractious Calit by the hand. The little boy, too young to be real, nonetheless observed everything from sharp, intelligent eyes that couldn't seem to be any more still than the rest of him. Enli sighed. You never knew what sort of children you would get. Gentle Ano, for instance, had produced not only the obedient Fentil but also Enli's niece, Obora, who was easily the noisiest child in Gofkit Shamloe. Azi placed an offering of zeli fruit twined with trifalitib on the altar.

The next offering surprised Enli: a man in the tunic of the Household of Voratur. Last year Pek Voratur had sent no offering. What could have happened in the Voratur household to lead Pek Voratur to reconsider? Probably Enli would never know. The Voratur offering was a beautifully made but not ostentatious flower tapestry, which the messenger draped to hang over the front of the stone altar.

Enli came last. When it was clear there were no more presentations, she pushed her way to the altar. A few people recognized her, those who had been in the root cellar that day, and smiled. Many others were strangers, mostly young people, drawn to the ceremony primarily for the dancing and feasting that would follow. Young people were young people.

The crowd was growing restless, but their attention sharpened as Enli unwrapped her offering and laid it atop the Voratur tapestry. "Aaaaahhhhhhh," they said again, but with a different tone than when they had appreciated old Pek Callin's wreath. Enli had brought a flower remembrance, the finest money could buy in Rafkit Seloe. She had been saving for it for three years. Her wish had been that Ano come with her to present it in Tabor's name, but Ano—who had accompanied Enli to last year's ceremony—was pregnant again and very near her birthing time.

The flower remembrance was blown glass, with the exquisite and sophisticated curves that marked it as the work of World's finest glassblower, Avino Pek Molarian. This rural crowd had never heard Pek Molarian's name, but they recognized the subtle beauty of the intricate glass tunnels. Through them the bright liquid metal, flowersoul, ran over and between two perfectly preserved Terran rosib. The rosib came from the Voratur flower trade, captured forever in the glass.

Enli whispered, for her presentation was meant only for Pek Allen's spirit. "From Enli Pek Brimmidin of World and Tabor Pek Brimmidin among his ancestors."

"May all your gardens bloom in joy," the priest of the First Flower said, again raising his arms, and the ceremony was over. The crowd began to disperse. The young people gathered on a flat clear patch of ground well away from the altar; in a few moments the sound of dancing flutes rose on the warm air. The visitors from Reality and Atonement mounted their bicycles for the return ride to the capital.

Azi pulled her cart over to Enli. "May your flowers bloom, Enli."

"And yours, Azi." Enli smiled.

"Do you stay for the dancing?"

"No, I must return to my sister. She's near her time."

"My garden rejoices for her. Then would you like—Calit! Stop that this moment!"

"He is beautiful, Azi."

"And a headpain all by himself. You look well, Enli."

"Thank you," Enli said. She knew she did not look different than she always had been: large, plain, undistinguished. But compared to how Azi had seen her the day of the sky sickness, Enli knew she must look wonderful. So would Azi always see her.

Calit had found an odd-shaped rock to study. In the moment of peace, Azi said suddenly, "Enli—do you think they will ever return? The Terrans?"

Enli stared at the flower altar, bearing the remembrance that had cost her most of three years' wages in her restored life. No one, not even Ano, had understood why she had insisted on a flower remembrance from the famous Avino Pek Molarian, and Enli had not explained. She had learned much from living among the Terrans, in that brief terrible time: There were things you could not explain. She now knew, as Ano and Azi and even the servants of the First Flower did not, that there were many realities. Some of those realities were what Pek Gruber had called *highprobability,* some were *lowprobability,* terms for which no World words existed. Some realities even both existed and not-existed at the same time, until someone like David Pek Allen, through sheer force of will, brought them about.

The Terrans had always known that, and now Enli did, too. The knowing set her apart; already she could feel the headpain starting. But it was her reality.

Azi waited. "I don't know," Enli finally said, "if they will ever return or not. That's for the First Flower to decide."

Azi nodded; she was a priest herself. "Would you like to come to my house for a glass of pel before you return to your sister?"

"Yes," Enli said, "I would like that."

She picked up the second shaft of the farm cart, Azi dumped a protesting Calit and his odd-shaped rock into the cart, and the two women pulled together for Azi's house in the village.

Look for . . .

PROBABILITY SPACE

By

NANCY KRESS

*Now Available in Hardcover
from Tor Books*

---

*Turn the page for a preview of
Nancy Kress's latest*

Heaven from all creatures hides the book of fate,
All but the page prescribed, their present state.

—ALEXANDER POPE, "AN ESSAY ON MAN"

PROLOGUE

MARS

July, 2168

Bellington Wace Arnold of Arnold Interplanetary, Inc., arrived late at his opulent office. Beyond the top-floor window and the piezoelectric dome of Lowell City, the sun was already well above the Martian horizon. Not much dust today. The sky was only faintly pink, and Arnold could see all the way to the hard clutter of the spaceport.

"System on. Messages."

"Yes, Mr. Arnold. Five messages." It meant five for-your-ears-only transmissions; Arnold's staff would have handled everything else. The wall screen brightened to visual. As he listened, Arnold settled into his desk chair and scanned the printouts his secretary had deemed important enough for his personal perusal. The chair, big enough to encase his impressive size, was made of imported Earth leather from calves genetically altered to produce hides in his favorite blue-gray.

The first four messages did not need his entire attention, even though two of them involved billion-credit transactions. There was a lot of money to be made in wartime, if you knew how. The longer the war with the Fallers went on, the better for Arnold Interplanetary.

The fifth transmission made him look up. There was nothing to see; this message was voice-only.

"Cockpit recording, personal flyer registration number 14387, transmission date July 3, 2168." Yesterday.

And then the voice of Arnold's son, Laslo Damroscher: *"Thass not 'sposed to be there."*

Slowly, pointlessly, Arnold rose from his expensive chair. Every line of his big body tightened.

The flyer had been a gift to Laslo on his eighteenth birthday. Arnold knew he did not love this son. Laslo, weak and whiny and easily led, was hard to love. A strange son for Bellington Wace Arnold to have, but then Laslo wasn't his son only. It still took two people.

Arnold had other, better, legitimate sons. Still, he had always provided well for Laslo, even though the idea that Laslo might ever need money was laughable. He was his mother's sole heir.

It had seemed a good idea to know where Laslo took his birthday-gift flyer, and what he did along the way. It might prevent danger, or embarrassment, or lawsuits. To that end, the flyer, unknown to Laslo, had been equipped with automatic continuous record-and-send equipment. A smart program flagged and relayed only those recordings that met certain parameters. None of the parameters meant anything good.

"Thass not 'sposed to be there." Laslo's voice, very drunk.

"What isn't supposed to be where?" Another young man, sounding marginally less drunk. *"Just an asteroid."*

"Isn't 'sposed to be there. Hand me 'nother fizzie."

"They're gone. You drunk the last one, you pig."

"No fizzies? Might as well go home."

"Just an asteroid. No . . . two asteroids."

"Two!" Laslo said, with pointless jubilation.

"Where'd they come from? Isn't supposed to be there. Not on computer."

"N-body problem. Gravity. Messes things up. Jupiter."

"Let's shoot 'em!"

"Yeah!" Laslo cried, and hiccuped.

"What kinda guns you got on this thing? No guns, prob'ly. Fucking rich-boy pleasure craft."

"Got . . . got guns put on it. Daddy-dad doesn't know. Illegals."

"You're a bonus, Laslo."

"Goddamn true. Mummy doesn't know either. 'Bout the guns."

"You sure 'bout that? Isn't much your famous mother don't know. Or do. God, that body, I saw her in a old—"

"Shut up, Conner," Laslo said savagely. *"Computer, activate . . . can't remember the word . . ."*

"Activate weapons. Jesus, Laslo. YOU gotta say it. Voice cued."

"Activate weapons!"

"Hey, a message from th'asteroid! People! Maybe there's girls."

"You are approaching a highly restricted area," a mechanical voice said. *"Leave this area immediately."*

"It don't want us," Conner said. *"Shoot it!"*

"Wait . . . maybe . . ."

"You are approaching a highly restricted area. Leave this area immediately."

"Fucking snakes," Conner said. *"Shoot it!"*

"I . . ."

"Fucking coward!"

"THIS IS YOUR LAST WARNING! YOU HAVE INVADED A HIGHLY RESTRICTED AND HIGH-DANGER AREA. LEAVE IMMEDIATELY OR YOUR CRAFT WILL BE FIRED ON!"

And then a fourth voice, speaking rapidly, *"Unknown craft . . . SOS . . . Help! I'm being held prisoner here—this is Tom Capelo—"*

A very brief, high-pitched whine.

"End flagged recording," said Arnold's system. *"Transmission complete."*

Arnold stood in the middle of his silent office. He tried to think factually, methodically, without haste.

The electromagnetic impulse carrying the flyer's last conversation would have sped at c toward the nearest far-orbit data satellite, of which Mars had thousands. There the information had been encrypted and relayed through closer satellites toward Mars. It had taken only a few minutes to arrive last night, when Arnold had been asleep. The transmission would have traveled ahead of the shock wave. The brief whine at the end of the transmission had been a proton vaporizer.

Laslo Damroscher was dead.

Arnold couldn't blame whoever had shot Laslo down. Laslo had been where he shouldn't have, had been adequately warned, had been old enough to understand that warning, had defied it anyway. Laslo, "Conner," and that boy in the other craft, "Tom," playing at war games when there was a real war on, pretending to be somebody famous to boost his own pathetic ego . . . irresponsible. All three of the boys. A corporation or a government had the right to protect its property. That was just reality. Most likely the restricted area had been government-controlled armaments, and in that case, Laslo's death would not even rate a trial. Not in wartime.

The irresponsible behavior that had gotten Laslo killed had not come from Arnold's genes. Arnold had made only one mistake in his entire life, and that mistake had produced Laslo. Whatever else Laslo's death might be, it was not Bellington Wace Arnold's fault. The responsibility lay elsewhere.

But . . .

To his own surprise, Arnold couldn't maintain his factual objectivity. Sudden memories flooded him: Laslo's birth, the beautiful baby in the arms of his preternaturally beautiful mother. Laslo toddling across the floor of this same office, holding out his small arms to be picked up. Laslo riding a toy red car, laughing and laughing. Laslo proudly printing his name for the first time, even though it was not his, LASLO D. ARNOLD . . .

Unexpected tears scalded Arnold's eyes. He stumbled back to his chair. It seemed he had loved his lost son, after all. Although never as much as the mother who had cosseted Laslo and spoiled him and ruined him.

At the thought of Magdalena, Arnold's tears vanished. He

would have to call her, tell her. Send her the recording. For years Arnold had avoided any contact with the bitch. Well, it was going to be only minimal contact now: a prerecorded message. Her reaction to Laslo's death would undoubtedly be violent, irrational, vengeful. Dangerous.

He could at least spare himself Magdalena.